Hope Springs™

THE
WARRIOR
MAIDEN

Hope Springs™

THE VIRTUE CHRONICLES

THE
WARRIOR
MAIDEN

By Paul McCusker

AUGUSTINE INSTITUTE
Greenwood Village, CO

Augustine Institute
6160 S. Syracuse Way, Suite 310
Greenwood Village, CO 80111
Tel: (866) 767-3155
www.augustineinstitute.org

Cover design: Ben Dybas

ISBN 978-1-950939-99-2

Printed in Canada

Dedicated to the Maiden herself.

THE WARRIOR MAIDEN

Andrew Perry stood in the middle of a room full of clocks. There were clocks of all kinds hanging on the walls, sitting on shelves, standing like soldiers in perfect rows.

He rubbed his eyes. His legs were unsteady. He felt as if he'd just stepped off a moving train.

A loud and solemn chime began behind him, coming from a man-sized clock in the corner. The hands on its ornate face showed 3:20. Why was the clock chiming at 3:20?

It was odd. But then again, everything Andrew had just experienced was odd.

How am I going to explain this to my parents? he wondered.

The other clockfaces in the room peered at him. They announced a different time: 11:03.

He now remembered the clocks chiming eleven o'clock when he first entered the room to find Eve. The clocks had to be wrong.

His eye went to his coat draped across an antique chair nearby. When had he put it there? According to the clocks, it would have been only moments ago. That was before he'd followed Eve through the door of the giant clock and gone back in time.

It was crazy to think about now. *Back in time*. Not just a few minutes or a couple of years, but several *centuries* to England, to the time of Robin Hood. Andrew and Eve had spent days and days there.

He could still feel the humidity and heat of the forest. The smell of the damp green lingered in his nostrils. The chirping of the birds was like a distant song in his ears. It was a sharp contrast to the dry, crisp air and the street noise of Hope Springs, Colorado, just outside.

"Are you leaving?" Eve Virtue asked.

Lost in his thoughts, Andrew had forgotten she was there. He also hadn't realized he'd picked up his coat and now held it in his hands.

"I have to go home and talk to my parents," he said.

Eve looked at him with an anxious expression. Her cheeks were flushed, as if she'd been running. Her dark, short-cropped hair was disheveled. Her eyes were wide, and Andrew wondered yet again what color they really were. Were they blue, green, azure, hazel? Eve herself didn't know.

Those eyes, along with her hair and the shape of her face, reminded Andrew of a pixie.

"You're going home?" she asked.

"I was gone a long time. They'll be worried."

"You weren't gone a long time," she said. "Remember? Time moves differently in the past than it does here." To prove her point, she took hold of the back of his arm and guided him to the open doorway. "See?"

Andrew looked out at the vast main floor of the Virtue Curiosity Shoppe. It was filled end to end with tables, shelves, racks, and display cases overflowing with antiques, knickknacks, and collectibles.

Catherine Drake stood behind a counter near the front door of the shop. That was exactly where she had been when Andrew and Eve first went into the room of clocks. Mrs. Drake was Eve's aunt and the owner of the shop. She looked over at them and smiled. Then her attention went to a customer coming through the front door.

"Why does it feel like I just woke up?" Andrew asked.

"That can happen with time travel," Eve said.

She would know, Andrew thought. She had been jumping back and forth in time for a while.

"England, Robin Hood, the sword fights and battles … weren't a dream?" Andrew asked, just to make sure.

"No. All of it really happened."

Andrew shook his head. "I have to go home and tell my parents."

"Let me show you something first," Eve said quickly. She wiggled a finger for him to follow her.

They made their way along the rear wall of the shop.

"Wait!" Catherine Drake called out to them.

"Oh no," Eve whispered as she froze in place.

"Eve, Andrew. Come here for a minute," Mrs. Drake said.

Eve rolled her eyes and groaned. "Let's get it over with."

"What? What's going on?" Andrew asked.

"You'll see."

Still clutching his coat, Andrew weaved his way around the tables and stands. The customer who had just entered stepped around the front counter to greet him.

"This is Dr. Vince Howard," Mrs. Drake said. "He teaches history in Denver."

Dr. Howard was tall, with a narrow, pleasant face marked by deep wrinkles on his forehead and the corners of his eyes. A salt-and-pepper-colored goatee adorned his mouth and chin, matching his shaggy gray hair. He wore a tan shirt and a brown waistcoat, jeans, and cowboy boots. All he was missing was a cowboy hat, and he would have looked as if he'd just come from a rodeo.

Dr. Howard shook Andrew's hand. Andrew noticed rough calluses on the man's palms.

"A pleasure to meet you, Andrew." Dr. Howard had a deep voice. "Catherine tells me you like history."

"Dr. Howard often comes to Hope Springs to shop for antiques," said Mrs. Drake. "He's interested in our local history. Just like you are."

Dr. Howard looked closely at Andrew. Then his eyes went up to an enormous painting hanging on the far wall. Andrew's gaze followed along. In the painting, two men posed in front of a large bookcase. An oversized globe of the world stood between them. The men were Alfred Virtue and Theodore Perry, ancestors of Eve and Andrew.

Looking as they did in the 1920s, the men were dressed in suits with long jackets and vests, stiff collars, and dark ties. Alfred Virtue sported a moustache and wore gold wire-framed glasses. Theodore Perry was clean-shaven and had wavy sandy-colored hair. His lips were pressed into a slightly embarrassed smile. Each man had a hand on the oversized globe. Alfred Virtue and Theodore Perry were business partners and best friends.

"You could be twins," Dr. Howard said to Andrew, nodding to Theodore Perry.

Andrew nodded. "Everybody says that."

"We should compare notes about your family history," Dr. Howard said. "My great-grandfather lived here around the time of Alfred Virtue. I think they did business together. He probably knew Theodore Perry, too."

Andrew gave him another nod. "Okay."

Dr. Howard's gaze went to Eve, who was standing just behind Andrew. "Hello, Eve. Are you hiding?"

"Hi," Eve said in a flat tone. "We were just about to go downstairs," she added quickly and tugged at Andrew's sleeve. "Let's go." She began to back away.

"Good to meet you," Andrew said, moving in Eve's direction.

"Likewise," said Dr. Howard. Then he turned his attention back to Mrs. Drake. She leaned on the counter and smiled at him like a schoolgirl.

Eve picked up her pace. Andrew hustled alongside her and whispered, "What's wrong with you?"

"Nothing," Eve said sharply.

They reached the far corner of the shop and rounded a tall bookcase. Half hidden behind it was a short hallway with a water fountain, two public bathrooms, and a stairwell leading downstairs. A metal Employees Only sign hung on a thin chain that stretched across the entrance to the stairs.

Eve unhooked the chain from the sign. They rattled loudly. She stepped into the stairwell and gestured for Andrew to do the same. He moved past her and down a few stairs while she hooked the chain again.

"You don't like Dr. Howard?" Andrew asked as they walked down the stairs.

Eve shrugged.

Andrew came to a landing and stopped. "Does your aunt like him?" he asked.

Eve shot him an annoyed look, then continued down the next set of stairs.

"Where's your uncle?" Andrew asked as he followed her.

"He died before I was born."

"So she's allowed to have a boyfriend if she wants."

Eve frowned. "He's not her boyfriend."

"Then why don't you like him?"

"I never said I don't like him." She reached the bottom of the stairs and stopped. "I don't think he's right for her."

"Oh," Andrew said, still thinking there was more to it than that.

"I live with Aunt Catherine," Eve explained. "If she marries him, then ..." She didn't finish her sentence. Instead, she pushed through a fire door and into a wide, dimly lit hallway.

"Where are your parents?" Andrew asked.

"They're not around." Eve walked ahead of him.

"Where are they?"

"Somewhere that isn't here," she said, her tone sharp again. "Aunt Catherine is my legal guardian."

"Why?"

"Forget about it," she snapped. Her voice echoed down the hall.

"Okay, then how about telling me where we are," he said, aware that the hallway was lined with various doors.

"The old bank had offices down here. And two vaults." She stopped at a large square iron door that stood open against the wall. The mechanics of its locks were an elaborate system of rods, levers, and boxes. "This is the main vault."

To the left of the open door was the vault itself, with bars protecting a room filled with safety-deposit boxes. In the middle sat a metal table and chairs. All of them were covered with file boxes, stacks of ledgers, and small plastic containers. A rack of clothes stood off to the right.

"My aunt uses the vault for storage," Eve explained.

"Is there anything in the deposit boxes?" Andrew asked.

"They were cleaned out when the bank closed down," Eve said. "If there's any treasure, it'll be in *this* one."

They came to another vault door. Unlike the first, this one was closed and smaller. It was painted a shiny black, with a gold border around the edges. In the center of the door was a detailed painting of a forest and stream at the foot of the Rocky Mountains. Below the painting, cursive lettering said *Theobold Safe & Lock Co., Denver.* To the left was a combination dial. Next to that was a large handle with a lock for a key. A design of black and gold pedestals and flowers adorned the sides. Matching gold trimmings crowned the top.

"There's a treasure in there?" Andrew asked.

"Nobody knows. That's the mystery," Eve said. She grabbed the door handle and gave it a tug. "Alfred Virtue had this specially built. We haven't found the combination or the key."

"Why don't you get a locksmith to break in?" asked Andrew.

"The family has tried over and over. Years ago they brought Mr. Theobold down from Denver. He said Alfred Virtue designed it so the only way to break in is to blow the whole thing up, which would destroy whatever is inside."

"Nobody knows what's in it?"

Eve shook her head. "That's why no one wants to risk damaging it. Alfred Virtue could have all kinds of valuable stuff in there."

"What about all those X-ray, sonic, infrared, whatever-they're-called machines?"

"They don't work," Eve replied. "In fact, the whole building messes up tech equipment like that. Computers glitch up. Cell phones can't get signals . . ."

"Why?"

"I have a theory. Come to the office and I'll show you." She moved away.

Andrew hesitated. He put his hand on the black iron door. It was smooth and cool to the touch. "I guess nobody has figured out the combination—or where the key is to get in," he said.

"No." Eve gave him a knowing smile. "Alfred Virtue only left a few clues."

"What kind of clues?"

"The kind no one has ever figured out," Eve said. "But *we* will."

"We?" Andrew asked, following her down the hallway.

Eve stopped at an open doorway. "You went back in time with me and met Robin Hood, and you don't want to help me find out more?"

Andrew gave a small shrug. "Yeah. But I—" He stopped. He wasn't sure how far he wanted to dig into the mysteries of Alfred Virtue and the Radiant Stone or this mysterious vault.

Eve put her hands on her hips and glared at him. "What do you want to do—go home? Tell your parents? Great. Go ahead. And you know what? They won't believe you. And if they do, they won't let you near the Radiant Stone ever again."

Andrew flinched at her sudden outburst. "What's wrong with you?" he asked. He felt annoyed that she was so annoyed.

"I'm tired of people being so flaky," she said. Her eyes were now a dark and stormy purple color.

"I'm not being flaky," Andrew countered. "*You* dragged me into this whole time-travel thing, remember? I haven't had any time to think about it."

"You had days and days in England!" Eve argued.

"How was I supposed to think *there* when we were running all over the country? And we've only been home for a little while! What do you want from me?"

"Nothing," she said with a grim look Andrew had come to know. "Go home. Tell your parents, if that's what you want."

Was that what he wanted? He wasn't sure. Changing tactics, he asked, "What did your Aunt Catherine say about you jumping around in time?"

"She knows about the stone," Eve said as a gotcha. "She says she likes my sense of adventure. She thinks traveling in time is kind of like going to school, but even better than learning algebra. She's Alfred Virtue's great-granddaughter, you know. She's a lot like him. What will your parents say?"

"How am I supposed to know?" Andrew replied. "Why are you so mad?"

She paused, then lowered her head. "Because I'm tired of doing this on my own." She turned away, then stepped through the doorway, disappearing into the darkness of the room behind her.

"You're not on your own," Andrew said. He lingered in the doorway. "I'm here now, aren't I?"

Her voice brightened. "Then come in."

"To where?"

"Alfred Virtue's private office."

There was a telltale click when Eve flipped a switch inside the dark room. Old bulbs hanging from wires in the ceiling flickered into a dull yellow and then brightened to a harsh white.

The room was crammed with tables and filing cabinets, metal and wooden shelves, and racks of glass beakers. Papers, books, and ledgers covered the surface spaces. A desk in the middle of the room held a microscope, various hammer-like tools, a pile of yellowed newspapers, and science magazines from the 1920s. Near the microscope was a stack of three notebooks.

"Those are Alfred Virtue's journals," Eve said. "I'm pretty sure there are more than those three, but I haven't found them. Maybe they're locked in that vault."

Andrew hooked his coat on a rack stand next to the door. A dusty gray smock draped down from one of the pegs. A black hat hung on another.

He turned back to the desk and picked up one of the notebooks. Flipping past the rough leather cover, he carefully touched the mass of scrawls handwritten in pencil and black ink. Some pages had drawings and diagrams of the Radiant Stone with arrows pointing to the various facets. Others had math equations and formulas. Still others had sketches of rocks and gems.

"You read all of this stuff?" Andrew asked.

"Over and over again," Eve said. She reached up to her neck and pulled out the silver necklace with the silver case that held the Radiant Stone.

She looped it over her head and placed it on the desk. "For some reason, this thing feels heavier in our time," she said.

The case always reminded Andrew of an oversized pocket watch. He pressed a stem on the top. The silver cover clicked open. Small clasps at the top and bottom of the case held the Radiant Stone in place. The stone glowed like a shiny jewel under the white electric light. The facets shimmered with different shades of blue, red, green, black, and even specks of yellow.

"What are you doing?" Eve asked.

"Just looking," Andrew said as he propped open the notebook he had picked up. A drawing of the stone covered most of a page. He leaned over to compare the drawing with the stone itself.

"Don't touch the stone," Eve said quickly.

"I *know*!" Andrew snapped. Touching any of the facets would send him back in time. *Where* he was sent depended on which facet he touched. Alfred Virtue had spent months, maybe years, figuring out which facet linked to which time and place. The drawing had arrows with notes written in a neat cursive.

Andrew looked at the stone, then the drawing. Then a question came to his mind. "If all I have to do is touch a facet to go back in time, why did I have to follow you into the big clock?"

"Because that's what Alfred Virtue said to do."

"But *why*? Why did we need the clock?"

Eve said, "It gets our bodies ready."

Andrew was baffled. "How?"

Eve grabbed another journal and flipped through the pages, as if trying to find a particular entry. She finally gave up and tossed the journal back on the desk. "Radonite."

"What?"

"Radonite," she said again. "The numbers on the big clock and the pendulum and the frame are all made of a rock called *radonite*. It's the rock Alfred Virtue found around the Radiant Stone."

Andrew shook his head. "I don't understand."

"How can I explain it?" she muttered to herself. Then she said, "Okay, so you know how a diamond is usually found in a rock called *kimberlite*?"

"No."

"Well, I looked it up. Trust me, it is," she said. "The Radiant Stone is like that. It was found in a weird rock that looked like coal, but nobody'd ever seen it before. Alfred Virtue brought some to Hope Springs and showed it to a local rock expert. The expert said it was unknown and unnamed. So Alfred Virtue called it *radonite*. He later found out that it acts like a kind of stabilizer. It makes time travel easier on our bodies."

"Like travel medicine?" Andrew said.

"Kind of," said Eve. "Alfred Virtue brought in *a lot* of radonite and put some into parts of this building and the mystery vault and some of the clocks you saw in the Clock Room."

"What happens if we use the Radiant Stone and there isn't any radonite around?" Andrew asked.

"It'd be like dropping fast in an airplane, or going down into deep water pressure," she explained. "Our bodies won't have time to adjust. We'll feel really sick."

Andrew was worried. "What kind of sick? Is our hair going to fall out? Are we going to get cancer?"

"Nothing like that," said Eve. "Maybe an upset stomach. Sometimes headaches and dizziness. You feel achy like you have the flu."

Andrew picked up another notebook. It opened to a section where a few pages had been roughly torn out. He held it up to Eve. "What happened to these pages?"

"I don't know." She pointed to words written at the top of one of the tears: *Beware of* . . . .

"Beware of what?" Andrew asked.

"Look at the page right before."

Andrew turned the page. A sketch of the Radiant Stone took up most of the sheet. Alfred Virtue had drawn an arrow pointing to a facet just left of the center.

"Beware of this facet?" Andrew asked. "Where does it go?"

Eve looked closer. "It must be written on the missing pages."

Andrew turned his attention to the Radiant Stone, still lying in the open case. He leaned down to look at the facet. It flickered in the light, and he thought he saw an image. "Is that a *castle*?"

Eve bent down to look. "What?"

"There." Andrew pointed. His forefinger moved close to the facet.

"Don't touch it!" Eve snapped at him.

Later, the two of them would argue over what happened next. Andrew would claim that he didn't intend to touch the stone, but Eve reached over to grab his hand and pushed his finger against the facet. Eve would insist that he touched the facet with the tip of his finger just as her hand made contact with his.

Either way, Eve was touching Andrew's hand when his finger pressed against the facet of the Radiant Stone.

And that was that.

A brilliant flash of light caused Andrew to yelp. Eve gasped. They instinctively lifted their hands to cover their faces.

The musty smell of the office gave way to fresh, crisp air. Andrew heard the sound of trickling water nearby. Farther off came the voices of men and women and the low murmur of a crowd gathered somewhere.

Andrew lowered his hands. He blinked, trying to regain his sight. His senses told him that he was sitting on soft earth with his back against rough stones.

"Ouch," Eve said to his right.

Andrew glanced over. Eve was standing, stretching, blinking her eyes, and looking as confused as he felt.

They were on a riverbank of grass and mud. A river flowed past only a few feet away. Andrew turned to see that he was at the base of a stone bridge. Broad arches rose high above him. They stretched from one fat stone pillar to another, all the way across the river to another bank. On both sides of the bank, steep inclines led to the top of the bridge.

Andrew started to stand, but a dull ache rolled through his body. Every muscle hurt. Then a razor-sharp pain went through his head. "My head hurts," he said, pressing his temples.

"Mine, too," said Eve. She looked pale and swayed unsteadily.

Bracing himself against the closest stone pillar, he tried to get to his feet.

"Oh no," he said as a sudden wave of nausea hit him. He bent near the pillar and threw up. Not once, not twice, but three times.

Eve made a face. "Ew."

He staggered a few feet, then dropped to his knees in a patch of mud. "Is this—?" he started to ask, but he hurled one more time before he could finish the question.

"This is what happens when we touch the stone without the radonite," Eve said. She held out her hand to him. "Let's go back before we have any worse side effects."

He grabbed her hand. She pulled him to his feet. Another wave of nausea hit him, and he had to close his eyes until it passed. He took a deep breath.

"Hurry," she said, still holding his hand. "Use the Radiant Stone."

Andrew let go of her hand and looked at her, puzzled. He showed her both of his hands. They were empty. "I don't have it," he said. "Don't you?"

Her eyes widened. "No!" She touched her neck. The chain wasn't there. Frantically she checked her pockets.

Andrew spun one way, then another. He looked on the ground near his feet. Then they both scrambled back and forth, searching along the riverbank and the water's edge.

The Radiant Stone wasn't there.

"What does this mean?" Andrew asked. "We're here. It must be here too."

Eve shook her head. "You touched the stone, but you weren't holding it. It's still sitting on Alfred Virtue's desk."

Andrew's head throbbed. He couldn't think straight. "What does that mean?"

"It means we can't go back to our time," she said. Her wide eyes filled with tears.

"There has to be a way back," Andrew said.

"How? The Radiant Stone was our only way back!" she cried out.

Andrew sank onto the wet grass. He thought he might throw up again.

Eve sat down next to him. She lowered her head. Andrew could hear her whispering, along with an occasional sniffle. It sounded as if she was praying.

Andrew closed his eyes and joined her.

Suddenly she stood up and wiped the tears from her face in a decisive "I'm done crying about it" gesture. "Let's see where we are," she said.

They looked up. The bank on the opposite side of the river inclined to an open horizon. Behind them, the ground rose more gently to uneven ledges covered with bushes. At the top was a short wall of stone.

Andrew craned his neck. He thought he could see the peaks of various roofs. Above and beyond them was a high wall and what looked like the towers of a castle.

"Are we back in Robin Hood's time?" he asked.

"There's a path," Eve said, pointing to a break in the bushes.

Andrew stood up, but his head started spinning. He doubled over, sure he was going to vomit again.

"Wait here." Eve darted to the path, then disappeared into the bushes. He caught glimpses of her as she made her way to the top of the hill.

Andrew sat down again until the wave of nausea passed. He focused on the sounds coming from somewhere overhead. He could hear muttering voices mixed with the clip-clop of horses' hooves on what must have been a dirt road. There was also the familiar rattling and creaking of wooden carts. It was a sound he had come to know from his time with Robin Hood.

He lowered his head, hoping that the bad effects of time traveling had passed.

A few minutes later, Eve returned. "We're dressed all wrong," she said, grabbing fistfuls of mud and smearing it on her jeans and pullover. She did the same to her tennis shoes, almost covering the tops with the brown muck.

"What are you doing?" Andrew asked.

"We have to blend in with the people up there."

"What are they wearing?" he asked.

"Definitely *not* jeans, tennis shoes, and shirts with factory-made stitching." She scooped up a handful of mud and threw it at him. A big brown splotch hit the middle of his shirt.

"Hey!" he cried out.

Eve began to tear at the stitching on her sleeves. "We have to disguise ourselves to look like peasants."

"Peasants? Like the ones we saw in England?"

"They look almost the same," she said. She tore a small hole in the fabric near her shoulder. "But I think they're speaking French."

Andrew gasped. "French! But you said we can only go to places in history where the stone has been."

"It's not what *I* said. It's what Alfred Virtue said."

"I don't care who said it. The Radiant Stone was from England. How can we be in France?"

"How am I supposed to know?" Eve shrugged. "The stone must have been in France at this point in history."

"At what point? What year is it?"

She frowned at him. "It's not like I could go up and ask someone, 'Excuse me. What year is it?' All the clothes look alike to me. It might be the thirteen or fourteen hundreds."

She knelt down and started rubbing more dirt on Andrew's clothes. Then she stood up and said, "Let's go. Something is happening up there. People are crowding along the bridge."

Andrew rolled around on the ground. He was beginning to feel better. He got to his feet again and presented himself. "How do I look?"

"Disgusting. How about me?"

"Like you've been mud wrestling with pigs."

"Good," Eve said. "I think we'll fit in."

Together they ascended the bank on a narrow path through the thick bushes. On level ground, Andrew saw what Eve had seen: a crowd of people were pressed together on the long bridge. They didn't seem to be moving in any particular direction. It looked as if they were waiting for something to happen.

Andrew saw a tall arched gate to his left. The road from the bridge continued past guards and into a town. Stretching away in the other direction, beyond the bridge, were green fields and a forest.

The people on the bridge looked a lot like the peasants Andrew had known in the time of Robin Hood. They wore rough and ragged clothes in dull colors of browns, blues, and blacks. The men wore long-sleeved shirts, tunics, breeches, and leather shoes laced around their ankles. A few heads were covered with hoods that draped onto the men's shoulders.

Some of the women wore long dresses with V-shaped collars. Their waists were belted with thin straps. Other women wore wool skirts and plain tops under leather vests pulled together by leather laces. The women wore their hair long and braided or tucked their hair into funny heart-shaped headdresses.

"We could be almost anywhere at any time in the Middle Ages," Eve whispered to Andrew.

"I guess fashions didn't change a lot back then," he said. Cocking his head slightly, he listened to the crowd. Fragments of sentences and words came to his ears. He was pretty sure the peasants were speaking French, just as Eve had said.

"Which way should we go?" Andrew asked.

"Across the bridge to the woods," Eve said.

Andrew looked at the crowd on the bridge. "We won't make it through that," he said. He shot a glance through the gate. Guards inside were nudging the people to keep moving and stay off the main road. "Let's go that way. Maybe there's a way out if we follow the road through the town."

Just then an old woman near Eve turned slightly, just enough to see Eve's face. She suddenly gasped and spun around. "*Qui est-ce? La Pucelle? Jeanne? La Sainte Fille!*"

Eve backed up, shaking her head. "No. No. I am not," she said.

The woman became more excited. "*Jeanne! Jeanne!*" she shouted and pointed at Eve.

Heads turned. The crowd pushed in to see what the fuss was about.

"What's going on?" Andrew asked Eve, backing away with her.

She looked alarmed. "I think they're freaked because I'm a girl dressed like a boy."

Andrew heard words and exclamations like *pucelle!* and *fille habillée en garçon!* and *la Sainte Fille!* and *jeune fille du Christ* and *vierge de Domrémy.*

Slowly he began to understand what they were saying. "They're calling you a girl saint from a place called Domrémy," he said to her.

"No!" Eve shouted to the mob. She waved her hands and cried out, "*Je ne suis pas qui vous dites que je suis!*"

Andrew looked at her, shocked. "You spoke French!"

"I did?" Eve said, looking equally shocked.

"You said you're not who they say you are," Andrew repeated, then realized he knew what the French words meant in English. He gasped and put a hand over his mouth. *How do I know that?* he wondered.

The crowd surrounded Eve, pushing Andrew away. He was in danger of losing her. He began to shove and elbow everyone around him.

"Stop!" someone shouted from behind the mob. The voice was commanding enough to stifle the chaos. A tall old man plowed through the crowd. He waved a long staff, as if he might strike anyone who wouldn't yield. "Fools! Step aside!" he roared. "Go away!"

He wore a long cloak made of a rich scarlet-colored silk. The fringes of the cloak were lined with gold. White hair crowned the man's head, and his thick beard flew out in wisps like white cotton candy. His face was a web of wrinkles that framed dark circles under angry eyes.

The peasants scattered, muttering under-the-breath curses as they withdrew.

The old man towered over Eve and stabbed his staff into the dirt. "Now then," he said, eyeing her face. He fixed his gaze on her eyes, tilting his head one way and then the other.

Andrew knew he was trying to figure out her eye color. It's what everyone did.

A perplexed look crossed his face. "What are you?" he asked.

"My name is Eve," she replied.

The old man's eyes then moved to her clothes and on down to her shoes.

"What are *those*?" he asked, pointing to her shoes with the tip of his staff.

She looked down. "Shoes?" she said, as if it was a trick question.

Andrew realized that her sneakers, even covered with mud, looked unlike anything anyone would wear at that time.

The old man bent down to look more closely. Then he suddenly grabbed her foot. She fell onto her back.

"Stop it!" Eve said and kicked at him.

Andrew rushed forward, ready to leap at the old man. But the man was quick and jabbed at Andrew's shoulder with his staff, knocking him away.

"Let me go!" Eve shouted, kicking harder at the old man with her free foot.

"What goes on here?" another voice called out. A guard dressed in a gold helmet, chain mail, and boots stormed up. His hand rested on the hilt of the sword attached to his belt. "What are you doing?"

The old man let Eve go and stood up to his full height. He was a giant next to the guard.

The guard looked at him and went pale. "A thousand apologies, commander!" he said, saluting as he backed away.

The old man turned to Eve again. His eyes were sharp like an eagle's. "Where do you come from?" he asked.

"Far away," Eve said.

Andrew stepped forward again. "What is wrong with you?" he asked, rubbing his aching shoulder.

The old man gave him a once-over, grunted, and then addressed Eve again. He pointed at her with a bony finger. "Child of Satan, you do not belong here." He lifted his staff.

Fearing the man would strike Eve, Andrew threw himself between them. He held up his arms to protect her.

The old man lowered his staff again. "I know what you are," he said quietly, then turned quickly and marched away. The crowd parted for him once again.

"What was that all about?" Andrew asked as he helped Eve back to her feet.

Eve looked shaken and said softly, "We have to change our clothes."

"We'll never get across the bridge," Andrew said. "Put your head down. Let's go into the town and figure out where we are."

Eve agreed. Lowering her head, she came close to Andrew as they walked through the gate. The guard scowled at them as they went past.

"There," Andrew said, leading Eve alongside a rickety old cart being pulled slowly by a heavily bearded man.

The man glanced at them. "Try to steal anything and I'll cut your hands off," he said.

Andrew peered into the back of the cart. It was full of what looked like piles of manure. "You do not have to worry about that," he said and continued on.

The narrow streets were congested with people who seemed to be watching for someone or something, like spectators waiting for a parade.

What is going on here? Andrew wondered.

He looked up at buildings in various sizes and shapes made of wood and stone. Some were leaning as if they might tip over. Crude signs hung from doorways, announcing the presence of bakers, butchers, weavers, and cobblers. But many of the shop doors were closed and the windows shuttered.

Even though Eve tried to keep her face hidden, people still gawked at her. Andrew heard whispers behind their backs.

"Is it?"

"No, it isn't. It can't be. She wouldn't enter the town on foot, would she?"

"No! She is coming on horseback with her soldiers."

"This was a mistake," Eve said to Andrew from the side of her mouth. "We should have gone across the bridge to the woods."

"We won't find any clothes there," Andrew said.

"We won't find any here either," she countered. "Unless we plan to steal them."

Andrew hadn't thought of that. "There must be a way out of town if we keep going," he said.

He saw a heavyset man wearing a stained apron standing in a shop doorway. Andrew pulled Eve out of the flow of people and went over to him. The smell of rotten meat lingered in the air from the open door behind him. Andrew assumed the man was a butcher.

"Pardon me, sir."

"I am not open for business today," the man said.

"I do not want to buy anything. I want to know where we are," Andrew said.

Big bushy eyebrows lifted high on the man's forehead. "Are you an *imbecile?*" the butcher asked.

"We are strangers," Andrew explained. "We have come a long way."

Eve came closer and added, "We are lost. That is why we do not know the name of the town."

Andrew realized they were both talking to the butcher more formally.

The butcher gave them a wary look. Andrew noticed that his eyes paused on Eve's eyes and then on their clothes. Slowly he said, "This is Chinon, on the river Vienne." He gestured up at something behind them.

Andrew turned and saw the castle peering at them over a high ledge.

"That is the home of the Dauphin, our king. How could you not know?" the butcher asked.

"Is that why everyone is on the street? Is the dolphin coming?" Andrew asked.

"*Dauphin*," Eve corrected him, pronouncing it *doe-fan*. "It's the word they use for a prince."

Andrew gave her a "How do you know that?" look.

"My Aunt Catherine loves Shakespeare," she said with a shrug.

A puzzled look from the butcher. "What are you saying?"

"Why are the people in the street?" Eve asked him. "Who is coming?"

"*She* is coming. The Maiden of Domrémy." He gestured to Eve's hair and clothes. "The one you are dressed as. You are a girl wearing the clothes of a boy. You have done it for her, yes?"

Eve smiled without answering.

The butcher raised his grimy hands. "Be careful, child. There are those who say it is a sin for a girl to dress as a boy. They will box your ears."

"Someone already tried that," Eve said.

Andrew asked, "How do we get out of town?"

"That way is the bridge," the butcher said, pointing to the left.

"It is too crowded," Andrew said.

The man pointed to the right and said, "Then follow this road to the gate. But it, too, will be crowded. She will be coming from that direction."

"*Merci*," Eve said and pulled at Andrew's arm.

Andrew also thanked the butcher. Then they continued on.

"A girl dressed as a boy is a big deal, I guess," Andrew said.

"And a girl with short hair," Eve affirmed.

"They were calling you the Maiden of Christ and a saint, too. I don't get it," he said.

"They don't know me." She gave him a coy smile.

At last, the street led them to another arched gate. They passed through and found themselves jostled by a crowd that didn't seem to know which way it was going. A group of people spread out onto an open meadow to one side of the gate. A field led to the river on the other side. Violet and yellow wildflowers showed their colors in spite of being trampled by the feet of the many campers.

Eve nudged Andrew and pointed. A forest stood in the distance ahead. The sun shone brightly, a sharp contrast to the shadows inside the town. She picked up her pace. "Hurry."

"What's the rush?" Andrew asked, following her through the crush of people. He knew the answer even as he asked the question. The woods were like home to Eve. He had noticed it during their adventure with Robin Hood.

They walked against the traffic of merchants and pilgrims headed for the town. The glances and double takes continued. Then the crowds thinned, and Andrew and Eve eventually came to an open stretch of road.

Eve sped up to a jog. Then she sprinted toward the trees.

"Slow down," Andrew complained. He worried as much about rushing into the woods as he did about rushing into a strange building. They never knew what might be waiting for them. Robin had taught them that.

Several yards along the road that cut through the forest, Eve slowed down. She turned her head this way and that. Then she dashed away from the road into a denser part of the forest. A canopy of branches and budding leaves softened the morning light.

Andrew tried to keep up as she dodged brush and branches. Then she leapt over a fallen tree and disappeared from his sight. He scrambled onto the top of the log and found her sitting on a floor of old leaves. She had already eased her back against the log and closed her eyes.

"What are you doing?" Andrew asked. He stood over her.

"Resting for a minute. We have to think."

Andrew slid off the log and dropped down next to her. He caught his breath and then asked, "I want to know how we were speaking French."

"It's something the Radiant Stone does," Eve said. She looked at him out of the corner of her eye. "Didn't you wonder why we could understand what people were saying in Robin Hood's time?"

"I figured it was because they were speaking English," Andrew said.

Eve sighed like Andrew's mom sometimes did when he wasn't paying attention.

"Have you read any books in Old English at school?" she asked. "*Canterbury Tales* by Chaucer?"

"One of the nuns read us parts of it," he said. "The words were kind of like ours, but with a lot of 'eths' and extra 'esses' and 'foresooths' and stuff like that."

"That's how they talked when we were with Robin Hood."

"I remember some 'thees' and 'thous,' but…." Andrew's voice trailed off as he slowly remembered. "When we first got there, it sounded strange. But I figured I just got used to how they were talking. It made sense to me."

"It wasn't you. It was the Radiant Stone."

"I don't get it."

"Alfred Virtue wrote that somehow the Radiant Stone makes our brains work differently. It *translates*." She sat up and leaned on her elbows. "He figured out in his time travels that people in the past were talking the way they always talked, but he heard them in a way he could understand. And when they heard him talk, they understood him as if he was speaking in their languages."

Andrew thought about it. "You mean like in the Bible on the day of Pentecost, when the disciples were talking in languages they didn't know?"

"Something like that," Eve said. "Alfred Virtue wondered if the Radiant Stone was a piece from the Tower of Babel. That's how everyone could speak in one language."

"That's crazy."

"It was just a theory," she said.

"It's still crazy."

She giggled. "All of it is crazy."

They sat in silence for a moment. Then Andrew stood up and checked their surroundings. It was another habit he'd picked up from his time with Robin Hood. He looked in every direction and listened for any sound of movement. A few birds called, but otherwise the forest was still. He breathed in the fragrance of the damp wood, decaying bark, and old smoke.

"I feel sick, and tired," Eve said without opening her eyes.

Picking up a broken branch, Andrew wondered if he could sharpen it into a weapon. He tested its thickness, but it snapped too easily to be useful. "We need a plan," he said.

Eve groaned. "How can we plan? We're stuck somewhere in time. We don't even know where. We have the wrong clothes and no money and ..." She leaned back against the log again and draped her arm over her eyes. "What are we going to do?"

Andrew didn't say anything for a long time. He didn't know what to say. He couldn't imagine that they were really stuck back in time.

God won't leave us here, he thought. He struggled against a feeling of despair. He prayed, *Dear God, please get us back to our own time.*

A bird called from somewhere deeper in the forest. Andrew turned. A single shaft of golden light had broken through the trees. A deer stood in the middle of the brilliant shower of rays. It seemed to be watching him. Then, with a nod, it bounded away.

Eve stirred. "What are you looking at?"

He didn't see the point of trying to describe it. "What if God put us here for a reason?" he said. "What if there's something He wants us to do in this time and place?"

Eve sat up. She wrapped her arms around her knees. "Remember the number-one rule of time travel: *we don't belong here.*"

"That was Alfred Virtue's rule," Andrew countered. "But God is God, and He can do whatever He wants."

"You think God put us here?" she asked.

"I think we made a mistake, but God can use our mistake to do something good." Andrew had often heard his parents say that very thing.

"What's good about living and dying where we don't belong?"

"That's what we have to find out," Andrew said.

At that moment, a violent shout came from another part of the forest.

Andrew and Eve were on their feet in an instant. In her hand Eve held a tall branch that had the makings of a good long staff.

Surprised, Andrew asked, "Where did you get that?"

"It was on the ground next to me," she replied. She pounded the end of the branch against the ground. It gave a sturdy thud.

Another shout came from the direction of the road.

"Are we going to help?" Andrew asked, giving Eve a knowing look.

Based on their past experiences, their instincts were to help someone in need.

"You need a weapon," Eve said.

"I'll find one on the way."

The skills Andrew and Eve had learned from their time with Robin Hood in the English greenwood served them well. They navigated the forest easily, leaping over nature's obstacles.

They raced toward the road, deeper into the forest and farther away from the town.

They could see movement through the trees ahead. "Something is happening on the road," Eve said, slowing down.

Crouching behind the wide trunk of a gnarled tree, Andrew peered around one side while Eve checked the other.

A dozen men on foot, dressed as peasants, were blocking the passage of seven people on horseback. Some of the riders were wearing armor. Swords and spears were held high on both sides. It looked to Andrew like a standoff.

"Outlaws," Eve whispered.

"Whose side are we on?" Andrew asked. The outlaws were the good guys in Robin Hood's time.

"I'll bet the ones on foot are the bad guys," Eve said.

As if to prove her point, one of the men on the ground thrust a long staff at the horses. The horses reared up, but the riders held firm.

"We come on the king's business," a man on horseback said with a voice like a bass drum. He struggled to control his black stallion.

"What king?" came the response from a scrawny man with wild red hair. "The fool in the castle? He is no king."

"Traitor! He is your king and mine!" came a much lighter voice from the riders.

Eve turned to Andrew. "That sounds like a girl," she said.

Andrew searched around the fat roots of the tree for any stones he might find. A couple of handfuls would do the trick. Even the smallest pebble hurt if thrown hard enough. He stuffed what he could find into his pockets.

"If you are going to the king, then you must have treasure," the red-headed outlaw said.

"Silver and gold we do not have," said the lighter voice. "Our treasure is word from God, to be delivered to the king alone."

The outlaw snorted. "Are you pilgrims?"

"Of a kind," the deep voice replied.

"We come from the court of Robert de Baudricourt in Vaucouleurs," another rider said. "Leave us in peace to go on our way."

Coarse laughter burst from the outlaws. "The business of any king, duke, or the pope himself is no matter to us. We will leave you, but not in peace."

"We know whose side we're on," Eve said. She lifted her makeshift staff. "I'll crawl to that bush by the road and cause a distraction. Can you get close enough to do what you need to do?"

Andrew nodded. "There's a tree overlooking the road. I'll climb that."

Eve dropped low to the ground and made her way forward. Andrew bent down and half crawled, half walked, ahead. They crept toward the road as silently as two bugs crawling on a leaf.

Eve reached a large holly bush that was positioned just behind the outlaws.

Andrew came up behind a fat tree. Well hidden from the road, he pulled himself to the lowest branch. Then he swung up to the next one and another higher than that. He reached a height overlooking the standoff. Circling around to the front of the tree, he crawled along a thick branch until he reached a good vantage point. The leaves were tiny, but the branches were full enough to give him cover. He perched there and began to take the stones from his pockets, lining them up on the flat surface of a nearby branch.

The band of thieves now brandished knives and spears. They slowly formed a half circle around the horseback riders.

Still crouching behind the bush, Eve was only a few feet from the outlaw closest to her. She held her staff with both hands. She looked up at Andrew and gave a small wave. Only then did he realize that he should have asked how she planned to cause a distraction. Whatever it was, she had to do it quickly. The outlaws were now in position to attack the riders.

At that moment, Eve stabbed her staff into the nearest outlaw's leg. She hit him hard enough to bring him down to one knee. He cried out angrily and twisted around to grab his leg. Eve jabbed quickly just under his ribs, knocking the wind out of him. He doubled over.

The outlaws spun to their fallen comrade. Andrew used the moment to throw his first stone, striking one of them square in the forehead. The thief staggered backward from the blow. Andrew sent another stone rocketing to the red-headed outlaw who had turned to help the man Eve had brought down. The stone caught him near the temple. He staggered and fell to his knees.

Eve sprung up, shouting and swinging her branch. The outlaws who were still standing spun toward her. "Ha!" she cried out, then raced back into the woods.

Andrew let fly a third stone, catching another outlaw just above his ear. He reeled to one side.

The outlaws turned this way and that, as if they couldn't figure out which direction their attackers were coming from.

The horseback riders looked astonished at the chaos. Suddenly the light-voiced rider cried, "Forward!"

With shouts, the riders spurred their horses and plowed through the outlaws. The band of thieves scattered with profanities and cries of pain.

The party on horseback disappeared around a bend in the road. The sounds of galloping horses' hooves soon faded away.

Andrew scrambled down the tree. Eve was there, her staff still in hand. They pressed close together behind the trunk.

Two of the outlaws had left the road and were searching around the bush where Eve had hidden.

"Who attacked us?" one shouted. "Find them!"

"I cannot see anyone!" another yelled.

"Let's get out of here," Andrew whispered.

Crouching low, they made their way back into the deepest part of the forest as silently as they'd come.

5

"We should go back to the town," Andrew said to Eve when they'd stopped to catch their breath in a thick clump of bushes. "It'll be safer."

The two peered over the top of the bushes. Andrew heard shouts far away but saw no sign of the outlaws.

Eve tipped her head at Andrew. They sprinted on, staying parallel to the road while keeping a safe distance.

"I wonder where the riders went," Andrew said.

"To the castle gate, if they're smart," Eve replied.

She had barely finished speaking when Andrew heard the snort of a horse just ahead. He held up a hand to Eve. They crouched down.

"The riders?" Eve said.

The uneasy shuffle of hooves on the forest floor was unmistakable.

They carefully made their way forward.

"Why did the riders leave the road?" Andrew whispered.

They crept onward. Soon, the view through the trees answered Andrew's question. An armored rider was using a knife to scrape at one of his horse's hooves.

"If my horse has been crippled, those scoundrels will pay dearly," the rider growled.

He was short and burly, with a thick head of black hair and a full beard. He wore armor on his upper body and gray hose on his lower body. More armor was strapped around his knees, lower legs, and feet.

"We'll have to go around them," Eve whispered. "They might think we're the outlaws and attack."

"Or we can hide here until they move on," Andrew countered.

"Or you may join them," a man said from behind.

Startled, Andrew spun around. A hand caught his arm in a vicelike grip. He looked into the face of the second armored rider, a young man with a shock of brown hair on top of his shaved head. His beard was thin and his skin was a sunbaked brown. He looked at Andrew with lively brown eyes.

A set of arms quickly encircled Eve and lifted her from the ground. She cried out, kicking at her assailant.

"Be calm," the one clutching her said. "If you are the ones who gave us aid, then you need not fear. We are in your debt."

Andrew relaxed. Looking at Eve, he signaled with a nod.

Eve stopped struggling. The riders released them both.

"Come along," said the young man. "We have food and water, if those are of any interest to you."

The man who had grabbed Eve was tall and clean-shaven with a shaggy head of hair that splayed out from under a green cap. He wore a dark-green tunic, brown hose, and leather boots strapped around his legs. He reminded Andrew of Robin Hood.

The two men kept Andrew and Eve between them as they walked to the other riders. Andrew casually reached into his pocket and took out one of the few stones he had left. He slipped it into his fist. He noticed that Eve held her staff with both hands. Just in case.

The rest of the party stood inside the circle of horses. Two men wearing blousy tunics and dark hose down to their leather shoes rubbed the horses' backs and flanks. Andrew assumed they were servants to the men in armor.

Another man stepped from behind a horse. He wore a red cap that flopped down the side of his head. His tunic matched the cap. A dull yellow cloak around his shoulders gave him the look of a servant from a royal court. Dark knee-high boots covered his legs.

"What have we here?" The question came from the rider with the light voice, who now stepped out from between the two servants. It was a young woman. She seemed small and frail compared to the rest of the group. Andrew figured she might be a little over five feet tall. She wore a black wool cap above her slender face and had a round nose and full red lips. She was dressed in the clothes of a squire: a gray tunic, a black shirt, dark hose and breeches, and riding boots. Her large, determined eyes rested on Andrew. He shuffled nervously.

A smile crept onto her lips. She pulled the cap from her head, revealing black cropped hair. "How is it that two children are alone in the forest?"

"And how is it that two children have the cunning to ward off highway robbers?" asked the burly man.

The young woman held up her hand. "We are being discourteous. First, tell us your names."

"I am Andrew," he said, giving a slight bow.

"I am Evangeline." Eve curtsied.

The young woman's eyes darted to Eve, then sharpened. "Come here. I want to see you more closely."

Eve stepped over to her. They stood facing each other. Andrew was astonished.

"Good Maiden," said the burly man with a laugh, "she could be your sister."

"Why is she dressed as a man?" asked the younger armor wearer in the group.

The young woman asked Eve with a playful tone, "Do you mock me?"

Eve shook her head. "I cannot mock someone I do not know."

The young woman peered closely at Eve's eyes. "You have the eyes of an angel," she said softly. "Perhaps God has sent you to help me with my mission."

"Who are you?" Eve asked.

"I am Jeanne d'Arc of Domrémy."

Jeanne d'Arc? Andrew thought. *Why does that sound so familiar?*

"You are the one the townspeople are waiting to see," Eve said.

Now Andrew understood.

"The townspeople are waiting to see *me?*" asked Jeanne.

The red-capped man rolled his eyes. "Someone in the castle has spread the word."

"The entire countryside knows," said the burly man. "Did you truly believe our journey would be kept a secret?"

"There are crowds all over the town," Eve said.

Jeanne looked dismayed. "It is Laetare Sunday. I do not want to distract the people from their Lenten disciplines. They should be praying, not waiting for me."

"I fear no Lenten observances will thwart them from coming to see you," countered the man who looked like Robin Hood. He now had a longbow slung over his shoulder to complete the resemblance.

"Perhaps we should wait until tomorrow to enter the town," Jeanne said.

"You would keep the Dauphin waiting?" asked the red-capped man.

Jeanne smiled. "I cannot believe he is sitting idly on his throne waiting for me."

"Let us wait until noon, after the Mass has been celebrated," the burly man suggested.

Jeanne looked thoughtful, then said, "Back home the children will be celebrating Laetare Sunday with picnics at the miraculous Gooseberry Spring. They will hang wreaths on the Fairy Tree." A sad look crossed her face. "The fairies are no more. But to drink from the spring will keep the children free from fevers for an entire year."

Andrew heard in Jeanne's voice the tone of a young girl. *How old is she?* he wondered. *Fifteen? Sixteen?*

"Good Maiden," said the burly man, "it is well that you drank from the spring for so many years. Few women would have the strength to ride a horse for as many leagues as you have."

"My strength comes from the One who sent me," she said.

Suddenly she turned and waved to them all. "Let us not be inhospitable to our two angels. I have given my name; now you must each do the same. Declare yourselves."

The burly man gave a grand bow, his armor clanging as he did. "I am Bertrand de Poulengy, and this is my servant Julien."

Julien, in a red and blue tunic, also bowed.

The younger guard gave a quick nod. "I am Jean de Metz, squire to Robert de Baudricourt, with my servant Jean." The servant wore a dark-blue tunic and also bowed.

Too many Jeans, Andrew thought.

The man with the longbow stood up straight. "I am Richard l'Archer."

"And I am Colet de Vienne, a royal messenger," the man with the red cap said as he swept it off his head and gave a low, dramatic bow.

"These good men have brought me safely from Vaucouleurs," Jeanne said. "Now we must share what food and drink we have before we enter the town. I know you are angels, but you must be hungry and thirsty."

They gathered in a small circle, and Jeanne prayed for them all. Then the servants passed around morsels of bread and cheese. Andrew noticed that Richard l'Archer and the two servants kept their eyes on the surrounding forest. Watching for the outlaws, he assumed.

Bertrand asked, "Tell me, children, why you are alone in the forest. Where are your parents? Are you beggars? Orphans?"

Andrew and Eve gave the simplest and most truthful answers they could. Their parents were not with them, they said. So they traveled alone as wayfarers who only came to Chinon that day.

"Then you must travel with us," Jeanne exclaimed happily. "By the grace of God, we will meet the gentle Dauphin."

"Is that your mission?" Eve asked.

Jeanne nodded. "I am to tell him that he must allow me to drive the English away. Only then will he be crowned as the true king of France."

Andrew and Eve looked at each other.

"Drive the English away?" Eve asked. "Are they here?"

Bertrand snorted. "Here? They are all over France as unwelcome invaders. How could you not know that?"

"It is for me to persuade them to go home," Jeanne said.

"You mean you are going to fight in a war?" asked Andrew, worried.

"Only if the English will not heed my warnings to depart on their own," came her reply.

"And if they do not?" asked Eve.

Jeanne's eyes were wide and innocent. She said earnestly, "Then I shall wage war. God has willed that it must be done. So I shall do it."

After they had all eaten, the riders prepared to enter the town. The men checked their weapons and inspected the condition of their clothes. Jeanne went off alone to pray.

Andrew sat down next to a nearby tree and nestled in where the roots clawed at the ground like bony fingers. One of the men said something about the wet spring they'd had. The damp mulch under Andrew's bottom proved it. He'd also learned that it was now early March—March 5th, in fact. Jeanne and her company had been traveling from some other part of France since February 23rd. It was a miracle that they had come safely through parts of enemy country, until they met the highway robbers.

"We are in no fit state to see the Dauphin," Colet de Vienne announced.

"Surely he will be forgiving, knowing how far we have traveled," said Jean de Metz.

"I suggest we go to an inn first to make ourselves presentable," Colet said.

A debate followed about whether to stay in the forest or at an inn. Finally the decision was made. They would stay at an inn. Bertrand's servant, Julien, climbed onto his horse and rode off to Chinon to make the arrangements.

Andrew looked at his own mud-covered clothes. He knew that if they were washed, he'd have a bigger problem explaining them. He shivered. Though the sky was blue, the air was cold and damp. He wished he'd brought his coat, strange as it would look. He thought of it now, hanging uselessly in Alfred Virtue's office.

Eve stepped over to him, a blanket pulled around her.

"Where did you get that?" he asked.

"One of the servants gave it to me." She sniffed. "It's a horse blanket."

"I wish I had one. It's cold," he said.

"Share?" She sat down next to him and shrugged a corner of the blanket from her nearest shoulder.

He hesitated. In spite of all they'd gone through in the time of Robin Hood, they still knew very little about each other.

Eve must have noticed his reluctance. "Or you can stay cold," she said simply.

He pulled the blanket around his shoulder. Side by side, they sat in silence for a moment.

"Do you know the story of Joan of Arc?" Eve asked.

"I remember a little from history class." He thought for a moment. "She was sent by God to make the Dauphin the rightful king of France."

"You're only saying that because *she* said it." Eve elbowed him.

He laughed, then asked, "Who is the king now?"

"Someone from England. One of the English Henrys, I think." She picked up a small stick and scraped at the mud on the side of her shoe. "I can't remember why an English king is ruling France."

"The two countries fought all the time," Andrew recalled. "Henry the Fifth invaded them and kicked their rear ends at a place called Agincourt."

Eve looked astonished.

Andrew smiled. "Your Aunt Catherine isn't the only one who likes Shakespeare. My parents love the movie about Henry the Fifth. Though I forgot the part about the Dauphin. He was an annoying little weasel."

Eve sighed. "I wish we'd gone back to England instead."

"We could have found Robin," Andrew said, brightening up.

Eve shook her head. "We're a couple of hundred years too late. He's dead by now."

Andrew groaned. "We just saw him this morning, and now he's been dead for a couple hundred years?"

Eve tossed her stick aside. "So what are we going to do?" she asked.

"About what?"

"About being stuck here."

"How am I supposed to know?" Andrew said. "You're the expert on time travel."

"And *you're* the one who said God put us here."

They fell into a quiet sulk. "Maybe we're here to help Jeanne," Andrew eventually suggested.

Eve glanced around as if to make sure no one was listening. "How can we help? Don't you remember?" She leaned in close and whispered, "They burn her at the stake. You think God put us here to light the match?"

"Maybe He wants us to blow it out."

"We can't change history," Eve stated. "If we try, time will mess us up."

"Then we'll have to figure it out as we go along," Andrew said hopefully.

"For the rest of our lives?" she asked.

Andrew shrugged. "We'll get home somehow. I don't believe God will leave us stranded here."

Eve turned to him. "What if He does?"

Andrew tried to think of an answer but couldn't come up with one. Then he noticed that Jeanne and her escorts were looking at them.

Jeanne nodded to Bertrand, then strode over to them. She knelt down. "What are we to do with you, my angels?" she asked. "Your clothes are ..." She gestured to their jeans and sneakers. "Of what are these made?"

"Cotton," said Eve.

She pointed to their shoes. "What make of leather are these?"

"The plastic kind," said Andrew.

Jeanne looked confused, as if she hadn't heard correctly. "*Plass-teek*? From what country do they come?" she asked. "I have never seen such a thing in France."

Andrew said, "My clothes came from a shop. I cannot say how they were made."

Bertrand joined them. He said to Jeanne, "Dear Maiden, it is enough of an offense for you to be dressed in a man's clothes, but for this girl to do the same is sheer folly. Their clothes betray a foreign tailor. The court of the Dauphin will suspect a plot. They may believe we are in league with those who would do harm to him."

"This is easily remedied," Jeanne said. She went over to her horse and opened a worn satchel. From it she retrieved a red dress and, with further digging, a pair of leather shoes.

Jean de Metz saw the dress and cried out, "How is it possible? I gave orders to burn that dress!" He scowled at his servant.

The servant spread his hands. "She was unyielding, master! She refused to part with it."

"Just as well," said Jeanne. "It is good we have clothes for our angel." She handed the dress and shoes to Eve.

Eve stood up. The dress looked as if it might fit. She moved away to change.

"What of the boy?" Bertrand asked.

Jean de Metz pointed to his servant. "For his disobedience, he will find suitable clothes for the boy."

"Me?" the servant asked. "Where will I find them?"

"In Chinon."

"Master, the shops will be closed," the servant complained.

De Metz gave him a stern look. "That is a problem for you to solve."

With a pained expression, the servant bowed.

———————➤

At midday, Jeanne and her guards walked their horses to the road, then mounted them. Andrew assumed that he and Eve would follow on foot, but Jeanne insisted that Eve ride with Richard l'Archer and Andrew ride with Jean de Metz.

The red dress and shoes were awkward for Eve. She had to ride sidesaddle.

With a commanding "Forward!" Jeanne spurred her horse on.

They rode at a slow but steady pace. Coming out of the forest, Andrew lifted a hand to shield his eyes from the bright sun overhead. As his eyes adjusted, he saw the town ahead. It sat like an obedient servant at the foot of the castle walls, towers, and turrets. The Vienne River curved like a blue ribbon to the left. Furrowed fields spread far away to the right.

"God's glory!" Jeanne cried out.

Chinon came alive as they approached. Word spread that *Jeanne la Pucelle* was coming.

A rider sped toward them from the town. It was Julien, Bertrand's servant. He reined in his horse alongside his master's. "I have found an inn for us," he announced.

"Then I shall go directly to the castle to inform the Dauphin of our arrival," Colet said.

"May God grant you speed," Jeanne called out.

Colet urged his horse on and galloped away.

As the riders came to the gate of Chinon, the townspeople called out much as they had earlier: *Jeanne of Domrémy, Maiden of Honor! Virgin Saint!* Some shouted out to her as the savior of France. A few shook fists and declared her to be a false prophetess. Andrew heard others complain that she was dressed as a man.

Jeanne seemed unconcerned. She rode with her shoulders erect and her head held high.

They followed Julien around a corner to a side street. Each rider dismounted in front of a ramshackle building made of dark wood and plaster. They eyed the place with concern.

"Sneeze and it will collapse," Bertrand said.

"With apologies, sir," said Julien. "It is the only inn that would have us. The madame seems like a good-hearted woman."

"We have not come this far to be fussy," Jeanne said. She pushed the wooden door. The rusty hinges squeaked loudly. The door listed as if it would fall off.

They stepped into a low-ceilinged room with a few tables and chairs. At the far end was a counter made of an old door and two sawhorses. It was covered with bottles and cups.

"Ah!" a woman exclaimed, bustling around the counter. She was thin, with a bony frame that resembled an assembly of matchsticks. Her tunic and skirt looked as if they'd swallowed everything but her head. "I am Marie de Loire. Welcome!"

"Greetings," said Bertrand.

The woman knelt in front of Jeanne and lowered her head. "Welcome, saintly Maiden."

Jeanne reached down and touched her shoulder. "None of that, dear mother. Stand up," she said.

The innkeeper smiled, then stood and waved for everyone to sit down. They made themselves as comfortable as they could on the rickety chairs. Cups of drink were quickly placed in front of them. Plates of bread, cheese, and suspicious-looking meat were delivered by a somewhat harried girl who looked like a younger version of the innkeeper.

Andrew ate slowly and carefully. Eve held up a piece of cheese, inspected it, then put it down again. Jeanne did not eat at all.

"I have rooms for you," Marie de Loire said.

"*Merci*, but no," protested Jeanne. "We need only clean ourselves up. The Dauphin will summon us soon."

The woman laughed. "You will not see him today, sweet girl. His advisers will not allow it. They must discuss and debate long before they will welcome you into their sacred company."

"But he summoned us," Jeanne said. "It was he who—"

"Trust me, child," the woman interrupted. "You will want the rooms. You, with your maidservant." She gestured to Eve. "The men will share the largest room I have."

"*Merci*," said Jean de Metz.

The woman added proudly, "I have prayed for my cats to drive away the rats, and by the grace of Saint Gertrude, they have. You will be undisturbed. But the rats up there"—she nodded toward the castle—"are another matter."

The other Jean, the servant of Jean de Metz, asked her where he might find a change of clothes for Andrew.

Marie de Loire gave Andrew a once-over, then said, "I have clothes that will fit him. They belonged to my son. He donned armor to fight for our country. Killed, he was, by the English murderers in Burgundy. Come!"

The innkeeper was right. The clothes fit Andrew perfectly—a wool tunic that draped down to his knees, wool hose, and leather boots that laced up the front. A leather belt cinched around his waist, with a loop to hold a knife.

"Perfect!" she said with a clap of her hands.

It bothered Andrew to wear the clothes of a dead person. It bothered him more when the harried servant took his clothes away to be washed.

Jean de Metz also gave the servant girl Eve's modern clothes to wash. Eve shot Andrew a worried glance.

Colet returned from the castle and delivered the disheartening news that the Dauphin would not grant an audience with Jeanne until he consulted with the wisest of his court.

Marie de Loire flashed a knowing smile at Jeanne. "You see?"

"I fear we have come for nothing," Colet complained. "The Dauphin is surrounded by men of doubtful intent."

"What men?" Jeanne asked.

"Georges de La Trémoille is a wily character. He will not readily serve your mission if it interferes with his own desires. The Archbishop of Reims plays one side against another, as it suits him."

"What are we to do?" Jeanne asked.

Colet said in a reassuring tone, "As a royal messenger, I must stay at the castle. There, I will discern who will aid your cause."

After Colet left, Jeanne said to her small group, "God desires to teach me patience."

Marie de Loire laughed. "I fear God has little to do with the goings-on in that castle."

"Mind your tongue, old woman," Bertrand warned her.

"I speak plainly," the innkeeper snapped back, her hands on her hips. "Was it not God's will for us to suffer defeat at the hands of the English again and again? Do you not remember the tales of the battle at Crécy, when the English King Edward's out-numbered soldiers defeated our French army with mere *arrows*? Or when Edward's son, the Black Prince, destroyed the French army at Poitiers? It was not so long ago that King Henry the Fifth conquered us at Agincourt."

"What are you suggesting?" Bertrand asked sourly.

"These victories must have been the will of God. Why else would He allow the Dauphin to live as an exile in his own country? Why else does the Duke of Burgundy dance like a puppet for the English boy-king Henry, the sixth of that name? Why does He allow the English to rule us at all?"

"Perhaps it was the will of God for us to be humbled," said Jeanne. "Now it is His will for the true king of France to be crowned in Reims. It is time for France to be French again, without the foreign invaders."

"Reims!" the lady cried. "How will you dislodge the coward from Chinon to crown him in Reims? Have you forgotten that you must first pass poor Orléans to reach Reims? The English hold that city under siege."

"By God's power, I will free Orléans," Jeanne said.

The woman's jaw dropped. "*You*, dear child?"

"God has said it will be so," Jeanne replied.

Marie de Loire closed her mouth and said very little for the rest of the day.

Afternoon slipped away. Jeanne and her companions did not dare to go outside, fearing the crowds would mob Jeanne. Instead, they prowled around the inn. The men scrubbed their clothes and stitched any tears they found. Then they gave their weapons a detailed shine.

Evening chased the daylight from the inn. Lamps were lit in the various rooms. Jeanne led everyone in evening prayers, then said goodnight. Eve went with her into a small room at the back.

Andrew joined the five men in a large open room with two beds and a pile of thin straw mats. Bertrand and Jean de Metz claimed the two beds, since they were paying for everything from their own pockets. The two servants deferred to Richard l'Archer, allowing him to pile two of the mats on top of each other so he might sleep more comfortably. They gave "Andrew the Angel" the remaining mat, which was only slightly better than sleeping on the hardwood floor.

At dawn, Andrew awakened in time to see Bertrand hand Richard l'Archer a pouch of money. Richard saw that Andrew was awake. He gave a quick salute, then left.

"Where is he going?" Andrew asked.

"Home to Vaucouleurs," Bertrand said. "His work for us is finished."

The two servants busied themselves by bringing bowls of water so the men could wash and shave.

A little later, Andrew bumped into Eve in the narrow hallway between the rooms. She looked tired.

"You didn't sleep?" he asked.

"Jeanne prayed for part of the night. Sometimes out loud," Eve said, then smiled. "I tried to join her but kept falling asleep. See? I am not a holy maiden."

"Are you Jeanne's servant now?" Andrew asked.

Eve shrugged. "I'm following along to see what happens. Isn't that the plan?"

"I guess so," Andrew said. What else could they do?

Marie de Loire greeted them in the main room, then cautioned them about going outside. "The people are already crowding the lane to see the Maiden. If they know you are with her, they may mob you."

"We are getting used to it," Eve said.

Bertrand, Jean de Metz, and the servants sat down at a table. A few minutes later, Jeanne joined them.

Breakfast—if it could be considered breakfast— consisted of a watery kind of porridge and warm bread. Only Andrew, Eve, and the servants ate. Jeanne and the two soldiers refrained.

"Why will you not eat?" Andrew asked Bertrand and Jean de Metz.

"A meal first thing in the morning is for peasant workers, women, and children," Bertrand replied.

"I fit those categories," Eve said, then dipped a piece of bread into her bowl of porridge.

"Me, too." Andrew laughed and upended his bowl of porridge into his mouth.

The men looked at him, unimpressed.

Suddenly Jeanne put a hand over her mouth and giggled. Then she laughed outright. For a moment, Andrew saw the young peasant girl from a small village somewhere.

How did she wind up here? he wondered.

———————————————➤

Later that morning, some men arrived from the castle. The innkeeper became very excited and dashed to a back room to find refreshments. The two servants, Jean and Julien, raced to tell their masters.

"Look," Eve whispered as three men came through the door.

Andrew was surprised to see that one of them was the white-haired old man who had assaulted Eve on the bridge the day before. "He's from the court?"

The old man went to a corner table away from the others. He sat down without speaking. The other two men invited Jeanne to be seated so they could talk.

One of the men was bald, but he sported a brown beard that hung down to the middle of his chest. The other was clean-shaven and had thin, curly white hair matted against his scalp. Both wore long cloaks. They introduced themselves with elaborate titles that went on so long, Andrew had lost interest by the time they reached their names.

Andrew noticed that the old man at the table wasn't looking at Jeanne. His eyes were on Eve. Slowly his gaze shifted to Andrew.

Andrew stared back at him. The old man's eyes were dark and showed no emotion. Andrew looked away.

Bertrand and Jean de Metz entered from the back of the inn. The two men gave them quick nods of greeting. The bald one held up his hand for them to stay back.

"The Dauphin has sent us to inquire about your mission here," the bald man said.

"My mission is for his ears only," said Jeanne.

"As we are here in his name, you should treat us as you would him," the curly-haired man said to Jeanne. "If not, then you will never be granted an audience with him."

Jeanne paused as if weighing her options. Then she said, "The King of Heaven has sent me to lift the siege of Orléans and to lead the Dauphin to Reims for his coronation."

The eyebrows of both men lifted up. The old man at the table leaned forward. His gaze shot from Andrew to Eve and then to Jeanne.

"You have come to inspire the Dauphin with these words?" the bald man asked. "You hope to entice him to attack Orléans?"

Jeanne shook her head. "It is not for him to attack Orléans. God has sent me to do it."

"*You?*" the curly-haired man asked, his eyebrows lifting.

"Who put this idea into your head?" the bald man asked.

"Messengers from God," said Jeanne.

"What messengers?" asked the bald man.

"Saint Michael and his angels," Jeanne replied.

The two men scooted back in their chairs, as if they feared a bolt of lightning might strike her. One exclaimed something that Andrew's mind couldn't translate, and the tone made him glad of it.

"We have heard rumors of this but dared not believe it," said the bald man.

The curly-haired man held up a thick finger. "How do you know it was Saint Michael and his angels? Perhaps it was a devil and its legions?"

"I would have recognized one from the other," Jeanne said. "Saint Michael would not allow me to be deceived."

The bald man snorted. "Arrogant child! Was it not a widow in Champagne who entertained both? Women are easy prey to the wiles of the devil."

"Some women, perhaps, but not I," Jeanne said calmly. "I can prove what I say."

The bald man waved his hand. "How? Will Saint Michael appear to us now?"

"That is his business, not mine," said Jeanne. "I have a message to deliver to the Dauphin. It is something only he can know, because it is from his prayers."

"You know what he prays?" the curly-haired man asked.

"The messengers told me," Jeanne replied.

"We shall see about that," the bald man said.

The curly-haired man turned his sights to Bertrand and Jean de Metz. "You are the two escorts from Robert de Baudricourt?"

"We are," Bertrand answered.

"The Dauphin wishes to speak with you," the bald one said.

"When?" asked Jean de Metz.

"Now." The bald man stood up. The curly-haired one did the same.

Jean de Metz and Bertrand looked at each other.

De Metz gave a quick bow to the men. "As you wish," he said.

"What of my audience with the Dauphin?" Jeanne asked, slowly rising.

"In time, if he desires it," the bald man said.

Out the door they went, with Bertrand asking the two men, "May we seek compensation from the Dauphin for bringing the girl safely to him?"

The old man slowly stood up, as if in pain. With stooped shoulders, he followed the others. He turned at the door as if to say something, but then he shook his head and walked on, latching the door behind him.

Marie rushed out from a back room. She fanned an apron at her flushed face. "By the saints!" she cried and collapsed into a chair. "Never have I entertained members of the royal court."

Jeanne frowned. "Why does the Dauphin delay? Is he playing games with me?"

"Dear child, he is a scared rabbit," Marie said. "He has been played the fool too often. He fears you have come to do the same."

"How can I assure him otherwise if he will not see me?" Jeanne lamented.

"How indeed?" Marie asked.

Jeanne attempted to disguise herself to attend Mass but was easily recognized. The crowd pressed in to touch her, pushing Andrew and Eve aside.

During the Mass, Andrew was distracted by all of the looks and whispering. Finally the priest shouted for the parishioners to cease their disrespect for God.

Back at the inn, Jeanne complained, "The people clamor to see me, but not the Dauphin."

So they sat and waited and prayed. To pass the time, Andrew and Eve played a game of stacking small sticks of wood to see how high they could go without toppling. The game ended when the innkeeper used the sticks as kindling for a fire.

Jeanne watched the sticks burn, with a somber expression on her face.

Supper included potatoes, bread, and another unidentifiable kind of meat.

"When did they invent french fries?" Andrew whispered to Eve.

"They didn't. French fries are American," she whispered back.

"Then why are they called French?" asked Andrew.

"It has something to do with cutting the potatoes in long strips, or something like that," Eve explained.

"Give me a knife and I'll invent them now," Andrew said.

Eve laughed. "They don't have deep fryers yet."

"I'll invent those, too," said Andrew.

In the middle of the meal, Bertrand and Jean de Metz returned from the castle.

Jeanne stood up as they came in. "Well? Tell me of your audience with the Dauphin."

"Please be seated, good Maiden," Bertrand said. He and Jean de Metz sat down. Their servants busied themselves setting food in front of the two men.

"The king asked us about our travels," de Metz explained. "He had heard rumors of miracles."

"It has been said that rivers parted for us," Bertrand said, smiling.

"He also heard that an ambush was foiled," said Jean de Metz.

Jeanne looked at Andrew and Eve. "And so it was."

Bertrand gulped down a tankard of ale, then wiped his mouth with the back of his hand. "The only miracle I saw was that we brought you safely through enemy lands, defying even the foul weather. That is miracle enough for me."

"It will be a greater miracle if we are compensated for our efforts," Jean de Metz added.

"When will the Dauphin see me?" Jeanne asked.

Bertrand gazed at her sadly. "In his own sweet time."

It didn't take as long as they feared.

Serving as the royal messenger, Colet arrived the next afternoon with three guards from the castle. With a wary smile, he bowed and said, "The Dauphin bids you come. He will see you, even against the advice of many in his court."

Jeanne lifted her hands and said, "Thanks be to God! Hurry! Gather your things. We must go."

"Not everyone," Colet said. "*You*."

Jeanne froze. "What of my angels? I cannot go without them."

Colet waved a hand at Andrew and Eve. "Your two angels may go as your servants. The others must remain— or depart. It is up to them."

"Depart! We must be compensated," insisted Bertrand.

"I am assured you will be," Colet said. "However, our Maiden must be seen first."

Jeanne bid farewell to Bertrand de Poulengy and Jean de Metz, her guides and protectors. "God will reward you for what you have done," she said. "I hope we will see one another again."

De Metz came close to her and said, "If ever you are in need of help, send a messenger to us. We will come."

Bertrand gave her a reassuring nod.

"*Merci*," she said, touching their hands like a blessing.

The servants of Bertrand and Jean de Metz retrieved Jeanne's horse from the stable, saddling it for the short journey up to the castle. Jeanne thanked them for their dutiful service to her.

Getting to the castle gate up the steep and dusty hill was a slow process. The people of Chinon gathered around Jeanne's horse, reaching out to touch her leg or foot. Colet, also on horseback, shouted at them to get back. The three castle guards shoved them aside, demanding that they make way.

Andrew and Eve were given a horse of their own and trailed behind the others. The crowd pressed in again. Andrew hoped they wouldn't get knocked off or trampled.

The procession came to the main gate. Reaching a drawbridge, the crowds were forced to stay back or risk falling into the moat below.

"Tell me of the castle," Jeanne said to Colet, now that she was able to be heard.

"There are *three* castles behind these walls," Colet explained. "To the west are the towers of the Fort du Coudray. Then, in the middle, is the Château du Milieu. The Dauphin resides there, in the chamber of Saint Louis.

It is next to the Grande Salle, the great hall, where you will be received. The garrison is in the stronghold to the right."

"Is there a chapel?" Jeanne asked.

"Yes, dear Maiden. It is just beyond this gate. The second Henry of England built it, under the patronage of Saint George. You know of Saint George?"

"A valiant knight," Jeanne answered. "He slew a dragon and saved a king's daughter, though he was still martyred for his faith."

Colet nodded. "Bound to a wheel with terrible spikes, like Saint Catherine. But the wheel miraculously broke, so he was murdered with an axe."

Once inside the gate, they entered a courtyard. Soldiers and workers alike turned from their duties to see the young woman on horseback.

A coarse-looking man staggered toward them. He was half dressed in his guard uniform and reeked of alcohol. He leered up at Jeanne. "Give me time, and I will put you in a different condition than you are."

Jeanne slowed her horse and gazed down at him. "Why do you use your time to offend God, when you are so near to death?"

The man opened his mouth to respond, but he suddenly went pale. He pressed his lips together and stumbled back as if she had struck him.

"Clear the way!" Colet shouted. "Or the Dauphin shall hear of it."

With the sounds of shuffling feet and rattling armor, the men drew back. Suddenly, a robed friar pushed through the crowd and called out, "*Jesu Maria.*" He lifted his hands and blessed Jeanne as she went past.

They crossed a second drawbridge and came to yet another courtyard. Colet dismounted. Servants suddenly appeared and helped Jeanne do the same. She waved them away and climbed down herself.

A man in a lavish red robe with a fur-lined collar stepped forward. He bowed low. "I am the Count of Vendôme, Louis de Bourbon. I have been given the honor of escorting you to the king."

Jeanne curtsied, which looked strange for someone in a man's clothes. "*Merci*, good count."

Led by the count, Andrew and Eve followed the entourage through a set of large doors. Andrew felt lost as they trekked down various hallways. They climbed a broad staircase and finally reached a set of huge wooden doors.

"His Highness is inside," the count said.

The doors seemed to swing open on their own.

Andrew would always remember the sight of Jeanne framed in that massive arched doorway, a tiny figure facing a great giant. Beyond her was a long meeting hall that stretched to a gigantic fireplace. Hundreds of people were gathered, dressed in the colorful clothes of the wealthy, the clergy, and high-ranking soldiers. Tapestries covered the walls, separated by dozens of lit torches hanging on iron rings. The room smelled of sweat, perfume, and burning oil.

The Count of Vendôme walked quickly ahead of the company and seemed to melt into the crowd. Jeanne slowly entered. Her black-and-gray clothes looked dull compared to all the colors around her. The assembly went silent.

Andrew and Eve stayed several feet behind Jeanne. Andrew searched the faces of the gawking crowd. Some looked at Jeanne with expressions of disdain. A few smirked. Most looked at her as if she were part of a freak show that had arrived to entertain them. Andrew then caught sight of a tall figure behind the others. It was the old man who had grabbed Eve on the bridge.

Jeanne's head turned slowly to the left and the right. She paused, stopping in front of a young man wearing robes far more royal than any of the others. He smiled at her.

The Dauphin, Andrew thought.

But rather than bow, as Andrew expected, Jeanne only nodded and walked past the young man.

Ahead was a large chair, the size of a throne. In it was a man sitting regally, his hands clasped in front of him as if waiting for her to come and pay homage. Surely that was the Dauphin.

Jeanne only glanced at the man, then turned toward a small cluster of men and women off to the side. A white-haired woman wearing a black, ornately jeweled dress was there. She smiled kindly at Jeanne.

"Pardon me," Jeanne said to the woman, then stepped past her. Andrew heard Jeanne say "Ah" to another young-looking man dressed in a modest tunic. He had a thin, pale face, with small eyes and a large nose. His thick lips hung like two sausages over a weak chin. Bony, hose-covered legs gave him the look of a stork.

Jeanne knelt at his feet.

The man on the throne stood up with an indignant expression. "What are you doing?" he called out.

Andrew and Eve looked at each other. *It has to be a mistake,* thought Andrew. *Poor Jeanne has come all this way and is kneeling in front of the wrong man.*

Then it got worse.

"Gentle Dauphin," Jeanne said, her head lowered. "May God give you a long life."

The pale stork of a man looked at her helplessly. His small eyes darted one way, then another, as if he wanted someone in the crowd to stop the embarrassment. He rubbed his nose nervously.

"Why do you speak to me?" he asked, then pointed to the man in the large chair. "There is your lord."

Jeanne did not bother to look toward the chair. "In God's name, noble Dauphin," she said, "it is you and none other."

A sound like a childish giggle came from the man's throat. Then the man relaxed. "I am your Dauphin," he said.

Jeanne smiled up at him. Laughter echoed around the hall.

"They tried to trick her," Eve whispered to Andrew.

"Pray, who are you?" the Dauphin asked. He reached down and gently lifted Jeanne to her feet. "Why have you come to me?"

Jeanne stood before him, her voice strong. "The King of Heaven sends me to you with this message: You shall be anointed and crowned in the city of Reims. You shall be the king of France, the lieutenant of the King of Heaven."

Whispers rolled through the crowd, followed by a stern look from the Dauphin. The gathering fell silent again.

"In my heart I yearn to believe you," he said. "Give me cause to do so."

"Sire, if I tell you things so secret that you and God alone know them, will you believe that He has sent me?" Jeanne asked.

"I will," said the Dauphin.

Jeanne looked at the assembly, all straining to hear her.

The Dauphin saw her expression and, taking her arm, led her to the far end of the hall near the massive hooded fireplace.

Andrew wasn't sure they should follow. Without looking to anyone for permission, Eve did. Andrew tagged along.

The Dauphin gave the two children a suspicious look as they approached.

Jeanne ignored them, a signal that the Dauphin should do the same.

"What, then, is the secret?" the Dauphin asked. "I have so few, with spies watching me at every turn."

Jeanne said softly, "Remember, sire, last All Saints' Day. You were alone in your oratory, in the chapel of the castle at Loches."

The Dauphin's small eyes widened. Andrew could see his mind working. He was trying to figure out how a peasant girl could know anything about his chapel in the castle at Loches or his whereabouts months before.

"I remember it well," he said, his voice a dry rasp.

"You asked three things of God," she told him.

The Dauphin's mouth fell open.

"Have you spoken of these things to a confessor or to anyone who might have betrayed them to me?" she asked.

"I have not," he said.

"Then hear me, gentle Dauphin. Your first request of God was that he should remove you from the throne if you are not France's true heir. You do not desire to be the cause of prolonging a war that brings so much suffering."

The Dauphin slowly nodded. "It is so. And the second?"

"The second was that you alone should be punished if your sins have caused the many troubles the people of France are forced to endure. You said you are willing to die, if God requires it."

Tears came to the Dauphin's eyes. "It is as you say. Speak to me of the third."

"The third request was that the people should be forgiven, and God's anger appeased, if their own sins are the cause of their misery."

The Dauphin lowered his head for a moment. Then lifting it up again, he said, "You have spoken the truth."

He wiped his eyes, then turned suddenly and marched to the center of the hall. All eyes were on him now, as the people anxiously awaited his verdict.

"God has sent her to me," he announced.

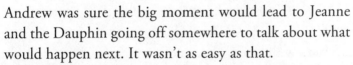

Andrew was sure the big moment would lead to Jeanne and the Dauphin going off somewhere to talk about what would happen next. It wasn't as easy as that.

With the Dauphin's announcement, a clamor rose from the crowd. Various men stepped forward, appealing to the Dauphin to be cautious and wise. They demanded that Jeanne be tested further to prove that she spoke for God.

The Dauphin looked conflicted. Finally he raised his hands to quiet them. "Please! Be still!" With an apologetic expression, he turned to Jeanne and said, "Dear Maiden, you will be taken to the Tower of Coudray."

Jeanne looked bewildered.

Andrew was shocked. *How could the Dauphin put her in a tower?* From his history lessons, he thought that being taken to a tower was the same as being put in prison.

An escort of servants and guards came forward and escorted the three of them to the western side of the grounds. At the base of a large tower, they were met by a man who introduced himself as Guillaume Bellier, the chief steward of the Dauphin. Next to him was his wife, Madame Bellier, an elf-like woman with a glowing smile.

"The tower is the royal residence for honored guests," said the steward.

Andrew was relieved.

Madame Bellier bowed to Jeanne. Then she looked at Eve and said, "Dear child, I have never seen eyes that color."

"She is my angel," Jeanne said, then gestured to Andrew. "This boy is her helper."

Andrew flinched. "I am not her helper," he said.

Eve shot him a grin.

A young man—maybe fourteen or fifteen years old—stepped forward. He had brown hair cut in the shape of a bowl, and a round face that was scarred with acne. He bowed his head.

"This is Louis de Coutes, our *Minguet*," Monsieur Bellier said to Jeanne. "He is to be your page during the day. My wife will see to you at night."

Wicks and torches were lit; then they entered the tower. Inside it looked exactly as it did outside: round. The staircase rose like a corkscrew around an edge of stony shadows. They passed various doors along the way.

"A round room is on every floor," Monsieur Bellier said.

"Dignitaries often stay here when visiting," Madame Bellier explained, then added cheerfully, "The king must think of you as a dignitary."

"Why am I to stay in this tower?" Jeanne asked with an impatient tone. "There is too much work to be done for me to be idle here."

Madame Bellier gave her a sympathetic smile. "Dear child, Saint Paul tells us to test the spirits that come our way. We must be discerning. Our prince would be a fool to follow the vision of every person who stands at the gate and claims to speak for God."

"I am not 'every person,'" Jeanne said. "*God* has sent me with this message."

"You ask too much of those who have not seen or heard what you have," Madame Bellier countered. "Allow us to prove your message."

"While you prove it, the English are spilling French blood," Jeanne said sharply.

"French blood has been spilled for a hundred years under the eyes of God. What is another day or month to Him?" Madame Bellier asked without losing her pleasant tone.

Jeanne frowned. For a moment, Andrew saw the face of a young girl sulking.

They stopped at a doorway. Monsieur Bellier said, "Minguet, you and the servant boy—"

"My name is Andrew," he cut in.

"Yes, *Andrew*," Bellier continued. "The two of you will stay in here. Jeanne will stay with her angel and Madame in the room above you."

Madame Bellier continued to lead the ladies upward. Monsieur Bellier followed them, explaining how King

Philip the Fourth held the Knights Templar captive in the castle one hundred years before. His voice faded away.

Louis stepped into the room. Andrew lingered at the doorway. He thought he heard a noise from somewhere down the stairs. He turned and, from the corner of his eye, saw movement just around the curve. The shadow of a man stood still against the wall. Then it slowly retreated until it was out of sight.

8

"I'm sure it was the old man from the bridge," Andrew said to Eve the next morning.

They were standing outside the chapel of Saint Martin. The Dauphin had commanded that it be reserved solely for Jeanne and her company.

"What does he want?" Eve asked. "I had a dream last night about that wild look he had in his eyes when he came after me. I think he's crazy."

"He's definitely creepy," said Andrew.

Eve stepped back and eyed him from head to foot. "You're wearing new clothes."

Andrew had on a dark-gray tunic with black leggings and shoes. A leather belt was buckled around his waist.

"Monsieur Bellier gave them to me this morning. He said I have to look appropriate for the court."

"And me?" Eve asked, spreading her arms and turning slowly. She was now adorned in a long white tunic with a dark-blue dress underneath.

"Pretty," he said.

She tugged at her dress. "I would rather wear my real clothes."

The door to the chapel opened, and Madame Bellier stepped through.

Jeanne came out a few seconds later. She was wearing the same black-and-gray outfit.

"Thanks be to God for the Dauphin's kindness in providing us with a private chapel," Jeanne said. She turned to Madame Bellier. "When may I see him again?"

"First, you must meet with Madame de Trèves and Madame de Gaucourt," said Madame Bellier.

"Who are they?" Jeanne asked.

Madame Bellier looked surprised. "How do you not know? Madame de Trèves is the wife of Robert Le Maçon of Trèves, the chancellor and one of the king's most trusted advisers. Madame de Gaucourt is the wife of Raoul de Gaucourt, the captain of Chinon and bailiff of Orléans."

Jeanne nodded. Andrew thought she was trying to look impressed but really didn't care.

Madame Bellier seemed to realize Jeanne's feelings and added, "The queen of Sicily has arranged everything."

Jeanne looked puzzled. "Of what interest am I to the queen of Sicily?"

"She is Yolande of Aragon, the Dauphin's mother-in-law. Surely you have heard of her. She certainly has a keen interest in you."

"Does she?"

"Oh yes. She greatly desires your success in God's mission. That is why she wants everything proven."

"How am I to be 'proven' by these good ladies?" Jeanne asked, bristling.

"Madame de Trèves and Madame de Gaucourt will get to know you. Then they will be able to assure the Dauphin that you are who and what you say you are."

Jeanne sighed. "If it will satisfy the Dauphin, I will comply. *Then* may I see him?"

"Of course you may," Madame Bellier assured her. "Once the council speaks with you."

Jeanne's shoulders slumped. "Is it necessary?" she asked.

"It is by the Dauphin's command," Madame Bellier said.

Jeanne nodded and straightened up. "Then let us begin."

"What would you like me to do?" Eve asked.

"You must stay by your lady's side," Madame Bellier replied. "Wait patiently, nearby, wherever she is. Louis, our Minguet, will be with you."

Louis suddenly appeared from around a corner and gave a quick bow.

"What am I supposed to do?" Andrew asked.

Madame Bellier turned to Andrew as if she had forgotten he was there. "What are your skills? Have you ever served in a royal court?"

"No," he said.

"As a page or a squire?"

"No."

She gave him the smile of a teacher who didn't know what to do with a misfit student. "I suggest you explore the castle and its grounds. Louis will train you in the ways of a page when he is not attending to Jeanne. Perhaps my husband will invent a purpose for you."

Andrew watched the four of them walk away. He felt annoyed. Why would God put him in this time and not give him anything to do?

He looked around and decided to take Madame Bellier's advice. How often would he have the chance to wander around a real castle without worrying about getting in trouble? Now was a very good time to explore.

He learned quickly that in many ways, a castle was like a busy city. Messengers raced in all directions. There were carpenters fixing wooden beams and masons chiseling on stone. Blacksmiths hammered on anvils, while groomsmen brushed the horses. Cooks chopped at vegetables on wooden tables and stirred the contents of large cauldrons with iron spoons.

Chickens got under Andrew's feet. The occasional cat meowed at him. Dogs chased each other. Children scampered and played in corners, out of the way of scowling soldiers. Guards stood at attention or strolled with their spears held like walking sticks, their hands on the hilts of their swords. Cadets sparred with one another using wooden swords or stood with their bows, shooting arrows at targets tied to bales of hay. The air was filled with the smell of damp straw, smoke, animals, and sweat.

Suddenly, a peasant woman rushed from a doorway, her hands covering her face. She sobbed loudly as she passed Andrew. He watched her rush off, then turned to see a robed man just inside a nearby room. The man was standing over a dead body stretched out on a slab. Andrew was sure he'd seen the face of the dead man before. It was the guard who had been so rude to Jeanne when they arrived at the castle the day before.

The robed man saw Andrew staring. He stepped to the door and said, "Take heed and learn from this man. This is what happens when you drink too much."

"What happened to him?" Andrew asked.

"The fool fell into the river last night," the man said, then closed the door on Andrew.

As Andrew walked away, he remembered Jeanne's words to the drunken guard. She had rebuked him for disrespecting God when he was so close to death.

Had Jeanne known the man was going to die, or was the man punished for being abusive to her?

Bored of exploring the courtyards, Andrew found his way to the main castle, where the Dauphin lived and kept court. He hoped he would bump into Eve. He went to a doorway he thought they had used when they first arrived. A guard gave him a cautious look.

"I am a servant of Jeanne," Andrew said. "The Maiden?"

The guard pushed the door open. Andrew entered a passageway that ended in a set of stairs. He followed them up to a wide hallway where small groups of people stood chatting softly. Servants flitted here and there. They were better uniformed than the ones in the courtyard.

Women adorned in satin, velvet, and lace dresses seemed to float in and out of various doorways. Men in regal-looking tunics and robes walked with their heads close together in quiet consultation.

Andrew was hardly noticed. Only the guards saw him and gestured for him to move on or warned him not to go down a particular hallway. He heard doors opening and closing and voices echoing from other places. He wandered down one passage, then another. Soon he was lost.

Behind him, a gruff voice asked, "Who are you? What are you doing here?"

Andrew ignored the man and picked up his pace as if he hadn't heard. The footsteps behind him quickened. Andrew darted down a side corridor. He saw a door standing slightly ajar and slipped through. He pulled the door behind him and waited. The footsteps came rushing up, then past.

Andrew leaned against the door and caught his breath. He turned to see what kind of room he'd entered. It was a narrow stairwell. Somewhere up above, men were talking. Then Andrew heard a girl's voice. It was Jeanne.

Creeping to the top of the stairs, Andrew found himself in the shadows of a low-ceilinged balcony. He went to a wooden rail and carefully peeked over. The room was a large rectangle with tall arched windows and banners. Men in brightly colored robes sat around an oversized table. At the far end of the table, Jeanne stood with her hands clasped in front of her. She looked like a prisoner in front of a panel of judges.

He took another step, and the floor creaked loudly beneath his foot. He backed up to make sure he wasn't seen. A hand fell on his shoulder and another clasped over his mouth.

"Shhh," a woman's voice said into his ear. "You must not give us away."

Andrew relaxed. The woman took her hands away. He turned and recognized her. She was the white-haired woman the Dauphin had hidden behind when he'd tried to trick Jeanne.

"I am Queen Yolande of Aragon," she whispered.

She reminded him of a queen. She wore a dress of white and gold with pearls sewn into the collar and sleeves. A white covering on her head framed her slender face. She had a petite nose and thin lips that were now pressed into a smile. Her eyes were sharp and alert, like a bird's.

Andrew remembered the name. "You are the Dauphin's mother-in-law."

"Indeed. And you are Andrew, one of the Maiden's angels."

"How do you know that?" Andrew asked.

"There are few things I do not know," she said. She leaned back, and Andrew saw that she was sitting in a small chair. She nodded to the proceedings below them. "The Maiden is doing well against the council. I have seen men quiver from fear when facing those men. She, however, has great courage."

"Do they believe her?" he asked.

"Does it matter what they believe?" Queen Yolande asked. "Men hold their petty positions of power, but women hold the most important positions of influence. They may tell the king what they think, but the king will listen to me."

"I was thirteen years old," Andrew heard Jeanne saying. He turned to the edge of the balcony.

"That was when you first heard a voice from God?" a man asked Jeanne.

"Yes. The first time made me fearful," she said.

Another man asked, "Was this at night? Were you sleeping?"

"No, sir. It was noon. I was in my father's garden. The Voice came from the direction of the church. A brightness came with it, a great light. The Voice was clear. I understood everything I was told."

"What did the Voice tell you?" asked the first man.

Jeanne said, "I was told to be virtuous and attend church as often as I may. Then the Voice told me that I must leave my home, in secret, because of my mission."

"Leave your home to go where?" the same man asked.

"To Robert de Baudricourt at the fortress of Vaucouleurs."

Another man asked, "For what purpose?"

"The Voice said that Robert de Baudricourt would provide me with the means to reach the Dauphin with a message from God."

"How did you know the voice—or the message—was from God?"

"Saint Michael gave me assurance."

"Saint Michael! How did you know it was Saint Michael?" asked the first man.

"By his voice. It was the voice of an angel. He spoke as an angel," Jeanne said, as if the answer should have been obvious.

"You are skilled in the languages of the angels?"

Jeanne gave a slight laugh. "No, sir. But I knew immediately when I heard him speak. He told me that Saint Catherine and Saint Margaret would come to me with advice, and I should take action on what they said."

"Did you speak to anyone about this?" asked yet another man.

"Only Robert de Baudricourt, to persuade him that I was not insane."

"Did he believe you?"

"No. He told me to go home. Later I returned, and he agreed to give me the men to lead me here."

"Tell us again, clearly, what mission the Voice gave you," asked the first man.

"I was told to raise the siege that has laid low the city of Orléans, so the Dauphin may be crowned king at Reims."

Jeanne's statement caused an immediate reaction. The men began talking all at once. The sounds of stomping and banging around the table shot through the rafters.

After everyone had calmed down, a different man asked, "Are you skilled with the sword? With leading men in battle?"

"No," Jeanne said calmly. "I told the Voice that I was a poor girl who knew nothing of these things. But I later thought of the unskilled peasant men and women our Lord uses for His purposes."

"You are thinking of our Holy Mother Mary?" a kindly voice asked.

"Yes."

"You dare to compare yourself to the Holy Mother?" a harsher voice exclaimed.

"No. I only compare myself as a poor peasant girl to other peasants who heard God and sought to serve Him."

"That is enough for today," the first man said.

"For today?" Jeanne asked.

"We will speak again," he replied.

"But sir—" Jeanne began to say.

The first man interrupted her and said firmly, "We will speak again."

Chairs were pushed back. Voices fell into low mumbles and whispers. The meeting was over.

Andrew heard a noise behind him and turned. Queen Yolande of Aragon was gone.

Andrew found his way back to the tower. Eve was sitting alone on the bottom step.

"What are you doing here?" he asked.

"Jeanne is meeting with the Dauphin now," she said. "I thought I'd come back and rescue you from your dull and dreary life. Where have you been?"

"Wandering the castle, like Madame Bellier said."

"Did you see anything interesting?"

"A few things." Andrew told her about the dead guard, and spying on the king's council meeting, and Queen Yolande of Aragon.

"I saw her too," said Eve. "When Jeanne met with Madame de Trèves and Madame de Gaucourt. I think the queen has a lot of power around here."

Andrew agreed.

Eve stood up. "Have you been to the top of the tower?"

"Not yet."

"Louis took me there earlier. The view is amazing."

"You went to the tower with Louis?" Andrew asked. "By yourselves?"

Eve nodded. "Did you know that Louis speaks French and English, and a little bit of Spanish?"

"No," Andrew said.

The two of them made the slow journey up the tower stairs. Eve chattered on about Louis's family and how they had been in the service of the House of Orléans for more than one hundred years. They were great warriors, she said, and Louis's mother was from a noble Scottish family. Sadly, Louis's father had died a year ago and left the family to fend for themselves. One of the sisters got married to the governor of a place called Châteaudun, which helped. Finally, the Duke of Orléans gave them the money to survive.

Andrew glanced out of a small window in the tower. He guessed they were only halfway to the top. His legs hurt, and he was tired of hearing about Louis.

He said, "Since we're stuck here, maybe you should *marry* Louis. Then you can hang around with all the rich people and not worry about being a peasant, like I'll probably be."

Eve stopped in her tracks and frowned at him. "You had to ruin it, didn't you?"

"Ruin what?" he asked, confused.

"Never mind," she growled. "I don't feel like going to the tower now. You go." She retreated a few steps.

"What did I do?"

"I made a friend," Eve said, retreating a few more steps. "But then you spoiled it by talking about being stuck here and getting married."

"I was joking!"

She picked up her speed and rounded the corner out of sight. He could hear her shoes padding against the stone steps and fading until the slam of a door cut them off.

He looked at the steps winding up and away from him. He had a long way to go.

He sighed. What else was there to do?

The view from the roof of the tower was amazing, just as Eve had said. The roofs of Chinon were directly below. The bridge over the river Vienne snaked from east to west. Green fields, forests, and vineyards stretched out in all directions. The lands to the north rolled away like waves. Roads leading to other towns and villages spread from the castle like roots from a tree.

Andrew leaned on the parapet and looked down. The sheer drop to the ground below made him dizzy. He stepped back.

"It would be easy to fall" came a low voice from behind him.

Andrew spun around. The white-haired old man from the bridge stood between Andrew and the door to the stairs. His sword was drawn.

"What do you want?" Andrew asked.

"Tell me how you think you will escape," the old man said. Drawing closer, he held the sword up to Andrew's chest.

Andrew swallowed hard.

"How will you escape?" the old man asked again. The point of the sword now touched the fabric of Andrew's tunic.

"I do not know," Andrew said.

"Then why did you put yourself at risk?" the old man asked.

"I did not know I was at risk. I came for the view," Andrew said feebly.

"You are always at risk in this world. You will not survive if you do not understand that." The old man grunted, then lowered his weapon. "Where is your sword? Do you have a sword?"

"No."

The old man snorted. "How do you *not* have a sword?" he yelled, raising a hand to the heavens. "How old are you? Eleven or twelve? And you have no sword?"

"Why are you yelling at me?" Andrew shouted.

"Because someone needs to," he snapped. "You must be prepared."

"Is that why you attacked my friend on the bridge? To prepare her?"

He shrugged. "What else am I to do with a sorceress?"

"She is not a sorceress!"

"She has the eyes of a sorceress."

"They are the eyes of a *girl*. She is only a girl!" Andrew said.

"And you are only a boy?" the old man said. "I think not."

"What else do you think I am?" Andrew asked.

The old man stepped closer. "I was looking from the bridge by the river. I saw no one. *No one.* And then I saw someone. *Two* someones. A boy. A girl. They appeared from nowhere. Out of nothing. They were not there, and then they were."

Andrew was speechless. *The old man saw us arrive from our time! No wonder he was spooked.*

"Do you think I am a lunatic?" the old man asked.

Andrew didn't dare answer.

"Some think so. I know what they call me behind my back. *La Démence*—demented, insane. *La Rage.*" He shrugged. "Maybe so. There are times when I think so myself. There are times when I remember things that cannot be part of my memory. Do you understand?"

No, Andrew thought. He stood frozen where he was.

"You and your friend are like bugs buzzing in my head," the old man continued. "You tease at my thoughts. You make me want to remember what I cannot call to mind."

Andrew swallowed hard. "Like what?"

"If I knew, I would not be wasting my time with you!" he said angrily. He suddenly grabbed Andrew's wrist and pulled him to the door. "Come. You must train."

"Train? To do what?" Andrew pulled back, digging his heels into the gravel of the tower roof.

"To fight."

Andrew struggled, but the old man's grip was too strong.

"I do not want to train you," he said. "But Madame Bellier has told me I must. She said you have no skill. I will give you skill."

"Ah!" Andrew said. *Madame Bellier arranged this.* "You should have said so. Now, please let go."

The old man looked down at his hand on Andrew's wrist as if he didn't know how it got there. He released his grip. "I am sorry. I am not doing it on purpose," he said.

Andrew rubbed his wrist.

Stepping back, the old man gave a curt bow. "I am Simon Le Fantôme."

Andrew bowed without taking his eyes off the man. "I am Andrew ... Le Perry."

"Well, Andrew Le Perry, we will find you a sword, and you will train to fight. Then when you are leaning over the side of a tower and someone sneaks up from behind to attack, you will be prepared."

"Does that happen a lot around here?" Andrew asked.

"Once is more than enough," the old man said. "Come. We have work to do."

They began the long descent down the stairs.

"Are you a royal trainer?" Andrew asked along the way.

"Not at all!" the old man said, as if the idea were preposterous. "Some believe I should never be allowed to hold a weapon. One does not know what I will do with it."

Andrew took no comfort from that statement.

Simon gave Andrew a sideways glance. "In war, there is no better man to have by your side than me. I fought with the fifth Henry at Agincourt."

Andrew gasped. "You fought with Henry the Fifth *against* the French?"

"Of course I did! I am from England . . ." He hesitated, then frowned. "Or so I believe."

"But you sound French. And you are in the castle of the Dauphin who wants to get rid of the English."

Simon shrugged. "I go where there is work," he said.

"What work? Are you a soldier-for-hire?"

"I am a jeweler," he replied. "Have you seen the Dauphin's clothes? The jewels around his neck, on his sleeves, around his armor—they are my handiwork. But I am also a soldier. One must be to survive. You will learn."

Simon Le Fantôme took Andrew to the courtyard where soldiers were still training. Simon disappeared through a doorway, then returned a few minutes later with a sword about the length of Andrew's arm. It was surprisingly light.

"Now we begin," Simon said, drawing his sword. "Basic skills."

He showed Andrew how to position his feet, body, and arms while holding a sword. Then he guided Andrew through the movements of stepping back and forth and from side to side. Simon complained about the weakness of Andrew's wrists and the lack of muscle control in his arms and legs.

"The goal is simple," the old man said. "You must stop your enemy. To stop him means you must be prepared to kill. For that, you must aim here." He hit his chest with the flat of his palm.

"Can I not wound him in the arm or leg?" Andrew asked.

"Imbecile!" Simon cried out. "Arms and legs move about quickly. How will you hit them? You must strike at the largest part of his body." He slammed the palm of his hand against his chest again. It made a loud thud. "Do not talk. Listen to me. Watch."

Simon began to go through slow movements, showing Andrew the stances he must take and the different ways to thrust the sword.

Andrew lost track of the time. He thrashed at a bale of hay, lunged at a man of straw, and finally exchanged blows with Simon himself. All the while, Simon taunted him. "Not that way; *this* way" and "Again! Again!"

Later Andrew caught sight of Eve and Louis standing off to the side, watching him. The glance away from Simon cost him a jab to his arm.

"Foolish boy," Simon shouted. "Concentrate!"

Andrew scowled. Then, with a roar, he lunged at the old man with his sword held high. Simon knocked him on his backside.

"That is all for today," Simon announced.

Andrew sat on the muddy ground. His muscles ached and his head hurt.

Eve brought him a cup of water. He noticed that she was looking cautiously at Simon from the corner of her eye. Simon glanced at her, then turned to a nearby barrel and used his hands to splash water on his face.

"It *is* him," Eve whispered as she handed Andrew the cup.

"Simon Le Fantôme," Andrew said. He took a long drink, then added, "Madame Bellier asked him to train me."

She knelt next to Andrew. "Did he tell you why he attacked me on the bridge?"

"He saw us arrive from our time," Andrew whispered.

Eve's mouth fell open. "He *saw* it?"

"He thinks you're a sorceress." Andrew pointed to her eyes. "*Those* convinced him. I don't know what he thinks I am."

"Keep that sword with you at all times," Simon said loudly as he approached them.

She cringed.

He tossed a leather sheath at Andrew. "Put this around your waist. Get used to your sword's weight and where it is on your body. It must become to you like another limb."

Eve stood up and glared at the old man. "I am *not* a sorceress!"

Simon's hairy face twitched. He said, "Then what are you?"

"I am just a girl!" she shouted.

Andrew struggled to his feet, in case the old man did something crazy.

"Then how did you come here?" Simon's voice grew louder as he spoke. "Tell me how you appeared beneath the bridge! If you are not a sorceress, then what are you?"

"A guest of the Dauphin!" Guillaume Bellier yelled from a doorway.

Simon came to attention, then quickly bowed. "Monsieur," he said.

"All this time in the castle, and you still have the manners of a brute," Bellier said. "Go on. The Dauphin has need of you."

Simon stood to his full height, towering over Bellier. "In another time, you would not have spoken to me in such a tone."

Bellier did not move, but his eyes betrayed concern. "Do not keep the Dauphin waiting."

Simon pointed at Andrew. "Practice," he said, then marched away.

Andrew fumbled with the sheath for his sword.

Bellier snapped his fingers. Louis rushed forward. "Sir?"

"Show him," Bellier said, then walked off.

Louis fastened the sheath around Andrew's waist. Then he showed Andrew how to slide the sword into the sheath without hurting himself. "It will take time," he said.

Eve watched them, then asked, "What about me? When will I be trained?"

Louis chuckled. "You?"

"Yes, *me*," Eve snapped. "If I am to travel with Jeanne, then I should know how to defend myself."

Louis flinched. "You are right, of course," he said. "I would be delighted to teach you."

Andrew didn't like the idea of the two of them training together. "Maybe you should learn from Simon," he quickly suggested.

Eve shook her head. "He scares me."

"He scares everyone," said Louis.

"Then why is he here?" Eve asked. "What do you know about him?"

Louis held up his hands. "He is a mystery. The stories are told that he was once a jeweler to the royal court in London. One night he was attacked by someone seeking a precious stone he possessed. His wife was murdered in the fight. They say it unhinged his mind. He seeks revenge through battle."

"He told me he fought with Henry the Fifth at Agincourt," Andrew said.

"So the legends say," Louis agreed. "They also say that he fought with kings *before* Henry—in Scotland and England."

"Why is he now with the French?" Andrew asked.

Louis shrugged. "No one knows for certain. It is whispered that he is eyes and ears for Queen Yolande of Aragon. She trusts him."

"Should we be worried about him?" Andrew asked.

"Worried? No. But I would not trust him readily," Louis said, then added, "Trust *no one* readily. The Dauphin's court is a den of well-dressed vipers."

"Can we trust you?" Eve asked him.

He gave her a coy smile. "Trust *no one* readily," he said again.

That evening Jeanne and her cohorts were served dinner in a dining room near the tower. The Dauphin's kitchen offered a variety of meats: beef, lamb, chicken, mutton, pork sausage, heron, and bizarrely, peacock and swan. Andrew couldn't bring himself to eat the peacock or swan. Eve tried them, but only because Louis insisted. She smiled at Louis as if she liked the taste of both. When he turned away, she made a disgusted face at Andrew.

The meal also included leeks, onions, turnips, cabbage, and some kind of bean soup. Fresh bread and various kinds of cheeses were laid out. Madame Bellier made a fuss about the presence of salt for the table. Andrew didn't realize that salt was rare.

As they sat around the table, Andrew thought of his family back in Hope Springs. An ache touched his heart. *I might never see them again*, he thought. He took a deep breath and fought back a sudden feeling of panic.

"What's wrong?" Eve whispered to him.

He shook his head and pushed his plate away. He'd lost his appetite.

After the meal, they all went to the chapel. Jeanne led them in evening prayers. Andrew prayed that God would help him not to worry or be afraid. *I'm here for a reason*, he told himself. *God will take care of us—and then He will show us how to get home.*

Jeanne remained in the chapel as everyone else filed out. Andrew was the last to leave. He glanced back and saw Jeanne kneeling with her hands clasped tightly in front of her. He was sure he heard her softly crying. He closed the door.

The room Andrew and Louis shared was windowless, though heavy curtains hung along the circular wall to block any drafts. There were two small beds of straw, small tables with small lamps, small pitchers with small cups, small chairs, and small rugs. Andrew felt cramped and wondered why the room was so small when the tower was so big. Compared to the width of the tower, the room seemed small. And there was no fireplace. The only means of warmth came from large fur blankets. Though it was now spring, the rains made everything feel damp.

Andrew sat on the edge of his bed and rubbed his aching legs.

Louis gave Andrew a stone.

"Why?" Andrew asked.

"Use it to sharpen your sword," Louis said. He sat down and began scraping a stone against his own sword. "The lunatic will look it over tomorrow and knock you on the head for not doing it."

Andrew watched Louis, then copied what he did.

It was a good thing.

The next day Simon Le Fantôme inspected the sword. He looked disappointed that he couldn't knock Andrew on the head.

11

In the days that followed, Jeanne met with various women the Dauphin had sent to examine her. They judged that she was a virtuous young maiden. She then submitted to more questions from the council and met privately with the Dauphin. Andrew was not told what they talked about.

Eve stayed by Jeanne's side. When Eve wasn't needed, Louis taught her how to use a sword. Andrew continued his training with Simon. Not only did they practice with the sword, but Simon taught him about history and politics and the culture of France.

"The river Vienne makes Chinon ideal for trade," Simon explained one afternoon while parrying with Andrew. "Centuries ago, the Romans built a camp here. Then Saint Mexme, a disciple of Saint Martin, established a monastery not far from here. The town was built after that. Then the English came and took it over for decades. Now the Dauphin is here. For how long, God alone knows."

Andrew grunted at him. He didn't know what to say.

"You think this is the prattling of an old man?" Simon asked. "Heed me, boy. The glory of man comes and goes. I have seen it for myself. In the span of time, we are great only in our own eyes."

"How old are you?" Andrew asked.

"I do not remember." Simon sheathed his sword, then walked over to a large barrel of water. Tugging at his shirt, he let it fall to his waist and began to splash water on his face and body.

Andrew's eyes widened. Simon's back was covered with scars.

The old man turned to him, scrubbing his face with his hands. Simon's chest was wide and muscular. It was the body of a younger man. But it was also scarred. Simon saw the boy's gaze.

"Battles," the old man explained. "A mere jeweler should never bear such scars."

"Why do you?" Andrew asked.

"A man must fight for what is right," the old man said.

"What is right?"

Simon paused, stroking his bushy beard. "If the English kings who claim this land would pay the same devotion to their own land, the people would not suffer as they do."

"Do you believe Jeanne will drive the English out of France?" asked Andrew.

"Jeanne has an important role to play." He pulled his shirt on again. "It will cost her everything," he said in a very dark tone.

There was a commotion beyond the courtyard, at the main gate. A moment later a rider galloped in on a beautiful black steed. The rider was dressed all in red and leapt from his horse before it had come to a full stop.

"Where is she?" he called out. He had dark hair and a hero's face—slender, with a firm jaw and confident eyes. "The girl from God! Where is she?"

When none of the gathering crowd answered, Andrew stepped forward, "I believe she is with the Dauphin now."

The man gave Andrew a quick look-over; then his eyes went to Simon and narrowed. "Simon Le Fantôme," he said, scowling. "I thought you were dead."

"Thought or hoped, my lord duke?" Simon asked with a bow.

"It is all the same to me," the man said. He pointed at Andrew. "Take me to the Dauphin."

Andrew hesitated. "Me? But—"

Simon pushed Andrew forward. "Do not keep the Duke of Alençon waiting," he said. "No doubt he sacrificed a day of boar hunting to join us."

"It was quail, actually," the duke said with a wry smile.

Just then, two servants rode up, looking as if they'd just lost a race. They were covered in dust. Andrew guessed they had been trying to keep up with the duke's horse.

"Stable the horses," the duke said to the servants. To Andrew he said, "Lead on!"

Andrew prayed he would remember the way to the Dauphin's chambers. He had gone with Eve a couple of times but now worried he would take a wrong turn.

"Are you being tutored by Le Fantôme?" the duke asked as they walked.

"Yes, my lord," Andrew said.

"He is an untrustworthy scoundrel," said the duke. "He fought alongside our enemies at Agincourt. My father was killed there."

"I am sorry, my lord," said Andrew.

"Le Fantôme also fought for the Duke of Bedford at the Battle of Verneuil," the duke continued, his tone filled with venom. "I was taken prisoner then by the English. They held me for ransom for five years."

Unsure of what to say, Andrew repeated, "I am sorry, my lord."

The duke seemed to be fuming. "I would happily kill Le Fantôme if he were not under the protection of Queen Yolande—and the Dauphin, of course. They see his value in ways I do not."

They came to the hall of the Dauphin's private residence. Eve and Louis were sitting close together in chairs along the wall, talking in low voices. At the sight of the duke, they leapt to their feet. Eve gave Andrew a puzzled look.

"Announce me," the duke said to Andrew. "Tell the Dauphin that John the Second, the Duke of Alençon, has come for an audience."

Louis opened the door for Andrew. Andrew gave Eve a pained look before stepping through the doorway.

He realized now that he'd never actually been inside this room. First, he came to a curtained area. He moved the curtains this way and that until he found a door. He carefully pushed that open and entered a small chamber with a few pieces of furniture. No one was there. Then he heard laughter coming from the other side of another door. He slowly opened that door and was met by lush green curtains hanging just inside. Pushing through them, he entered an ornately decorated meeting room.

The Dauphin was sitting at a table with a book the size of a Bible open in front of him. Jeanne stood nearby, her hands clasped behind her, as if she had been waiting.

"My angel!" she cried out to Andrew.

The Dauphin looked up. "What is it you want?"

"Sire, the Duke of—"

Andrew didn't finish the sentence, since the duke himself now strode in. He winked at Andrew as he passed and gave a swift bow to the Dauphin. "God grant you peace, my king!"

The Dauphin rose quickly, arms outstretched. "John!"

Jeanne watched the two men embrace and asked, "Who is this?"

The Dauphin hooked an arm around the duke and led him to Jeanne. "This is John, the Duke of Alençon!" he announced grandly.

Jeanne bowed. "You are most welcome, my lord duke. The more we gather together the royal blood of France, the better it will be."

The duke took her hand and, bowing, kissed it lightly.

Seeing Andrew again, the Dauphin waved him away. "Go, child."

Andrew bowed and tried to leave. First, he got tangled in the green curtains and then had a near miss with the door. Eventually he returned to the hall.

Eve looked anxiously at him as he came out. "What was that all about?" she asked.

"He's a duke," Andrew said.

"Do you not know the Duke of Alençon?" Louis asked.

"Should I?" asked Andrew.

"He is one of the greatest men in France," Louis said. "There are those who would make him the king, if they could."

"The Dauphin might have a problem with that," Andrew said. He shot a look at Eve. "I am sorry for interrupting your *date*."

Eve looked at him aghast. Then she blushed.

Louis looked baffled. "Date? What is a date?"

Andrew gave a slight shrug, then walked away, hiding his grin.

The next morning, Andrew, Louis, and Eve were allowed to join Jeanne for the Dauphin's Mass in his private chapel. The Duke of Alençon was with them, along with Madame Bellier, and a man Andrew had seen before: Georges de La Trémoille. La Trémoille was the one who had sat in the royal chair when Jeanne first met the Dauphin. He was one of the Dauphin's closest counselors. He had a horse-like face with a small mouth, a long nose, and small eyes set too close together. Andrew was immediately struck with an uneasy feeling of distrust. La Trémoille joined the others in the Mass, kneeling and praying earnestly. Andrew felt guilty for judging him.

After the Mass, Jeanne told the Dauphin, "I have a message for you."

The Dauphin waved for the small group to depart. "Not you, my lord duke. Nor you, La Trémoille."

Madame Bellier shuffled out with a worried look on her face. Louis followed her.

Andrew and Eve hesitated.

Jeanne said, "My angels must stay."

The Dauphin nodded.

Andrew and Eve went to the chairs lining the back wall of the chapel and sat down.

"What is this message?" the Dauphin asked. "From whom does it come?"

"God," Jeanne said.

The Dauphin glanced at the duke and La Trémoille. "What has God told you?" he asked Jeanne.

"My gentle Dauphin," Jeanne said. "Give your kingdom into the hands of the King of Heaven, and the King of Heaven will return it as a gift to you, as He has often done for your predecessors. You and all that should be yours will be restored."

The Dauphin waited, but Jeanne said no more. He looked unsure of how to respond. "Ah. Well. *Merci.*"

Then, as if there was nothing more to say, he clapped his hands together. "Shall we eat?"

Andrew wasn't sure what to think. Did the Dauphin really believe Jeanne? Would he entrust his kingdom to the King of Heaven?

No answers came that day.

The Dauphin invited Jeanne, the duke, and La Trémoille into his royal chambers to talk. Eve and Louis waited outside the doors as usual. Andrew, with nothing to do, went off to find Simon Le Fantôme. He was not in his usual places around the courtyard. Finally, a guard pointed Andrew to a row of doors at the edge of the courtyard. They were the officers' quarters.

"Fifth from the right," the guard said.

Andrew walked over and knocked. He heard a muffled sound inside. Hoping it was a summons, he slowly opened the door.

The room was a mere cell, small and dark. There was a bed, a large trunk, a nightstand, a table covered with weapons, and a shelf holding papers and a few books. Simon sat on the side of the bed, his head in his hands. Next to him was a small wooden box with the lid open. A black cloth hid whatever was inside.

Simon's head snapped up. "What do you want?" His hand went to the box and closed the lid.

"Are we training today?" Andrew asked, stepping back through the doorway.

"No. Go away." Even in the dim light, Andrew saw that Simon's eyes were puffy and red-rimmed.

Andrew hesitated. "Are you all right?"

"What is it to you?" Simon asked, sneering. "If I say yes, will you be satisfied? If I say no, will you be able to help me?"

Andrew shuffled his feet where he stood.

Simon began to pound his fists against his temples. "There is a pain here."

"I will find a doctor."

"No doctor can ease this pain," Simon said.

"I can find a priest."

"No!" Simon shouted. "I am beyond absolution. Not even God can help me."

"God can help anyone who asks Him," Andrew said.

Simon stood up and glared at him, his fists raised. Andrew backed up another step, then another, until he stumbled onto the pavement outside. Simon scowled at the boy, then slammed the door in his face.

"He must be crazy," Eve said quietly.

Andrew had found her in a meadow behind the castle. She was there with the Dauphin, the Duke of Alençon, and other members of the royal court. They were all watching Jeanne, in full armor, riding on the duke's black steed. She carried a long lance in her arms and rode back and forth in front of a straw man that had been fastened to a pole. She came at the straw man with the lance, hitting it squarely in its center.

It was an afternoon of clear blue skies and a warm springtime sun. Eve and Andrew stood with three other servants. They were several paces behind the Dauphin and the duke, who sat in high-backed chairs. Food and drink were spread out on a table in front of them.

"Maybe pain is making Simon crazy," Andrew suggested. He was beginning to feel sorry for the old man.

"He makes me nervous," Eve said. "I wish you did not have to go near him."

Jeanne called out with a loud *Ha!* She had knocked the head off the straw man. She laughed like a young girl at play.

Andrew noticed Louis standing at the far edge of the meadow, ready to run for the lance if Jeanne dropped it.

"She is both graceful and skilled," Andrew heard the duke say. "But she must have a proper horse if she is to go into battle." He leaned toward the Dauphin. "Will she go into battle?"

The Dauphin bit into an apple. "I await my council's report."

"Even so, she may have my horse. He is perfect for her," said the duke.

"You are generous," the Dauphin said.

The duke watched Jeanne for a moment, then said, "Sire, you must give her relief from all of the questioning. It is overwhelming for a peasant girl. Allow me to take her to meet my wife. It will be restful."

The Dauphin sighed. "It would be a relief to me, dear John. I know she is impatient. So yes, take her home with you."

"You are gracious, as always," said the duke.

The Dauphin snapped his fingers, and a servant rushed forward. "Bring her to me," he said.

The servant ran out into the meadow, waving his arms. Jeanne rode up to him, heard his message, then guided the horse toward the Dauphin. She took off her helmet. "Yes, my Dauphin?"

The prince told her about the duke's offer of the horse and the visit.

Jeanne's face lit up. "My lord duke! You are too kind to me."

The duke smiled. "It is a small gesture."

Louis ran up to Jeanne. She tossed him the lance, then dismounted. Louis pulled at her gloves and took her helmet. Jeanne said to the duke, "I would be most pleased to meet your wife. I know she is the daughter of the Duke of Orléans. He is still being held hostage in England?"

"I am sorry to say that he is," the duke replied. "You are well informed."

"He is a brave and courageous man." Jeanne's face was radiant. "My lord, I would have your wife know that God loves her father and will keep her father safe. If necessary, I will cross the English Channel myself to fetch him back to France. Please tell her."

"You may tell her yourself," said the duke.

Jeanne was insistent that she go alone to the duke's residence at the Abbey of Saint-Florent-lès-Saumur. "It would do us well," she explained to Eve. "For me, it will take my mind off the Dauphin's indecision. For you, it will ease the burden of watching me pace impatiently."

Andrew was relieved to learn that Louis would return to other duties while Jeanne was away. He said to Eve, "We'll have time to explore the castle."

"I *have* explored the castle." Eve was sulking.

Now what? he wondered. Was she sulking because she couldn't go with Jeanne, or because she wouldn't have time with Louis?

"Have you been to the secret balcony that overlooks the Dauphin's council?" he asked.

She lifted an eyebrow. "No."

"Come on. I'll show you."

Even before Andrew and Eve reached the top of the steps to the balcony, they could hear shouting from the council room below.

Eve paused. "Isn't this spying?"

Andrew continued on. "Trust me."

They came to the chair where he'd seen Queen Yolande before. It sat empty in a half shadow.

The two of them edged forward to the rail. They peeked over. Several men sat at the table below. Eve gave only the quickest look, then withdrew. "I've seen it. Let's go," she whispered.

"His Royal Highness wants a report about Jeanne!" Andrew recognized the sneering tone of Georges de La Trémoille.

Eve froze at the mention of Jeanne's name. She slowly approached the rail again.

"What excuses can we give for our delay?" La Trémoille demanded.

A fist slammed against the table. Then a different voice said, "We must be wise. She comes from a frontier town very near to our Burgundian enemies. They may have sent her to lure our lord into a trap."

"We have spoken to her again and again," La Trémoille said. "Do any of you truly believe she is a spy?"

"The girl is without guile, innocent even in her determination," said another voice.

"Caution!" an older, raspy voice said. "Keep the girl at a proper distance. She is too close to the Dauphin. It is good she has gone away. That allows us more time."

"Time? We have had enough time!" cried one man.

The raspy-voiced man asked, "Are *you* convinced, my lord La Trémoille? If you were to give a report to our lord right now, what would you advise?"

La Trémoille was quiet.

"You see?" the voice said. "Still you cannot decide."

"I am not a learned theologian." La Trémoille's tone was silky smooth. "I may debate the prudence of the politics, or the military strategy. But the Dauphin's first question is one of spiritual trust."

"A question of this importance is beyond us as a council," another member said.

"Is that what we will say?" La Trémoille asked, then mocked them. "'Forgive us, sire, but after days of debate, we have concluded that we are fools who cannot decide.'"

There was silence for a moment. Then the raspy-voiced man said, "The greatest theological minds of our nation are refugees in Poitiers. Let *them* meet with her. Let *them* advise the Dauphin about what to do. Is that not their purpose? What else have they been doing since they were banished from Paris?"

Andrew could hear the shuffling of bodies and the creaking of various chairs.

"I see," said La Trémoille. "If they advise him to heed the girl, and she fails to save Orléans, then the blame rests with them. If they advise him to ignore the girl, then they take responsibility for better or worse. We are off the hook."

Murmurings followed that Andrew couldn't hear well. But the tone told him the council agreed.

"I shall tell the Dauphin," La Trémoille said. Then the meeting ended.

"Poitiers?" Eve whispered.

"*Fools!*" came a harsh whisper from behind them.

Eve gasped loudly. Andrew turned, already knowing who had spoken.

Queen Yolande of Aragon sat in the shadows.

How does she do that? Andrew wondered.

She leaned forward, part of her face in a half light. "They are no better than Pontius Pilate, washing their hands of the matter instead of making a proper decision. Have they asked themselves why God would send a peasant girl to us now? Have they considered that God is finally answering our prayers, as He once did for the Hebrew slaves? Might this be the rescue they have long desired, ever since God allowed Henry to bring down His judgment at Agincourt?"

"Is the Dauphin supposed to be Moses?" Andrew asked.

Queen Yolande slowly shook her head. "Love him as I do, I confess that he is not. He has been in a crisis of faith and purpose most of his life. Until the Maiden arrived." Her eyes went to Eve. "You must be Evangeline."

Eve curtsied.

The queen gave her a sharp look. "You are Jeanne's angel. What do you believe?"

"I believe she is a messenger from God," Eve said.

The queen turned to Andrew.

Andrew nodded. "So do I."

"As do I." Queen Yolande sighed. She knit her fingers together in her lap. "The members of the council hope to save their own skins. They would rather cower under the rule of the English than disturb their ease. So the girl must go to Poitiers for more questioning. God have mercy on her."

Andrew wondered how the queen got in and out of the balcony without being seen. He asked, "Is there a secret door behind the chair?"

Queen Yolande smiled at him. "Yes. Would you like to see it?"

13

The secret door was hidden in the wood paneling behind the chair. Andrew and Eve followed Queen Yolande into a cramped passage. The queen reached into a wooden box fixed to the wall. A moment later, she used a flint device to light a small lamp.

The queen whispered, "The castle is filled with hidden passages. One could easily become lost. It has taken me a long time to learn where they all go."

"Why are they here?" Eve asked.

"The kings of old wanted to move freely to meet privately with trusted advisers. Secret passageways have been used for less noble purposes as well," she said.

A narrow hall went off to the right and another to the left. They continued straight. Eventually they came to a set of creaky wooden stairs. Descending to another floor, they reached a landing with more steps that led downward.

"What is down there?" Andrew asked.

"A courtyard and the soldiers' quarters," Queen Yolande said. "The men-at-arms have used this passage to position themselves for battle."

"All of the soldiers know about this?" Andrew asked.

"A few of the officers. It would not be a secret passage otherwise," the queen replied. She guided them to the right, down a long passage with various corridors to other parts of the castle. Finally she stopped and lifted her candle. A small latch was attached to the wall in front of them.

"Where are we now?" Eve asked.

"Where you should be," she said. She carefully lifted the latch and slowly opened the door. Stepping back, she gestured for the children to go through.

Eve and Andrew stepped into a room that looked like a storage closet.

"Where is—?" Eve started to ask, but Queen Yolande had closed the door. It seemed to disappear into the plaster of the wall.

The storage room was filled with shelves of linens and various crates. Another door stood on the opposite side of the room. They slipped through and found themselves in a hall. From there, they made their way back to the courtyard and then the tower.

Later in the afternoon, Eve and Andrew walked along the castle wall overlooking Chinon.

"I want my clothes," Eve said suddenly. "I may be stuck here forever, but I want my clothes."

Andrew had forgotten all about them. "They're at the inn. We left them there to be washed."

"Can we get them back?" Eve asked.

"Sure."

They made their way to the main gate. The guard gave them a long look as they approached. "You are with the Maiden?" he said.

"Yes, sir," Andrew confirmed. "We have to go into the town to pick up some clothes."

"Be back before sunset," he told them.

It was as easy as that.

Marie de Loire, the innkeeper, greeted them happily when they arrived. "I thought I would never see you again," she exclaimed. "Sit! Tell me everything! I have made a fresh stew."

Andrew and Eve sat down while the innkeeper dished out large bowls of a stew with venison. She asked them endless questions about life in the castle.

When they'd finished telling her all they could, Andrew remembered why they had come. He asked the innkeeper, "Do you still have our clothes? You took them away to be washed when we arrived."

"Yes, of course," she said. "But they are not here. I gave them to the tall, hairy man from the castle. He came one day and asked oh so many questions about the two of you. As if I would know the answers! Then, seeing as he lived at the castle, I asked if he would please give you the bundle of your clean clothes. He promised he would."

Andrew and Eve shared a glance.

"Simon?" Andrew asked.

"He never said his name," she replied.

"He did not give them to us," Eve said.

"Ah!" Marie de Loire said. She looked worried.

"He is a busy man," Andrew suggested. "Maybe he has forgotten."

"Yes, yes, I am sure he is," Marie said with a nod.

As Andrew and Eve walked back to the castle, Eve asked, "Why would Simon take our clothes?"

Andrew shrugged.

Back inside the castle grounds, Andrew went to the door of Simon's room. Eve kept her distance.

Andrew pounded on the door. No answer. Another pounding. Nothing.

"Where is Simon Le Fantôme?" Andrew asked a soldier standing nearby.

The soldier held up his hands, like a shrug. "He comes and goes as he pleases."

Andrew decided to see if the door was locked. He lifted the latch and pushed. The door creaked open.

He glanced back at Eve. She gave him a "What are you doing?" look. Andrew held up his forefinger for her to wait; then he stepped into the room.

The room was much as it had looked before, though tidier. Weapons that had been on a table now hung from hooks on the walls—a crossbow, a sword, and a plain silver shield, dented and scratched. Pieces of armor lay piled in a corner.

Where would he put our clothes? Andrew wondered.

His earlier tour of the secret passageway made Andrew look closely at the back wall. It was a combination of dark crossbeams and plaster. Toward the corner, he saw faint horizontal and vertical lines that looked like cracks—or the outline of a door. He pushed the panel. Nothing happened. He ran his hands along the rugged wood, wondering if there might be a hidden latch. Nothing.

Then he saw a bronze hook where two of the beams met. He pulled it down and then tried to turn it to one side and then the other. It didn't budge. He pushed it up. Suddenly it slid into the wall. There was a soft click. The panel cracked open slightly.

Andrew opened the door wider and peered into the darkness. A corridor ran to the left, directly behind the walls of the garrison. Thin shafts of light shone randomly through cracks in the walls of other rooms. Wooden shelving had been built from floor to ceiling just to the right of the entrance.

Adjusting his eyes to the darkness, he saw the shelves filled with dust-covered junk. There were old brown bottles and jugs, an oil lamp with flint next to it, frayed leather pouches, and a rusty knife. On the ground sat boxes of varying sizes, packed with rusted tools, chains, old spikes, and wooden posts. He noticed one crate with a clasp and lock on it. But there was no sign of their clothes. Satisfied, he pushed the secret door closed again.

He turned back to the room. *Maybe our clothes are under the bed*, he thought. Kneeling down, he gazed at the bed cover. It was uneven and lumpy. Something was underneath. Then he saw something sticking out from under the edge of the cover. Blue denim. Andrew pulled the cover back. There, spread on the bed, were their clothes.

It looked as if Simon had laid them out to examine each one. The stitching on the shoulders and sleeves of their shirts had been picked at. The rivets on their jeans were torn, along with sections of the seams. Their tennis shoes were there as well, sitting upside down. Deep lines were scratched in the soles and heels. It looked as if Simon had cut them with a knife in an attempt to figure out what they were made of.

Eve coughed loudly out in the courtyard. Then Andrew heard the deep sound of Simon's voice. He gasped.

"Monsieur Le Fantôme, I have come to ask you to train me with a sword," Eve said loudly.

Panicked, Andrew quickly threw the bed cover over the clothes. What was he going to do? Hide under the bed?

"I do not train girls," he heard Simon say gruffly. His voice was closer to the door now.

"I am a fast learner," Eve said. She was stalling him.

Thinking fast, Andrew grabbed the bronze hook and opened the secret panel again. He stepped inside the passageway, then clawed at the inner wood to pull the panel closed. His fingers caught hold of a small ring. He used it to shut the door. The latch clicked.

He heard Simon throw open the door to the room. Eve was pleading with him to train her. Simon was adamant. *No girls!*

"Who has been in my room?" Simon shouted. The door slammed.

Andrew retreated into the corridor, nearly banging into the shelves. Dust billowed from the junk lying there. He stepped back, afraid he was going to sneeze. His heart raced.

Simon banged around in the room, muttering to himself.

Andrew moved a few feet farther along the wall, touching the shelves to guide him in the dim light. His hand brushed against smooth wood. Looking closer, he saw that it was the wooden box he had seen next to Simon on the bed. Andrew reached for it just as he heard the click of the latch on the other side of the wall.

Simon is coming! he thought.

Andrew tiptoed as fast as he could before the secret panel opened. He pressed himself against the wall at the far end of the shelves. He hoped it was enough to hide him. The light from Simon's room cast the old man's shadow onto the opposite wall. Andrew heard Simon step into the secret corridor. The shadow grew larger. Andrew held his breath.

The shadow turned toward the shelving. There was a soft grunt and something scraping against wood. Simon's shadow shrunk again as he returned to his room. From the outline, it looked as if the old man had retrieved the box from the shelf. The panel closed and the shadow disappeared.

Relieved, Andrew stepped out from the wall. He looked at the shelf. The box was gone. Squinting, he turned and slowly made his way down the secret passage. Thin shafts of light from the various rooms helped guide his way. He hoped that if he went far enough, he would find a way out.

The passageway seemed to go on and on. Muffled voices came from the other side of the wall, along with an occasional bump or bang. He reached a dead end. Fear rose up within him. Then he saw that the passage continued in deep darkness to the left. He would have to grope his way forward.

As he looked at the yawning black passageway, he thought he saw a flicker of light ahead. He decided to take the chance and walked carefully with his hands in front of him.

The flicker of light took shape as he got closer to it. It was a vertical line that shone through another secret door. He paused and listened. No sound came from the other side. He pushed on the door, but it wouldn't move. He ran his fingers around whatever edges he could feel. His hand brushed against something metal. Pushing up, he heard a familiar click, and the hidden door opened slightly. He nudged it farther and peeked out.

He stood behind a wall of stacked barrels. He followed them to an opening that led to a large room filled with tables and benches. It was empty of people now, but Andrew imagined it was a room for the soldiers to sit and drink. He crossed to a single door on the other side of the room and followed it through to an arched passage. To the left was a long alley leading to stone stairs. To the right was an entrance back to the courtyard.

"Thank God," he said.

Andrew found Eve waiting for him in the courtyard.

"You're covered with cobwebs," Eve said and dusted him off with her hand. "I was afraid Simon would catch you."

"He never saw me. I hid in a secret passage."

"Did you find our clothes?" she asked.

"Yes," Andrew said. "And it looked like he was trying to take them apart to figure out what they are. I'm worried. He's too curious about us." He went over to a barrel of water and splashed some on his face and neck.

"What if he takes our clothes to the Dauphin?" Eve asked. "Anyone who looks closely enough will know they're all wrong. The rubber on our shoes will give us away."

"It'll be worse if Simon tells them how we appeared out of nowhere. They'll burn *us* at the stake," Andrew said.

Eve plucked a strand of cobweb from Andrew's shoulder. "What should we do? Run away?"

"To where?" Andrew asked.

Simon Le Fantôme suddenly emerged from his room several yards away. "I have changed my mind." He was looking at Eve. "I will train you both."

Eve shuffled uneasily. "I am not sure if I—"

"Tomorrow at dawn," he commanded, then spun on his heels and disappeared from view.

Eve groaned to Andrew, "Great. That's the last thing I need."

"You asked."

"It was the only thing I could think of to stall him." She scowled. "I want my clothes back."

The next morning at dawn, Simon met them in the courtyard. He handed Eve a sack. "I am not here to be your errand boy," he said.

Eve opened the top and looked in. She opened it wider for Andrew to see. Their clothes were inside.

Simon handed Eve a small sword. "You will need time to catch up," he said, then added as a taunt, "Though it will not be hard. This boy is not very good."

Andrew rolled his eyes.

The training began. Andrew watched Eve move quickly with her thrusts and dodges. She was light on her feet. He remembered how skilled she was with a staff in their days with Robin Hood.

Simon looked impressed as well. Though grunts were the best he could manage as compliments.

The entire time, Andrew wondered if and when Simon would ask them about the clothes.

The training finished midmorning. Simon never asked.

Back in the tower, Andrew and Eve took their clothes out of the sack. The shoes were still scarred, but the clothes looked as if Simon had made a clumsy attempt to stitch the seams to look as they had. A few rivets were missing from the jeans.

"What should we do with them?" Andrew asked.

Eve shoved the clothes back into the sack and took it over to a battered trunk in the corner. "I'll keep them here until we can find a better hiding place," she said, then dropped the sack inside.

Andrew watched her close the lid. He wondered if they would ever wear those clothes again.

Jeanne returned from her visit with the Duke of Alençon and his wife a few days later. She was rosy cheeked and seemed happy. She told stories of quail hunting and long walks, meals full of conversation, and laughter and playfulness.

The Dauphin summoned the Maiden. Andrew and Eve went with her. They watched from the back of the royal chamber. Louis soon joined them and whispered, "Back to work."

With a thin smile, the Dauphin told Jeanne that he had made up his mind about allowing her to fight at Orléans. She was delighted. Then he crushed the moment by explaining that *first* she would have to travel to the city of Poitiers to meet with the professors and theologians there.

Andrew saw the look on her face. Her eyes glistened. He imagined the arguments she wanted to give against this delay. Instead, she stood up straight and said, "Then let us go at once."

The group of travelers quickly grew from just Jeanne and her company to the Dauphin himself, along with Regnault de Chartres, the Archbishop of Reims. Andrew recognized the Archbishop from the council meetings and an occasional glimpse of him in the halls of the castle.

The Archbishop had a lean face, with large eyes and a hooked nose. A gray beard spilled over the front of his collar. He was officially robed in white, with an embroidered gold cape and a white fur-lined collar. He often wore the traditional miter but traded it for a simpler skullcap for the journey.

The Dauphin and the Archbishop rode in separate carriages, surrounded by the royal guard. Though he was not an official member of the guard, Simon rode along with the caravan. Hardly anyone noticed him, though Andrew was watchful. The old man kept pace at the rear, wearing a hooded cloak over his armor. He looked more like a hermit than a soldier.

Andrew, Eve, and Louis settled in the back of a wagon, driven by one of the guards. Jeanne rode the black steed that the Duke of Alençon had given her. She refused to change into traditional women's clothes, wearing instead the garb of a page. Though she kept her head held high, she looked grim. Eve told Andrew that Jeanne had complained the night before about being forced to endure yet another round of questioning.

"What will it take for them to believe?" Jeanne had asked again and again.

Along the way, Andrew learned that the city of Poitiers had often been part of the tug-of-war between the English and the French. It was now the capital of the Dauphin's territory. He had installed his parliament there. Though, according to Louis, parliament had nothing to do, since there were no laws to pass or court cases to hear.

"For all of the glory of the buildings there, the counselors themselves are poor," Louis explained. "They say the families of those holding high positions wear rags and walk barefoot."

"Why will the Dauphin not help them?" Eve asked.

Louis looked around to make sure no one was listening. "How? The Dauphin has no money."

"But he is the ruler," Eve said.

"The ruler of what?" Louis growled. "He rules over the scraps that the English have left for him." He nodded to Jeanne. "But *she* will change all that. She will make him a true king."

The caravan moved at a slow and maddening pace, stopping in a field overnight and reaching Poitiers in the middle of the next day. At a distance, Poitiers looked like a magnificent city, dominated by the spires of a cathedral and the square towers of a castle.

Dignitaries from the town greeted them at the edge of the city. Andrew, Eve, and Louis were told to walk as part of a formal procession behind the Dauphin, the Archbishop, and Jeanne to the city center.

In the press of the procession, Andrew wound up next to Simon.

"A farce," the old man said sourly. "A dozen men will interrogate her—and then what? They might believe her or declare her a witch and have her burned at the stake."

"They will not burn her," said Andrew.

"That will come later," Simon said, his gaze on something far away.

Andrew was surprised. "How do you know that?"

Simon looked at him. "Know what?"

"That Jeanne will be burned at the stake," Andrew said, keeping his voice low.

Simon's bushy eyebrows lifted. "Will she?"

"You just said so."

Simon frowned. "Did I?" He shook his head violently as if trying to get rid of a bad thought.

Andrew was confused. Did Simon really say what he heard him say? Andrew replayed the conversation in his mind a few times later—and then gave up.

As the procession entered the city, lines of people gathered, raising their hands to welcome the dignitaries. Andrew saw that their clothes were little more than rags. Their faces were pinched, their eyes set in dark circles. He realized that many were lifting their hands not to honor the Dauphin but to beg for his help.

In contrast, the buildings looked majestic. There were churches with names like *Notre-Dame-la-Grande* and the *Saint-Pierre Cathedral*, which was still being built. Nearby was a rectangular-shaped church called *St. John the Baptist*, which Louis said was the oldest Christian building in France. And there was also the Saint-Hilaire-le-Grand church, built over the tomb of Saint Hilary.

The procession labored along the narrow streets and finally came to a stop in front of a mansion. Speeches were made. Then one of the city officials, a lawyer named Jean Rabateau, invited Jeanne and her company into the Hôtel de la Rose.

"We're staying at a hotel?" Andrew whispered to Eve.

Eve shook her head. "I think they use the word *hotel* for a house with a lot of rooms," she said.

The Dauphin, the Archbishop, and the royal guard continued on to their official residences.

Though the Hôtel de la Rose was impressive from the outside, Andrew thought it looked run-down inside. He later learned that Rabateau was a poor lawyer, in part because he refused to take bribes. Even the mansion was not his but was borrowed from another family.

Jean Rabateau's wife and a handful of meager-looking servants met Jeanne and her company in the large foyer. Jeanne was taken to a room with Eve. Andrew and Louis shared a room across the hall from them.

Jeanne asked if there was a private place where she might pray. Madame Rabateau directed her to a small chapel in another part of the mansion. It had a simple altar and benches.

"This will do perfectly," Jeanne said.

A large sitting room had been set up for Jeanne's interrogation. Jean Rabateau told her that the professors and clerics would arrive the next day. Jeanne looked anxious. She didn't eat that evening. Instead, she went to the chapel to pray.

When Andrew and Eve saw her a few hours later, she told them, "The blessed Saint Catherine came to comfort me and remind me that she had to defend the Gospel against more than fifty pagan doctors."

She explained that Saint Michael had also appeared to her. He said she would be "victorious in her trial and made worthy of 'our Lord Jesus Christ, the hope and crown of those who strive for him.'"

The next day, Andrew and Eve were allowed to sit in on the interrogation. The officials, clergy, and theologians assembled on one side of a long table, facing Jeanne. She sat in a chair opposite them, looking slight and pale.

A priest called Brother Jean Lombard began by saying, "We desire to know what led you to come to our king."

Jeanne sighed as she told yet again how a Voice had spoken to her when she was younger, saying, "God has great pity on the people of France. Jeanne, you must go into France." She explained, "On hearing these words, I began to weep. Then the Voice told me to go to Vaucouleurs, where a captain would take me to the Dauphin."

Another brother asked, "The Voice told you that God will deliver the people of France from their distress. But if God will deliver them, why does He need soldiers?"

It sounded to Andrew like a silly question.

The Maiden looked frustrated but restrained herself. "In God's name," she said, "the soldiers will fight, and God will give the victory."

One theologian demanded to know why Jeanne insisted on calling the king her "gentle Dauphin" instead of by his true title. "He is Charles the Seventh, proclaimed king upon the death of his father, the beloved Charles the Sixth."

Her answer was straightforward. "I will not call him 'king' until he is anointed and crowned at Reims. To that city I intend to take him."

And on it went.

By the end of the first day, Jeanne looked worn out. She confided to Andrew and Eve that she despaired of the days to come, not knowing how long the examination would take or who would show up to ask her questions.

The days dragged into weeks.

None of the questioners were overtly rude to her, but they asked many of the same questions over and over. At times she became irritated and gave curt responses. Andrew sometimes winced but had to remind himself that Jeanne was a teenager being hammered by more than a dozen men who were two or three times her age.

Andrew noticed that Jeanne relaxed when she was in the chapel, or walking in the nearby fields. She also enjoyed hanging out with the soldiers and servants. They said they had faith in her. Andrew noticed that she told them stories about the Voices of Saint Michael, Saint Catherine, and Saint Margaret that she never mentioned to the officials.

When Andrew asked her why, Jeanne said simply, "I was not sent to them. They are not why I came. I came with a message for the Dauphin, not for them."

Again and again, Andrew heard Jeanne tell her interrogators, "I come from the King of Heaven to raise the siege of Orléans and take the Dauphin to be crowned and anointed at Reims." It was as simple as that.

Andrew sometimes stayed in the room after Jeanne had been dismissed. The officials did not notice him as they debated among themselves. A priest named Gérard Machet, the Dauphin's own confessor, stated that he believed Jeanne was the fulfillment of a prophecy about a maiden coming to help the king of France. A weighty discussion followed about the role of prophetic women in the Holy Scriptures and throughout history.

A few of the officials objected to Jeanne wearing men's clothes and cutting her hair short. They debated Old Testament verses about the sin of women wearing men's garments.

"They were an abomination to God," one old priest argued. "Saint Paul himself wrote against cutting a woman's hair."

Others countered that Jeanne was acting from pure motives out of modesty and not to defy God or the Scriptures.

"Why will they not believe God?" Jeanne complained to Andrew and Eve privately. "They want proof, they want a sign, but the proof and the sign will be God's victory. How can I show them Saint Michael, Saint Catherine, or Saint Margaret unless they appear for themselves? They are not at my beck and call to summon as I wish."

It was as if it never occurred to her that others would doubt the revelations she had been given so freely, especially men who claimed to serve God.

Brother Séguin was one of those men. He told her, "God would not have us place faith in your words without a miracle to prove that you are acting by His command. Without that, how can we advise the king to turn over an army to you and risk the lives of so many soldiers on your claims?"

"In God's name," Jeanne cried out, "it was not to give a sign that I came to Poitiers. But take me to Orléans, and I will show you the signs I have been sent to give. Give me soldiers—it does not matter how many—and I will go to Orléans!"

During all of this, Andrew and Eve began to feel like prisoners in Poitiers. They could not go out, for fear of being mobbed by those who wanted to meet Jeanne. The only people they saw were the servants and soldiers around the hotel.

Andrew overheard one soldier talk about two men who had escaped from the English siege of Orléans. The men were told about Jeanne and her mission and raced back to tell the people of the city. Appeals were sent to the Dauphin. He had to make a decision.

Andrew also learned that the interrogators had sent priests to Domrémy to ask about the Maiden. They inquired about her birth, her life, her behavior, her purity, and her soundness of mind. The responses were consistent. Jeanne was a young woman of simplicity, faith, honesty, devotion, humility, and purity.

The day finally came when the officials presented their report to the Dauphin. They had determined that the prayers of the poor people of France and all who sought peace and justice might well be answered. The Dauphin should not reject Jeanne, they advised. Instead, they should allow that God had sent her to bring the people comfort. Though Jeanne had not provided a miraculous sign, her life and testimony were enough for them to trust her. "We find no evil in her," they proclaimed.

They concluded that the king should not hinder Jeanne from taking an army to Orléans. He should trust God to do as He had told her He would.

When the report was made public, shouts and celebrations filled the streets of Poitiers. Andrew imagined that the same would happen everywhere else once the news spread throughout France.

He thought, *If hope had a voice, this is what it would sound like.*

———————————————▶

Jeanne was on her knees in the private chapel at the Hôtel de la Rose when a message came from the Dauphin. She must travel immediately to the cities of Tours and Blois.

"Why Tours and Blois?" Eve asked her.

The Maiden beamed. "Because that is where I'll find the commanders, troops, and supplies for my army. Finally I can do what God has sent me to do."

The next day, Andrew and Eve sped with Jeanne and the entire company back to Chinon. There, they both learned what it meant to be servants. Eve worked long hours assembling uniforms, sewing buttons, and packing various crates and trunks. Andrew often ran from one end of the castle to the other as a messenger. When he wasn't doing that, he gathered weapons and whatever provisions of food he could find and carried them to the transport wagons.

In the midst of it all, Simon either ignored Andrew or exhausted him with sword training. There were no odd moments, nor any questions about the clothes. The old man maintained a fierce look as he stayed focused on the battle ahead.

A contingency of soldiers was assembled in Chinon to escort the long procession to Tours. The Dauphin had two-wheeled and four-wheeled wagons loaded with everything from wine, clothes, and armor to bedding, a mattress, kitchen utensils, and chapel furnishings. The horses were saddled for the higher-ranking members of the court.

Andrew discovered that Queen Yolande actually *owned* the city of Tours. In fact, it was only one of many towns and lands in France that rightfully belonged to her. Few knew how rich she really was, but it was rumored that the Dauphin would have been penniless without her help. It was also rumored that she was funding Jeanne's mission with her own money.

Jeanne was to ride next to the Dauphin at the front of the convoy. Eve was invited into the queen's carriage. Andrew made his way to a wagon at the rear. He would ride with Louis and a handful of soldiers.

"Have you seen Evangeline?" Louis asked.

"She is with Queen Yolande."

Louis shook his head. "A servant from the queen was just here asking for her."

Andrew was concerned. When and where had he last seen Eve?

"I last saw her in the tower," Louis said.

Andrew dashed to the tower. He took the steps two at a time to Jeanne's quarters. The door was open, but no one was there. He wasn't sure where to check next. He made a snap decision to check the very top of the tower.

With a sharp stitch in his side, he pushed through the door to the tower roof. Eve wasn't there. *Where did she go?* He fought to catch his breath as he leaned on the parapet.

He held on to the stones as he tried to think of where she might have gone. He glanced at the town below and then at the surrounding fields. *This might be the last time I enjoy this view*, he thought.

His gaze drifted over to the bridge. He stood up straight. There, on the side closest to the town, he saw a figure pacing along the bridge. A figure in a red dress.

It must be Eve, he thought. He took a deep breath and gathered his strength to rush down the stairs.

"Do not leave without us," he shouted to Louis as he raced past the caravan and through the main gate.

"They will not wait!" Louis called after him.

Andrew's legs felt wobbly as he ran down the hill, through the town, and out to the bridge. Eve was not there. He groaned, leaning against the railing of the bridge. He looked down at the north bank, where they appeared when they had first arrived. Then he saw her.

"Eve!" he called out, but it was little more than a croak. Holding his side, he pushed himself around to the path that would take him down to the riverbank.

The water had risen since he was last there. The bank was only a narrow slip of rock, dirt, and grass. Eve stood near the water's edge with the sack of their clothes cradled in her arms.

"What are you doing?" Andrew wheezed as he stumbled from the bushes. "Everyone is about to leave."

Eve had a grim expression on her face. Her eyes were red. "What are we doing?" she asked.

"We're helping Jeanne," he wheezed in reply.

"We are about to go into a *war*," she said. "We could die."

"We're kids. No one expects us to fight," he countered.

"Look at some of the soldiers and the squires and the pages. They're only a little older than we are. *Jeanne* is only a little older than they are."

There was no point arguing. "Okay. Fine. What are you saying?"

Eve's lower lip trembled. "I want to go home."

"How?" he asked. He felt frustrated. "I don't get it. You weren't like this when we were running all over the place with Robin Hood."

"We had the Radiant Stone there," she said. "We could leave whenever we wanted. We can't do that now."

"You want to leave Jeanne?"

"They're going to burn her at the stake," she said. "What if they burn us, too?"

Andrew shook his head. "They won't."

"That's what *she* probably thinks."

"God will keep us safe."

"That's what she thinks too."

"It's her time, not ours. We don't belong here. The rules are different, remember?" he said.

"We don't know all the rules. We don't know how many people touched that stone, went off in time, and died," she said. She hugged the sack and shivered. "I'm afraid."

"We are *not* going to die here, Eve," he said firmly.

"Is that faith or stupidity?" Eve asked. She turned away and began to search along the bank.

"What are you doing?"

"I'm going to hide our clothes here," she said. "I put a message inside."

"What kind of message?"

"I'm asking for help." Eve moved close to the pillars that held up the bridge.

Andrew followed her. "Who is going to help us?"

"Alfred Virtue."

"*What*?" Andrew asked, dumbfounded. "How is he supposed to help us?"

She scrambled onto a ledge at the base of the nearest pillar. "We know he found the Radiant Stone, right? And it must have been connected to this spot, or we wouldn't have come here, right? So maybe if we hide our clothes and a message for help, he'll find it and come back to help us."

"But he is, like, *six hundred* years away from us," Andrew said.

Eve stepped along the large blocks of stone that shored up the bridge. The river coursed to her right.

Andrew carefully followed her, still unsure of what she was doing. "Do you have any idea what the chances are that he'll get your message?" he asked. "The river could wash the sack away. The weather might ruin it. It might turn into dust. Lots of people might find it in the meantime, and ..."

Eve turned and glared at him. "Don't tell me all the reasons it won't work. I have to try. It gives me hope."

She looked up at the stonework. The underside of the bridge stretched out above them. Something flapped its wings in the darkness.

"Where are you going to put the sack?" he asked, coming close to her.

"There's a gap just a few feet up." She clenched the leather strap at the top of the sack between her teeth.

"Ew," said Andrew.

Finding footholds in the rough surface of the stonework, Eve climbed as high as she could go. With one hand, she grasped the jagged edge of a stone. Then with her other hand, she shoved the sack into a space out of Andrew's sight.

Andrew was sure she'd fall into the river. She didn't. She climbed back down, and they returned to the riverbank.

It won't work, Andrew thought. He actually felt sorry for her.

From somewhere on the bridge, a woman shouted, "You must hurry! The Maiden is about to leave."

"I am hurrying, I am hurrying!" an irritated man replied.

"We have to go," Andrew said. "Are you coming?"

Before she could answer, a voice said, "Of course she is coming."

The two of them spun around. Simon Le Fantôme stood by the path, his face twisted in rage.

Eve gasped and staggered back.

"What do you want?" Andrew asked.

Simon's eyes were wild, his face twisted into pure rage.

Andrew looked for a way to escape, but there was nowhere for him and Eve to go. Except into the river.

The old man took a few quick steps, then grabbed the collars of their tunics. He jerked the two kids up, half carrying them under his arms like a couple of small animals.

"Put us down!" Eve cried. She punched at him.

Simon squeezed harder and lurched back to the path. He slowly lumbered up to the bridge. Once there, he threw Andrew and Eve onto the ground, then quickly drew his sword.

"What is wrong with you?" Eve demanded.

Andrew half crawled a few feet away, then clambered to his feet. He clawed at the hilt of his sword, fumbling to get it out of its sheath. "Stop!" he shouted.

"I heard what you said," Simon snarled, his voice raw. "This is not your time. What do you mean? Whose time is it?"

"How am I supposed to know?" Eve asked, still sitting on the ground.

Simon raised his hands, ready to grab her. "Will we die at Orléans? Tell me, *witch*!"

"Back, old man," Louis said as he strode toward them from the bridge. He held up his sword.

Simon scowled at him. "Mind yourself, boy."

Louis took a fighting stance. "On guard," he said.

"What would the Maiden say if I were to kill her servant here?" Simon asked.

Louis smiled. "What *would* she say? I do not think she would look upon you kindly. Though no one would miss *you* should I strike you down."

The old man's face suddenly relaxed. The feverish look in his eyes softened. He grunted at Louis as he sheathed his sword. "See to your charges," he said, then pushed past the lad.

"What was that about?" Louis asked.

"How should I know? He is insane," Eve said. "*Merci*."

"The caravan is ready to depart," Louis said. He slid his sword into its sheath. "Jeanne said she will not depart without you. Everyone is angry. Are you coming?"

"I am," Andrew said. He looked at Eve for her answer.

Eve took a deep breath and stood up. "So am I. God help us."

———————————————►

The caravan reached the city of Tours that afternoon. Jeanne was mobbed yet again by crowds that wanted to touch her. They grabbed at her legs, wanting to kiss her feet in honor. It was slow going.

Andrew saw the castle, with its round, rocket-like tower. Then he gazed at the great cathedral, which dominated the other churches, houses, and shops around it.

Louis nudged him, gesturing toward the many buildings they passed. "It is no coincidence that we are here," he said. "Tours has some of the finest craftsmen in France. There are weavers of silk, craftsmen of silver and gold, forgers of coats of mail and armor. Our Maiden will be equipped with all she needs."

Jeanne and her company were taken to the house of Jean Dupuy. Dupuy was a friend of Queen Yolande, a member of her council, and a leader in the city. He lived in a great manor house and welcomed them warmly.

Later in the afternoon, the Duke of Alençon arrived in Tours. So did Jeanne's dear friends and escorts Jean de Metz and Bertrand de Poulengy. It seemed like one happy reunion after another.

That night, Andrew heard a commotion downstairs. He raced down to see Jeanne embracing and weeping over two men who had just arrived. The men were Pierre and Jean, her brothers from Domrémy.

"I thank God I may welcome you," she said to them. Jeanne feigned a serious expression. "Our father has not sent you to drown me, has he?"

Her brothers laughed.

Jeanne turned to Madame Dupuy, who had also been watching the scene. "My father said he would rather they drown me than allow me to leave home for this mission," Jeanne explained.

"He has since changed his mind," said Pierre. "He is thankful to God, and proud of you."

Jeanne looked touched and hugged him.

Andrew could see their resemblance to Jeanne. There was a light to their eyes, especially when they smiled, he thought.

Jeanne was surrounded by able-bodied men, each worthy to be called a military commander. Louis de Coutes was assigned to her for as long as she needed him, along with another fifteen-year-old boy named Raymond. Together they would serve as pages to the warrior Maiden. Two heralds named Guyenne and Ambleville also joined their ranks to deliver messages.

Jean d'Aulon would serve Jeanne as a proper squire to bear her shield and armor. D'Aulon was tall and muscular, with thinning brown hair and blue eyes. Andrew guessed he was around forty years old. Though he seemed friendly enough, he bore a look of hard determination that came from years of experience in battle.

With her military staff in place, Jeanne now had to decide about her weapons, clothes, and armor.

The Dauphin's master armorer brought craftsmen from the city to measure the Maiden for a breastplate and backplate. They would be made of wrought iron. Various models of helmets were tried on her head to see which size would fit. She was presented with different styles of armlets; elbow pieces; gloves that covered fingers, hands, and forearms; shoes; and steel protection for her thighs, knees, and shins. She was also shown fabric for the loose coat she would wear over it all.

Jeanne argued that she wanted nothing fancy. "The armor may be white and unadorned," she told them again and again.

The Dauphin also commanded that a banner be made for her out of a durable white cloth and silk fringe. The Dauphin's own artist, from Scotland, would design the banner according to Jeanne's instructions.

Jeanne prayed and then reported that the Voices had told her the banner should show the image of Our Lord sitting in judgment in the clouds of Heaven. Jesus was to be placed upon His throne, blessing with His right hand

and holding in His left a globe of the world. Jeanne also wanted angels on both sides of Jesus, the image of the *fleur-de-lis* and the names *Jhesus* and *Maria* at the top. The background was to be strewn with royal lilies in gold.

"I will carry the banner into battle myself," Jeanne announced.

Jean d'Aulon asked, "How will you fight with your sword if you carry a banner?"

"If I carry the banner, then I will not use my sword," she replied.

D'Aulon cocked an eyebrow. "Then you will not need a sword?"

"I must have a sword," she said. "Though the sword I bear must come from the hand of Saint Catherine herself."

"How am I to find a sword that Saint Catherine used?" d'Aulon asked. "She had many. Do you want the sword she brought from Alexandria in Egypt? The one the Prince of the Franks gave her?"

"I want the sword that has five crosses engraved on the blade."

Jean d'Aulon tossed up his hands in exasperation. "Where am I to find this sword?"

Jeanne looked as if she could not understand why d'Aulon was so upset. "It is at the Church of Saint Catherine's in Fierbois. Behind the altar. Saint Catherine has told me so herself."

The squire rolled his eyes and said, "Of course. That makes perfect sense."

Later, Andrew went with d'Aulon to seek advice from a master armorer named Espee.

With a face permanently darkened by soot and smoke, Espee merely shrugged. "I have heard of no such sword. But if it is battle worthy, then she should use it. Shall we go to Fierbois and see?"

So Master Espee, Jean d'Aulon, and Andrew went to the Church of Saint Catherine in Fierbois to find the sword.

Though Fierbois was only eighteen miles from Tours, the journey took longer than it should have because the armorer and Andrew were clumsy riding horses. The armorer complained that all the bouncing on the horse caused him a lot of pain.

Andrew had never ridden a horse at such a high speed. He clung to the reins with white-knuckled fists and lifted his backside to ease the pounding he got from the galloping. But then his legs ached and finally gave out. D'Aulon alone was the skilled rider and smiled patiently each time they had to stop.

They found two priests serving at the Church of Saint Catherine. Father Robert was short, with white hair. Brother Gilles was slender and had dark hair. Both wore black robes.

Alarmed by the arrival of the three strangers, the priests were even more alarmed by the letter Jean d'Aulon handed to them. Jeanne had given instructions about where to find the sword.

Father Robert read Jeanne's letter, then handed it to Brother Gilles.

"There has been a mistake," Father Robert said. "The Maiden describes a sword with five crosses engraved upon it. There is no sword of that kind here."

"Come inside," Brother Gilles said.

The five of them went into the church. Andrew gasped. Shields, armor, and swords adorned the entire length of the walls. "It looks more like an armory than a church," he said.

Father Robert spread his hands in a "What can we do?" fashion. "When the men of our country were faced with danger, they called to Saint Catherine for help. When she saved them, they would come here and offer their armor and weapons as a sign of thanks. We hang them for all to see."

"And sell the rest to feed the poor," Brother Gilles added. He tapped the letter. "The Maiden writes that Saint Catherine's sword is behind the altar."

"I can assure you, there is no sword behind the altar," Father Robert said.

"See for yourselves." Brother Gilles led them down the center aisle of the church. Andrew's eyes went from the weapons and shields to the beautiful stained-glass windows, then up to the arched roof far above him.

They reached the altar and searched the stone walls, the ledge beneath the stained-glass window, and then every inch of the altar itself.

"You see? No sword," said Father Robert.

Andrew thought about the secret passageway at Chinon and wondered if the sword was behind a hidden panel. The walls were solid. He knelt and rubbed his fingers along the stone tiles on the floor. "Why is this tile larger than the others?" he asked.

"I had not noticed it," Brother Gilles said. "Odd, since I have often scrubbed these floors."

D'Aulon drew a knife and shoved the point into a crack between the larger tile and the smaller ones around it. The knife pushed through to open space below. He worked the blade all the way around the edges. "Help me," he said.

The priests ran off and returned with thin pikes. It took a lot of effort to find the right angle without destroying the tile, but eventually they were able to lift it up. Beneath was a long, rectangular space no more than a foot deep. In the darkness, they saw a rough cloth.

"A rag?" Brother Gilles said, then reached into the space. "No, it is more."

He carefully brought out a moldy cloth that was wrapped around something long and thin. He laid it down and pulled the rag away.

Inside the cloth was a rusty sword with five crosses engraved on the blade.

Father Robert performed the Sign of the Cross. "Saint Catherine, save us," he said.

The armorer picked up the sword, using his fat thumb to scrape at the rust. Small brown flakes fell. "It is beautiful workmanship," he said and held the sword up. The blade caught the sunlight and glowed.

"How could the Maiden know?" Father Robert asked.

"Saint Catherine told her," said Jean d'Aulon.

The two priests decided they must journey back with d'Aulon, Andrew, and Master Espee to present the sword to Jeanne.

"Allow us time to prepare it," Father Robert said.

"Pray, stay the night," said Brother Gilles.

The three men were given a meal and places to rest in the small house next to the church. Meanwhile, the priests busied themselves preparing the sword. They also asked the townspeople to help with what needed to be done.

The next morning, Jean d'Aulon readied the horses for the journey back to Tours. The townspeople gathered around him. Brother Gilles carefully slid the sword into a sheath of red velvet with a fleur-de-lis symbol embroidered on the side. He then wrapped the sword and sheath in a sturdy black cloth.

"Let us say a Mass of Thanksgiving," Father Robert announced. "Then we will deliver the sword to its new owner."

The return to Tours took on its own kind of pageantry. Word about the "miracle of the sword" went ahead of the travelers. By the time they reached the city, people were clamoring to see the newly discovered Sword of Saint Catherine.

Jeanne received the sacred weapon at the castle. "This is the sword Saint Catherine said I should have," she announced and held it high for the Dauphin's court to see. Shouts of celebration went up.

"This is the sign the officials in Poitiers yearned to see," Queen Yolande said to Andrew with an ironic smile.

Walking back to the manor house of Dupuy, Jeanne said to Jean d'Aulon, "The sheath for this sword is too fancy. It is made for show, not for battle. Please find me a simple leather one to use."

The next day, Andrew found Jeanne pacing in the front hall of the house. Eve stood nearby, watching her mistress with a doleful expression.

"What is wrong?" Andrew asked quietly.

Eve shook her head. "Something is bothering her."

Jeanne stopped and looked at them. "Why do my angels whisper?"

"We whisper because we do not want to disturb you," Eve said.

"You whisper a lot," Jeanne said. "Why do you whisper now?"

"I asked why you are pacing," Andrew said.

"I am pacing because I desire to confess my sins to a priest I can trust," Jeanne said. She gazed at them eagerly. "Now tell me. What do you whisper about at other times? What weighs on your hearts?"

Andrew and Eve glanced at each other.

"Sometimes . . ." Eve began, then hesitated.

"Go on," coaxed Jeanne.

Eve continued. "I want to go home, but I do not know how to get there."

Jeanne suddenly sat on the floor and leaned her back against the wall. "I know that feeling." She beckoned them to sit down next to her. "Two of my brothers have come, which should make me happy. Yet when I look at them, I think of Domrémy and the fields in which I ran, and the games I once played as a child. When I think of these things, I feel a quickening in my heart for those simpler days. I know I will never see them again. God may give me a year for this mission. But I fear I will have no more time than that."

Andrew was sitting cross-legged. He looked down at his hands, wanting to avoid eye contact with her. He feared she would see something there that betrayed what he knew about her future.

"Are you afraid?" he asked.

"I am not afraid. God is with me. I was born for this," Jeanne replied. She said to Eve, "Now, what do you think about?"

Eve said, "I think about our town and the beautiful mountains and the joy of discovering new things. I miss them."

"And you?" Jeanne asked Andrew.

"I think about my family," he said. "I wonder if I will ever see them again."

Jeanne smiled. "Are your parents good? Are they kind? Do they love Jesus and His Church?"

"Yes."

"Do you have brothers and sisters?"

"I have a sister named Elizabeth, a brother named Nicholas, and another sister named Samantha." Andrew took a deep breath. Talking about his family caused a swell of emotion in his chest. It threatened to slide up to his eyes and come out as tears.

"Do you love your sisters?" Jeanne asked.

Andrew nodded. "One of them is like you," he said.

Jeanne giggled. "You are in trouble, then."

Eve turned to Andrew. "What do you mean?"

Andrew thought for a moment, then said, "My sister Elizabeth has a … I am not sure how to say it. She has a special relationship with God."

"Do Voices speak to her?" asked Jeanne.

"It would not surprise me," he said. Then he revealed something he had never told anyone. "She has seen her guardian angel."

Eve blinked as if she hadn't heard right. "Is that possible?"

"It is for her." Andrew quickly regretted saying anything. "You cannot tell anyone. Ever. It is a family secret."

Jeanne looked solemn. "As her brother, you must not mock or doubt her. If what you say is true, then she will suffer a pain few others will ever know."

"What pain?" Andrew asked.

Jeanne sighed. "Loneliness. The pain of separation. To see and know what others cannot see or know sets her apart. It makes her more different than any other kind of difference a man or woman may feel. She must find her consolation from God alone, and what morsels of comfort you may give her."

Andrew lowered his head as Jeanne spoke. His eyes burned. "If I ever see her again, I will remember what you said."

"Why will you not see her?" Jeanne asked. "Is she far away?"

"Very far."

"We are stranded here," Eve added.

"Stranded?" Jeanne said the word as if contemplating its meaning. "As in a shipwreck? Marooned?"

"Something like that," Eve said. "I do not think we will ever see home again."

Jeanne reached out and took both of their hands in hers. "Oh, my angels. We feel as one. Never will I see Domrémy again. Yet our true home also awaits us."

The burning in Andrew's eyes wouldn't stop. He heard Eve sniffle.

"No matter how far away we may be," Jeanne said, "we are never abandoned. God is with us always. And He often sends someone to remind us it is true."

Just then, there was a loud pounding on the large front door. A maid appeared from a side room and pulled it open. A young man in a gray robe entered.

"What is it you want?" asked the maid.

The man looked around, as if lost. "I am seeking"— his eyes caught Jeanne, Andrew, and Eve sitting on the floor—"the Maiden and her two angels! Just as I expected to find them." He drifted past the puzzled maid and knelt before Jeanne.

Jeanne stood up. Andrew and Eve did the same.

The man continued. "God told me to come to this house. He said I would find the Maiden and her two angels sitting on the floor."

Jeanne laughed.

The gray-robed man looked up at her. He explained that he was a monk from the Augustinians, an order that had taken their rule from Saint Francis himself. "I have been traveling the countryside, and everyone I meet has said I must find you. I went to Chinon, but you had already left. I came to the abbey here in Tours, and it was while I prayed that I was told to come here."

She waved for him to stand up. "You are Brother Jean Pasquerel," Jeanne said.

The monk looked surprised as he stood.

"I have heard of you from those I trust," she explained. "They have told me I will like you when I know you."

"Who told you about me?" the monk asked.

Jeanne answered by gesturing to the sky, then said, "I would be honored for you to hear my confession."

He gave her a warm smile. "It is what I have come to do. Today, tomorrow, and to the end of our lives, if God wills it."

18

Jeanne and her company spent their remaining days in Tours assembling more supplies and weapons for the move to Blois. Jeanne became more excited. The city of Blois put them thirty miles closer to Orléans. At Blois, she would finally meet with the Dauphin's military commanders and troops.

The morning of their departure, Jeanne was again placed at the front of the procession, arrayed in the splendor of her new armor. The Sword of Saint Catherine was at her side. The gentle wind unfurled her beautiful new banner.

Outside of Blois, a sprawling military camp spread out across the green fields. Andrew saw white, red, and blue tents dotting the landscape. It looked as if hundreds or even thousands of soldiers were there. Some were gathered near the tents, tending to cauldrons and campfires. Some were on horseback, churning up the ground as they practiced their maneuvers. Some marched while others honed their skills in sword fighting or archery.

Andrew was surprised to see jugglers, jesters, and troubadours plying their trade for any coins the soldiers might throw their way. Women also moved freely around the camp. It looked almost like a carnival.

Monks were there to give the men spiritual counsel, hear confessions, or conduct Mass on makeshift altars.

The city of Blois itself sat sunbathed on the north side of the Loire River. Like Chinon, the streets threaded uphill, leading to a castle. Soldiers and wagons bearing provisions poured in and out of every gate.

Once inside the city, the procession had to stop more than once until a soldier scooted away a cow or a pig, a few sheep, or some wayward chickens. Animals seemed to run everywhere. The people saw them and came out of their homes with outstretched arms. Laughing children darted on and off the street.

The castle grounds were also overrun with troops. Most were officers who commanded underlings to put this barrel over here and that crate over there and those boxes on top of that one. It was then Andrew realized that the march to Orléans wasn't only to battle the English. It was a rescue mission to get food to the starving citizens under siege.

The members of the procession from Tours scattered in different directions. Andrew and Eve went with Louis to a meeting hall, where the Dauphin's military commanders had been assembled for Jeanne's arrival.

Andrew wondered, more than once, what these hardened men of battle thought about following a teenage peasant girl. What was she to them? Definitely not a professional soldier. She wasn't even a man, though she dressed like one. She was just an inexperienced peasant girl who might or might not have been sent by God to lead them in battle. How would she cope in battle, where a lot of the fighting would be hand to hand against men twice her size? How would she respond to the filth, sweat, and blood?

The commanders were watchful as they stood there waiting for Jeanne. Andrew followed Eve and Louis to one side of the hall, where they could see the meeting unfold.

"Who are all these men?" Eve asked softly.

"That is the Marshal of Sainte-Sévère," Louis said, pointing to a stout, ruddy-faced man in silver armor. "And that creepy-looking man next to Sainte-Sévère is Gilles, the Baron de Rais.

Andrew was amused. The Baron de Rais had long black hair and a trimmed beard dyed blue.

Louis nodded to another man who had close-cropped hair; a long, combed beard; and a face that looked more like it belonged to a librarian than a soldier.

"That's Ambroise de Loré," Louis said. "He is celebrated for destroying an English regiment not far from one of the English governors. Few have ever made it that close."

Andrew recognized the silver-haired and leather-faced Captain Raoul de Gaucourt from Chinon. It was his wife who had inspected Jeanne when she had first arrived there.

A crash came from the back of the room, followed by angry shouts. Heads turned. A man with a wolf-like face and lean body stood over a hapless young soldier who had dropped a tray of wine.

"Fool!" the man shouted, adding words that Andrew knew were bad at any time and in any language.

Louis chuckled. "That is Gascon Étienne de Vignolles, though everyone calls him 'La Hire.'"

"Why La Hire?" Andrew asked.

Louis shrugged. "I am not certain. Because he is prickly like a hedgehog?"

"What does La Hire have to do with a hedgehog?" Eve asked.

"It is a play with words," Louis said, as if no further explanation was needed.

La Hire was still ranting at the poor soldier when Jeanne strode into the hall, the Duke of Alençon at her side. Silence fell on the assembly, leaving only La Hire's voice and foul words shaking the rafters.

"Enough of that, sir," Jeanne said sharply to La Hire.

The old soldier spun to face her. He looked as if he might strike her for interrupting him. But when he saw Jeanne, his expression changed to one of open astonishment. His eyes, narrow from rage, grew wide.

To everyone's surprise, the man stammered as he bowed to the Maiden, "Forgive me, Holy Maiden."

Jeanne laughed lightly, touching his shoulder. "It is not for me to forgive," she said. "But I beg you ..." Here she turned and raised her voice to the entire assembly. "I beg all of you to go to confession. Cleanse yourselves with God's absolution. No more swearing or blasphemy, from the highest ranking commander to the lowliest soldier."

This announcement caused whispers and murmurs to roll through the men.

Jeanne continued. "Those who wish to join this fight must attend Mass twice daily. None will be forced against his will. However, anyone who refuses will be released from our service."

The Baron de Rais cried out, "Dear Maiden, you must be reasonable."

Jeanne gave him a steely look. "I would also have you release all women from the camp."

Gasps and loud protests came from the soldiers.

"Hear me, men of valor!" Jeanne called out, silencing them. "We go to Orléans as the army of God. The fate of France is in the hands of the pure."

Andrew expected at least one of the captains to complain further, but they all fell quiet and merely nodded as Jeanne passed among them. She took her position behind a large table covered with maps. Looking up, she calmly faced the men sent to help her.

"Good men, what must I know about Orléans?"

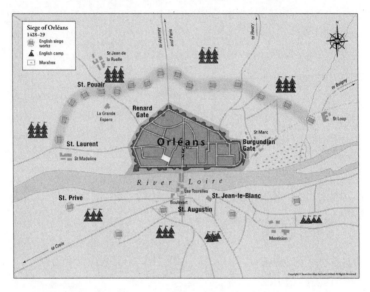

A barrage of reports and opinions followed. Orléans should never have been taken by the English while the duke was still a prisoner in England, the commanders told her. To take it was to defy the laws of war, which said that the land of a prisoner was protected so the prisoner could pay his ransom. Yet Orléans was besieged. The French protested. The English didn't care.

The Duke of Alençon explained that the English king's commander, the Earl of Salisbury, attacked Orléans because of its position on the river Loire. If the English captured the city, they would have control over the supply

lines into France and a sure passage into the Dauphin's
territory.

La Hire pointed to the map. "The Earl of Salisbury has
attacked and claimed towns up and down the river from
Orléans. But Orléans has its high walls and some thirty
watchtowers. And it has a great stone bridge that serves as
the single entrance across the river from the south, should
the other gates be closed. That is how the city has escaped
a complete capture."

Jeanne moved some of the papers around on the table
and came to a sketch of Orléans. "I see it. The fortress at
the end of the bridge. *Les Tourelles*, it is called."

"It is like a castle unto itself," said La Hire. "Salisbury
was able to take the Tourelles, but the valiant men of
Orléans damaged the bridge so the English could not
cross to the gate. Taking Tourelles was the death of him."

At this point, Louis leaned over to Andrew and
explained that Salisbury had been killed by a French
cannonball while he was looking from the window of the
tower to the city. Another English commander, the Earl
of Suffolk, replaced Salisbury. Suffolk quickly realized he
did not have the troops to surround the city completely,
nor could he capture the bridge. So he settled down for
a long and grueling siege, hoping to starve the people of
Orléans into surrendering.

"So they are stuck?" Andrew asked.

"More or less," said Louis. "Suffolk has had to take over
the surrounding buildings and construct small fortresses

all around Orléans to watch for our army. He brought in Sir John Talbot to command the English forces in Tourelles."

"Have the French tried to attack them?" asked Eve.

Louis nodded. "The Dauphin sent his cousin Jean de Dunois and the ferocious La Hire to save Orléans. But alas, the two could not rally enough men to defeat the English in open battle. Instead, they looked for weaknesses on the English side by engaging in skirmishes. They also attacked the English supply lines from the north. Their efforts annoyed Suffolk but did not help Orléans."

Andrew's attention went back to Jeanne as he heard her say, "For months, forty thousand people have been trapped inside a city that was built to hold only fifteen thousand."

"It is true, Maiden," La Hire said. "And English arrows and cannon fire bombard them relentlessly. The stress of constant danger and the despair of death oppresses them."

The Duke of Alençon reminded everyone that his father-in-law, the Duke of Orléans, had written a well-known ballad explaining the misery of the French people. "Their suffering is a chastisement for their sins of pride, gluttony, laziness, dishonesty, and injustices. The people must renounce their sins, live holy lives, attend Mass, and appeal to Mary and the saints for help."

"Have they done this?" asked Jeanne.

"They have, dear Maiden," said the duke.

"And what do they believe God will do in response?" she asked.

The duke smiled at her. "They believe that a young maiden is coming with a fresh army to liberate them. They have heard that much-needed food and supplies are on the way. For the first time in months, the people have hope."

Jeanne had a steely-eyed look. "Now the people's suffering will end," she declared to her commanders.

Many of the men cheered. The Duke of Alençon gazed at her proudly.

"The English troops are spread thin," said La Hire. "They are weary and diseased. That great traitor, the Duke of Burgundy, has removed his soldiers from the siege and sent them to other parts. Yet the Duke of Suffolk does not dare give up his position, though they do not have the strength to attack. It is all they can do to maintain the siege. God has given us the right moment to strike."

Jeanne now turned her attention to the issue of supplies. She learned that wheat, sheep, pigs, cows, and other foodstuffs had been gathered. She assigned their safe delivery to Marshal Saint-Sévère and Gilles, the Baron de Rais. "Good men, how will you get the provisions to the people of Orléans?"

Gilles stepped forward. "The English are positioned on the north, west, and south of Orléans," he said, pointing to the map on the table. "Even now, the eastern gate of the city is open to merchants. They attempt to bring into the city whatever they can carry on their backs and on small wagons."

The Marshal of Sainte-Sévère said, "The English still have troops scattered in strongholds along the roads approaching from the east. They sometimes attack the merchants."

"What do you propose we do?" Jeanne asked. "How will we approach the city if the roads are open to attack?"

Gilles replied, "We will not use the road. We will use the river Loire itself. The officials of Orléans will send barges eastward on the river to the town of Crécy. We will meet them there and transport the provisions quickly back down the river to Orléans."

"Go immediately," Jeanne ordered. "Assure the city officials and their people that we are coming."

The rest of the meeting dealt with the battle itself. Jeanne and the commanders gathered around the table and marked the positions of seventy-one cannons along the walls of Orléans. They discussed the lack of master gunners to fire them. They debated the skill of the English archers and the need for more French shields to protect the soldiers from the arrows. The commanders finally settled on the grim reality that most of the battle would be fought hand to hand at Tourelles.

"How can a woman fight against brute strength?" Louis asked Andrew and Eve. "There will be men with swords and lances, iron clubs and battle-axes. How can she enter such a battle?"

"By the grace of God," said Eve.

As the preparations for the march from Blois to Orléans were finalized, Jeanne spent more and more time in prayer. Eve joined her, while Andrew helped distribute supplies to the soldiers and load more provisions into wagons.

One afternoon, Andrew had a rare moment with Jeanne and Eve in Jeanne's quarters.

"The English must be given a chance to repent and depart peacefully," Jeanne announced. "I must now send a letter of terms."

Andrew and Eve sat with heart-pounding admiration as Jeanne, who could not read or write, dictated a stern letter to the king of England and all his commanders in France. She warned them that God had sent her to restore the royal blood of France to its rightful place on the throne. She told them to hand over the keys to the cities they had violated, confess their sins, and pay back what they had stolen or destroyed. In exchange, she would allow them to depart in peace. If not, she promised to bring about a great injury to them. She begged them not to bring about their own destruction.

It was clear to Andrew that Jeanne hoped to avoid war, if possible. But he suspected the English would only laugh at her.

Jeanne listened to her herald Guyenne read back the written appeal. Then she ordered him to carry the letter to Sir John Talbot, the English commander at Tourelles. "Our attack will affect him more than anyone," Jeanne reasoned.

Looking very worried, Guyenne bowed, then departed.

The next morning, Jeanne dressed in her full armor of white. Eve was at her side, wearing her red dress. Andrew thought they both looked calm, even peaceful.

La Hire approached the Maiden, suggesting they tour the camp. "The sight of you will encourage the men."

Jeanne agreed and went off with him.

Eve walked over to Andrew, who had been watching them from the back of a supply wagon.

"Are you okay?" Andrew asked as he leapt down.

"Yes," she said. "Jeanne and I were praying in the chapel, and I felt ... I'm not sure what I felt. It's too hard to explain. It was like God put His arms around me and held me close. Now I'm ready for the battle."

"You aren't going into battle," Andrew said.

"I'm not staying *here*," Eve said.

Andrew was stunned. "What? The commanders have said clearly that they don't want any inexperienced fighters tripping them up during the battle. We are to stay with the wagons behind the archers."

Eve nodded. "Then I'll stay with you and watch."

"You shouldn't be near the battlefield at all!" Andrew said. "What if the English break through? What if we get pulled into the battle itself?"

"Then we'll fight," Eve said firmly. "But I must be wherever Jeanne is. I will *not* hide here in Blois while she is fighting there."

Andrew knew it was better not to argue.

A Mass and prayers were offered that night. They would march to Orléans the next morning.

Andrew heard from Louis that La Hire himself had prayed, "Lord God, please do for La Hire what La Hire would do for you if you were captain and La Hire was God."

Some of the men laughed at the prayer, sure it was a joke. Andrew thought it was the sincere prayer of a man who prayed very little but prayed honestly when he did.

The Maiden slept in her armor that night—if she slept at all.

Veni, Creator Spiritus,
mentes tuorum visita,
imple superna gratia
quae tu creasti pectora.

Under the banner of the cross, priests and monks chanted, *"Come, Holy Spirit, Creator blest, and in our souls take up Thy rest; come with Thy grace and heavenly aid to fill the hearts which Thou hast made."*

A long line of horsemen followed, with Jeanne at the head, her banner held high. The Duke of Alençon rode with her, along with Jean de Metz and Bertrand de Poulengy. Jeanne's brothers, Pierre and Jean, rode behind them with various squires and pages. The assembly of commanders came next, looking fierce and determined.

The priests sang out,

Qui diceris Paraclitus,
altissimi donum Dei,

fons vivus, ignis, caritas,
et spiritalis unctio.

"*O comforter, to Thee we cry, O heavenly gift of God Most High, O fount of life and fire of love, and sweet anointing from above.*"

They continued with ...

Tu, septiformis munere,
digitus paternae dexterae,
Tu rite promissum Patris,
sermone ditans guttura.

Andrew heard the words "*Thou in Thy sevenfold gifts are known; Thou, finger of God's hand we own; Thou, promise of the Father, Thou who dost the tongue with power imbue.*"

More than five hundred soldiers marched behind the assembly, with spears pointed to the heavens. Bows and other weapons with leather straps were slung over shoulders or held firm in tight fists.

The priests chanted,

Kindle our sense from above,
and make our hearts o'erflow with love;
with patience firm and virtue high
the weakness of our flesh supply.

Andrew and Eve sat next to the driver of a horse-drawn wagon that was burdened with food and more weapons. More wagons followed, some pulled by horses and others by servants.

The priests continued,

Far from us drive the foe we dread,
and grant us Thy peace instead;
so shall we not, with Thee for guide,
turn from the path of life aside.

Oh, may Thy grace on us bestow
the Father and the Son to know;
and Thee, through endless times confessed,
of both the eternal Spirit blest.

Now to the Father and the Son,
Who rose from death, be glory given,
with Thou, O Holy Comforter,
henceforth by all in earth and heaven.
Amen.

The final *Amen* was now a distant sound, nearly lost in the tramping of feet and hooves and the rattle of wooden wagon wheels.

The day wore on. Dark clouds gathered overhead. The procession stopped for the night in a large field. Andrew didn't know where. Tents and campfires were quickly set up. Jeanne made sure they had an altar to celebrate Mass.

That night, Jeanne again slept in her armor, though the burden of it was beginning to show on her face. Her shoulders seemed slumped.

Eve wanted to unstrap sections of the armor to lessen the weight.

Jeanne shook her head. "It is my cross to bear for our Lord. Dare I refuse it?"

In the morning, with the sun rising over their shoulders, they marched on to the besieged city. Clouds rolled in, and an unhelpful rain fell heavily on the entire region.

Andrew understood from the wagon driver that they were circling wide around Orléans from the south side. The plan was to avoid any skirmishes with the English forces that manned the posts closer to the city.

"We will drive to the southeast of the city and assemble there," the man explained.

Andrew assumed it made sense to go that way. But as they ascended the rising lands around the town of Olivet, Jeanne seemed agitated. Andrew and Eve crested a hill with her. Even through the rain, they had a clear view of the belfries and towers of Orléans, just across the Loire River.

The army was marching toward the river. Andrew watched as the livestock and carts of provisions split away from the main formation of troops and headed east.

"Why are we here and Orléans is over there?" Jeanne asked. "What were they thinking? I want to speak with my commanders *now*!" She stormed back down the hill.

La Hire barked at a handful of foot soldiers to put up a tent. They hastily erected a few poles and a large tarp in the middle of the field. The rain poured down. Jeanne went inside the tent and waited for her commanders to arrive.

Andrew joined Eve and Louis near the edge of the tent, just under the roof to get out of the rain. Brother Pasquerel stood next to them, his hands clasped as if in prayer. Andrew wondered what was about to happen. Jeanne was visibly upset.

Once she had their attention, Jeanne asked her commanders, "Why are we on the south side of the river? Why are we not on the north side?" She had to speak loudly to defeat the loud tapping of the rain on the tarp. "I see the walls and towers of Orléans over there, but we are here. Are we lost?"

Captain de Gaucourt spoke first. "No, good Maiden. We are not lost."

"No? Then what is this deception? Why have you tricked me?" she asked.

"It is no trick," La Hire offered, taking off his wet helmet and cradling it under his arm. "The English forces are stronger on the north side of the river. We are not ready to battle them. We came around the south and to the east—"

"Not ready to battle them? Why are we not ready to battle them?" Jeanne shouted angrily, cutting him off.

"We have only five hundred men," La Hire reminded her.

Jeanne looked at him in disbelief. "What of the three thousand I saw at Blois?"

"They remain in Blois," said the Duke of Alençon. "The Dauphin did not want his entire force to join us yet."

"Why are we here, if not to take Orléans?" Jeanne asked, her voice strained.

"We are delivering the provisions," said Marshal Sainte-Sévère. "That is our first act. Then comes the battle."

Andrew thought Jeanne might cry with rage.

Sainte-Sévère added in slow, measured words, "Dear Maiden, please remember that the provisions are to be transported from Crécy."

"Remind me, where is Crécy?"

"A few miles farther east along the river," said Gilles de Rais. "It places us safely out of the reach of Lord Talbot and his English army."

"We have not come this far to be out of their reach!" Jeanne glared at the commanders. "You have known all along that you would come this way. You did this even though God Himself made it clear to me that we must march on the other side and attack the English. You have deceived me."

Andrew watched the faces of the commanders. At that moment, he realized they did not really believe Jeanne was in charge of this battle. What could a peasant girl know about war—God or no God?

La Hire was undaunted. "To fight now would be folly. Let us first engage the English as they have engaged Orléans—by siege."

"We came to defeat them in battle, not to wait until they grow old and die," Jeanne snapped.

"*Pucelle*," Marshal Sainte-Sévère said, "we understand your disappointment. But delivering the provisions from Crécy is vital to our success."

There was a blast of wet wind. The top of the tent strained at the poles, threatening to blow away.

Andrew heard the decisive sounds of a horse racing to the tent. Then a muddied page pushed open the tent flap and entered. With a bow, he announced that Jean de Dunois, the defender of Orléans, was even now at the river's edge with some of the city's officials. He had just landed in a small boat from Orléans and would soon join them.

"Was he part of your plan?" Jeanne asked.

"The plan was mostly his idea," said the Duke of Alençon. "He is the son of the Duke of Orléans, the defender of the city."

"He will send boats and barges from Orléans to Crécy to bring back the provisions," Marshal Saint-Sévère explained.

Jeanne fumed while they waited.

Jean de Dunois soon arrived. He was tall and broad shouldered and wore a simple cloak with a cap adorning his narrow, clean-shaven face. Even drenched with rain, he looked noble and dignified.

He smiled at Jeanne as he took off his dripping cap and bent low to greet her. "Sweet Maiden," he said, "I rejoice that you are here."

"You are the defender of Orléans?" she asked.

"I am." He looked up at her, rain sliding down his face.

"Was it by your order that I was brought to *this* side of the river rather than the side that would allow us to fight Lord Talbot's army?"

Dunois stood and looked kindly at the girl. "Our council deemed it the wisest decision."

"Would you not agree that our Lord is wiser than the wisest of your council?" she challenged him. "The King of Heaven has sent me to help you, and He is greater than any captain or army you hope to trust." Jeanne gave her commanders a sharp look. "You would all do well to heed me. Not for my sake, but for the sake of God Himself, who was moved to pity by the appeals of Saint Louis and Saint Charlemagne for your city."

Dunois made the Sign of the Cross and said, "I admit my mistake, kind Maiden."

Jeanne was clearly surprised by his admission. "Let us begin afresh. Tell me the plan so I may consider it properly," she said.

Dunois looked at the other commanders. When none of them spoke, he said, "Your provisions will be transported to Crécy, where our barges will meet them and then bring them back downriver to Orléans. It will be safer than the road, since the English have strongholds between us."

"How far is Crécy?" she asked.

"Five miles."

"The barges have departed?"

Dunois pursed his lips and looked slightly embarrassed. "The barges have not departed for Crécy yet." He gestured to the sky. "The wind is against us."

"Is it?" Jeanne asked. The tapping of the rain had all but stopped. She marched past her commanders out into the open air. Facing the river, she said, "The wind will change soon."

Dunois came to her side. He shook his head. "Dear Maiden, it has only just begun to blow from the east and will do so for several days."

"It will change," Jeanne said again. "God's mission will not be thwarted by the wind."

The commanders gathered around them. Andrew and Eve followed Brother Pasquerel to the edge of the crowd.

"We will meet your boats in Crécy today," Jeanne declared.

"But the wind—," said Dunois.

"It will change." Jeanne looked at him with eyes of fire.

Suddenly, it was as if the sky slowly exhaled its last breath. There was a strange stillness to the air. Then the wind gently resumed, touching their damp skin.

"The wind is coming from the west," Brother Pasquerel whispered to Andrew and Eve.

Jeanne raised her hand, feeling the breeze. "Sail your boats and barges to Crécy. We will meet you there," she said to Dunois.

Andrew watched the faces of the commanders. Some seemed astonished; others looked fearful. He imagined they were wondering, *Does Jeanne have the power to change the direction of the wind?* He wondered the same thing.

With a look of delight, Dunois gave another low bow and said, "Sail with us, Maiden. Then return with me and the provisions to Orléans."

"How will you prevent the English from setting upon us all when we return from Crécy? They could easily come around from the northwest side of your city," Jeanne asked Dunois, though the question went to her captains as well.

"A company of my men will feign an attack to distract them," Dunois replied.

Jeanne gave him an approving nod.

Dunois drew closer to Jeanne. "Come, dear lady, sail with us to Crécy. Bring a few of your captains. Then I would have us enter Orléans together, so the besieged citizens can see you. It will renew their hope."

"I must not leave my army," Jeanne said.

"Why not?" Dunois asked, nodding to the group of commanders. "Are they not enough to lead your men?"

"The soldiers are in a state of grace, ready for battle," she said. "I fear for their waywardness if I am not with them."

"Brother Pasquerel will represent you," Captain de Gaucourt said. "We will command the men to remain worthy of your banner and their duty to God."

Jeanne looked uneasy. A reassuring smile from Brother Pasquerel caused her to relax.

"As you wish," she said.

She summoned her brothers, her squire, and Andrew and Eve to come with her. Bertrand de Poulengy and Jean de Metz followed along. Louis carried her banner.

Once they gathered on the boat, Dunois commanded the sailors to make all good speed for Crécy.

Jeanne watched as they moved farther away from Orléans. She sighed. "I am delayed yet again."

Dunois arranged for Jeanne and her companions to stay the night in Crécy at the home of his fellow soldier and friend Guy de Cailly.

In spite of her frustration, Jeanne allowed herself to be freed from her armor, eat a proper meal, and even have a bath.

Eve told Andrew later that Jeanne still fretted about being away from the army. "She was like a worried mother who left her kids with a babysitter," Eve said.

Jeanne retreated to her room alone to pray.

Later, La Hire arrived at the house.

Jeanne rushed to the dining room, where La Hire sat at the dining table picking at a plate of pheasant. Eve followed Jeanne and quietly joined Andrew, who was standing by the wall. She rolled her eyes at him, as if she knew what was to come.

La Hire half stood to greet Jeanne, then sat down again.

"Why have you come? Why are you not with our soldiers?" she asked him.

"They have departed for Blois," he said, pushing small bones around the plate with his stubby fingers.

"Blois!" Jeanne cried, the blood rushing to her cheeks.

La Hire reached for a chalice, saw that it was empty, then put it down again. "Now that we know the strength of the English and their positions around Orléans, we decided it is time to bring the remainder of our forces to the city."

"*We* decided?" she said.

La Hire grunted. "We have kept enough soldiers to ensure that you and the provisions reach Orléans for your grand entrance."

Jeanne sat down in a large chair across from the commander. She clenched her hands tightly on the table. "Another plan without my consultation."

La Hire stayed focused on his plate of pheasant.

A servant entered carrying a jug. She poured wine into the empty chalice in front of La Hire. He quickly drained it.

Andrew saw Dunois slip through a doorway at the other end of the room and linger there, watching the scene play out.

Jeanne said, "You sent our troops all the way back to Blois, for no other purpose than to retrieve the soldiers who should have come with us to begin with?"

La Hire nodded.

"How will they cross the river when they arrive here?" she asked. "The defender of Orléans has said that his barges will be of no use for so many men."

"They will not cross here," La Hire said simply. "There is a bridge at Blois. They will cross there."

Jeanne spoke slowly, like a small child trying to work out a math problem. "So. The army will cross the river at Blois. They will then come to Orléans on the *north* side."

"Yes."

"That was my original plan," she reminded him.

La Hire eyed his plate. "So it was," he admitted. He lifted his gaze and smiled at her.

Jeanne cried out and dropped her face into her hands.

Dunois now stepped forward. "Dear Maiden, we wage a war that is as much of the mind as of might. To come from the north, we would have had to drive through the English army to reach Orléans. To come around from the south, as you have done, allows us to deliver you and the provisions to the people of Orléans, building their spirits. Let the English become aware of you. Let them wonder all the more about your mission. Let them believe their forces have us outnumbered. Let them see our forces march away, so they will think we have retreated. Let them feel confusion about our plans. Then let them see with great terror, the three thousand men returning, ready to fight for the French witch."

"*Witch!*" Jeanne said, lifting her head.

"It is what they believe you are," Dunois said. "Our spies tell us the English fear you. They are perplexed that our armies will follow you into battle. They think you have bewitched us."

Jeanne pounded her fist on the table. "I have appealed to them in the name of the saints! How can they think such a thing?"

La Hire laughed. "They are arrogant fools."

Jeanne rose from the table, her eyes darting from La Hire to Dunois. "Was it too bothersome for you to consult with me about your plan? Or have you just made this up, using your honey tongue to calm me?"

"We made a mistake," Dunois said. "I ask your forgiveness."

Jeanne glared at him. "Then here is *my* plan. I will not ride a barge back to Orléans. We will take the road."

Dunois shook his head. "Sweet Maiden, there are English strongholds along the way."

"So?" she asked like a dare, then walked out. Eve gave Andrew a wary look and then followed her.

Andrew stayed where he was and watched the two men.

La Hire chuckled. "She is unpredictable," he said.

Dunois leaned on the table. "Do you believe?"

"Believe what?" La Hire asked.

"That the Maiden has been sent to us by God?"

La Hire chewed on a small bone. "God has sent her to us, I am sure. But He also sent us to her to use our wits and skill to accomplish her mission."

Dunois remained calm. "We must give her our loyalty and faith, or we will *fail* as we failed before. Have you forgotten?"

La Hire looked away. "I have not forgotten," he said.

Jeanne spent the next morning watching the provisions being loaded onto barges. She urged the soldiers to work speedily. "The people of Orléans need us," she said.

At midday, fifty soldiers arrived from a garrison in another part of France. They had heard about Jeanne and had marched for two days from Gâtinais to fight with her. They carried unusual weapons made of long poles with spikes and iron tops bent like hooks. The handles on the sides were used to swing the poles like scythes in a field, except these scythes would cut down the enemy rather than wheat.

Jeanne welcomed the men and prayed for them.

Once the provisions were ready, Dunois signaled for the barges to depart. Jeanne wore her white armor and was given a white horse to ride, since her black steed had remained with the troops returning to Blois.

"You ride the steed of the great heralds and archangels," Dunois said.

The procession was small but impressive. Jeanne was again at its head, along with Jean de Dunois. Behind them was Jeanne's squire Jean d'Aulon, then her brothers Pierre and Jean, Louis, La Hire, Bertrand de Poulengy, and Jean de Metz, along with only a handful of soldiers and the men from Gâtinais. Andrew and Eve shared an old horse that Guy de Cailly had provided.

Night came as they marched, and torches were lit.

They passed the Bastille Saint-Loup, which contained a church and a convent. The English had turned the convent into an outpost.

All eyes in the procession were on the doors, windows, and tower of the bastille. Would the English soldiers launch an attack?

The answer proved to be no. Instead, dim lamps flickered inside the stronghold. Shadows moved. A face appeared quickly over the top of the tower, then disappeared again.

"It was shrewd to travel at night," La Hire said with a chuckle. "The English are too scared to fight the French demon."

Jeanne gave him a knowing smile.

The procession marched through the Burgundian Gate on the east side of Orléans. The crowds pressed in a fevered frenzy around Jeanne and her company. The faces of the townspeople were like flickering masks of shadow and yellow in the torchlight.

It was the same as every other city Jeanne entered: hands reaching out, the occasional rush forward to kiss her feet, screams for her attention, and tearful shouts of praise to God. Church bells rang, and from the distance came the muffled sounds of cannon fire.

Jeanne held high the Sword of Saint Catherine. The pole of her banner had been tied onto her saddle, so the banner waved freely at her side. She kept a look of resolve on her face, though Andrew was sure he'd seen a smile creep onto her lips from time to time.

As they approached the cathedral, a corner of the banner fell onto a lifted torch and caught fire. The crowd screamed and reared back. Jeanne calmly reached over and smothered the flame with her gloved hand. The applause for that small act was wild and enthusiastic, as if she'd performed a miracle.

Dunois ordered the soldiers to clear a path into the cathedral. There they could give thanks to God. The leading lords, nobles, and captains of Orléans met Jeanne on the steps, bowing and kissing her hand in welcome.

She strode down the long aisle to the altar, then knelt to perform the Sign of the Cross. She bowed her head in silent prayer. The others crowded inside and did the same.

Occasionally, Andrew heard the sounds of a battle raging outside the city as French forces distracted the English.

From the cathedral, the company marched to the Renard Gate, which faced the English forces to the west. The mansion of Jacques Boucher, the treasurer to the Duke of Orléans, was nearby. It was one of the largest and most beautiful mansions in the city, with enough rooms for Jeanne and her party.

Jacques Boucher bid his guests enter. According to tradition, Jeanne was given a room to share with her hostess, Madame Boucher, and her daughter, Charlotte. Eve would also stay with them. Andrew, on the other hand, was given a room nearby with Jean d'Aulon and Louis.

As they settled in, Andrew heard a servant say to Jeanne, "It is as if the siege has already ended."

"Only in our hearts," said Jeanne. "The real battle is now to come."

The hardest work for Jeanne was having patience.

Dunois had told her that the barges would reach Orléans quickly. The river was swollen from all of the rain, he explained, and would move them speedily. The English troops in Saint-Loup could not attack from the riverbank, since the banks were tree lined. And if the trees did not hide the barges, the night would.

Dunois was right. The barges arrived in the middle of the night. They were guided to the riverbank at the southeastern corner of the city, then moored in the moat closest to the Burgundian Gate.

The city became festive as the supplies were brought inside by the soldiers. The hard-pressed townspeople were delighted to see all of the livestock and the many crates of dried goods.

Many began to call it "the Maiden's bounty" and rushed to the mansion to thank Jeanne for saving them.

Jeanne spent most of the next day with Dunois at his residence. Andrew noticed that while she was there, the commanders met privately at Boucher's hotel.

What are they planning without her now? Andrew wondered.

He helped Jean d'Aulon clean Jeanne's armor. They sharpened her sword, then polished her horse's saddle. Andrew sensed that something was stirring in the city. Crowds began to surround the mansion.

"What is wrong with them?" he asked.

"The people of Orléans are restless," d'Aulon said. "Like Jeanne, they do not want to wait for days and weeks to drive out the English. They want to attack now."

Later, Jeanne returned to the Boucher mansion with Dunois. La Hire cornered them both and suggested they allow the people to release their pent-up anger.

"How?" asked Dunois.

"Let them attack the small stronghold of Saint-Pouair. It is a mere eight hundred yards from the city," La Hire replied.

Jeanne looked unsure. "We cannot attack the English until they have been given the chance to leave peacefully."

La Hire howled with laughter. "The English will not leave peacefully!"

"What of my letter to Lord Talbot?" Jeanne asked. "I sent Guyenne to deliver it. Did he not arrive? Did the English not receive it?"

"Ah, about that," Dunois said, clasping his hands together. He cleared his throat. "Dear Maiden, they received your letter and took your herald prisoner."

"What? That is not in keeping with the rules of engagement," she said.

"It is worse," Dunois continued. "They claim they will burn Guyenne at the stake, since he is in league with you, the French witch."

Jeanne cried out, "No! We must save him! Where is Ambleville? He serves as my second herald."

Ambleville was summoned and bowed low to Jeanne. "Yes, my lady."

Jeanne told him, "You must go to the English with a message. Tell their great commander, Lord Talbot, that he must free Guyenne to me immediately. Then he must take his army back to England."

Ambleville's eyes grew wide. He swallowed hard and said, with a loud gulp, "My lady?"

"Write down my words," she said.

With trembling hands, the herald recorded a new letter from Jeanne that restated what she had said in her first letter.

"Take the letter to Lord Talbot. And do not come back without Guyenne," she said.

With a fear-filled look, Ambleville bowed, then departed.

"It will not be as easy as that," Dunois said to Jeanne.

"We shall see."

It was a few hours before Ambleville returned. He was a sickly white. His clothes were dirty and torn. "They threatened to take me prisoner as well," he said and held out a response from the English.

Dunois grabbed the letter from Ambleville's hands before Jeanne could see it. After reading it to himself, he held it behind his back.

"There is no cause for you to read it, good Maiden," he said. "They have responded to your letter with contempt and abuse."

"What of my herald?" Jeanne asked.

"They will not release him, nor will they leave."

La Hire rubbed his hands together. "Now allow me to lead that skirmish at Saint-Pouair."

Jeanne grew more distressed and shook her head. "It is not enough. Where is the closest point to the English?"

"The Bridge Gate," La Hire said. He looked confused about what she was asking.

"I will speak to them myself," Jeanne said, then marched off.

Dunois and La Hire tried to stop her, but Jeanne would not listen. She went to the Bridge Gate and stepped out in full view of the English troops that held Tourelles at the far end. She didn't stop there but continued walking along the ruined bridge, navigating around deep cracks and holes from the earlier battle.

D'Aulon, Andrew, Louis, and Eve stayed on her heels.

On the bridge, they reached a rampart called *La Belle-Croix*. D'Aulon caught Jeanne's arm and said, "Good Maiden, go no farther. They can hear you from here."

Ahead, Andrew could see the English soldiers gathering in the windows of Tourelles.

Jeanne climbed the rampart and shouted in a voice louder than Andrew thought she was capable of: "Tell me! Who is there?"

A low voice shouted back, "I am Captain William Glasdale. Is that the witch of France?"

Jeanne ignored the insult. "Surrender in God's name, and I will grant you your lives!"

A barrage of blistering insults came from the captain, with his soldiers joining in.

Andrew blushed at their words. Eve put her hands over her ears.

Finally the captain said, "If ever I get my hands on you, I will burn you alive, witch that you are!"

Jeanne looked shaken, stepping back as if he had struck her. In a voice that once again reminded Andrew that she was only a teenage girl, Jeanne shouted "Liars!"

She climbed from the rampart and stormed back to the city gate. Her company followed her, walking backward. They were afraid that the English might rain arrows down on them.

La Hire looked amused when they returned. "Is that enough for you?" he asked Jeanne.

"Do what you must," she said, fuming.

As the afternoon waned, La Hire led a small company of citizens and soldiers from Orléans to dislodge the English from the fortress of Saint-Pouair just north of the city.

The company looked more like a mob of rioters than a coordinated army. They carried clubs and shovels and threw rocks at the wooden stronghold. The English inside seemed bewildered by this sudden random attack.

Soon the band of fighters was close enough to the fortress to set it on fire. Kindling was laid at the base of the wall. La Hire called for a lit torch.

Suddenly the English army gave a ferocious cry, "In the name of Saint George!"

The French reared back, stricken with fear. Invoking the name of Saint George had been the practice of the English before their greatest victories against the French. The small band from Orléans raced back to the safety of the city.

Once inside the gate, La Hire merely shrugged and said, "I hope they got that out of their systems."

The next day was Sunday. Combat was forbidden.

After the morning Mass, Dunois joined Jeanne at the Boucher mansion. He expressed his dismay that no word had come from Blois about the whereabouts of the troops. "Let us hope the Dauphin is not holding them back."

"Surely he would not restrain us," Jeanne said. "Not now."

"I will see for myself."

"I will go with you," Jeanne said.

Dunois shook his head. "Dear Maiden, you must stay here to command."

Jeanne laughed. "When have I ever been in command? What is to prevent you from taking the army into battle yourself, before I have been told of their arrival?"

He gave her his most charming smile. "In good faith, then, allow your squire to accompany me. Let him be your eyes and ears."

Jeanne nodded. "Go, then."

Within an hour, Dunois and d'Aulon left Orléans with a company of soldiers as an escort. La Hire rode with them until they were safely beyond the reach of the English.

When La Hire returned to Jeanne an hour later, he looked puzzled. "We have given the English many opportunities to attack, but they do not. Is it stupidity? Fear? Or do they have a plan?"

"Let us pray they are fearful of God, if not of us," said Jeanne.

Andrew began to feel besieged. The people of Orléans often surrounded the mansion, calling for Jeanne to come out. Mothers wanted her blessing on their children. Young girls wanted to hear words of inspiration. Men of all ages wanted to view this saint-in-the-making.

"They will break down the doors," Jacques Boucher complained.

"Saddle my horse," Jeanne said to Louis. "If they want to see me, then let them."

"They may tear you apart," warned Boucher.

"I will be safe enough," Jeanne said.

Mounted on her horse, she emerged from the stable and rounded the front of the mansion. The crowd saw her and cried out. Andrew expected them to mob her. Instead, they suddenly fell silent. A few of them dropped to their knees.

"Come, my friends." Jeanne spoke calmly as she slowly rode away from the mansion.

The people followed with puzzled expressions on their faces.

"What is she doing?" Andrew asked Eve as they walked along.

"I have no idea," Eve said.

"Will you lead us into battle now?" a man called out.

"A battle of a different kind," Jeanne said to him.

She led them to the cathedral. Remaining on her horse, she said, "I would ask you to enter this holy place and pray for me. For our battle is not only one of flesh and blood but of spirit. Seek out a priest and confess your sins. To some, I would ask that you go to the places of the poor and give them comfort. Find the sick and infirm and pray for healing."

From there, Jeanne rode throughout the town, listening to the people and giving them words of encouragement and consolation. They emerged from their houses and shops to cheer her on, to touch her, and to receive her blessing.

Jeanne returned to the mansion, satisfied that the people would calm down. She retreated to the chapel Boucher had set up for her. Only a little time had passed when she emerged again with a fierce look of determination on her face.

"I want to speak with the English again," she announced as she strode to the front door.

"I will find La Hire," Louis said.

Jeanne spun to him. "No!"

Louis stepped back, his arms raised in surrender.

"La Hire has his secret plans, and I have mine," Jeanne said.

Andrew and Eve tagged along as Jeanne left the mansion and walked the short distance to the Renard Gate. The gate faced the English on the western side of the city. The guards stationed there were confused by her sudden arrival.

She demanded that they open the gate. Flustered, one captain insisted that they needed permission first from his commander. She argued that she was equal to any commander.

A crowd gathered as Jeanne demanded that she be allowed to pass through. One of the guards ran off to find someone in charge. The other guard gave the order to open the gates.

The growing crowd looked on as Jeanne thanked him, then walked through the gate. Peasants followed from the city, along with a few soldiers. They marched west along the main road. Andrew looked to the left and right as they passed the burnt shells of houses. He worried that English soldiers might be hiding there.

Jeanne marched decisively. She kept her eyes fixed ahead. They came close to one of the English forts. It was little more than a tall pile of rough-hewn logs. A wide trench had been dug around it to serve as a moat.

Andrew saw men with torches moving on the parapets. He imagined archers lining up to release a volley of arrows at them.

"My lady, do you want to die here?" an uneasy soldier asked.

"No one will die tonight," Jeanne replied firmly.

A door opened at the front of the fort. An advance guard of English soldiers marched out to the edge of the moat. "What is your business?" an armored man called out. He had a round face and bushy beard.

"I have come with a message for your commander," said Jeanne.

"I am the Duke of Granville, the commander here," he said. "Speak the message from where you stand."

"I beg you to retreat before the hosts of the Lord! Surrender, and your lives shall be spared," she shouted. "In God's name, go back to England. If you will not, I will make you suffer for it."

The duke laughed. The soldiers on the parapet joined him.

"Would you have us surrender to a woman?" asked the duke.

"You surrender to God Himself," Jeanne replied.

More derisive laughter came from the English soldiers, then rude insults telling the country girl to go home and tend to her cows. The French soldiers in the crowd moved forward, pulling at their swords.

Jeanne sternly waved them back.

"Since you have come as a messenger, we will not kill you," shouted Granville. Then he taunted the French soldiers. "Your witch may protect you tonight, but she will do you little good when we burn her."

"It is enough," Jeanne said. Then she signaled for everyone to return to the city.

When they had reached safety and closed the gate behind them, one of the soldiers asked Jeanne, "My lady, why did you go to them?"

She said sadly, "In God's name, I would have them willingly submit to peace before they are forced to submit to death."

That night, Eve and Andrew found themselves alone with Jeanne after prayers in the private chapel.

Eve asked, "Jeanne, how did you know the English would not kill you?"

Jeanne looked solemnly at Eve. "My angel, these things I know for certain from the Voices who guide me: I will break the siege of Orléans. I will be wounded in the battle, but not fatally. I will lead the Dauphin to Reims for his coronation."

"You will be wounded in battle?" Andrew asked. "You know that?"

"I have seen it as in a dream," Jeanne said. "I do not want you to be alarmed when it happens. Though I may cry from the pain, I will recover."

"Have the Voices told you anything else about your future?" Eve asked.

"They have not, nor have I asked them," Jeanne said. "The weight of the future is too much for any of us. Perhaps that is why God mercifully keeps it hidden from our eyes."

Jeanne bid them good night and went off to her room.

Eve remained with Andrew in the chapel. Her eyes were awash with tears. "The longer I'm with her, the more it breaks my heart to know what will happen to her."

Andrew sighed. "I wish I knew what will happen to *us*."

Another day of tense waiting came and went. No word had come about the expected troops from Blois.

Jeanne paced in her room, refusing to eat. Then she prowled around the mansion praying for a messenger to come from the Dauphin. When nothing happened by late afternoon, she announced to Louis that she wanted her horse saddled again. "I will not wait idly by."

"Where will you ride to?" Eve asked.

"I want to see the strength of the enemy."

Once again Jeanne went to the Renard Gate. Once again Andrew and Eve followed her as she trotted through its archway. A small crowd of townspeople followed the Maiden as well. No one seemed to care that they were moving within range of the English archers.

"God will preserve Jeanne, and He will preserve us," a woman said.

Jeanne stopped in the fields surrounding Orléans, gazing at the English fortresses and camps as if she was making mental notes of their positions.

The English watched her every move. Andrew could hardly imagine what they were thinking. Jeanne moved this way and that, with the small crowd tagging along.

It looks like she's giving a guided tour, he thought.

La Hire rushed out of the Renard Gate with a handful of soldiers. He positioned them along the walls of Orléans, weapons ready.

Then Jeanne suddenly turned and announced, "It is time for vespers. Let us go to the cathedral."

Just as the crowd had followed her out of the city, they now followed her back, collecting more of the townspeople along the way.

That evening the cathedral was overflowing.

Eve and Andrew stepped out of the cathedral after the Mass. Eve squeezed Andrew's arm.

Andrew looked at her. "What's wrong?"

She was staring openmouthed at the cathedral square.

Andrew followed her gaze. People were milling around as usual. Then he saw what had stopped Eve. Simon Le Fantôme stood in the middle of the crowd, with people flowing around him like water around a large rock. Simon's eyes were on Andrew and Eve. Then, as if satisfied that they had seen him, he turned and walked away.

Andrew watched as the old man strolled to the edge of the square. He glanced back at them again, then continued over to the doorway of a closed shop. He turned to face them, his expression like a dare.

"He wants us to follow him," Andrew said.

"So he can attack us again?" Eve shook her head. "Not a chance."

"Then *I'll* go," Andrew said. He made his way across the square, hoping it wasn't a mistake.

A half-lit torch hung on a nearby iron ring. It splashed yellow and red on Simon's shaggy face. Andrew tried to recognize from his expression if the old man was in his right mind.

"The girl does not want to speak with me?" Simon asked.

"Why would she? You attacked us the last time we saw you."

"Did I?" Simon gave Andrew a pained look. "I had hoped that was a dream."

"It was not a dream," Andrew said. "What do you want?"

"Sir."

"What do you want, *sir*?"

"Tell me, what will you do when the battle starts?" he asked. "Will you fight, or will you hide?"

"I will be wherever Jeanne tells me to be," Andrew said.

Simon looked around. "The English are preparing. Reinforcements and provisions are coming from the north to strengthen them. It will be a fierce fight on both sides." He stooped slightly to gaze at Andrew's face. "Have you ever been in battle?"

"Not like this one," Andrew replied.

He flinched as Simon put a heavy hand on his shoulder. "Remember, boy. Once you have seen a battle, you will never close your eyes without seeing it again."

Why is he giving me fatherly advice? Andrew wondered.

Simon added, "The English have summoned an assassin. I believe he is going to slay the Maiden."

Andrew was surprised. "How do you know that?"

"I see and hear what others do not." His hand went to the hilt of his sword. "Beware of strangers."

"I am surrounded by strangers," Andrew pointed out.

"You will know the assassin when you see him. He has a patch over his right eye."

"A patch," Andrew repeated. Didn't all of the villains he'd seen in movies look like that? "Why does he have a patch on his eye?"

"Because that is where I stabbed him," said Simon.

Andrew flinched. "You did?"

"He is known as Vincent the Ravager. Beware. Even to say his name is to invite death." With that cryptic warning, Simon nudged past Andrew and strode into the square.

Head and shoulders above everyone else, Simon was easy for Andrew to watch until the old man disappeared down a side street.

———————➤

Eve didn't wait for Andrew at the cathedral. He found her later at the Boucher mansion.

"You want me to tell Jeanne that a crazy man thinks she's being hunted by an assassin?" Eve asked after Andrew told her what Simon had said.

"It could be true," he said. "Tell her, just in case. I'll tell La Hire."

"But if we say the name, we'll be killed," Eve teased.

Andrew rolled his eyes. "I know it sounds overdramatic, but we have to be careful."

Eve glanced around to make sure no one was listening. "She won't die from an assassin," she whispered.

"But someone else might," Andrew said.

"Did Simon tell you why he stabbed the man in the eye?" she asked.

"I didn't have time to ask," Andrew replied. He frowned. "I have a nagging feeling about him, but I can't explain why."

"I have a nagging feeling too," she said. "It's called *fear*."

———————————————▶

The next morning, the head of worship at the Orléans cathedral organized a procession for the annual Feast of the Finding of the Holy Cross. Jeanne joined the procession, along with the city officials.

Andrew found himself searching the faces in the crowd for anyone with an eye patch.

Later that day, soldiers arrived from garrisons in Gien, Château-Renard, and Montargis to join the coming battle. Jeanne gratefully received them. But Andrew knew she was worried that the main army from Blois still hadn't come.

As the new soldiers marched through the Burgundian Gate, Andrew got La Hire's attention and repeated what Simon had told him.

La Hire looked grave. "If Simon has said so, then we would do well to believe him." The captain gave an occasional salute to the incoming troops. "Does he know who the assassin is?"

"It is someone called Vincent the Ravager."

La Hire jerked his head around quickly and muttered a few words that would have upset Jeanne. "The Ravager! I will alert our guards." He snorted. "The English must be desperate to summon that madman."

"Simon told me he stabbed the Ravager in the eye," Andrew added.

La Hire nodded. "A fight over a treasure, or some such thing. Simon lost his wife. Vincent lost his eye. That is as much as I know."

Later that evening, Andrew sensed an undercurrent of excitement in the city. Louis, who always knew what was being said, reported that rumors were spreading about the army from Blois. They were on their way and should arrive in the morning.

Shortly after dawn, the sentries in the watchtowers sent word that the lances and banners of the reinforcements could be seen. More word came from the watchtowers facing south that a caravan of provisions was making its way around to Crécy. Like the earlier supplies, they would be transported down the river on barges.

Jeanne and La Hire mounted their horses. They summoned as many soldiers as they could to ride out and meet their approaching army. Andrew and Eve went to the top of the wall to watch. Andrew noticed that the English did the same from their various bastions.

"Why will the English not attack them?" Eve asked.

Louis, who stood nearby, said, "It is rumored that the English are too frightened to attack Jeanne."

Ahead of the troops, Brother Pasquerel led a group of priests under a banner of the cross. The words of a psalm they were singing rose to the tops of the castle walls. Moments later, their singing was drowned out by the loud ringing of the cathedral bells.

Orléans was overcome with joy—and soon over-whelmed with soldiers. The new arrivals needed places to stay and food to eat. Already filled to capacity, the city looked as if it might burst at the seams. No one seemed to mind. The townspeople celebrated as if it was a holiday.

Jeanne looked pleased to see Jean d'Aulon again and brought him back to the Boucher mansion for a meal.

They talked privately, and by the time the plates were cleared away, Jeanne seemed annoyed. Andrew wondered if d'Aulon had raised her suspicions yet again that she was being left out of her commanders' decision-making.

All was made clearer when Dunois strode in with his usual swagger and bowed to Jeanne. She greeted him but seemed aloof to his charms.

"The provisions are coming on barges from Crécy, like before," he said. "However, we have received news that the notorious English captain John Fastolf is bringing reinforcements and provisions to the English as well."

"I want to know when he arrives," Jeanne said.

Dunois was hesitant. "My lady, is it so important for you to—"

"In God's name, I *command* you to tell me when he has arrived," she said angrily. "If you do not, I swear I will have your head."

Andrew was shocked.

Dunois's expression remained calm. "I assure you, I will let you know." He bowed, then walked out.

Jeanne slumped into a chair. Her face was flushed. "I am undone," she groaned.

D'Aulon admitted that he was exhausted from the journey.

"Then rest while you may," Jeanne advised.

"*Merci*," he said.

"You should rest as well," Eve suggested. Jeanne agreed, and they went up the stairs.

Andrew and Louis followed d'Aulon to his room and helped him out of his armor. At once, he dropped onto a couch and fell fast asleep. Louis sat on the floor, propping himself up in a corner. He closed his eyes. Andrew looked at them both, shrugged, then leaned back in a chair.

I'll close my eyes for just a minute, he thought.

Andrew was suddenly awakened by a commotion. Jeanne was in the room with them, shouting, "Where is my armor?"

Andrew leapt out of the chair. *How long have I been sleeping?* he wondered.

Jeanne was leaning over d'Aulon, shaking him roughly. "In God's name, my council has told me to go against the English, but are we fighting against their fortress or against Fastolf?"

"Dear Maiden," d'Aulon said, sitting up and rubbing his eyes. "Have you been dreaming?"

"My Voices have told me that a battle has begun! French blood is being spilled even now!" Jeanne cried out. "My armor! I must have it now!"

Two other servants appeared from the hallway and scrambled to Jeanne's room to help her into her armor. Eve looked at Andrew, mystified, then followed them.

D'Aulon was suited up again, looking bewildered as Andrew and Louis strapped his armor into place.

A short time later, the uproar moved downstairs as Jeanne now commanded for her horse to be saddled.

"Why did you not tell me that our blood is being spilled?" she asked Louis.

Louis stammered, "I did not know that it is." He dashed away.

Brother Pasquerel arrived in the midst of the chaos. "What goes on?" he asked.

"Cruel man! Why did you not tell me the blood of our people is soaking the ground?" she cried.

Brother Pasquerel looked as puzzled as everyone else. "What blood?"

"Where is my banner?" Jeanne shouted.

Brother Pasquerel put up his hands. "Jeanne, stop for a moment. Tell us what—"

Shouts in the street interrupted him.

Going to the doors, he threw them open. A crowd had gathered around a man lying on the steps. Blood covered the side of his head and had stained his tunic. Brother Pasquerel knelt next to him. Jeanne stood in the doorway, looking pale and shaken.

"There is a battle at Saint-Loup," the man said in a pained voice. "The English are killing us."

Louis rounded the corner with Jeanne's saddled horse. She raced along the steps and leapt upon its back, grabbing her banner from Louis's hands. She spurred the horse away. The crowds parted for her, and Andrew was sure he saw sparks flying from the horse's hooves on the stone street.

Jean d'Aulon, Louis, and Andrew hurried to find horses so they could follow her.

"What about me?" Eve called to Andrew.

"Help Brother Pasquerel!" Andrew shouted.

D'Aulon rode on alone. Louis found another horse that he shared with Andrew. They raced to the Burgundian Gate but were slowed by a solemn parade of wounded men being helped back inside the city.

Andrew saw Jeanne ahead. She, too, had been delayed. She turned on her saddle, looking at the injured soldiers. "Are they French?" she called out.

"Yes," came the reply.

"It makes my hair stand on end," she said, then spurred her horse forward.

Louis and Andrew galloped east on the main road to Saint-Loup, trailing d'Aulon and Jeanne. Andrew remembered passing the bastion there when they first came from Crécy. The English had been using it as an outpost.

Louis slowed their horse as they reached the rear guard of the French troops. The ground was covered with the wounded and the dead. Jeanne guided her horse among them. D'Aulon paused by the road.

"The English are slaughtering us!" someone cried to Jeanne.

"What is happening?" Jeanne asked.

"Our soldiers are preparing to retreat to Orléans," a man replied.

"No!" Jeanne shouted at the troops, her banner waving in the wind. "Boldly! Attack the English boldly!" She spun her horse around and bounded forward to the battle.

The soldiers who were still standing watched her go. They looked at one another and then raced after her with a warlike shout.

Andrew was astonished as the French soldiers rolled like a wave back into the field of battle.

Captain Raoul de Gaucourt was in the thick of the fight. At the sight of Jeanne and the return of so many of his men, he roared and raised his sword high. The soldiers around him did the same and threw themselves at the English with renewed strength.

With ferocious blows, the French forced the English soldiers back. Soon they were pressed against the fortress walls and had to withdraw inside. It was not enough protection. The French forces battered their way in.

"Preserve the church!" Jeanne shouted. "Take nothing for yourselves!"

Within an hour, the battle was won. Forced to surrender, the English lost their fortress and all their supplies inside.

The victorious French returned to a jubilant Orléans. The church bells rang. As one voice, the townspeople shouted praises to their heroes. It had been a very long time since they'd seen such courage, or the glory of such a triumph.

Jeanne did not celebrate. She walked among the French wounded, offering them words of comfort. She found Brother Pasquerel praying over the dead bodies of the English.

Kneeling and weeping, Jeanne said, "So many of the English men were killed without the benefit of confession. I beg you, dear brother, to remind our soldiers to confess their sins."

"They are drunk from their victory," Brother Pasquerel said. "They are not thinking about confession."

Jeanne stood up. "If they refuse, I will leave them to battle without me."

Brother Pasquerel bowed to her. "I will tell them so."

"Now, please hear *my* confession," she asked softly. "Then let us present this day to God in a Mass."

That night, Jeanne summoned the commanders to the mansion for a meeting. She demanded to know how the battle at Saint-Loup had started.

Dunois explained, "It was another diversion. We wanted to take the attention of the English away from the barges on the river."

"Why did you not tell me?" Jeanne asked.

Before Dunois could reply, La Hire burst into the room. He was in his full armor and dropped into a chair. He shouted for a drink.

"Where have you been?" asked Dunois.

"While you were seeking glory elsewhere, I was routing the English forces on the north side of the city," he said. "They had every intention of saving their fortress at Saint-Loup, but we stopped them. They turned back when they saw the smoke from the fire."

Jeanne asked, "What of the wounded and the dead?"

Dunois said, "Of the fifteen hundred French who went to battle, only one hundred have been wounded or killed."

"And the English?" she asked.

Captain de Gaucourt cleared his throat. "Most of the English were killed."

A shadow crossed Jeanne's face.

"It is the nature of war, dear Maiden," La Hire reminded her.

"This victory was greater than we could have hoped for," Dunois rushed to add. "We have not only reclaimed the abbey, but the English have abandoned their stronghold at Saint Jean-le-Blanc across the river to the southeast. And we have cut off their supply lines to the east. That side of the Loire River is ours."

"And yet you still could not be bothered to tell me of your plans," Jeanne said, her gaze falling on all of the commanders.

"Dear Maiden—" Dunois began to say.

Jeanne held up her hand. "It is better that you do not speak."

Dunois bowed, then took a few steps back.

"Tomorrow is the Feast of the Ascension of Our Lord," Jeanne said. "I will honor it by not wearing my armor. There will be no attack on the English. See to it that your soldiers make a good confession and stay pure. Otherwise, God may allow us to suffer defeat because of our sins."

"As you command," Dunois said.

Jeanne bid them good night, then left the room.

Some of the commanders raged against the girl.

"How dare she rebuke us for doing what we have come to do!" a sour-looking captain named Guillaume de Gamache said. "I despise her insolence against more experienced men! She is nothing more than a saucy child of low birth!"

La Hire called them to silence. "There are few things more wounding to old soldiers than to be embarrassed. You feel humiliated that you must yield to a mere girl."

The commanders agreed.

"Yet we are not dealing with a mere girl," he continued. "Will any of you deny that the battle for Saint-Loup was lost until she arrived? Will you argue the inspiration she is to our soldiers and the people of this city? Will you dispute that she confounds the English? Will you contest that her raw knowledge of military strategy is nothing less than remarkable?"

Somewhere in the muttering, the answer was a reluctant acceptance of what La Hire was suggesting to them.

"Then stop complaining! You dishonor yourselves," La Hire said. He caught Andrew's eye and winked at him.

Gilles de Rais stood. "We must seize the momentum of today's victory. We must meet tomorrow to discuss the battle against the English. How are we to do that when she has commanded us to take the day off?"

Dunois stood up. "She has not commanded that we all attend Mass," he reminded them. "Let us meet while she is there. *Then* we will submit to her our counsels for how and where to attack the English. I am sure she will approve."

They agreed.

Andrew was surprised that grown-ups could be so foolish.

As the meeting ended, La Hire caught Andrew by the arm. "You are not spying on us, are you?"

"No," Andrew said quickly.

"That is good," La Hire said. "If I thought you were, I would be forced to ban you from our meetings. Do you understand?"

Andrew swallowed hard. "Yes, sir."

Andrew decided not to tell Eve about the commanders' intentions. He knew she would have to tell Jeanne. Instead, he decided to watch everything play out, especially since Dunois was going to report to Jeanne anyway.

The next morning, Eve went with Jeanne to the Feast of Ascension Day Mass. Andrew followed La Hire to the town hall, where the commanders had planned to meet. As the defender of Orléans, Dunois led the meeting. The chancellor, Guillaume Cousinot, was there to represent the city officials.

Andrew overheard the chancellor say that his wife had invited Jeanne to lunch. It was not a coincidence. The chancellor's home adjoined the town hall. The idea was to make sure that Jeanne didn't accidentally find her captains having a meeting without her.

When the commanders finished their meeting, they sent Chancellor Cousinot and Dunois to inform Jeanne of what they had decided.

Andrew followed the two men to the chancellor's home.

Jeanne greeted them in the sitting room as if their arrival was a pleasant surprise. The two men sat down. The chancellor nodded to his wife, who stood up, curtsied, and left the room. Andrew found a chair next to Eve and sat down.

As soon as the men were comfortable, Jeanne asked, "Well? What news do you bring from your meeting?"

"Meeting, good Maiden?" Cousinot asked. "What meeting?"

"The meeting you had next door," Jeanne said, leveling her gaze at him.

He squirmed. "Well, yes, it is true. We met."

"To discuss the battle," Jeanne continued. Her gaze went to Dunois. "Without my presence."

"It seemed best to debate our plans and then present you with our suggestion," Dunois said, his tone dripping with charm.

"What is your suggestion?" Jeanne asked.

Cousinot signaled a servant to bring in a large parchment. He spread it out on a side table. Andrew saw that it was a map of the area around Orléans.

Cousinot explained how they planned to lure the English into a battle on the west side of the city—at the English fortress of Saint Laurent. "This will draw their troops from two of the fortresses on the south side of the river. If the English meet us at Saint Laurent to fight, it will leave Tourelles and the bridge without reinforcements. We shall then reclaim them."

Jeanne nodded. "Where will I be positioned?"

"You will join the troops and citizens at Saint Laurent," Cousinot said.

"I see." Jeanne stood up. She paced the room.

The two men watched her anxiously.

She stopped in front of them. "Now tell me what you have *really* decided to do. I assure you, I have kept far greater secrets than whatever you have schemed."

The chancellor's lips moved, but he didn't say anything.

Dunois stood quickly and said, "Dear Maiden, do not be angry with us."

"Why should I not be?" Jeanne countered, pointing at the map. "You would have me join a *ruse* battle at Saint Laurent when you know the *true* battle will be at Tourelles."

Dunois was undaunted. "We cannot fight at Tourelles if the English forces there have not been drawn away. Attacking Saint Laurent is the only way to do that."

"This is not a trick to keep me away from the real battle?" asked Jeanne.

"We would save you from battle if we could," Dunois said. "But we know you will not allow it."

"It is the best plan," added Cousinot.

"So it is," Jeanne agreed. "But I must give the English one more chance to leave."

———————————————➤

Andrew and Eve listened as Jeanne dictated another letter to the English. She reminded them that they had no right to be in France. She warned them that the King of Heaven was now commanding them, through her, to depart. She said that if they failed to leave, she would make a war cry against them that they would never forget. She signed the letter *Jhesus Maria, Jeanne la Pucelle.*

Then, just as the newest herald prepared to leave, she added a postscript: "I would have sent you my letter in a more honorable manner, but you have imprisoned my herald Guyenne and detained and mistreated my other herald. Please send Guyenne back to me, and I will return the English soldiers we captured at Saint-Loup."

The herald looked concerned. "My lady, I beg you not to send me on this errand."

Jeanne gazed at him for a moment. Then she said, "We will try another means."

She wrapped the letter around an arrow, tied it with a thread, and had an archer with a crossbow shoot it into an English camp outside Orléans.

She watched from the city wall as the arrow fell to the ground. The English sent a soldier to grab it up. When he returned to his company, the soldiers began to shout abusive words and foul names at Jeanne.

Andrew watched to see what Jeanne would do. The Maiden endured the abuse as long as she could, then burst into tears and retreated from the wall. She went to her room, where she later said that God had given her comfort. She also summoned Brother Pasquerel to stay near so that he could hear her confession first thing in the morning.

"It is done," Jeanne said to her two angels at the end of the evening. "At long last, I will fulfill God's mission to drive the English from Orléans."

The city was awake at daybreak. Mass was sung for Jeanne, her company, and all of the men about to fight.

"Jeanne won't let me go with her," Eve said to Andrew after Mass.

"Did you want to go?" he asked.

Eve gave him a shy smile. "No. But I thought I should offer."

"La Hire has told me to stay in the city too," Andrew told her. "He said to watch from the southwest corner of the wall. I'll be able to see what is happening on the west side at Saint Laurent and then move around to watch the south side at Tourelles. Come there with me."

They were about to set off when they happened upon Louis. He was struggling to strap the sides of his armor in place.

"I am off to a bad start," he said while Eve fastened the straps for him.

"What is wrong?" Andrew asked.

"Captain de Gaucourt has locked the Burgundian Gate and placed guards there to keep the townspeople from joining the battle."

"Why would he stop them?" asked Eve.

"To keep them from getting in the way of his army. The people are ready to riot. Jeanne has gone to calm things down." He groaned. "I would not want to be Captain de Gaucourt right now. Jeanne believes the people should be allowed to fight for their city."

"Done," Eve said, inspecting Louis's armor.

Andrew gave him a once-over. "Your armor looks a lot like Jeanne's," he said.

Louis smiled. "Good."

Eve suddenly kissed him on the cheek. "Be careful."

Louis blushed. "*Merci.*" He hurried away.

Andrew rolled his eyes at Eve.

"What?" she asked.

"Nothing," he said. "Let's go!"

Andrew and Eve struggled to stay out of the way as the guards raced to their battle positions on the city wall.

Looking out at the fields bathed in the morning sunlight, Andrew wondered if he was in the wrong place. Maybe he should be on the field with everyone else.

"Which is which?" Eve asked, pointing to the various enemy strongholds around Orléans.

Andrew pointed to the west. "That little fortress is called Saint Laurent. That's the one Jeanne is supposed to attack from the Renard Gate."

He moved his finger, following the land to an island in the middle of the river. There sat another English-made fortress. "That one's called Charlemagne."

Then he pointed across the river back to the land and yet another fortress. "That one is called the Champ de Saint-Privé."

"We have to conquer all of those?" Eve asked.

"That's just the beginning," Andrew said. He led her around to the south wall. "Keep down," he said, "just in case the English in Tourelles shoot their arrows at us."

Eve crouched, her eyes just above the top of the wall.

Andrew pointed to the damaged bridge leading from the south gate of the city. The castle-like fortress with multiple towers sat at the other end. "That's Tourelles," Andrew said.

"I've seen it before, remember?" Eve said.

"But do you know what's beyond it?" Andrew asked. "That's where it gets tricky."

Andrew explained that to get to the main fortress of Tourelles from the south, the French first had to take back a monastery called *Saint Augustin*. The English had captured it when the siege started. He pointed to the monastery, with its church-like spire on top.

"That doesn't sound so bad," said Eve.

"That's only the beginning," Andrew corrected her. "Then our army has to get past an obstacle course of defenses."

"Like what?" Eve asked.

"Well, first, the soldiers have to get over a wall made of tree trunks."

"Nice."

"Then they have to cross a trench to a sort of ledge called a *boulevard.*"

"Okay."

"Then there's a wide dry moat to get across."

"Uh-huh."

"Then they'll reach a forty-foot-high stone wall that leads to a small stronghold called a *bastion.*"

"And that's Tourelles?" asked Eve.

"No, the stronghold is across a drawbridge from Tourelles," Andrew replied. "Once they take the stronghold, they'll have to fight to get to Tourelles."

"The whole thing sounds like a video game I once played," Eve said.

"I wish it was as easy as a video game," Andrew said. "The whole time our army is trying to get into Tourelles, the English troops will be shooting arrows or cannonballs at our soldiers or dropping hot tar on their heads."

Eve shook her head. "Do we really believe Jeanne and the army can do all that?"

"They hope to do that much today," said Andrew. "Then the English might surrender Tourelles."

"What if they refuse?" Eve asked.

"Then it will be a hard battle tomorrow."

They moved back along the wall to a vantage point on the west side of the city. A trumpet sounded, and they watched as Jeanne, on horseback, led a company of soldiers and townspeople out of the Renard Gate. They crossed to the fortress of Saint Laurent.

"It looks like Jeanne won the argument about allowing the townspeople to fight," Andrew said.

"Something is wrong. Jeanne has forgotten her banner," Eve said, pointing.

Andrew looked. "That's strange."

As the French moved forward, the English in Saint Laurent gave a rousing cry and rushed out against them. Armor of gold, silver, and gray caught the morning light in bright flashes and dull flickers. The two sides looked evenly matched as they slammed together with a loud clashing of swords and shields. Andrew thought it sounded like cars crashing on an icy highway. A choking dust rose up and over them.

The battle for Orléans had officially begun.

Andrew lost track of time. Jeanne was waving her sword, but her company of soldiers held a solid circle around her to keep the English at a distance. For a while, the English forces prevailed, driving the French toward the Renard Gate. Then, for reasons Andrew could not figure out, the French got the upper hand and pushed the English back toward the stronghold of Saint Laurent.

All the while, Andrew remembered the plan. He gazed toward the Charlemagne fortress on the island, then checked the two fortresses on the south side of the river.

He watched to see if the English troops would come out to help their comrades at Saint Laurent. The soldiers were positioned on the walls, but the gates remained closed.

"They aren't taking the bait," Andrew said.

One of the guards on the wall behind him announced that Captain de Gaucourt had finally given the command to open the Burgundian Gate. The captain now led armored soldiers and plainly dressed citizens east around to the river. He had organized them onto anchored boats and barges that would ferry them across to the southern side of the Loire.

"Jeanne won that argument, too," Eve said, smiling.

"Come on," Andrew said, then moved east along the wall. But Eve didn't follow him.

"What's wrong?" he called back.

She pointed behind her. "I'm worried about Jeanne."

Andrew nodded, knowing he should do the same. But Jeanne was part of a ruse to distract the English from the main battle. The outcome of the day would happen in the south and southeast.

Andrew continued on, slipping through a line of archers who were preparing for their part in the battle. His eyes landed on the fortress called *Saint Jean-le-Blanc* that the English had abandoned. This didn't stop some of the townspeople from attacking it anyway. Axes and clubs in hand, they assaulted the main gate and cheered their victory when it opened easily.

Most of the army had now assembled on the south side of Orléans. There, they began their march to the Augustin monastery. The townspeople surged ahead of the troops, emboldened by their vain victory at Saint Jean-le-Blanc.

For several minutes, it looked as if the English had abandoned Augustin as well, but suddenly a terrifying roar came from inside the monastery. Then archers appeared along the top of the walls and unleashed swarms of arrows on the townspeople below.

Andrew raised his hands to his mouth in horror as the screams tore the air, and one man after another fell to the dirt. Panic overtook many of the townspeople. They turned and crashed into the seasoned soldiers, who were trying to move forward. Captain de Gaucourt shouted orders, but the cries of the wounded turned his words into whispers.

Volleys of arrows continued to rain down on the French. It was a blood-filled and chaotic scene.

Then came mind-numbing explosions. Cannons previously unseen now appeared at various portals. The stone balls smashed into the fleeing civilians and mowed down the soldiers.

Andrew pressed himself closer to the wall, terror-stricken by the slaughter. "Where are *our* cannons?" he cried out.

"The order has not been given," said a soldier next to him.

"Look at what's happening down there!" Andrew pointed at the battlefield. "That should be the order!"

The soldier raised a gloved fist to strike him, but held back. He turned away instead.

A fresh roar sounded amid a blast of trumpets. Andrew pressed against the edge of the wall to see the English troops now pouring through the gates of Augustin. They began to chase the scattered French forces. Clashing swords rang loudly, blades crashed against armor, clubs with spikes hammered against shields. The crude weapons of the heroic townspeople were no match for the real weapons wielded by the English soldiers. Men dropped to their knees; others fell lifeless underfoot. Arrows flew from all directions, and the pounding cannons sent stone balls mercilessly into the French warriors. Andrew felt sick at the unfolding slaughter.

He wasn't sure he could watch any more.

But then he caught sight of Jean d'Aulon. The squire had moved to the front of the retreating French line. He reached the fortress of Saint Jean-le-Blanc, along with a fighter Andrew didn't recognize. D'Aulon beckoned the scattered French soldiers to use the abandoned fortress as a base for the battle. French archers quickly took up positions and sent arrows flying back to the English. The English foot soldiers spun around to attack d'Aulon and his valiant company.

"The plan failed," Eve said at Andrew's side. Her cheeks were smeared with tears. "The English have captured Jeanne!"

"What? No!" Andrew shouted. "Where? How?"

"It was awful. The English surrounded her horse and pulled her to the ground," Eve cried.

"But that's wrong," Andrew said. "She can't be captured. Not today."

"I saw it," Eve said, her voice shaken by sobs. "The English broke through the circle of soldiers, yanked her from the horse, and dragged her back to their fortress at Saint Laurent."

Andrew stumbled along the castle wall to see for himself. She couldn't have been captured!

He looked to the southwest. The English troops on the island stronghold of Charlemagne were boating to land and circling around the western side of the city. The soldiers from the Saint-Privé fortress were dashing out to do the same.

"They are going to brag about their catch," Andrew said. *How could the battle go so wrong so fast?* he wondered. *Jeanne was supposed to win this battle!*

Horns blew to the southeast.

"What now?" Andrew asked. He moved along the wall and suddenly realized that Eve had taken hold of his hand. He held it tight as they returned to view the main battlefield. Together they peered over the wall.

Eve gasped.

It isn't possible, thought Andrew.

Galloping on their horses toward the English were La Hire and *Jeanne*—her banner flying high.

"How can she be *here* when I saw her captured *there*?" Eve asked, clearly baffled.

Andrew had an idea. "Louis dressed in armor that looked a lot like Jeanne's," he said.

"He was a decoy?" Eve asked. "They captured poor Louis?"

"He sacrificed himself for *that*," Andrew said, gesturing to the hundreds of soldiers who now joined Jeanne and La Hire in the battle below. They moved like a tidal wave behind the banners of Jeanne's commanders. French warriors seemed to be coming from everywhere.

The retreating French soldiers turned on their heels and rushed back into the battle. Even the wounded struggled to their feet and grabbed what weapons they could to fight.

The English troops stopped in their tracks. They nearly tripped over each other as they scrambled back toward the Augustin fortress.

"Fire!" Andrew heard from behind him. Before he knew what was happening, the cannons of Orléans erupted with deafening roars. He and Eve put their hands over their ears.

The cannonballs smashed the retreating English and cut off their escape to the fortress. The smell of gunpowder filled the air around Andrew and Eve.

Andrew now understood. The French had fooled the English on two fronts, scattering them to the west and the south. Not only were the English fooled, but the French retreat had lured them out of their fortresses so that Jeanne and her army could strike at them on the open field with superior numbers.

The surprise, as great as it was, did not make the fighting any less brutal. Andrew heard the din of pain and death. It was a grotesque clamor, dark and terrible.

Jeanne never drew her sword but sped on her horse from one part of the battlefield to another, urging the French to fight. The combat was slow going. It seemed as if this campaign was being won an inch at a time. The English shrunk in numbers as they fell. Some were able to retreat into the Augustin fortress.

Andrew feared this might be yet another turning point in the fight. Behind those walls, the English could regroup and begin a fresh attack. But the doors of the fortress were not strong enough to stop the oncoming French forces. They crashed through them as if the thick beams were made of mere sticks of wood.

It was impossible for Andrew to see what was happening inside the fortress. He caught glimpses of soldiers moving behind the windows and holes in the walls, through the open passages, and between the buildings of the monastery compound. Now and then, he saw English soldiers trying to escape through other doors and gates.

The English still held their fortresses at Saint-Privé and Saint Laurent to the west. It now looked as if they were not coming out to aid their comrades at Augustin.

Andrew and Eve were pushed aside as a company of French archers came to the wall. They let fly their arrows toward Tourelles, attempting to distract the English soldiers there from the main battle.

Andrew could no longer guess which way the fight was going. It seemed to surge in one direction, then another. There was a strange ebb and flow to it, like water splashing back and forth in a rocking tub.

"Look," Eve said, pointing to the middle of the field.

Simon Le Fantôme was in the thick of battle, his sword swinging and slashing at everyone around him.

"Do not stand there idle!" one of the archers shouted at Andrew. "Distribute arrows to the line of archers!" Then he turned to Eve. "*You!* Fetch drink and bread for these men."

"Yes, sir!" both children said, then went to work.

The evening darkness crept over Andrew and Eve almost before they knew it was there.

Andrew noticed that a fire had broken out inside the Augustin fortress.

"Are they going to burn it down?" Eve asked.

"No," said one of the archers. "We are purging it."

Jeanne appeared at one of the pinnacles of the fortress and waved her banner at the English in Tourelles.

And so the first day of battle ended with a French victory. But Andrew knew that the harder fight was about to begin. No ruses or combat tricks would breach the obstacle course that protected Tourelles. He also knew the English would not yield it. Tomorrow would require raw nerve, brute strength, and the faith of a child.

The soldiers and citizens of Orléans took positions between the captured fortress of Augustin and Saint-Marceau, a town to the south. They guarded what they had painfully gained from the English. Priests and nurses set up camps to tend to the wounded and offer prayers for the dead.

The rest of the French fighting forces wearily made their way back to the city for a much-needed rest.

Eve ran ahead of Andrew to greet Jeanne. When he caught up, he saw Jeanne limping through the gate and leading her horse by the reins. They learned that she had been wounded in the foot by some kind of foreign weapon made of sharp spikes. She looked pale and admitted she was overcome with fatigue. La Hire came alongside her, lifted her in his strong arms, and carried her all the way back to the Boucher mansion.

Jeanne was placed in a chair in the dining room, where Madame Boucher nursed her foot. Soup and bread were offered, but Jeanne only sampled it, claiming she wasn't hungry.

Eve admitted to Andrew that she felt anxious about Louis. He had been captured, but she had no idea what the English would do to him.

Andrew put the question to La Hire.

The old soldier shook his head. "They will be angry that they were deceived. Pray they do not abuse him all the more for it. The lad had a lot of courage to do what he did."

Dunois arrived, his gallant face smeared with dirt and blood. He knelt next to Jeanne's chair and said, "You are indeed a valiant warrior. Never have I seen such a display of bravery."

Jeanne gave him a weak nod. "Will you see to it that food, drink, and all things necessary are delivered to those who stayed behind in Saint-Marceau?"

"I have ordered the barges and wagons to operate throughout the night," Dunois assured her.

A moment of silence passed. Then Jeanne eyed Dunois. "Is there something else?"

"The commanders have met," he said.

"Again? Without me?" she asked.

"Some of them believe our victory today has given us the advantage," he explained. "The town of Saint-Marceau is well supplied. They suggest we do not go into battle tomorrow."

"Why would we not press our advantage?" she asked.

"To allow the Dauphin to send us more of his army before we fight again."

"Is that your suggestion?" Jeanne asked him.

He gave her a grim smile. "I suggest nothing. I am merely the council's messenger."

"They have their council, and I have mine," Jeanne said. "Mine will make good on His promise, whereas yours will come to nothing. Tomorrow we will rise even earlier than we did today. On the field of battle, we will do the best we can, by God's grace. There is much that remains to be done, and more to suffer."

Dunois nodded to her bandaged foot. "Is that not enough?"

"This is little more than a scratch," she said. "My blood will spill from a greater wound before this is finished."

"Surely not," said Dunois.

Jeanne gave him a grave look. "Bring me a map of Tourelles. Summon my captains. We must plan our attack."

Looking at the map, Andrew saw that the battle to capture Tourelles would be harder than he had described to Eve earlier. In fact, he thought it looked impossible.

The first obstacle was a wall made of tree trunks that stood over ten feet high. It was called a *palisade*. Jeanne's army would have to get past that to an initial drawbridge, which the English would raise. That would leave the French to deal with the first trench. It was at least ten feet wide and twenty feet deep. Worse, the sides of the trench were filled with soft earth so that any invaders would be unable to scale it.

At the top of the trench was the *boulevard*. It was twenty feet wide and circled around Tourelles like a horseshoe. But between the boulevard and Tourelles was a dry moat about twenty feet deep and more than thirty feet wide. The steep angle of the moat's walls made climbing difficult, even with ladders.

Then came the forty-foot-high stone wall of the outer stronghold, with a vast courtyard behind it. From there, the English could drop hot tar and oil onto the invaders.

On the other side of the courtyard was a moat filled with water from the Loire River. It was more than twenty feet wide and required a drawbridge to cross into Tourelles.

As Andrew had told Eve earlier, while the French army was attempting to get past all of these defenses, the English would be hitting them with arrows, spears, axes, and other kinds of sharp weapons.

Andrew looked from the map to Eve. She saw the same thing he'd seen and mouthed the word *How?*

"Can your Voices allow our soldiers to grow wings and fly over that?" La Hire asked.

"Perhaps they will, once we break down the palisade," said Jeanne.

"Our cannons will destroy the palisade," said Dunois hopefully.

"Then we will use the debris to fill the trench and cross over to the boulevard," Jeanne said. "Once we're there, we will use scaling ladders to climb the dry moat, all the way to the top of the first wall."

"The English will strike the first French head that appears at the top, or they will use poles to push the ladders away," said La Hire.

"Our archers on the walls of the captured fortresses will keep them too busy to succeed," Jeanne suggested.

"And then?" asked Gilles de Rais.

"We invade the stronghold, cross the courtyard, and fight to take Tourelles itself," she said. "That is the goal of our battle, is it not?"

The commanders nodded unhappily.

Jeanne gazed at each of their faces. "Sleep, men of stout hearts. Then rise to victory."

Andrew felt sluggish and thickheaded when the call to awaken came. It was still dark. The sun knew better than to get up so early.

He trudged down to the private chapel to join Jeanne and Eve for Mass with Brother Pasquerel. Eve looked as if she hadn't slept at all.

After Mass, they dressed for the battle ahead. Jeanne refused to eat any breakfast. As far as Andrew could tell, she hadn't eaten much at all since arriving in Orléans. Later, as they departed the Boucher mansion, a peasant woman brought Jeanne a fish and begged her to eat before she went into battle.

Jeanne smiled at her. "If God wills it, I will share this with an English prisoner when I return tonight. Bring it to me when I cross the bridge from Tourelles."

Captain La Hire gave Andrew new orders. "Put on a breastplate and come with us to the fortress of Augustin. You will hand out weapons, restock the ammunition, deliver water, and if necessary, bandage the wounded."

Andrew saluted and said, "Aye, aye, Captain."

Eve grabbed his arm. "If you are going, then I am going."

Andrew shook his head. "No."

"Why not?"

"Because you are—"

"A girl?" Eve was defiant. "So is Jeanne. I am going."

"But you said back at Chinon that you were afraid," Andrew reminded her.

"I am still afraid. But I am going anyway," Eve said.

They had to find breastplates and backplates that would fit the two of them. They struggled with each other's straps and buckles. Andrew felt as if someone had hung two heavy doors around his neck.

Eve tugged at one of the buckles. "How do they fight in these things?"

"I will be worn out before I even get to the fortress," Andrew complained.

The troops and townspeople marched to the Burgundian Gate with Jeanne in the lead. She waved her banner for them to follow. Once again, Captain de Gaucourt refused to open the gate.

"Why are you here?" he shouted at them. "Did you not learn your lesson yesterday? And you soldiers, go back. My orders were that there would be no fighting today."

Andrew wondered if the captains were conspiring against Jeanne. Were they trying to stop her from fighting a battle they didn't want to have?

Jeanne was furious. "You are siding with the devil against your own people."

De Gaucourt looked as if she'd slapped him. "Dear Maiden, I am here to serve."

"Then serve us now," she said. "I am commanding you to open the gate."

De Gaucort looked helpless. "Where is Captain La Hire? The defender of Orléans, Jean de Dunois? Allow me to send a messenger for clarification."

"While you do, we lose our advantage against the enemy," she said.

The townspeople roared against Captain de Gaucourt and his guards. They began to push and shove their way to the gate. The soldiers stepped aside, many of them looking defiantly at the captain. Andrew feared that a riot might break out.

Captain de Gaucourt considered the situation. "Open the gate!" he shouted.

By the time Jeanne and her initial company marched to the river to cross over, the other captains arrived with their various banners and troops.

Slowly the French forces made it to the south side of the river and joined the other companies still holding the land and fortresses they had captured the day before. Though everyone looked tired, they had been replenished by the food and provisions that were delivered throughout the night. Fresh arrows, hammers, axes, lead and powder for the cannons, and ladders had arrived. All eyes were on Tourelles.

Andrew heard a soldier say confidently that the battle should not take very long, since the French outnumbered the English inside the stronghold.

Captain La Hire said sharply, "Do not be a fool! The English commanders are shrewd. They know we cannot overwhelm Tourelles by our numbers. We must attack in smaller groups, making their numbers even greater than ours."

The soldier mumbled an apology, then skulked off.

La Hire shot a look at Andrew. "And what, pray tell, will the English to the west of us be doing? Will they renew their attack? Will they circle around to the Renard Gate and attempt to take the city while we are fighting for Tourelles?"

Andrew hadn't thought of that.

"May God grant us another trick," said La Hire. "If Louis has served us as we hope, the English may not know what to do."

"Louis?" Eve asked, perking up. "How is he serving you if he has been captured?"

La Hire gave her a roguish smile. "The English will question Louis about our plans. He is to tell them that we have soldiers hiding behind the Renard Gate. They will suspect that if they send reinforcements to the south of the city to fight for Tourelles, our hidden forces will rush out of the Renard Gate and attack their fortresses on the west."

Andrew understood. "Oh, but now they will think twice about attacking the Renard Gate to invade the city on that side because they do not know how many soldiers are hidden there."

"Do we have soldiers at that gate?" Eve asked.

"Not very many," La Hire replied. "But the English do not know that."

"So you *wanted* them to capture Louis?" Eve asked.

La Hire nodded. "His bravery is greater than anyone realizes."

Andrew and Eve looked at one another, impressed.

La Hire put on his helmet and turned his gaze toward Tourelles. "The fortunes of war are a mix of plans, accidents, and the hand of God. Pray today that the hand of God determines our victory."

The horns blared for the Battle of Tourelles to begin.

Andrew did not have time to watch the battle. He raced from one point to another in the Augustin fortress and on the battlefield, carrying weapons or water. Eve was sent to help Brother Pasquerel with the wounded. Reports came to him in bits and pieces about how the battle was going.

He heard that Jeanne's plan was going as they had hoped. Though the English bombarded the French army with arrows and cannonballs from inside Tourelles, the French destroyed the palisade. That allowed them to deal with the next obstacle: the trench. Using the logs from the palisade, they began to build a makeshift bridge.

It was slow going, but by late morning, they reached the boulevard and captured the few English who tried to defend it.

This brought them to the next obstacle: the dry moat. Long ladders were used to climb into the moat, and then they were moved to the other side for the soldiers to climb. The English attacked from the high wall of the stronghold with rocks, hot oil and tar, and even stones they pried loose from the walls of the fortress. The French covered themselves with shields as they struggled to scale the wall. Many were wounded or slain. The few soldiers who made it to the top of the ladders were beaten back with axes and clubs. Some fell to their deaths.

The French soldiers began to despair. The victory that some thought would be so easy to achieve now seemed like a vain hope.

At noon, the captains withdrew their forces to the shelter of the Augustin fortress to regroup. Andrew slipped into the room to hear what they had to say.

"It is as we feared," Gilles de Rais complained. "We should have waited until the Dauphin sent us more men. Waging battle today was a mistake."

"No!" Jeanne argued. "Keep heart! The fortress will be ours!"

To the surprise of the commanders, Jeanne handed her banner to a page standing nearby—a boy named Mugot. Then she dashed from the room. She raced out of the fortress and made her way to the front line of the battle. Mugot stumbled behind her but held the banner high.

Andrew watched, astonished, as Jeanne reached a handful of men carrying one of the scaling ladders. She shouted to them, "All who are with me, come now!"

Together, Jeanne and the soldiers carried the ladder to the dry moat. The French commanders were dumbfounded. La Hire and Dunois stepped forward, unsure of what to do. Captain de Gamache—the man who had called Jeanne a "saucy child of low birth"—was the only one to take action. He leapt on his horse and rode after her.

The English watched Jeanne from the stronghold wall. They loudly mocked and taunted her. Andrew expected them to attack, but they didn't. They seemed curious to see what this mere girl thought she was going to do.

With her soldiers, Jeanne disappeared from view into the dry moat. Captain de Gamache followed her.

The commanders still delayed, but Andrew joined a few other men in a mad dash to the boulevard. An eerie silence fell all around. It was as if both sides of the battle had stopped to see this wild act of bravery. The ladder was put in place against the wall, and Jeanne approached to make the climb.

Andrew looked up at the English. With growing fear, he saw a single archer lean over the parapet with his longbow.

"Watch out!" Andrew cried out.

But it was too late.

The archer released his arrow, and it flew straight at Jeanne, striking her in the chest. She spun backward, fell off the ladder, and crashed to the ground.

Captain de Gamache and the nearby soldiers surrounded her. They used their shields to protect her from anything else the English might send their way.

The English cheered. Some shouted praise that the witch was wounded. "Spilled blood will take her power away," they exclaimed.

French archers positioned themselves to provide cover while Jeanne was brought up from the dry moat. De Gamache and his soldiers carried her to the Augustin fortress. Andrew stayed with them. He couldn't tell if she was dead or alive.

Silence rolled like a wave through the ranks of the French forces. It was as if the entire battle had come to a halt.

Inside the Augustin fortress, they carefully placed Jeanne on the ground. The captains surrounded her.

Andrew saw that the arrow had struck her at an odd angle between her shoulder and right breast. Jeanne suddenly gasped and then began to weep from the pain. She reached with her left hand and grabbed the arrow. With a spine-tingling scream, she pulled the arrow out and threw it aside.

Captain de Gamache commanded that her armor be removed. Andrew pushed in to help, but two soldiers nudged him aside. They clumsily yanked her in one direction, then another as they loosened the various straps. Jeanne cried out.

"Be careful!" Andrew shouted.

One of the soldiers was muttering as he worked. Andrew realized he was speaking the words of some kind of spell.

"What are you doing?" Dunois asked the soldier.

"It will stop the bleeding," the soldier said.

"No," Jeanne said sharply to him. "I would rather die than save myself by sinning against God. Keep your charms to yourself."

Brother Pasquerel broke through the circle around her, with Eve hot on his heels. She looked at Jeanne and went pale. Andrew stepped over to her. She grabbed his arm to steady herself.

Brother Pasquerel knelt down, opened a small pouch, and took out a bottle of oil and a container of something that looked to Andrew like fat. He put both on the wound, then dressed it with a bandage. "This will do until we can get her back to the city," he said.

Jeanne closed her eyes. Her groans mixed with whispered prayers. Then she opened her eyes and proclaimed, "Saint Catherine and Saint Margaret have come, as I knew they would."

She relaxed.

Brother Pasquerel made the Sign of the Cross.

The commanders looked helplessly at one another. They began to move away, speaking in low tones. Andrew assumed the battle was finished.

Suddenly Jeanne sat up. "Help me with my armor," she said.

Brother Pasquerel laid a hand on her arm. "You must rest."

Dunois knelt next to her. "Hear your priest. We must stop now. Sound the retreat," he said.

"No! We have not finished what we came to do," Jeanne said. She used Brother Pasquerel as a brace to help her stand. "Where is my horse?"

Orders were given to the soldiers standing nearby to find Jeanne's horse.

"She can't go back into battle," Eve whispered to Andrew.

"Would you try to stop her?" Andrew asked. He moved into the gap and grabbed Jeanne's breastplate. It was smeared with blood. He struggled to put it in place and fix the straps on the sides.

Mugot, who had been carrying Jeanne's banner, helped with the other pieces of armor.

Captain de Gamache watched Jeanne, then bowed and said, "Maiden, I am sorry for my harsh words about you. Truly you are the bravest of captains."

"I bear no grudge," she said. "You are a brave and noble knight."

Dunois spread his arms in an appeal. "Dear Maiden, I beg you not to go. Rest. Eat. Drink."

"No," she said again. A shout came from outside. The soldiers had retrieved Jeanne's horse.

Andrew and Mugot came alongside Jeanne and helped her outside. With gasps of pain, she climbed onto her horse. Looking down at her bewildered commanders, she said, "Tell your men to take comfort and refresh themselves. We will take the English when I return."

"Return?" asked La Hire.

Jean d'Aulon ran up to Jeanne, carrying her banner. "I found this," he said. He looked at Jeanne sitting on her horse in her blood-stained armor. Then he noticed the befuddled looks on everyone's faces. "What have I missed?" he asked.

Jeanne smiled at him. "Hold on to my banner until I come back," she said. Spurring her horse, she turned and rode south, away from the Augustin fortress, Tourelles, and the battlefield.

"Where are you going?" Dunois called after her.

She did not answer but continued on to some nearby hills.

With a confused expression, d'Aulon looked at the banner and then at Dunois. "What is in those hills?" he asked.

Dunois shrugged. "Nothing but vineyards."

"Perhaps she is going to pray for us," Eve said.

Looking alarmed, Dunois said, "Let us hope so."

The French troops made a few half-hearted attempts to attack Tourelles during the afternoon, but without success. The worry on everyone's minds was if and when Jeanne would return.

As the afternoon waned, an impatient d'Aulon lifted Jeanne's banner and shouted, "Follow this blessed banner to victory!"

With the banner in one hand and his shield in the other, he ran for the stronghold wall. A group of soldiers saw the banner and shouted, following the squire.

Andrew watched from his position near the Augustin fortress. "What is this?" he heard Dunois ask. "Who gave the command to attack?"

The English in Tourelles let loose arrows and crossbow bolts at d'Aulon as he and the men entered the dry moat. Andrew expected the worst. He could not guess how d'Aulon and his brave men could protect themselves from the onslaught. Suddenly, Jeanne's banner came into view as d'Aulon climbed the ladder. He waved it at the French troops, trying to rally them.

The English archers turned their arrows on d'Aulon but could not seem to find the right position to strike him down. The French archers sent a slew of arrows buzzing at the top of the wall, driving the English back.

"They will kill him if we do not help," Andrew shouted. He was about to run for the stronghold when he heard a loud shout from somewhere behind him. He spun around to see Jeanne riding onto the battlefield at a full gallop.

"In God's name, you will enter soon. Do not be afraid!" she shouted. "The English have no more power over you! To my banner! Bring more ladders!"

At the sight of her, the soldiers seemed to come alive. As one man, they threw themselves again at Tourelles.

The faces of the English men on the wall betrayed their shock and fear. They retreated from view as French archers let more arrows fly.

Andrew watched with awe as the French raised a dozen ladders against the wall. Men crawled like spiders up each one, rising higher and higher. The English came forward to drop stones onto the soldiers, but the French arrows drove them back again.

Jeanne rode back and forth along the boulevard, urging the French soldiers onward.

Then came a riotous shout from the city of Orléans. Andrew ran from the Augustin fortress and followed the brow of a hill to get a better view. He saw the city gate to the great bridge open. Soldiers and townspeople flooded out with giant planks of wood. Even with his limited view, Andrew could guess what they were doing: the planks would cover the massive holes in the bridge so they could cross from the city to the north side of Tourelles. The English would now be attacked from two sides.

Jeanne cried out to the English, "Surrender now! Receive mercy!"

A man Andrew remembered as William Glasdale, the English commander, appeared on the wall. He looked down at her.

Jeanne begged him, "Hear me! For the sake of your men and their souls, yield to the King of Heaven!"

Glasdale scowled at her, then disappeared again.

Fewer arrows flew from the English side. The men on the wall had retreated farther into the stronghold. French soldiers breached the wall, climbing over the top.

A French boat came into view on the river. It was pulling a second boat that had been lit on fire. Both boats were sailing toward Tourelles. Andrew angled around the battlefield to see what the French were trying to do.

The men in the first boat allowed the flaming boat to come alongside them. Then using long poles, they pushed the second boat into the moat that flowed between the stronghold and Tourelles itself. Soon, flames from the vessel engulfed the drawbridge that connected the two fortresses.

Andrew was alarmed to see the main gate to Tourelles open. A small group of armored English soldiers ran onto the burning drawbridge. He guessed they were trying to escape. Instead, they crashed through the weakened wood on the bridge. One or two fell into the flaming boat. Others splashed into the moat. The weight of their armor ensured that they would never see the surface again. Andrew felt sick to his stomach.

"The commander has been killed!" came a cry from the stronghold. A captured English soldier stood there, pale-faced. He pointed to the water below. William Glasdale was one of the men who had just fallen to his death.

Upon hearing the news, Jeanne dismounted her horse and knelt down. Andrew learned later that she had prayed for the souls of the dead English.

The black of the night sky was stained red by the flames from the drawbridge. Soon, Tourelles itself was on fire. The remaining English soldiers attempted to fight their way onto the great bridge that led to the city, but the French forces caught them. Many of the English simply laid down their weapons and raised their arms in surrender.

The battle was over.

Later, the fires on the drawbridge and the fort itself were put out. The remaining English soldiers were rounded up. Andrew and Eve followed Jeanne and the weary French soldiers marching slowly through Tourelles and onto the great bridge back to Orléans.

Andrew remembered Jeanne telling a peasant woman that she would enter the city this way. He wondered if

Jeanne would share the peasant woman's fish with an English soldier, as she had said.

Otherwise, everything Jeanne had promised about the siege of Orléans had become reality.

The bells of the city began to ring. Somewhere, beautiful voices sang the "Te Deum."

Andrew and Eve looked at each other as they crossed the threshold of the gate.

"What next?" Eve asked.

Jeanne returned to the Boucher mansion to have her wounds treated properly. She was taken to her room, and the door was closed on the males in the house so Madame Boucher and Eve could undress her.

Eve asked a servant for some bread and wine. Andrew did not expect Jeanne to partake. As far as anyone knew, she had refused to eat for days. So he was surprised when Eve came back out to report that Jeanne had diluted the wine with water and dipped the bread into the mixture. She even asked for more.

A physician with a wrinkled face and a droopy moustache arrived later. As he came through the door, he announced that he would have to cleanse and cauterize the wound using burning rods. He sent servants to prepare the coals.

The physician went into Jeanne's room, then returned to the hall several minutes later with a mystified look on his face. "The wound does not need my services." He made the Sign of the Cross and added, "Someone with greater skill has already begun the healing."

Andrew learned later from Eve that Jeanne had gone into the hillside vineyards to pray. Her reappearance on the battlefield came after she'd been given renewed strength and comfort from her Voices.

That night, the ringing of the bells and celebrations in the city were not enough to keep Jeanne or her entire company from their sleep. Andrew fell onto his cot with a deep sense of joy.

Morning arrived sooner than Andrew expected. At dawn, d'Aulon shook him.

"Up, lad. The English are on the move," he said.

Andrew had forgotten that the army of the Duke of Granville and Captain John Talbot were still encamped on the west side of city. Were they planning to counterattack?

Andrew quickly dressed and rushed out of the room. He bumped into Eve on the stairs. Jeanne was ahead of them, along with her commanders. They all walked straight to the Renard Gate to see what the English were doing.

"We should attack *now*," said Captain La Hire.

The English army appeared to be very busy, but it was hard to discern whether they were preparing to attack or retreat.

"It is Sunday," Jeanne said to La Hire. "Bring an altar. We shall say Mass here."

"What if they attack?" La Hire asked.

"Surely they will not attack while we celebrate the Mass," Jeanne said. "If you are worried, then watch to see if they face us or turn their backs on us while we worship."

An altar was set up, and priests from the cathedral came out to celebrate the Mass. Jeanne would not look at the English troops. She kept her eyes on the chalice and paten, her face filled with a childlike anticipation at the sight of the Body and Blood of Jesus.

Andrew sneaked peeks at the English. They had paused in their work to watch the Mass. Then they turned their backs to Orléans.

"They're retreating," he whispered to Eve.

After the Mass concluded, Captain La Hire said unhappily. "I still think we should attack them now."

Jeanne said, "It is not the Lord's pleasure that we should fight them today. You will have the chance another time."

"By then, they may have the strength to kill us," La Hire grumbled.

Andrew later learned that more than four hundred English soldiers were slain in the battle for Tourelles. The French suffered the loss of over one hundred soldiers and civilians. He also heard that the English had left their sick and injured in the various strongholds they had abandoned. The French found food, ammunition, cannons, and mortars as well.

Guyenne, Jeanne's herald, was set free. So was Louis, who blushed when Eve gave him a long hug. The young page assured Captain La Hire that he had passed along the false information when the English questioned him. Together, they wondered if that was why Captain Talbot and the Duke of Granville did nothing to help their allies at Tourelles.

A formal procession with Jeanne, her commanders, and the city officials filed through Orléans. It stopped at the cathedral, where a service of thanksgiving was held. All there praised God for the end of the siege of Orléans.

All the same, Jeanne's commanders were nervous. Some of them believed the English would seek revenge against other French towns. Many of the men decided to leave Orléans and spread out in different directions to protect their territories.

In the evening, Andrew took time to explore the Boucher mansion. He found a small library with a selection of leather-bound books. He glanced at one after another and marveled that he could read the French and Latin words.

He had curled up in a chair to read an account of a woman called Eleanor of Aquitaine when Louis appeared at the door. "There you are! I have been looking everywhere for you."

Andrew laid the book on a side table. "Is something wrong?"

"Come with me," Louis said softly. "There is someone who needs to speak with you."

"Who?"

"Simon Le Fantôme," Louis replied.

Just hearing the name made Andrew feel anxious. "What does *he* want?"

"He was wounded."

"During the battle?" Andrew asked.

"During the battle but not *in* the battle," said Louis. "You should hurry."

They slipped out of the mansion and made their way through the city. Though Sunday was meant to be a day of rest, celebrations were still being held in some of the homes, public inns, and taverns.

"Simon was found near the vineyard behind Saint Jean-le-Blanc," Louis explained as they walked. "That is where Jeanne rode to after she was wounded."

"What was Simon doing there?" Andrew asked.

"Let him explain."

After turning onto one street and then another, they came to an alley. A single wooden door sat at the far end. Louis knocked. The door opened, then slanted to one side as if it would fall off its hinges. A man with dark, curly hair and equally dark eyes looked at the two boys. He recognized Louis and, with a grunt, bid them enter.

The place was one large shadow that smelled of rotten wood, sweat, and old vegetables. They walked down a short hall to a closet-sized room, where they found Simon Le Fantôme stretched out on a cot. His long legs hung off the end. A single lamp burned on a bedside table. But no amount of light could have put color into Simon's pale face.

As sick as the old man looked, his eyes darted to them as they entered. His hand went to his right side. Andrew suspected he had a knife hidden under the rags that covered him.

Simon nodded to the dark-eyed man, who retreated into the hall. Louis took a few steps to the back of the room and stood in a half shadow with his hand on his sword.

Andrew moved nearer to the cot. "What happened to you?" he said.

"Have you seen him?" Simon asked, his voice a strained rasp.

"Who?"

"The assassin," he said as if it should have been obvious. "The Ravager. Vincent."

Andrew was alarmed. "He is here?"

" 'Twas he who did this," Simon said, then threw the left side of the ragged cover aside.

Andrew saw a blood-soaked bandage draped over Simon's hip.

"He followed the Maiden to the vineyard," the old man continued. "I saw him and stopped him from his evil intent. He escaped with a wound equal to my own." Simon pulled the cover back over his chest. "If there is justice in God's world, he will die slowly and painfully from that wound."

"He went there to kill Jeanne?" asked Andrew, his mouth going dry.

A single nod from Simon, his eyes closing.

"What can I do about it?" Andrew asked as fear laid a cold hand on his heart.

"You are her angel. You must be vigilant," Simon said, his voice fading. "He is looking for ..." The words disappeared.

"What is he looking for?" Andrew asked.

Simon's eyes opened slightly. "Hope Springs."

Andrew felt a jolt as if an electric current had gone through him. "What did you say? He is looking for Hope Springs? Is that what you said?"

Simon's eyes were fully closed. The old man's chest rose and fell with labored breaths.

Andrew turned to Louis. "Did you hear that?"

Louis nodded. "I heard him say 'hope springs.' Does he mean the hope that springs within us?"

The dark-eyed man came to the doorway. "You must leave now."

"Is he going to die?" Andrew asked.

The man snorted. "Him? I do not believe anything can kill him. But this will add another scar to his collection."

Andrew and Louis ventured back to the Boucher mansion. Andrew walked silently, confounded by what Simon had said. Had Andrew ever said those two words to him? Was it a coincidence?

As he walked, he realized that he was looking at every face in the crowd, wondering if the Ravager would suddenly appear. He gripped the hilt of his sword so tightly that it hurt his fingers to let go when he finally reached the safety of the mansion.

"Perhaps Eve will know why he said 'hope springs,'" Louis said.

"Do not tell her," Andrew said.

"Why not?"

"There is no reason for both of us to worry," Andrew replied.

Jeanne could not sit still. She announced Sunday night that she would leave first thing in the morning to speak with the Dauphin. "We have kept faith and freed Orléans. Now we must see the Dauphin properly crowned in Reims."

Dunois begged her to wait. "You must rest."

As he sat against the wall in the meeting room, Andrew felt drained. Eve looked at him. She looked exhausted. Waiting and resting sounded like the perfect plan.

"How am I to rest when the mission is not yet completed?" Jeanne asked. "We have already lost too much time."

Andrew and Eve shared a glance. Wherever Jeanne went, they went.

"I will accompany you to the Dauphin," Dunois promised. "Once we find out where he is."

It was rumored that the Dauphin was in Chinon. They knew that much because he had written letters from there to announce the wonderful news about Orléans. Then they heard he had moved to Blois, and then Tours.

"Will someone *please* find him!" Jeanne begged, clearly exasperated. "I do not understand why he has not sent for me already."

"The Dauphin is surrounded by people who do not like Jeanne," Eve said to Andrew later. "La Trémoille is one. The Archbishop of Reims is another. You watch. They will do anything to stall her."

———————————————▶

Knowing they were going *somewhere*, Jeanne's company packed the next morning. When the city officials heard that she was going to depart, they came to the mansion to express their thanks for all she had done. They offered her gifts as a reward.

"I am here for God and whatever reward He may give me later," she said. "I cannot accept your gifts."

A messenger arrived in the early afternoon and reported that the Dauphin was at his castle in the small town of Loches. He agreed to receive Jeanne if she wanted to come.

Andrew noticed that the Dauphin still had not actually summoned her.

Jeanne hardly took time to say goodbye to her many friends. Andrew learned that Bertrand de Poulengy and Jean de Metz were returning to Vaucouleurs to take on other duties. Louis had been ordered back to Chinon to serve Guillaume Bellier once again. Jeanne's brother Jean had said he would return home to Domrémy, though Pierre was resolved to continue on with Jeanne.

The squire Jean d'Aulon remained as part of Jeanne's company, along with Brother Pasquerel. Dunois, of course, had his own business to attend to.

As Jeanne and her company departed, the people of Orléans crowded the streets. They wept with joy and shouted their praise to her. She waved and thanked them until the travelers were well beyond the Burgundy Gate and out of earshot.

From a distance, Loches looked small compared to the other towns Andrew had seen. It sat at the foot of a rocky mount, with a castle perched on top and a monastery nearby. The town itself was not walled in but spread around the castle like moss around a tree. The spires of various churches sprung up like pointed arrows. Like so many other towns and cities in France, it sat near a river.

Jeanne pushed them to move faster as they came closer to the town. "We must not keep the Dauphin waiting," she called out, making sure to hold her banner high.

Andrew and Eve shared a horse that d'Aulon had found for them. Riding at a gallop, Andrew was sure one of them would bounce off. Dunois kept pace with Jeanne, probably fearful of what the Maiden might do when she greeted the Dauphin.

Just outside the city was a large company of men on horseback. The Dauphin had come out to greet her. He sat regally on a black stallion, wearing a brightly colored tunic. Seeing Jeanne, he broke the line and rode across the field, meeting her halfway.

Jeanne brought her horse to a halt and quickly dismounted. She took off her cap and bowed as far as she could.

The Dauphin climbed off his horse and, with a great smile, reached down and gently encouraged her to stand. She obeyed. Still smiling, he suddenly wrapped his arms around her.

Andrew reined in his horse only a couple of yards away.

"Did he *kiss* her?" Eve asked, craning to see.

"It is too hard to tell from here," Andrew said.

Soon they were surrounded by members of the Dauphin's court: a scowling Archbishop of Reims and a disdainful La Trémoille. Their sour expressions told Andrew that they did not like the Dauphin's open show of affection for Jeanne.

The Dauphin invited Jeanne and her companions to his royal lodge in Loches so he could hear her account of the battle at Tourelles. Andrew was glad that the Dauphin gave Jeanne so much attention and respect. Even the members of the royal court seemed to appreciate her. Sadly the feeling was short lived.

Over the next several days, the Dauphin's counselors squeezed Jeanne out of his schedule. She reminded them that they must now march to Reims to crown him as the one true king. In response they insisted that the subject needed further discussion. The Dauphin himself was indecisive.

"See?" Eve said to Andrew. "They are stalling everything."

Theologians and scholars wrote long and involved essays about Jeanne and sent them to the Dauphin for consideration. They concluded that the Dauphin should "do what the Maiden commands and prudence directs. For everything else, give yourself to works of piety and prayers of devotion."

Meanwhile, the military captains fumed again about taking commands from a girl like Jeanne. La Trémoille and the Archbishop of Reims did all they could to thwart Jeanne's influence on the Dauphin.

A servant in the royal court told Andrew and Eve that La Trémoille had advised the Dauphin "to allow the *average* people and soldiers" to draw inspiration from her. "*You* are above that," he told the Dauphin.

When Jeanne wasn't waiting for the Dauphin, she was answering yet more questions from the council. Privately she met with Brother Pasquerel to pray and study. He began to teach her to read and write. She also went into the fields to hone her sword-fighting skills and learn to use a battle-ax. The exercise helped restore the strength in her chest and shoulder. Andrew discovered that her greatest pleasure was riding her horse alone in the nearby forests. Otherwise, she regularly made her confession and attended Mass with Brother Pasquerel. Andrew often saw her weeping.

He learned from Jean d'Aulon that the council's latest argument centered around the expense of an ongoing war. They claimed the royal treasury could not afford it. Yet they also understood that the victory at Orléans would be lost if they did not continue the fight to drive out the English. But how were they to be driven out? Every positive statement was met with a dozen negative responses.

Eve reported that Jeanne often paced in her room like a lion.

"I may live a year, barely longer," she said. "Why does the Dauphin destroy my time with delays?"

One day Andrew overheard Jeanne tell Brother Pasquerel that she had been given four things to do: Deliver Orléans—which she had done; see the Dauphin crowned and anointed at Reims; drive the English out of France; and rescue the Duke of Orléans from the hands of the English.

"How am I to do any of those things waiting here?" she asked.

"Had God not given her this mission, she would have been the holiest of women in a convent somewhere," Brother Pasquerel later said to Andrew and Eve.

Meanwhile, the Duke of Alençon was promoted to the rank of lieutenant general of the Dauphin's armies. He and Dunois went off with the troops to fight. First, they marched to the besieged town of Jargeau to get rid of the English there. They believed they would be victorious, just as they were at Orléans. They weren't. The high waters of the river Loire flooded the trenches, blocking their access to the fortress. The French forces unhappily returned to Loches.

"They would have won if they had taken Jeanne," Eve said.

Jeanne was deeply distressed. Unable to wait any longer, she stormed to the Dauphin's chambers. Andrew and Eve followed closely, afraid of what was about to happen.

Bursting through the doors, Jeanne found the Dauphin meeting with a few of his council members. The councilmen leapt to their feet, appalled at the interruption.

Jeanne dropped to her knees and begged, "Gentle Dauphin, do not continue with your tedious councils, but come with me to Reims to claim the crown that is yours!"

The Dauphin politely said, "Do not be impatient. You know better than most that the will of God will be accomplished in His good time."

"I know that," Jeanne countered, then gestured to the council. "But do they?"

Christophe d'Harcourt, an arrogant nobleman whose lips always seemed to purse into a frown, asked, "Is interrupting the Dauphin in his chambers your idea or the idea of your council of angels and saints?"

"My heavenly council has urged me forward," Jeanne replied.

"Show us," d'Harcourt said. "Here, in the presence of your king, show us how your council speaks to you."

Andrew was surprised to see Jeanne blush.

The Dauphin held up his hand. "Jeanne, does it please you to answer this request here, publicly?"

Jeanne glanced at the Dauphin, then fixed her gaze on d'Harcourt. "I know what you want and would provide it willingly, if I could. However, I am at the beck and call of my Voices. They are not at mine."

"A good answer," said the Dauphin.

She turned to him again. "Gentle Dauphin, I am sad that you and your council do not believe me. Yet the Voices of *my* council comfort me and say, 'Daughter of God, go, and we will be your help.' These Voices fill me with so great a joy that I would stay in that condition forever, if I could."

Andrew sensed that something had changed in the room. It was as if the light of the sun had somehow penetrated the thick walls and bathed Jeanne in a beautiful radiance. Her eyes were filled with tears, but her expression had a look of peace that Andrew would never forget. Then, almost as quickly as the change had appeared, it faded again.

Wide eyed, Andrew turned to Eve. Her expression told him that she had felt it too. He glanced at the faces of the council. They all looked astonished.

D'Harcourt put a hand on his heart and said, "Good Maiden, I apologize for any doubt I have had in you."

The other council members looked unsettled. Even a heavenly light was not going to stop them from their meeting.

"Your Highness, I beg you to allow us to resume," one of them said.

"Yes, yes," the Dauphin stammered.

The moment was gone.

Jeanne knew it. Without another word, she bowed to the prince and left the room.

Eve and Andrew followed close behind, eyeing each other with the same question: *What just happened?*

Whatever had happened in the room impacted the council. Soon after, they gave their approval for a great army to be gathered at the city of Selles-en-Berry, south of Blois. Jeanne would be reunited with the Duke of Alençon and her fellow Orléans commanders, including Jean de Dunois, La Hire, and Gilles de Rais. From Selles-en-Berry, they would march again on the English-held towns along the river Loire, learning the lessons from their failure at Jargeau.

The challenge from the royal council was simple: *If* Jeanne and the French army conquered the English strongholds and cleared the passage to Reims, the Dauphin would go there to be crowned.

Jeanne looked delighted. It was what she had hoped to do all along.

"Why did it take them almost a month to decide?" Eve seethed.

Jeanne and her company journeyed to Selles-en-Berry. It was another small town, hardly able to sustain the many soldiers who had come to fight. The military camp spread out from the city limits along the river Cher.

The troops were well assembled by the time Jeanne arrived. She greeted the men she already knew and was introduced to a few new captains who had come to join the fight. One was an old friend of La Hire named Jean Poton de Xaintrailles. He was a stern-looking man with jet-black hair, a matching moustache, and dark, penetrating eyes. He gave her a swift salute.

Two of the new men were young brothers, Guy and André de Laval. Both were noblemen. Yet Andrew noticed that Guy actually blushed when he met Jeanne, and he stammered like a fan meeting a famous rock star. Andrew thought it was funny. Eve said she thought it was "sweet."

Jeanne reminded the commanders of their duties: the soldiers must make a regular confession and go to Mass, no women were allowed in the camp, and there was to be no swearing. Considering the victory at Orléans, the men readily agreed.

Wanting to waste no more time, Jeanne marched the army to Orléans, the starting point for their campaigns along the river.

It's almost like coming home, Andrew thought as they passed the wreck of Tourelles and crossed the great bridge to the gate into Orléans. The people cheered, more bells rang, and the cannons thundered to welcome them.

The Bouchers greeted Jeanne as one of the family. They even put her back in the room she had shared with Madame Boucher and her young daughter, Charlotte.

In no time at all, the commanders were in a heated argument about where to attack first. Jargeau was the obvious choice, if only to finish what Dunois had started. But rumors had reached them that the English had recently brought in a great number of reinforcements.

"We must be cautious," one of the captains said.

Jeanne had heard enough. "Friends! Do not be afraid. No matter the numbers against us or the difficulties ahead of us, God leads this work. If I were not sure of it, I would be home tending sheep rather than enduring this. We must go on *now*!"

The next day they marched to the English fortress at Jargeau. The rumors about reinforcements turned out to be false. But the English commander, the Duke of Suffolk, had used the time following Dunois's attack to prepare for an invasion.

On the first day, Andrew and Eve were told to stay near the supply wagons. They watched as the townspeople from Orléans unwisely rushed ahead of the army to attack the fortress on their own. As had happened before, many lost their lives for their reckless bravery. A company of French soldiers, young and inexperienced, also attacked in a disorganized frenzy. Many were wounded and driven back.

It took Jeanne to bring order to the chaos. Riding in with her banner, she led a renewed attack. The Duke of Suffolk took the hint and sent a message to the French commanders.

"Give us fifteen days to surrender," Suffolk offered. "If reinforcements come in that time, then we will fight. If not, we will surrender."

The commanders considered the idea. It was part of their military tradition to allow such an offer.

Jeanne was furious. "No!" she said. "Tell them to leave *now*, with the clothes on their backs, if they want to live. Otherwise, we will continue our attack."

Suffolk refused Jeanne's demands. The next day, the battle began again. Both sides stood strong, no closer to victory. Once again Jeanne rode from one end of the field to another, urging the French soldiers on.

The story was told later that she had found the Duke of Alençon with his men trying to establish a new position near the city wall. Jeanne told him to move or he would surely be killed. He was surprised enough to obey her advice. Later, another captain took the same position and was struck down by cannon fire.

At the end of the day, the English waved a white flag for another round of negotiations. They demanded the same terms as before. Jeanne refused. The fight would continue.

Andrew watched as she personally directed the placements of the French cannons and catapults. With a renewed bombardment, she sped to a wall with a company of men carrying a ladder. As she began to climb, a stone was thrown down, knocking her to the ground. Her banner flew from her hand. From where Andrew stood with the supply wagons, it seemed as if everyone froze where they were in the fight.

Jeanne leapt to her feet and raised the banner again. She shouted for the French troops to move ahead. The English recoiled as the French forces thundered their way toward Jargeau. La Hire used the time to position a catapult even closer to the fortress. He let fly three huge stones, each one slamming into the tower and turning it into a jagged ruin. The French forces now entered the city.

The English abandoned the wall and fell back among the houses and shops. Many hurried to the river. The French chased them wherever they went. Finally, the Duke of Suffolk was captured and the battle ended.

The army returned to a jubilant Orléans. Jeanne expressed thanks to God for the victory and urged everyone to attend Mass.

That evening, Dunois came to Jeanne with servants carrying a trunk.

"A present for you from my father, the Duke of Orléans," he said. "Though he remains a hostage in England, he arranged to send this to you."

Jeanne opened the trunk with the happy look of a young girl at Christmas. She took out a beautiful red cloak and a green tunic fringed with white silk.

"The colors of our house," Dunois explained.

Jeanne was clearly touched by the gesture and promised to wear those colors proudly when the time was right.

"But for now," she said, returning to business, "we must move on to the next English stronghold."

"The men must rest," Dunois said.

"I will give them two days," she conceded.

The campaigns to defeat the English strongholds on the way to Reims became a fuzzy memory to Andrew. Each one was a variation of floods of soldiers in glistening armor and colorful banners, stone walls and ladders, flying arrows and cannon fire, swords and lances, shouts and screams, blood and death.

"We're only twelve years old," he complained to Eve one night. "How are we supposed to cope?"

Eve, looking pale, nodded. "In our time, generals push buttons and fire long-range missiles. We hear about the numbers of casualties on a list or see on a map what cities were captured. If we had to fight this way all the time, maybe we wouldn't fight so often."

Andrew shook his head. "The commanders here see how terrible it is, and they still fight all the time. It isn't the way we fight; it's the way we are."

Outside of a town called Meung-sur-Loire, the French army captured a bridge that would allow the troops and their supplies to move freely between the north and south.

They moved on to the ancient town of Beaugency, passing through lush vineyards, colorful gardens, and stretches of cornfields before reaching a few outlying homes.

The English were ready for them. Guards had been posted among the houses, waiting to attack. It worked. The French began to retreat. Once again, Jeanne rallied them to push forward.

The English quickly withdrew into the town and its castle. Rather than fight any further, the English commander presented terms for their immediate surrender. Jeanne agreed that they could leave the next day, taking their horses and personal property with them, if they promised not to fight again for ten days.

Jeanne's commanders were surprised. Why would she allow the English to leave?

Andrew knew the answer: Jeanne had a soft spot for any who would surrender.

That same day, Andrew heard about a different problem.

"Another French army has shown up," Eve explained to him, after hearing Jeanne talking with her captains.

"Another French army is good, right?" he asked.

"But this army belongs to Arthur de Richemont. He is the constable of France. Though, he had a falling-out with the Dauphin, and no one is sure if he is here to join us or fight us. Jeanne said we should attack him before he attacks us."

"What do the commanders say?"

"They told Jeanne that if she attacks the count, their soldiers will not fight with her."

Andrew found that hard to believe. "What is Jeanne going to do?"

"Ride out to meet him," Eve said. "The Duke of Alençon will go with her. So will Dunois and a couple of others. The duke wants us to go too."

"Us? Why us?"

"Because we are her angels. He thinks she will be less hotheaded if we are with her."

"It has not worked so far," Andrew said.

Eve smiled. Andrew had not seen her do that in a long time.

Andrew could feel the tension as Jeanne and her company rode out from their camp to meet Arthur de Richemont. The adults had their own horses. Andrew and Eve shared one.

The constable of France sat on horseback at the head of a vast army. He had at least as many men as Jeanne had on her side. If it came to a fight, it would be a terrible one.

De Richemont was dressed in royal colors and wore a dark cape along with a broad hat that had a long feather sticking out of it. He carried a sword at his side. Andrew noticed that he did not bother to wear any protective armor.

The constable spurred his horse and trotted away from his army to greet Jeanne. As they drew closer together in the middle of the field, Andrew saw de Richemont's face. He had sad eyes and a long nose that seemed to pull his face down, setting his mouth in a permanent frown.

When they were only a few yards apart, de Richemont reined in his horse and dismounted. Jeanne did the same. Andrew saw Dunois's hand slip over to the hilt of his sword.

De Richemont took a few steps and looked surprised when Jeanne came close and then knelt down in front of him.

He made the Sign of the Cross and urged her to stand. She slowly got to her feet.

He said, "Jeanne, I have been told that you want to fight me. I do not know whether you come from God or not. If you come from God, I do not fear you in any way, for God knows my good intentions. If you come from the devil, then I fear you even less."

"Then let us talk, my lord," she said.

The two of them strolled away. De Richemont clasped his hands behind his back and lowered his head to listen to Jeanne. They stopped at a distance where no one else could hear them. He nodded as Jeanne spoke. Then Jeanne listened to him and she, too, nodded.

They returned a few minutes later. The constable mounted his horse and rode back to his army.

Jeanne watched him, then turned and announced to all, "We have peace."

There was a collective sigh of relief.

She mounted her horse and said with a smile, "He has offered the best of his men to fight with us."

When they returned to their army, Jeanne and her captains received a report from a nervous-looking French soldier. He had overheard from the departing English troops that Sir John Talbot and Sir John Fastolf were leading six thousand English soldiers from Paris.

Andrew knew that the French already feared Talbot, but the mention of Fastolf struck absolute terror in their hearts. They would never forget that Fastolf and his army had brutally defeated them in what had become known as the Battle of the Herrings.

"Even now the English troops are headquartered at Meung," the soldier said.

Andrew listened as the French commanders argued again for caution. Jeanne should wait, they said. Better yet, she should retreat to a safer position. Anything would be better than to face Fastolf and his army.

Andrew couldn't imagine that they had been fighting alongside the warrior Maiden all this time and still didn't know her. The pattern always seemed to be the same: news would come, they would react, and she would act.

"I do not care what numbers they bring," Jeanne said. "God has sent us as His rod of iron to discipline them."

To Arthur de Richemont, she sent a message: "I was not responsible for your coming, but since you have come, you are welcome." The arrival of de Richemont's army would bolster their mission, she told her commanders. Retreat was not an option.

"We will not wait for the English army to attack us," Jeanne insisted. "Let us go and drive them out at sword point."

The commanders reluctantly accepted her order. The French army marched on to Janville.

As they passed fertile fields and great thick forests, Andrew heard Dunois warn the others, "There are many places for the English to hide. Watch for a surprise attack."

Jeanne agreed. "By God, if they were hanging from the clouds, we would have them by now." But she quickly added, "Still, my council has assured me that they will be ours."

Along the way, news came that the English forces had already been marching in *their* direction and had established positions on the vast Beauce plains a few miles ahead.

Jeanne was unafraid.

The French reached a broad hill that gave them a clear view for miles around. In the distance, they could see the town of Patay. They also saw evidence of the English army's presence. Just ahead of a narrow pass between two woods, a long line of pikes had been staked into the ground. The points were sloped toward the enemy.

It was the same kind of barricade the English had used at the Battle of Agincourt. The pikes prevented a charge on horseback.

Dunois frowned. "The English are hiding in the woods behind those pikes. Their longbowmen will slaughter us."

Two English messengers appeared behind the pikes. They passed through the blockade, crossed the field, and eventually ascended the hill. Bowing to the French commanders, they issued a challenge from Talbot. "If you have the courage, come down and fight us."

Jeanne smiled at this obvious lure into their trap. "God and Our Lady willing, we will see you face-to-face at noon tomorrow."

The messenger nodded, then returned the way he came.

"Noon?" asked La Hire.

Jeanne shrugged. "Would you prefer we engaged them sooner?"

"Not when I do not know where they are," La Hire replied. He nodded. "Noon it is."

The French spent the rest of the day preparing for battle.

"There is much we cannot see" became a common refrain among the commanders. "The English could be hiding their archers anywhere in the hedges and forest."

Andrew kept hearing the name *Agincourt* whispered among the troops.

The French captains met to assess the situation. "How do we fight what we cannot see?" was the question they asked.

"We must draw them out," said La Hire.

"How?" asked Dunois.

"God will show us," Jeanne said, her eyes alight.

Andrew could see that her words were not comforting the captains.

She stepped away, stating that she wanted to spend time thinking and praying. She signaled for Eve and Andrew to walk with her.

They strolled back along the road to Beaugency, passing soldiers who now rested on the roadside or in the neighboring fields.

A disturbance caught their attention. Across a field, a group of soldiers had circled around a stag that had unwisely ventured from the forest. With swords and spears ready, the soldiers were about to kill the poor beast.

"We shall eat it when we are victorious," one of the soldiers said proudly to Jeanne as she approached with Andrew and Eve.

Andrew was amused. "I am sure you could lure the English out with one of those."

Jeanne turned to Andrew with a look of wonder. She then shouted, "Wait! Do not kill it!"

The soldiers groaned from disappointment.

"What do you want us to do?" one of the soldiers asked.

"Set it free," she said.

Once again, the soldiers groaned. "Why?" another asked.

Jeanne smiled. "By God's grace, it will be a gift to the English. *Then* we will have our victory."

The soldiers looked at her, perplexed. Then they slowly spread out. The stag stood tall and proud. Andrew noticed a jagged scar along its flank.

Another narrow escape, he thought.

The stag bounded away in the direction of the English army.

"I hope the English enjoy their feast," said the soldier.

"I doubt it," Jeanne said.

Andrew turned to Eve. She gave him a look that said "I don't know what she's thinking."

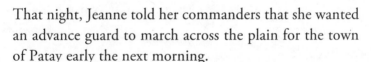

That night, Jeanne told her commanders that she wanted an advance guard to march across the plain for the town of Patay early the next morning.

"Stay in tight formation as you go," Jeanne said.

"To what purpose?" asked the Duke of Alençon. "Do you want the advance guard to attack early? Is that why you told the English messengers we would see them at noon?"

"How can they attack what they cannot see? I want the English to show themselves," she said firmly. "Once we know where they are hidden, the remainder of the army will follow, ready for battle."

The duke was not assured. "Are you suggesting that an advance guard will serve as bait to draw out the English?"

Jeanne looked at him calmly. "It is another kind of bait that will show us where the English are. My angel has said so." Her gaze went to Andrew.

Andrew suddenly realized that all of the commanders were looking at him.

His cheeks burned from the embarrassment. Especially since he didn't know what Jeanne was talking about.

"If this is your angel's plan, then he should travel with the advance guard," said La Hire, giving Andrew a coy look.

"Yes, he should see his handiwork," said Jeanne.

Andrew swallowed hard. *What handiwork?* he wondered. *What is she doing?*

"I will lead the advance guard," La Hire announced.

"As will I," said Captain de Xaintrailles. "I know this region."

Guy de Laval stepped forward with his brother. "André and I will take a company of men with them."

As the meeting broke up, Jeanne gave a final instruction to her commanders. "Wear your spurs, good men. You will need them to pursue the English as they run away."

The night passed at a painfully slow pace. Andrew couldn't sleep. His mind raced. He didn't fear traveling with the advance guard, but he couldn't figure out what

Jeanne had been talking about. What idea had he given her?

——————————————————➤

Before the light of dawn touched the sky, La Hire, Captain de Xaintrailles, and the two Laval brothers assembled the men who would form the advance. La Hire instructed them to stay in tight formation. "We do not know where the English are hiding, but our Maiden is certain we will find them."

Eve showed up while Andrew was putting on a few sections of armor.

"Will you be all right?" she asked as she helped him fasten his breastplate.

"How am I supposed to know?" he countered. "Did Jeanne tell you anything?"

"No," Eve said. "But I think it has something to do with that stag she set free."

Andrew shook his head. "I thought about it all night. I don't get it."

"Neither do I," Eve said. "But Jeanne does, and that's all that matters."

Andrew sighed as he slid his sword into its sheath. "I hope so."

La Hire and the other captains led the advance guard down the hill toward the plain. Andrew marched between La Hire and Captain de Xaintrailles. La Hire had insisted on it. "You should be one of the first to see whatever you put in the Maiden's mind," he said.

Andrew didn't reply.

The morning dew soaked their boots and helped to muffle the sound of their footfalls. The air was still. Not even a bird greeted them with a call.

Andrew thought the English barricade seemed farther away than it had looked from the top of the hill.

"The Battle of the Herrings was near the town of Patay only four months ago," La Hire said softly. "Fastolf was the victor there."

"Will this be payback?" Andrew asked him.

"Payback?" La Hire repeated, as if he had never heard the word before.

Andrew realized he probably hadn't. "Never mind," he said.

"Brace yourselves," whispered Captain de Xaintrailles. "Shields up."

Andrew heard the sounds of the soldiers' shields being gently raised. The barricade was closer. If the English archers were hiding nearby and prepared, then the arrows would come buzzing at them at any moment.

But the arrows did not come as they reached the barricade. It looked half finished. Andrew thought that with a single hard push, it might even collapse.

"The English are not prepared," La Hire whispered as they moved past it.

"Or it could be a trick," de Xaintrailles said.

The tension felt like electricity in the air all around them. They entered the path that cut through some woods. Birds sang to the left and the right. There was no hint of anyone hiding anywhere.

"This is unbearable," said de Xaintrailles. "Send a scout ahead."

La Hire nodded. He began to turn and signal one of the soldiers when Andrew made a quick decision.

"I will go," he said.

"I do not think the Maiden intended that," said La Hire.

Andrew began to unbuckle his armor. "I am a fast runner and smaller than any of your soldiers. I will go." He tossed his armor into the bushes nearby. He felt twenty pounds lighter.

"Brave lad," de Xaintrailles said. He clapped the boy on the shoulder.

"I want to end the suspense," Andrew said, half smiling.

A moment later, he was jogging up the path. He picked up speed, glancing back to see La Hire and the advance guard grow more distant. He hadn't thought about what might happen if he came upon the English. Would they shoot him? Take him prisoner? *Better not to think about it*, he decided.

The woods on both sides of the path seemed to thin out. It looked as if he was coming to another open field. He thought he could see the outline of a village far ahead. Was that Patay? He squinted at the shapes dotting a field ahead. There were hedges and what looked like carts of hay. Had something moved off to the left?

Still there was no sign of the English. Slowing down, he moved off the path into the protection of the trees. He watched for a moment.

The call of a bird caused him to turn. He saw a shaft of sunlight cutting through the trees several yards to his right. A stag stood in the middle of the golden rays. It reminded him of when he and Eve had first arrived. He had seen a deer standing in light just like that. And he felt then that maybe God wanted him in this time for some good purpose.

The stag took a few steps. Andrew saw a jagged scar on its flank.

He realized it was the stag that Jeanne had set free. *What are the chances of that?* he thought.

The stag looked at him. Then, with a nod, it leapt away and darted through the trees into the open field.

Andrew was surprised to hear a man shout. He was even more surprised to see several men with longbows suddenly appear from behind the hedges and carts. They were struggling to get their arrows in place to shoot at the stag. One or two arrows flew but missed the mark. The stag zigzagged and bounded onward, drawing more men out of hiding. Their English accents were unmistakable.

Andrew sprinted to the path. Then he ran with all of his might back to La Hire and the advance guard.

Seeing them up ahead, he put on the afterburners like a marathon racer sprinting to the finish line. He threw himself at Captain de Xaintrailles, who caught him and lowered him to the ground.

The world was spinning as Andrew choked out the word "Found!"

"Get your breath, boy," said the captain.

Andrew sat up and tried to breathe. "The ... English ... are ... just ahead. In ... a clearing."

"Have they set up a blockade? What are they doing?" asked La Hire.

"Hunting ... a ... stag."

La Hire gave orders to one of the soldiers to run back to the other commanders. "Tell them to hurry," he said.

De Xaintrailles pulled out his sword. "Shall we?"

La Hire gave a sharp nod. "*Attack.*"

The Battle of Patay, as it was later called, was won within two hours.

The English archers were completely surprised when the French advance guard came at them. They had expected a slow-marching army later in the day, not a smaller group of fast-running soldiers first thing in the morning. Worse, they had not completed their own preparations for the battle. They were still establishing their positions when the stag drew them out.

Jeanne and her commanders had fooled them in another way. Rather than come as one army straight toward Patay, they had sent companies of soldiers around to the left and the right in a flanking maneuver.

The fierce and feared Captain Fastolf had bounded upon his horse and fled. Captain Talbot was not so fortunate. He was captured and brought before the French commanders.

"You did not think this would happen," the Duke of Alençon said to him.

The captain shrugged. "It is the fortunes of war."

Those fortunes had changed very suddenly for the English in France. Upon hearing that no one was coming to protect them, the English commanders at other fortresses set fire to their strongholds and retreated.

Andrew heard La Hire say it was the French revenge for the Battle of Agincourt.

That evening Andrew was reunited with Eve and Jeanne. He asked the Maiden directly, "Did you know the stag would show me where the English were? Is that why you set it free?"

She gave him a slight smile and said, "How could I know such a thing?"

Andrew never heard what became of the stag.

The Dauphin sat on a thick-cushioned chair in front of Jeanne. She was on her knees before him. He had a bored expression on his narrow face.

Eve finally realized what it was about him that bothered her so much. He reminded her of a kid she once knew at school who became whatever the kids around him were. If he was hanging out with nice kids, he was nice. If he hung around the bullies, he acted like a bully. Right now, the Dauphin was hanging around the snobs.

Jeanne traveled with her company and the Duke of Alençon to the home of Georges de La Trémoille. His castle was only twenty-five miles east of Orléans at Sully-sur-Loire. She had gone from the wonderful victory celebrations in Orléans to the stifling indifference of the men who bent the Dauphin's mind whichever way it suited them.

Jeanne pleaded with anyone who would listen: "Talbot is captured. Fastolf is fleeing. The English army is scattered. We must march to Paris *now* and reclaim it for France."

In response, Jeanne was given various excuses.

"Wait. The time is not right."

"We do not have the funds."

"Our soldiers must rest."

"It is too risky."

"Speak first with the Dauphin."

"Do *not* speak with the Dauphin."

"You said he must be crowned in Reims next."

Other commanders, like the duke, sided with Jeanne. "Let us march to Paris!" he affirmed.

But they needed the Dauphin's blessing to do anything.

Now the Dauphin sat in his chair, with his bored expression, and said to Jeanne in a sympathetic tone, "I pity you because of the suffering you have had to endure. Rest now."

Eve felt like screaming.

Jeanne's eyes glistened. She did not work for the Dauphin's praise, but she was clearly upset by his response.

"Gentle Dauphin," she said, "you will receive the whole of your kingdom. You will be crowned."

Eve saw the briefest exchange of looks between the Dauphin and La Trémoille, who stood nearby.

Jeanne waited for a response. When the Dauphin said no more, she asked, "Gentle Dauphin, will you recognize the valiant work done by Arthur de Richemont at the Battle of Patay?"

The Dauphin flinched.

"Whatever has divided you in the past should be forgiven," Jeanne continued. "If nothing else, it would help to reunite the kingdom under you as king."

Eve saw the blood rush to La Trémoille's face. He pressed his lips together so tightly that they became thin white stripes.

"Yes, of course," the Dauphin said. "De Richemont is forgiven. But he will *never* again serve as a member of my court. I will find another way to reward him."

La Trémoille's lips twisted into a smirk.

This was his influence at work, Eve knew. She had come to learn that he disliked anyone and anything that would lessen his hold on the Dauphin. This mere maiden from Domrémy was no match for him. He would get rid of Jeanne if he could. That much was an open secret. But he would not dare. Not now. He would use her for as long as he could, then dispose of her when he was finished.

Eve had seen the royal announcements about the French army's successes. The Dauphin gave credit to Jeanne and the commanders of royal blood. But he did not mention Jean de Dunois, La Hire, Captain de Xaintrailles, or any of the other great men who had fought alongside Jeanne.

It's none of my business, Eve reminded herself, then fumed, *But it is my business.*

It had become her business after spending so much time with Jeanne. There was something about the Maiden that made Eve want to help her, no matter what.

When Eve first arrived in this time, her greatest desire had been to go home again. Now she did not want to leave Jeanne's side. Was it loyalty? Survival? No. It was more than any of those things. Eve had come to love Jeanne, which was a big surprise. It was a struggle for Eve to love anyone. To love meant to trust—and trust was something that her life's experience had taught her not to do.

Eve knew that Jeanne was in greater trouble now than she had ever been on any battlefield. Jeanne was now famous all over the known world. People in other countries were arguing over whether she had been sent by God or the devil. She was compared to David fighting against Goliath, and even the donkey's jaw that Samson had used to wipe out the Philistines. Jeanne's exploits were on the lips of every traveling merchant, monk, sailor, and soldier. Word had spread to the largest cities and the smallest villages. Men like La Trémoille hated her for it.

It made sense to attack Paris while the French army was strong. Paris was the heart of the nation. To reclaim it would be the final victory. But if Jeanne was not allowed to do that, then surely she should be allowed to accompany the Dauphin to Reims to officially crown him as king.

Eve admitted to Andrew that she didn't understand the importance of Reims, since the Dauphin had already declared himself the king after his father had died seven years before.

It was Brother Pasquerel who gave her the answer.

"Reims is where our kings have been crowned for hundreds of years," he said. "The sacred anointing with holy oil is the seal of the king's true position. And the cathedral is glorious, a place of majesty. It is the only place truly worthy of a king."

Eve heard stories that the English wanted to have a coronation of their own in Paris. Not the Dauphin's coronation, of course. The English Duke of Bedford planned to crown Henry the Sixth there. Henry was a mere boy, but that didn't matter. Bedford wanted a dramatic show to rally the people of Paris against the Dauphin. The event would also remind everyone of the role the Dauphin had played in the murder of the Duke of Burgundy's father.

"The Dauphin denies killing the father of the Duke of Burgundy," Eve told Andrew one evening.

"It's like a Shakespeare play," Andrew observed.

"I think it *was* a Shakespeare play," Eve said.

The one person who seemed thrilled by Jeanne's determination was the wily Archbishop of Reims. Eve did not like the Archbishop. There was something about his eyes that bugged her. They darted back and forth too quickly, like an animal looking for prey.

Jeanne once admitted that she thought the Archbishop was "very clever and sharp-minded but loves money a little too much."

Brother Pasquerel added that the Archbishop was a shrewd man who knew how to play every situation to his advantage. He was allied with La Trémoille and manipulated the Dauphin behind the scenes. On the other hand, he had put up a lot of his own money to defend Orléans. Though some said he did this not because he believed in Jeanne's mission but because he knew it would help his standing with the Dauphin.

After Jeanne's indecisive audience with the Dauphin, she went off to pray. She dismissed Eve to go off somewhere to walk, think, and play.

Eve considered taking a walk but dreaded going outside. The castle sat like an island in the middle of a large moat. The only way in or out was a single bridge that led to the town. It was too much effort.

She had to admit that the castles and manor houses all began to look the same to her. They were impressive from the outside. But inside, the hallways and rooms were variations of the same kinds of walls and floors.

After considering climbing one of the towers, she decided to look for Andrew. She stood in a large corridor and tried to remember in which direction his room was. Suddenly he ran around the corner and nearly fell when he saw her.

"We're leaving," he puffed breathlessly.

"What? Why?" she asked.

"The Dauphin has finally agreed to be crowned in Reims."

In a day, everyone was on the move—not only Jeanne and her company but the Dauphin and his court. Carriages, wagons, and horses were loaded. They departed Sully-sur-Loire in a long procession destined for the town of Gien, more than seventy miles southeast.

"Why Gien?" Eve asked Andrew. "Isn't that the wrong direction from Reims?"

"The Dauphin has a castle there. And that's where the army is being assembled," he explained.

The castle at Gien was a relatively modest one and was soon overrun by tailors, seamstresses, and various craftsmen tasked with making sure everything was prepared for the coronation. Even Jeanne wanted her banner cleaned for the occasion.

Queen Yolande arrived, explaining that her daughter Marie was the Dauphin's wife and had to be properly dressed. Eve was glad to see the queen again, though it now meant running errands for her and other ladies of the royal court. She had no idea that people could spend so much time discussing the lengths of a robe or the shoulder width of a cloak or the choice of satin versus silk. It became dizzying trying to understand whether this red would match that gold or this yellow would go with that purple.

"There is one thing you can do for me," Queen Yolande said to her one afternoon while they were comparing fabrics. "The royal jeweler is here, working on a broach for the Dauphin's cape. Please ask him when he expects to have it finished."

Eve wandered the castle until she found someone to direct her to the royal jeweler's residence. It was in an unfamiliar wing. She entered a large room where men and women were busy cutting and sewing fabrics at long tables. In a small room in a back corner, she found an old man hunched over a desk with his back to the door. As Eve came around to his side, she saw his fingers working carefully with a thin silver tool. He used the tool to press a purple gem into a gold case.

"Pardon me," Eve said.

The man grunted at her.

"Queen Yolande wants to know about the broach for the Dauphin's cape," she said.

"This afternoon," he said in a low growl.

Eve had been watching the delicate way the man worked with the gem. Then her gaze went up to his face. She staggered back.

It was Simon Le Fantôme.

"Oh," she said, startled.

The old man's hair had been cut and his beard trimmed. And he now looked distinguished in a deep-blue robe. But even from the side, Eve thought his narrow face seemed aged and sickly pale.

He did not even glance up at her. His eyes were fixed on his work. "You are still here," he said.

She wasn't sure what he meant. "Where else would I be?" she asked.

He grunted again. "Did your 'servant' warn you about the assassin?" he asked.

"You are the only assassin I am worried about," Eve said, then rushed out of the room.

In the hallway, she leaned against a wall and tried to calm herself. Seeing Simon was the last thing she had expected. She had hoped he'd gone away for good.

She took a few deep breaths, then pushed away from the wall. She had almost forgotten why she was there. She shook her head sharply and ran off to deliver the message to Queen Yolande.

And then she was going to have a talk with Andrew.

Eve eventually found Andrew in the small closet that served as his bedroom. She told him about her unhappy surprise.

He looked sheepishly at her.

She realized what the look meant. "You *knew* he was here?" she asked. "Why didn't you tell me?"

"I didn't want you to worry."

"I would rather be worried than surprised," she said, frowning.

Andrew looked at her. She could tell he was thinking about something else.

"What?" she asked.

"There's something else I haven't told you."

"What?"

"I saw Simon in Orléans after the battle. He was wounded."

"A lot of people were," Eve said.

"He said something to me that I haven't been able to figure out."

"He says a lot of things that no one can figure out."

"Will you stop throwing my words back at me?" Andrew snapped. "This is why I didn't tell you about Simon."

"Say something that makes sense!" Eve complained.

Andrew gazed at her, then rushed to get the words out. "Simon was delirious. He said he had been wounded trying to stop the Ravager from killing Jeanne. And then he said the words *Hope Springs*."

Eve flinched. "Why?"

"I wish I knew."

"You must have mentioned it to him," she offered.

Andrew shook his head. "I've thought it over. I never did."

"Then ...?"

Andrew groaned. "I think he said 'Hope Springs' because ... he knows."

"Knows what?"

"That it's where we came from."

Eve was doubtful. "How can he know that?"

Andrew shrugged. "That's the hard part. I think ... he's from the future. Maybe he's from Hope Springs."

"No," she said. "That isn't possible."

"Just like it isn't possible that we're from a town called Hope Springs in the future? Or that we're now living in medieval France?"

Eve shook her head.

"He saw us arrive," Andrew reminded her.

"Okay," Eve said, trying to sound reasonable. "If he is from Hope Springs, then why not say so?"

"He's been here for *years*," Andrew said. He held up a finger like a teacher presenting a theory. "Maybe that's why he's crazy. He's been here too long. Alfred Virtue said it might happen, right?"

"He didn't say it *would* happen."

"But it *could* happen."

"And what? He's forgotten all about his life in the future? How could anyone forget something like that?"

Andrew frowned. "It was only a guess."

Eve felt drained talking about Simon. "Next time, *warn* me when you know he's around," she said. "No more secrets."

"No more secrets," Andrew said.

The Dauphin was committed to going to Reims. But he wanted assurances that there would be no English assassination attempts or uprisings by those still allied to the English. He would be traveling through two hundred miles of territory that had been loyal to England, after all. It could be dangerous.

Jeanne didn't share his worry. She assured him that God would give the French the power to push back the English and their supporters. To ease his mind, she sent letters to officials and nobility alike, appealing to them to give their hearts to God and their loyalty to the Dauphin. She invited them to the coronation in Reims to personally witness God's blessing on their sovereign.

She also wrote, by her own hand, a letter to the dreaded Duke of Burgundy. The duke was England's greatest ally in France and hated the Dauphin. In the letter, Jeanne begged him to embrace the will of the King of Heaven. "Come to the coronation of France's *true* king," she wrote.

Guyenne and Ambleville, the Maiden's heralds, were kept very busy.

The Dauphin also sent letters. He assured the town governors along the way to Reims that he would forget any past betrayals if they gave him their obedience now. If not, they should expect trouble.

For all of their efforts, Jeanne still felt as if the Dauphin was stalling. She became exasperated and left the castle, choosing to sleep in the fields alone.

"Should I not go with her?" Eve asked Brother Pasquerel.

"Why?" he said. "She'll come back when the Dauphin finally gets on his horse to ride to Reims."

It happened two days later.

Eve would never forget the sight of the Dauphin sitting on his royal steed at the head of his vast army. Following

Jeanne's victory at Patay, men came from all over France to join the coming fight.

"Where are we supposed to be in the procession?" Eve asked Andrew as she looked at the long line of people.

"Somewhere back here," he said.

Together they walked past the Dauphin, with Jeanne next to him. The Duke of Alençon was on her other side. Eve saw the Archbishop of Reims, then Dunois, La Hire, and Captain de Xaintrailles. La Trémoille was there but had been relegated to a spot even farther back and didn't look happy about it.

Finally they came to a collection of wagons carrying provisions for the commanders and nobility. Jean d'Aulon sat at the head of one and offered them both a hand up so they could join him. Eve turned to look at the spectacle behind them. The column of soldiers stretched on and on, out of sight.

It was more than a day's march to the first city: Auxerre. The people there had taken the Dauphin's earlier letter very seriously and responded quickly with money and supplies to keep the peace. Against Jeanne's wishes, the Dauphin's army stayed there for three days before moving on.

The people of Troyes, on the other hand, were not happy to open their gates to the Dauphin. The city had sworn allegiance to the Duke of Burgundy and the English. It also had a garrison of several hundred soldiers ready to fight for that allegiance.

The Dauphin's commanders had to admit that attacking the city would be difficult, and a siege would be fruitless. The city was self-sufficient.

"They could stubbornly resist us for months," La Hire said.

"What are we to do?" asked the Dauphin.

They were considering their options when the officials of Troyes sent a new message. Before they would discuss terms, the officials had asked a friar named Richard to meet with Jeanne. They wanted assurances from the friar that Jeanne was not actually a witch who had put a spell on the Dauphin.

Eve heard rumors that Friar Richard had been a preacher in Paris and had cried out against Jeanne. He had called her the "Antichrist" who would come to destroy the people's souls. Now it looked as if he was going to find out if she really was.

The city gate opened, and Friar Richard walked out. He was a large man with a long beard. As he trekked across the field, he kept crossing himself and sprinkling holy water as if he were about to encounter a demon.

"This is ridiculous," Eve said.

"Do not be offended," Jeanne said. "I have heard good things about him. He preaches good works to prepare for the return of our Lord Jesus. They say the people of Paris were so moved by him that they gave up their sinful practices and turned to holiness."

Friar Richard came nearer.

"You see?" Jeanne called out to him. "I will not fly away. Approach boldly."

He took her hands and looked into her eyes. A smile slowly worked its way onto his grim, bearded face. "This is a time of marvels," he said. "I see in you great hope. The Lord Himself will establish His kingdom in France. And you, dear child, must lead His people to deliver the Holy Sepulchre in Jerusalem. Then we shall see the consummation of the ages."

"As God wills it," Jeanne said.

She invited Friar Richard to her tent. There, she dictated a letter to the officials in Troyes. "As a servant of the King of Heaven, I urge the people in Troyes to give obedience to the Dauphin." She turned to Friar Richard. "One way or the other, the Dauphin, as king, will enter all the cities and towns of France to bring peace."

Friar Richard took the letter back to Troyes. The city's council did not reply. Worse, they would not admit the Dauphin's own messengers through the gates.

"What are they up to?" La Hire demanded.

Dunois said, "The garrison in the town supports the English. The council is afraid of what the soldiers will do if they allow the Dauphin in."

The Duke of Alençon added, "Or they may be awaiting reinforcements from the Burgundians. Either way, they are stalling."

The Dauphin looked unhappy. "We cannot allow such a strong fortress to stand against us," he said. "They will cut off our return."

"We should attack them right away," La Hire said.

Dunois disagreed. "The city is too well defended."

Jeanne finally proclaimed, "Enough of this. We must not delay on a course that God has set. By love, by force, or by courage, I will lead the Dauphin through the gates of Troyes."

She climbed onto her horse and rode to the town gate. The soldiers followed. Jeanne gave the command to prepare for battle. The people of Troyes gathered on the walls to watch as archers were put into position. Brushwood was placed against the walls, and guns were mounted and aimed. Under blazing torches, Jeanne worked the men tirelessly through the night, giving the townspeople a clear view of what would come if they didn't surrender.

By dawn, Jeanne was adorned in her white armor. She was helped onto her horse and handed her banner. She lifted it up and turned slowly, giving every appearance that she was about to give orders to attack.

With loud shouts from the wall, the gates of Troyes were opened. Out came the town officials—and Friar Richard.

Much later, the story was told that Friar Richard had urged the city officials to surrender. He explained that Jeanne was a holy maiden, a true saint, who could bring all of the king's soldiers flying over the walls if it pleased her to do so. The officials were convinced to yield.

As promised, Jeanne led the Dauphin through the gates.

The soldiers of the garrison slipped away through another gate.

The bells rang for Sunday Mass, and Jeanne marched straight to the church.

News of the surrender of Troyes helped cleared the way to Reims. Town after town declared its loyalty to the Dauphin.

Twelve miles from Reims, the entire procession stopped at the fortress at Sept-Saulx. It had been built by ancestors of the Archbishop of Reims. The Archbishop invited them to rest there while he rode ahead to reclaim his place at the Reims cathedral, something he hadn't been able to do for more than a dozen years. It was his role to welcome the new king, even though they had been traveling together. Meanwhile, dignitaries from Reims came and went from the fortress, all assuring the Dauphin of their loyalty.

Eve went with Jeanne to a chapel in Sept-Saulx, and they prayed together. Afterward, Jeanne lingered, sitting quietly. Eve assumed she wanted to be alone, but Jeanne asked her to stay.

Eve sat down next to her on a wooden bench. The altar was lit by two candles in red holders. The crucifix had an amber glow.

Jeanne suddenly said, "I have come so far in such a short time. A peasant girl who has become ..." She couldn't seem to think of the word to describe herself. "Still, there are those who believe I am simple-minded. Perhaps that is what will undo me. My simple trust. Only those who trust can be betrayed."

"I understand," Eve said.

Jeanne continued. "Now that we are so close to the fulfillment of what was promised, I fear that the simplicity of my mission will change. The affairs of state and the intrigues of politics will become a loud scream to me, drowning out my Voices. Then what will become of me?"

"God knows," Eve whispered.

Jeanne nodded. "Yes, my angel. God knows. I am safe with you nearby." She patted Eve's leg and added, "Watch over Andrew."

Eve was surprised. "Why?"

"Combat can be intoxicating for young men," said Jeanne. "They drink it in. It becomes part of them. It can impair their judgment."

"Has it done that to you?" Eve asked.

Jeanne was silent for a moment. "The taste of that drink does not appeal to me. If I could have completed this mission by methods of peace, I would have been happier. For soldiers of either side to die in their sins grieves me."

Jeanne stood up, genuflected, then walked to the door. "I must find Brother Pasquerel," she said. "I must give my confession."

Eve watched her go with a deep sadness. Once the Dauphin was crowned, they would be even closer to the end.

The Dauphin, with Jeanne at his side, led the long procession to Reims. Eve sat behind Andrew on a slow-moving nag of a horse. It smelled of dirt and manure and constantly flicked flies with its tail.

Peasants had trod the road for them along great fields of poppies and lilies. As the procession passed by, the people cheered and waved white handkerchiefs. Fathers and mothers lifted children up to be blessed—not by the Dauphin, but by Jeanne.

The procession came to the high road along the bank of the Vesle River. It was evening, and the view of the city was breathtaking. People lined the ramparts waving flags. Bells rang and cannons boomed. The drawbridge at the southern gate lowered, and the iron gates lifted up to greet them.

Inside, the crowds lined the streets with blazing torches. Townspeople waved hats and handkerchiefs. Trumpets and drums sounded in great fanfare. "Noel! Noel! Peace to our king!" the people shouted, but Eve noticed that their eyes were on Jeanne.

When the procession reached the cathedral steps, the Archbishop and the city's dignitaries formally received the Dauphin. The moon bathed the majestic building in pale white light. Eve looked in awe at its size. Twin towers stood like giant sentries. Three high arches crowned the front doors. Magnificent pillars and spires reached heavenward. A large stained-glass window, rounded and webbed like a giant flower, glowed with red and blue and purple from the burning lights within. After many speeches were made, the Dauphin was taken inside for private prayer.

The Dauphin and Jeanne were invited to stay at the Archbishop's luxurious palace. As Eve left to accompany Jeanne to her room, she gave Andrew an apologetic look. He was going to stay with Jean d'Aulon and the other squires in the servants' quarters.

According to tradition, the coronation had to take place on a Sunday. That was the next day. While the dignitaries slept, the cathedral workers spent the night making preparations. Eve had thought she might sleep a few hours, but the pounding of hammers woke her up.

As it turned out, no one around Jeanne slept anyway. Her armor and sword had to be polished. Tunics and tights were stitched and cleaned. Jeanne's banner was given another fresh scrubbing. Formal dresses were delivered, but Jeanne insisted on wearing her armor. Brother

Pasquerel and Friar Richard, who had accompanied them from Troyes, were ready to hear Jeanne's confession or offer her spiritual counsel at any time.

Louis de Coutes arrived from Chinon that night. Guillaume Bellier had given Louis formal permission to remain with Jeanne for as long as she needed him.

An even greater surprise came when Jeanne's father, Jacques, arrived at the palace door. He had traveled from Domrémy for the coronation. They had not seen each other since Jeanne set off for Vaucouleurs seven months ago. Eve thought Jacques had the hard look of a man who had spent his life working the fields. She could not imagine him being soft and emotional. Yet he embraced his daughter with great tenderness and a few tears.

Jeanne returned his embrace not as a young peasant girl but with the confidence of an adult. They moved off to talk in private. Eve later heard that Jacques had spoken to Jeanne about petitioning the newly crowned king to ease the tax burden on the people of Domrémy.

Jeanne offered to pay for her father's lodging in Reims. But she discovered that the people of Reims had covered the cost in her honor. They had also given Jacques a beautiful horse to take home.

———————————➤

Eve didn't know at what hour she was finally able to lie down. All she knew was that her eyes were open when the light of dawn shone through the small windows of her room.

Soon, a new commotion of activity began. Mass was celebrated and then a light meal was served. There was also a final check to make sure everything was ready for the coronation that would start at nine o'clock. Eve was given a dress of heavy red velvet to wear.

Jeanne wore her white armor, which had been polished to a radiant sheen. Over the armor was draped a cape of blue and red, woven through with gold thread. Jeanne's cropped hair had been combed back but still fell forward in places, as if invisible fingers moved it around.

"You look beautiful," Eve said.

Jeanne tearfully waved her away. "Go. Find Andrew. Seek out a place to watch the ceremony."

"Why are you crying?" Eve asked.

"Because my gentle Dauphin will finally be crowned king today," she replied.

Venturing into the city square, Eve was shocked to find the crowds already waving flags and pennants. She guessed they had been gathering all night. She squeezed into the cathedral, which was overflowing with nobility, officials, soldiers, and toward the rear, peasants.

The cathedral itself was more than Eve could take it. It must have been three or four hundred feet long with pillars lining each side. Vast arches rose up to smaller pillars and a vaulted ceiling of stone ribs. At the far end of the cathedral was an arrangement of stained-glass windows, dominated by one that looked like a kaleidoscope. Beneath that were more arches and stained-glassed images framed by two walls with countless statues of the saints. An ornate altar stood in the center beneath all the arches and windows. Banners hung to greet the nobles. The smell of hundreds and hundreds of flowers filled the air.

"Eve!"

The voice was a distant call amid the noise and echoes. She looked around.

"Eve!"

Her gaze followed the sound up to a gallery above her on the right. Andrew was there waving.

She held her arms up in a "What are you doing up there?" gesture.

Pointing with exaggerated effort, Andrew shouted. "Go under to the door! On the other side of the pillars. I'll meet you!"

Eve pushed her way through the crowd and came to a long aisle on the back side of the pillars. She had to maneuver through another crush of people as she searched for a door. There were a lot of doors. Then Andrew appeared at one and beckoned her over.

"This is crazy," she said, breathless.

He pulled her through the doorway and closed it quickly. They stood in a small passage, with dim light from somewhere above.

"You look good," he said, gesturing to her dress.

She curtsied as a thank you.

She saw that Andrew was wearing a bright-green tunic with gold stitching around the neck, and a belt of gold ringlets. The leggings were a dark-blue wool.

"These leggings itch," he said. "Come on."

They followed a narrow passage to yet more passages.

"This reminds me of the secret corridors at Chinon," Eve said.

"It was Friar Richard's idea to come here," Andrew explained. "There are upper galleries that'll give us a great view of the ceremony."

They eventually came to a staircase that ascended higher and higher, until they reached another door that led to an upper aisle. Guards were posted there. One of them recognized Andrew. With a nod, he signaled them to go through.

Friar Richard was right. The gallery overlooked the main part of the cathedral and the altar where the ceremony would take place.

It was hard for Eve to keep up with all the traditions of the day. She learned from Andrew that Gilles de Rais and three other knights from a nearby abbey had retrieved an ancient flask of holy oil at six o'clock that morning. The sacred oil of Clovis, named after the first French king, would be used to anoint the Dauphin as the true king of France. In a separate ceremony, the four knights escorted a bare-footed abbot to the cathedral and handed the oil over to the Archbishop.

Andrew learned about this firsthand because he was dragged out of bed to help with it all.

Following the delivery of the oil, the constable of
France brought the royal sword to the altar. A specially
chosen sword bearer held up the sword for the rest of the
coronation.

Andrew nudged Eve. "Look." He pointed down at the
crowd.

Eve looked, unsure of what she was supposed to see.
Then she spotted Simon Le Fantôme standing in the
midst of the crowd. Instead of watching the ceremony, he
was staring up at them. Eve shivered.

Trumpets sounded, echoing loudly throughout the
cathedral. The Dauphin had arrived, along with his
generals, clergy, officials, and delegates. They walked
slowly toward the altar as a choir sang. The Dauphin was
wearing a dark robe, open at his chest and shoulders to
reveal a dull-colored shirt. He had a sad expression on
his face. Eve thought he looked scrawny compared to the
nobles around him.

Jeanne also entered the cathedral carrying her standard.
She reached the sanctuary, bowed to the altar, then stood
a few feet away from the Dauphin. Her face was alight
with joy.

The Archbishop offered prayers, and then the Dauphin
took his place in front of the altar and swore an oath to
serve Christ and the nation. A pair of royal shoes was then
placed on his feet, and he knelt down.

The Duke of Alençon was given the royal sword. With
it, he knighted the Dauphin. Golden spurs were added to
the royal shoes.

The Archbishop then led a solemn High Mass with prayers and psalms. Afterward, he anointed the Dauphin's head, chest, shoulders, and arms with the sacred oil and loudly consecrated the Dauphin to God.

The people shouted in response, "Noel! Noel!"

The Dauphin was then dressed in royal robes and given a ring and scepter. Then the crown was placed on his head.

Again, the people shouted, "Noel! Noel!"

Even now, Eve thought the Dauphin looked small and miserable as he sat down on an ornately carved throne. From this moment on, he was no longer the Dauphin. He was Charles the Seventh, the true king of France.

Eve saw Jeanne kneel at the king's feet. She said something to him, then began to weep.

The ceremony continued with various lords and peers of France pledging their loyalty to their sovereign. Then, to Eve's surprise, a group of them lifted the throne high on their shoulders so that everyone could see their newly crowned king. Deafening shouts and cheers went up, along with chants of "Long live the king!"

The trumpets sounded again. The king and the nobles marched out of the cathedral in a grand procession. Five hours after the coronation ceremony had started, it came to a rousing end.

Eve turned to Andrew. He was leaning forward on the rail of the gallery, looking intently at the crowd below.

"Is Simon still there?" Eve asked.

"I'm not looking at him. I'm looking at ..." Andrew gasped, then stepped back from the rail. "It's him. I'm sure it's him."

"Who?" asked Eve.

"The assassin!" Andrew whispered. He moved forward again and pointed at a man wearing a dark cloak and hood at the edge of the crowd. "It's Vincent the Ravager."

From where she stood, it was hard for Eve to get a clear look at the man's face. He was making his way through the jostling crowd. Suddenly the hood slipped back. Eve saw a strap circling a shaved head. The man turned slightly. The strap was attached to an eye patch. A chill went down her spine.

"He can't be the only man in France with an eye patch," she said, hoping it wasn't him.

"He is the only man in the cathedral who was watching *Simon* instead of the coronation," Andrew said.

Eve looked again. As the man with the eye patch moved with the crowd, he was staring at Simon. Simon didn't seem to notice. His head was turned to the altar. He was watching Jeanne.

Eve kept her eyes on the Ravager. "Why is he here? Who did he come to kill?"

"I have to go down and warn Simon," Andrew said and sprinted away.

"Be careful!" Eve said.

But Andrew was already beyond hearing her.

Eve looked over the railing. Both Simon and the one-eyed man were out of her sight. She couldn't see Andrew at all. She wasn't even sure where he had gone. Now all she could think to do was warn Jeanne. With the crush of the coronation crowds, it wouldn't be an easy task.

———————————▶

Though the coronation ceremony had finished, the celebrations were just beginning. The king rode through the streets to hear the praises of the townspeople. Then he presented gifts to the Archbishop and the various officials of Reims for their services. He honored a few men with new positions. Gilles de Rais was made the marshal of France. La Trémoille was given the title of count. The Laval brothers were also made counts. La Hire was given as much land in the county of Longueville as he could reclaim from the English. Jeanne remained with the king at every moment.

With great difficulty, Eve drifted through the crowd, watching for Andrew or Simon or even the one-eyed assassin.

Later, the Archbishop hosted a lavish meal in an ancient banquet hall at his palace. Tradition demanded that the royal table stretch into the street to encourage feasting throughout the town. A bronze stag was placed in one of the courtyards and filled with wine so the people could drink from it.

Eve prayed that Andrew would suddenly appear and all would be well. But he didn't.

What could she do? There was no police station where she could file a missing-person's report. What could anyone do to help?

She kept her eye on Jeanne, who stayed near the king throughout the day. Once or twice she tried to get close enough to warn Jeanne, but the king's guards blocked her way. Even explaining that she was Jeanne's "angel" didn't make a difference. And screaming didn't seem like an option, since there was no imminent danger. For all Eve knew, the assassin was nothing more than a story a madman had made up and Andrew had believed.

It was late afternoon now. Eve watched as Jeanne slipped away from the king's table and disappeared behind a decorative screen. Maybe this was her chance.

She circled around to a doorway, but one of the Archbishop's guards stopped her. She explained that she was the Archbishop's guest and Jeanne's servant. The guard recognized her and allowed her through. It took a few minutes, but she eventually found her way back to Jeanne's bedroom.

Jeanne was sitting in a chair next to her bed. She had taken off her armor and dropped it on the floor at her feet. She now rubbed her face wearily.

"Jeanne—," Eve began to say, but Jeanne spoke instead.

"The Duke of Burgundy sent a delegation to the coronation today. They claim the duke wants to negotiate a peace. The king desires to meet with all of his advisers first thing tomorrow." Jeanne sighed a deep and weary sigh. "I fear it is a ploy. I am weary of ploys. I fear that hidden within all these ploys, there is treason."

She tilted her head back and closed her eyes.

Eve opened her mouth, but suddenly she didn't have the heart to bring up Andrew or Simon. What would be the point? What could Jeanne do? Even telling her about the assassin would not help. Jeanne had thrown herself into far more dangerous situations. And as it was, Eve knew that Jeanne would not die by an assassin's hand.

She realized it would be better for her to talk to Jean d'Aulon. Or Louis.

She nodded to herself. *That's what I'll do.*

Jeanne was looking at her. "Are you all right, my angel?"

"Are you going out again to the celebrations?" Eve asked.

"No. I want to stay here," she said. "I need to pray."

"Good."

"Why?" asked Jeanne.

"It may not be safe ... out there," Eve said.

Jeanne gave a small giggle. "It is never safe for me out there. And yet I am safe. God is my shield."

"Please pray that God will shield the rest of us," Eve said.

"Dear Evangeline, have you not seen that He already does?"

Throughout the evening and into the night, Eve exhausted herself searching for Andrew. It seemed impossible, with the city lights reduced to torches and bonfires. She was a stranger to Reims and knew nothing about its many streets or what might await her down the dark alleyways.

She approached random people to ask if they'd seen a boy in a bright-green tunic. They looked at her as if she was insane. How could they possibly spot a twelve-year-old boy in such a crowd? She then asked passersby about a man with a patch over his eye. No one had seen him.

She eventually found Louis outside the Archbishop's palace. He was alarmed to hear what had happened and promised to search for Andrew himself. He would also tell Jean d'Aulon if their paths crossed.

The revelries showed no sign of ending. Eve began to despair. There was no explaining Andrew's disappearance except to think that something bad had happened.

Finally Eve decided to go back to the cathedral to pray. Maybe stopping for a few moments would clear her wearied brain.

As she approached the steps to the great cathedral doors, she saw a dark figure in a long robe. The figure was pacing slowly back and forth in the half light of a torch. It could have been a monk, but her instincts told her it wasn't. The figure turned as she reached the top step. It was Simon.

She froze, just out of arm's reach.

"Where is Andrew?" she demanded.

"Your friend is a fool," said the old man.

"Where is he?" she asked again.

Simon looked annoyed. "By what manner of ignorance did he think he could approach a known assassin?"

Eve felt her heart lurch. "He went to find *you*. To warn you."

"The only warning I received was a message from Vincent," he said.

Eve swallowed hard. "What message?"

"He has taken Andrew hostage."

Eve slumped down on the cathedral step. "He kidnapped Andrew?"

Simon stood over her. "Vincent has been watching me. He has seen Andrew in my company. He assumed Andrew is worth a ransom to me."

Eve put her face in her hands. She couldn't believe this was happening. "What kind of ransom?"

"He wants something from me."

Eve looked up. "What does he want?"

"Something of mine that he has sought for years."

A realization came to her. "So he was here for you? He did not come to kill Jeanne?"

"He came for her. But he also came for me."

"You have to save Andrew. Give him what he wants," Eve said.

Simon snorted. "What is the boy to me?"

"He was trying to save you!"

Simon seemed unimpressed. "He failed."

"What if the Ravager kills him?"

Simon gave a slight shrug. "A man like Vincent can do far worse things than that. Terrible things."

"What are you talking about? What does he want?" Eve could not imagine it was worth more than Andrew's life.

"It is not for you or anyone else to know," he replied.

Eve was stunned. "You will let Andrew die?"

Simon walked down a few steps until he was eye level with Eve. "I do not believe he will kill Andrew."

"Why should I believe you?" Eve asked, avoiding his gaze.

"What other choice do you have?" the old man said.

"Then what is going to happen if you will not give the Ravager what he wants?" she asked.

"I will rescue your friend."

"How? Do you know where he is?"

"They are well on their way to Paris by now," said Simon. "It is there the assassin will want me to hand over my treasure."

Eve stood up. Knowing *where* Andrew was gave her hope. "Paris? How far is that?"

"Two or three days' journey."

"Can we run after them? If we catch up, then—"

Simon interrupted her. "Vincent is half a day ahead of us by now. He will not travel a normal route. He will take the boy somewhere secret."

"And then what?" she asked.

"I will send a message that I will pay a ransom."

"Where will you send the message?"

"There is an inn that we both know," Simon replied.

Eve clenched her fists. "Then we have to go there."

Simon shook his head. "Not *we*, child. *Me*."

"I am going with you."

"Oh? You will leave your Maiden?" His question was like a taunt. "What will become of her without her angel?" Simon asked.

"Do not tease me," Eve said.

"It is a serious question," Simon said. "Will she live without you? Will she live at all?"

Eve looked at him. Suddenly she had the feeling that he already knew the answer. "Do you know?"

He gazed at her without expression. "An imbecile can venture a guess," he said.

"Not a guess. Do you *know*?" She wondered if Andrew had been right about Simon.

He blinked, then shook his head as if he was trying to rid himself of an unwanted thought.

Eve's temper flared. "What if I say to you *Hope Springs*?"

Simon looked as if she had struck him.

"What does Hope Springs mean to you?" she persisted. "You said those words to Andrew. Why? Does it have something to do with the Ravager?"

Simon staggered back, his heel catching on a step. He stumbled and caught himself. "You are an enchantress!" he shouted. "You are sowing evil seeds in my mind!"

A man and a woman passing on the street stopped to look at him, then her. He glared at them.

Eve came closer to him than she had ever dared. "Help Andrew, and we will help you. We will figure out why words like *Hope Springs* mean something to you."

"I do not know what you are talking about!" Simon protested in a harsh voice. Then he turned and rushed away, fading into the shadows of the cathedral.

Eve's legs felt as if they were about to give out. She sat down on the step again.

"Are you all right?"

Eve turned to the sound of the voice. Louis was ascending the cathedral steps. His hand was on his sword.

"Andrew was taken hostage by the Ravager," she said.

Louis groaned.

Eve lowered her head. "And I just chased away the one person who can help him."

Louis convinced Eve that the only thing she could do now was get some rest.

He escorted her back to the Archbishop's palace. Music and laughter echoed down the many passages. She thanked Louis and went back to Jeanne's bedroom. Jeanne was sound asleep.

Stepping back into the hallway, she gently closed the door again.

There's nothing I can do, she thought. She slumped wearily to the floor. Cradling her arms on her knees, she put her head down. She was too drained to think.

A hand touched her shoulder.

She looked up into the face of Brother Pasquerel. "Are you well?" he asked.

Eve burst into tears.

Brother Pasquerel sat down next to her on the floor. He listened as she explained about Andrew.

"What could Simon Le Fantôme possibly have that the Ravager would kidnap Andrew to get?" he asked after she had finished.

"I wish I knew," Eve said.

"I will pray for wisdom," said Brother Pasquerel. "Given the right moment, we should also tell Jeanne. But I am afraid there is little any of us can do at the moment."

Eve felt tears coming again.

"It is difficult for me to say, but I am afraid you will have to trust Simon."

Eve looked at him. "Trust him?"

"The Ravager is part of Simon's world. He knows that world better than anyone. Simon may be the only hope you have of getting Andrew back."

Eve suddenly sat up in bed. She had fallen asleep, but for how long?

Throwing aside the bed covers, she went to the door and peeked into the adjoining room. Jeanne was not in her bed. The light streaming through the window suggested it was well into the morning.

She changed quickly from her nightdress into the plain red dress Jeanne had given her. She laced up her boots and ventured out to find the dining room where she'd had breakfast the day before. It was empty. The table was cleared of dishes, except a single bowl of fruit in the center.

Eve was about to leave when a door opened on the opposite side of the room.

Louis walked in. He saw her and smiled. "You are awake."

"Where is everyone?"

"I am here," he said, as if that should be enough.

"Where is Jeanne?"

Louis plucked an apple from the bowl on the table. "She is in a meeting with the king and his council. The Duke of Burgundy wants to negotiate a truce with King Charles." Louis took a bite of the apple. "The king wants to meet with the duke's emissaries. Some of us think it is a trick. The Duke of Burgundy and the Duke of Bedford are stalling for time while they build up their reinforcements in Paris."

"Paris?" Eve asked. "Are we going to Paris?"

"Not while the king meets with the duke's men." Louis looked at the apple, then took another bite. "Jeanne and La Hire have protested. The king will not listen."

"I will go to Paris on my own," she said.

Louis asked, "Do you know how to get there? Do you have money or food for the journey? How will you survive?"

Eve could not answer.

"Even if you reached Paris, how do you think you would find Andrew?"

Eve pouted. "I thought you were going to help me."

Louis put the half-eaten apple on the table and came to her. "I am. I know where Simon is. He has not left the city yet. I must say, he does not behave like a man who intends to go anywhere anytime soon."

"What am I to do in the meantime?"

"Be patient and wait," he said.

Eve felt as if she was going mad. Waiting was torture for her.

The king delayed his decision about Paris.

Louis reported to Eve that Simon was going about his usual business at the garrison as if nothing had happened.

Jeanne filled her time riding through the streets of Reims to meet the citizens. Though, privately she told Eve that she was becoming irritated by the king's indecision. She also felt as if the king and his counselors no longer cared what she thought. Now that Charles was officially the king of France, they assumed her mission was over.

Eve was with Jeanne one afternoon when she caught the Archbishop coming from a meeting with the king. The king had not changed his mind, he told her.

Jeanne said, "Then by God's grace, I wish the king would allow me to put aside this fighting and return to my father and mother. I would prefer the peace of keeping sheep with my sister and brothers. *They* will rejoice to see me."

The Archbishop merely smiled and walked on.

Three days later, the king announced that he and the Duke of Burgundy had agreed upon a truce of fifteen days. After this time, they would resume negotiations in the city of Arras.

"*Fifteen days!*" roared La Hire. "It is enough time for the English and the Burgundians to join forces in Paris."

King Charles was determined to give every chance for peace. Meanwhile, he would honor an age-old tradition for newly crowned kings: he would travel with his entire court to the Abbey of Saint-Marcoul de Corbeny. The abbey was founded by Saint Marcoul, who, according to tradition, could cure the evil disease of scrofula by the power of his touch. It was believed that the kings of France were given this same miraculous ability if they went to the abbey after being crowned.

"Sick people are waiting for me to come cure them," the king said.

Jeanne asked to accompany him. He agreed.

Eve did not want to leave Reims. She worried about all of the things that might happen to Andrew. Finally she told Louis that she wanted to talk to Simon again.

Louis led the way through Reims to the garrison near the castle. Many of the king's soldiers were quartered there. Simon was brushing a horse as they approached. He glanced over and saw Louis first.

"This is not the time for our fencing lesson, is it?" Simon asked.

Eve now understood how Louis had been able to keep an eye on him.

Louis nodded to Eve.

Simon looked at her and said, "What does she want?" He went back to brushing the horse.

"Is this all you plan to do?" Eve asked.

"I have not heard from the Ravager," he said. "What else am I to do until then? March to Paris? Search every house, room, and hovel until I find him?"

"You said something about an inn," Eve reminded him.

The old man turned to her. "I know what you are thinking. It will not work. If I go there before I am summoned, the Ravager will know it. Do you want him to kill your friend?" He spun back to the horse. "There is nothing to do but wait."

That night, Eve did not eat. She could not stomach any food while she thought about Andrew. Where was the Ravager keeping him? Was he tied up? Beaten? Was he fed?

Jeanne pushed her own plate away. A servant quickly appeared and took the plate from the table. Her glass of wine was refilled. Jeanne ignored it.

"Brother Pasquerel told me about Andrew," Jeanne said to Eve. "I have been praying for him."

"There must be something else we can do," Eve said.

"I would go to Paris myself to rescue him, but the king forbids me from venturing near that city. So I will go with him to the Abbey of Saint-Marcoul de Corbeny. I bid you come with me. To lose one of my angels is grievous. To lose both would break my heart."

Eve struggled with Jeanne's invitation to go to the abbey. Louis insisted that she go. He assured her he would stay at Reims and watch Simon. If anything happened, he would send a messenger immediately.

Eve unhappily agreed and traveled the next day to the abbey with Jeanne and the king's court. There, the king worshiped and presented offerings at the shrine of Saint Marcoul. Then he touched those afflicted with scrofula. Jeanne offered prayers and blessings for the many who asked. Eve got the impression that the king was not pleased to be upstaged by the Maiden.

News reached them that many of the nearby towns were pledging their loyalty to the king of France. King

Charles decided to visit each town to pay his respects. Eve found herself taken farther and farther away from Paris—and Andrew.

She wondered why she couldn't ask the king to help. Couldn't he send his soldiers to Paris to find Andrew?

She put the question to Jeanne, who answered that the king was as helpless as anyone. "Paris is in the hands of the Duke of Burgundy. Until the king decides to trust me rather than him, there is nothing we can do."

One night, Eve found Jeanne praying in the chapel of yet another manor house where they had been staying. Eve could not even remember which town they were in. Was it Soissons or Château-Thierry?

Eve knelt next to the Maiden and prayed for Andrew. Then she sat back and wished God would do *something*. Andrew believed that God had brought them to this time for a purpose. Was that it? Being held hostage by an assassin? Was this her purpose: sitting and waiting yet again for an indecisive king?

"The Voices are not clear," Jeanne said.

The statement yanked Eve away from her own thoughts. "What did you say?"

Jeanne sat on the bench next to Eve. "All along I have felt as if my Voices have been holding my hand, guiding me as a child. But now they have let go. They want me to decide for myself."

"Decide what?" Eve asked.

"What my place is now that the Dauphin has become the king," she replied. "You see? He has been my mission. Now I must think differently about why I am here. My Voices have gone silent, so I will think on my own."

Eve wondered if this had something to do with what she was just thinking about. "What if there is no purpose?" she asked.

Jeanne took Eve's hand in hers. "There is always a purpose with God. It is against His very nature not to have a purpose."

Eve thought about that for a moment. "What do you think your purpose is now?" she asked.

"To attack Paris."

———————————➤

Eve knew there was little hope of a lasting truce between King Charles and the Dukes of Burgundy and Bedford. She was now hearing that Bedford had been sending insulting messages to the king. He also made scathing comments about that "deranged woman who dresses like a man."

In recent days, there were a couple of close calls when the French and English armies came very near each other but backed off from actual combat.

Though more towns around Paris pledged their allegiance to King Charles, the city itself remained in the clutches of Bedford. The English duke did exactly what the French king's commanders had said: he reinforced his army in Paris.

One morning, yet another inflammatory letter arrived from Bedford. The king was finally offended enough to act. He ordered his commanders to claim the village of Montépilloy, just north of Paris. Jeanne joined them, but only as an adviser to the king.

When the French army arrived at Montépilloy, they discovered that the English had fortified their positions with their usual rows of sharpened stakes.

Jeanne urged the commanders to attack, but they were ordered to wait for permission from the king. The French and English forces sat stewing in the sweltering August heat.

King Charles arrived with La Trémoille. Together they rode around the battlefield and then left again that evening.

Reinforcements had arrived that afternoon from Reims. They brought with them complaints from the citizens of that city that the English would invade now that the king had left. Jeanne sent a letter promising that she would never abandon them, no matter what truces were made.

Louis and Simon were among the reinforcements. Eve was pleased to see Louis again, and asked if any word had come from Vincent the Ravager. The answer was no.

Eve insisted that Louis take her to Simon. They found him on the far edge of the camp.

"Why have you not heard from the Ravager?" Eve asked the old man.

"It is a war of nerves," Simon told her. "Much as you see with these two armies. Though we know who are the true masters."

"Who?" asked Louis.

"The Duke of Bedford has made the Duke of Burgundy the official governor of Paris," Simon replied, then mocked, "The king giveth, and the dukes taketh away."

———————➤

The next morning, Jeanne took to her horse and rode along the front lines, waving her banner and daring the English to attack.

They did not take the bait.

She dictated a letter to the English commander, warning him to prepare for battle. She did not receive a response.

Then, without warning, the English gave up Montépilloy and marched back to Paris. The entire confrontation was a waste of time.

"They are gathering their forces to strengthen the city," said the Duke of Alençon. "Paris will be harder to invade."

Jeanne was unconcerned. "Let them go to Paris. I would rather fight there than sit idly here for days on end."

Eve watched the English army march away. "I wonder if I could sneak into Paris with them," she said to Louis.

"Do not think about it," he warned.

She went to see Simon again. "We are so close," she said. "Why not go to Paris now to save Andrew?"

"Why are you bothering me?" Simon grumbled. "I have told you that *we* will not save Andrew. You are a wicked child. You must be patient. There are forces at work that you know nothing about. We will get closer to Paris before you expect it."

Furiously she asked, "But what happens to Andrew while we wait?"

"He also waits," said Simon.

"In what condition?" she asked. "What is happening to him?"

What is happening to me? Andrew wondered. He knelt on the cold stone floor and winced. There was little left of his leggings to protect his knees. Both the cloth and his skin were worn away. The open sores burned.

He grabbed a cloth, and a terrible stinging came back to his palms and fingers. Some of the blisters that had formed now broke open again.

"Work!" a raspy voice commanded. It was an innkeeper by the name of Henri, though Vincent the Ravager always called him Scab. The name suited him. Hardly a skeleton of a man, Henri had red scars on his forehead and cheeks that made his face look like a wound that would never heal.

Andrew grabbed the rag again and, ignoring the pain, scrubbed at the floor. He knew what would happen if he didn't. Scab owned a fat walking stick and liked to use it. If Andrew had a question, the answer was a blow with the stick. If he did a job poorly, a blow with the stick. If he did a job well, a blow with the stick. If he did nothing at all, a blow with the stick.

Scrubbing was Andrew's morning job. Later he would pick up cups and plates from drunken townspeople. Often he would have to mop up after soldiers who had gotten sick on the floor.

A large, dog-faced woman with dark whiskers on her upper lip forced Andrew to help her in the crude kitchen. He helped her make stew in a large pot, boil water in the kettle, cut vegetables, and make the bread. He never heard the woman's name. She never offered it.

The August heat outside and the infernal heat in the kitchen made Andrew thirsty. He was allowed one cup of stagnant water a day.

At night he was chained to an iron ring in the wall in a back room. The woman threw him some moldy bread to eat. There all alone, he often wanted to cry. But he refused. He didn't want to give Scab or anyone else the satisfaction of knowing he had done it.

One day as Vincent the Ravager watched Andrew work, he said, "You still have hope. That's good. Always have hope. Hope is what keeps people alive right up until I kill them. I enjoy the look on my victims' faces when hope drains away with their lives."

Andrew blamed himself for his situation. He had gone to warn Simon about Vincent, but then he saw the assassin leave the cathedral in the massive crowd. He stupidly decided to follow the man and find out where he was staying. He thought, unwisely, that he could report back to Simon.

Vincent had disappeared around a corner, and Andrew dashed after him. Vincent was waiting.

A hard knock on the head left Andrew stunned enough that he could be dragged off. He was taken to a storehouse, maybe. Somewhere with barrels and boxes. He was tied and gagged and put in a crate.

"Kick and scream all you want," Vincent had said in a voice like broken glass. "No one will hear you. But if you do make a commotion, you will suffer."

Andrew wasn't sure how many hours he was stuffed in the crate. Nor could he figure out where the crate was being moved to after it was loaded on a wagon. Vincent let him out from time to time, when they were away from anyone who might ask why a boy was tied up and locked in a crate.

They eventually came to a noisy city. Andrew was unpacked and put in the care of Scab until Vincent returned. Scab didn't ask where Vincent was going. Vincent never said. Andrew got the impression they had done this sort of thing before.

He overheard enough conversations to learn that he was in Paris. He also learned that he was being kept at an inn called the Captain's Cat. He was never allowed to venture beyond the door to look outside. He didn't know in what part of the city the inn was located.

Andrew looked for ways to escape, but Scab watched him constantly by day and chained him up at night. Scab warned him, "Do not let me catch you trying to escape. Do not let me catch you *looking* like you want to escape. Otherwise, you will not live long enough to know what the consequences will be."

Andrew believed him.

Scab only ever called Andrew "boy" or "the hostage." He often talked about how things would change once Andrew was ransomed. Andrew tried to explain that it was a waste of time. No one would ransom him.

Scab hit him on the back with the stick and said, "Why would you say such a thing? Do you want to die now? The ransom is the only thing that is keeping you alive."

Andrew kept his mouth shut after that. He said so little that most of the customers thought he was a mute. Instead, he listened.

It was from the soldiers that he heard rumors about the "pretender to the throne." They meant King Charles. They also talked about the "French peasant girl." Andrew figured they were talking about Jeanne. He heard them say how the Duke of Bedford and the Duke of Burgundy were making fools of them with all of their talk of a peace treaty.

Andrew overheard some of the peasants say that the French were marching near Paris. Then came rumors that they weren't.

The Duke of Bedford kept reminding the people of Paris that Charles was not really the son of the king. Worse than that, he had murdered the Duke of Burgundy's father. *Killed him in cold blood!* the duke cried.

All of this talk seemed to make Vincent the Ravager angrier. He and Scab had been convinced that Jeanne would march the French army straight into Paris after the coronation. Simon would come with them and hand over his treasure in exchange for Andrew. It was as simple as that. But the French army did not attack. Maybe it never would. Vincent would have to contact Simon and arrange another way to meet up for the exchange.

Andrew wished he knew his history better. Had Jeanne ever marched into Paris? Was this where they burned her at the stake? He didn't know.

Then the night before, Andrew had heard one soldier say that Jeanne and the Duke of Alençon had captured the town of Saint-Denis. It was only four miles outside Paris. The same soldier suggested that more French captains were on the march to Paris with hundreds, if not thousands, of soldiers. King Charles himself might even show up.

Vincent sat at a table, drank watered-down ale, and told Scab to beware. "Simon is bound to show up now, with or without the stone."

Andrew had heard the words *ransom* and even *treasure* before, but nothing about a stone. *What stone?*

Scab argued that Simon would not hand over something so precious. Not for Andrew, not for anybody. "Why should he care what happens to this boy?" He hooked a thumb at Andrew, who was scraping something disgusting from the leg of a chair.

"There is something special about the boy," Vincent said. "I do not know what, but it is enough for me to believe that Simon will come."

"If he does not?" asked Scab.

Vincent sneered. "Then we will sell him as a slave."

Chained again to the wall, Andrew spent the night thinking about all he had heard.

La Hire had told Andrew that Simon was married to Vincent's sister. They fought over a treasure. The sister was killed. Simon stabbed Vincent in the eye. For what? A treasure they called a stone. Was it a jewel?

What if it was a stone like the Radiant Stone? What if Simon had used it to travel back in time from the future? Maybe even from Hope Springs?

In the middle of the night, it all seemed possible. In the light of day, it all seemed stupid.

The next day, Andrew became aware of a lot of noise outside. It sounded like the whole city of Paris was in an uproar. There were shouts that the peasant Maiden was leading an attack *today*—a *holy* day—the Feast of the Nativity of the Blessed Virgin! Who but a witch would attack a city on such a day?

Even Scab took offense, and he was as profane as a man could be.

The cannon fire started around noon. Scab went to the door of the inn. "Look at them scamper," he said, laughing.

Andrew picked up a few cups near the front window. People were rushing into the streets. Soldiers ran in every direction.

Later came screams and shouts. "They have broken through the gate! All is lost!"

When he heard the thunderous sounds of more cannons, Andrew stopped scrubbing the floor and looked up.

Scab swung the stick at him. "Do your work!"

Andrew ducked.

Scab grabbed Andrew by the nape of the neck and dragged him to the small back room.

"I know what you are thinking," Scab growled. He fastened a manacle around Andrew's ankle and chained it to the ring on the wall.

"It does not matter who comes. You will not escape," he said. He walked out, pulling the wooden door closed behind him.

Andrew waited. It sounded as if Scab had gone to the front door again. Maybe he had left the inn to see the fighting for himself.

Looking down at the manacle, Andrew thought, *One way or another, I'm going to get out of here.*

He twisted his foot around, trying to squeeze it through the iron. The rough edge of the manacle scraped at his skin. He tried to grease his foot with some lard he'd been given to eat the day before. Slowly, painfully the foot was slipping through.

There was a loud crash. It was so loud that Andrew thought a cannon ball had hit the inn. He hadn't thought that he might die in a barrage. He heard voices and shouts from somewhere. He worked harder to get his foot free. He scraped at the skin, hoping the blood would make his foot more slippery.

Then the door burst open. Scab stumbled into the room with a look of utter disgust on his face. He hit the ground as dead weight.

A man in monk's robes stepped through the doorway and kicked the fallen villain. In the man's right hand was a bloody knife. He pushed back his hood.

"Simon," Andrew said, relieved.

"Where is Vincent?" Simon asked.

"Not here."

Simon looked at him, clearly annoyed. "I hope this was not a waste of my time."

This is nothing like the Battle of Orléans, Eve thought as she watched the campaign for Paris from a supply wagon on the hill.

The trumpets had sounded at noon. At the western gate of Saint-Honoré, Jeanne had raised her banner to lead the soldiers. Her courage was endless. Stones and debris were thrown down at them from the ramparts. Arrows and bolts buzzed. Artillery fire went back and forth.

Then the gate opened, and both English and Burgundian soldiers streamed out to protect the city. Savage hand-to-hand combat followed, with the terrifying noise of crashing armor and pain-filled cries. Neither side made any progress in one direction or another. Then the trumpets sounded for the enemy soldiers to retreat into the city.

Jeanne met with the commanders. "You must cross the moats now. Go forward, my friends! Do not give up the assault until Paris is taken!"

As they had done at Orléans, the soldiers now needed to fill the moat with wood. As many bundles as they could find. The soldiers dashed down to the moat, throwing more and more wood into the water below. But the water flowed from the river Seine and carried the wood away.

The English and Burgundian soldiers on the walls released more arrows and bolts. Jeanne urged her soldiers on. "Victory is yours if you persevere!" she shouted.

She also shouted to her enemies on the wall. "Surrender and be saved, or suffer death without mercy when we enter the city!"

Hour after hour this went on. Jeanne finally dismounted and raced for the wall to cheer on the flagging French soldiers. Her page Raymond stayed by her side, carrying her banner.

Eve watched, clutching her hands to her stomach, trying to calm her anxiety. Her eyes went to the top of the wall. She watched with horror as one of the English archers aimed his crossbow at Jeanne. He was clearly following her as she moved. Then she stopped to say something to Raymond. The archer released his bolt.

Eve screamed as Jeanne clutched her leg and dropped to the ground.

Another bolt flew, and Raymond fell. Eve was sure he was dead. But then the poor young man suddenly sat up. He tore off his helmet and clawed at the bolt sticking out of his foot. He had just caught hold of the bolt with both hands when another arrow buzzed from the wall. It struck him between the eyes. He slammed lifeless to the ground.

Captain de Gaucourt and another captain named Guichard Bournel scrambled to Jeanne. De Gaucort shouted, "Sound the retreat! Retreat!"

Eve took a few steps. Then before she realized what she was doing, she found herself running as fast as she could to Jeanne.

Meanwhile, another soldier picked up Jeanne's banner to rally the scattered men. It was too late. The trumpets sounded the signal to retreat.

De Gaucourt and Bournel put Jeanne's arms around their shoulders and lifted her up. The end of the bolt stuck out of her thigh. They began to move her off the battlefield.

She fought against them. "No! We must take the city! More wood into the moat! We can make a bridge!"

"The *king* commands you to retreat," Bournel begged. "The Duke of Alençon pleads with you to come away."

Eve was now running with them.

"Help me!" Captain de Gaucourt gasped to Eve. "Speak to her!"

Eve pleaded, "You must retreat, Jeanne!"

Jeanne pulled her arms from the shoulders of the two men. She limped a few steps for the city gate. "In God's name, the city can be taken!"

Bournel's face turned crimson with rage. "Stubborn girl! You risk all our lives!" He grabbed Jeanne's arm and yanked her back.

Jeanne fought him, but he was too strong. He pinned her arms with his. De Gaucourt reached down and grabbed her kicking legs.

"Please, do not hurt her!" Eve cried out.

With Jeanne firmly in their grip, the two men carried her away from the gate and joined the retreating troops.

Jeanne screamed the entire way, her cheeks covered with hot, angry tears.

Eve wept to see her so upset. And she wept because she had lost all hope of rescuing Andrew.

———————➤

At the camp, Eve watched as a physician dressed Jeanne's wound. The crossbow bolt had split the piece of armor meant to protect her leg and had sunk into her thigh.

Jeanne was heartbroken. "We would have won the city if only we had kept fighting."

Eve stayed with her throughout the night, pressing a cool wet rag to her forehead. Jeanne thrashed in her sleep, crying out words that made no sense.

The next morning, Jeanne was on her feet again, wincing as she struggled to get into her armor. "Victory will be ours today," she told Eve. "Where is my duke?"

Eve helped Jeanne to the tent of the Duke of Alençon. The commanders were all there to plan the next attack. They were divided as usual, with some arguing to delay a renewed attack. An hour passed. Then another.

Jeanne sat in a chair off to the side, excluded from the debate. Eve saw her fidget. Finally she hit the palms of her hands against the arms of the chair. "I beg you to stop arguing! Claim the victory that awaits you!"

A messenger arrived with news that a party of nobles was approaching the camp. One was the Baron de Montmorency. He was well known for switching his allegiance from the English and Burgundians to King Charles. With him were the Duke of Bar and the Duke of Clermont.

"This is good news!" Jeanne said. "Surely they have brought reinforcements to take Paris."

The three noblemen entered the tent, dressed as if they were going to a formal ball.

The captains gave them a respectful bow.

"What goes on here?" the baron asked.

"We are discussing our attack," the Duke of Alençon explained.

"Attack? There will be no attack today or any other day," declared the Duke of Clermont. "Have you not heard? King Charles has commanded that you retreat!"

The commanders were incensed. Jeanne tried to rise from her chair but fell back again.

"If you will not obey," the duke continued, "the king has commanded us to stop you by force. All of you must return to his court at Saint-Denis immediately."

Jeanne groaned as she sunk farther into the chair. "It cannot be."

The Duke of Alençon glared at the three nobles.

"See to it!" the baron said. Then the three turned and walked out.

The Duke of Alençon knelt next to Jeanne. "Ride with me to Saint-Denis."

She gave him a painful nod.

The Maiden tried to hide her agony as she and the captains rode the two miles on horseback to King Charles at the Abbey of Saint-Denis. Eve sat behind Jeanne and tried not to add to her pain by holding on to her too tightly.

When they arrived, King Charles was sitting at a table in a small room. La Trémoille stood nearby. Both men watched silently as the commanders entered and bowed. Jeanne held on to Eve and managed to lower herself into an awkward kneeling position.

The king rose to his feet. In a sudden outburst, he shouted, "*Fifteen hundred men* were killed! Fifteen hundred!"

His gaze went to Jeanne. For only a second, it softened. Then it hardened again.

Jeanne remained kneeling, her face twisted in pain. "Gentle Dauphin," she started to say, but the king held up his hand.

"Why do you call me Dauphin? Am I not your king?" he asked.

"You are," she replied. "Forgive me. I forgot myself."

"You forget much, my valiant warrior," he said. He scanned the faces of his commanders. "We are *ceasing* our campaign."

La Trémoille smirked at them.

"Paris is included in our new truce with the Duke of Burgundy," the king announced. "It is not our city to take."

"A new truce, my king?" the Duke of Alençon asked.

"It awaits my signature," he replied. "There is no need for further battle."

Jeanne fell forward and crawled to the king. She wrapped her arms around his knees. "I beg you, gentle king! If this is so, then please allow me to remove this armor and go home."

The king patted her head. "Alas, no, Jeanne. We have need of you yet."

Eve couldn't bear to hear anymore. She wanted to scream at the king, "I know how this will end! You will blame her for *your* mistakes. You will betray her and make her suffer for daring to speak for God!"

Instead, Eve waited silently. She could not leave Jeanne to struggle out of that room.

Eve helped Jeanne to a bedroom the king had provided for her. Jeanne did not speak as she limped through the abbey. She did not look at Eve as she eased onto the bed.

Eve slipped out of the room. She wanted to find a chapel where she could pray for Jeanne and Andrew. She wanted to ask God to ease her anger.

She followed one passage, then another. It was an abbey. How hard could it be to find a chapel?

Rounding a corner, she ran straight into Simon Le Fantôme. She did a double take. He was wearing something that looked like a monk's robe.

"What are you doing?" she snapped. "Why are you dressed like that?"

"You are a rude little girl," Simon said. He grabbed her arm and began to drag her down the hallway.

She struggled against him. "Let go or I'll scream."

"Scream. I do not care." He pushed open a door with his free hand and shoved her through.

She stumbled and was about to turn on him when she saw something out of the corner of her eye.

It was Andrew. He was sitting on a small bed, holding a bowl with bandaged hands. Brother Pasquerel sat in a chair next to him, putting ointment on his bloodied knees and feet.

Eve let out a little squeak, then put her hands to her mouth.

Andrew smiled at her. "Hi." His voice was weak.

She ran over to him and hugged him so hard that the soup in his bowl splashed onto his chest.

"Careful!" he said.

Eve knelt next to the bed. "What happened? How did you get away?"

Andrew nodded toward the door. "Simon went to kill Vincent and found me instead."

They turned to the doorway, but Simon was gone.

"Simon sneaked into Paris in disguise," Andrew explained to Eve. "He was supposed to join up with an underground movement of Carmelite monks. Their plan was to wait until a French attack started. Then they would run around the city claiming that the French army had broken through. They spread rumors that the French would kill them all if they didn't surrender. They had rebels ready to fight inside the gates."

Eve was astonished. She wondered if Jeanne knew.

"It was working," Andrew said. "The officials were discussing their surrender. But then our army retreated."

"I think I know who sounded the retreat," Eve said. "La Trémoille. Except he hid behind some noblemen."

"That was too bad. They were very close to capturing the city," said Andrew.

"If Paris fell, the English would have lost France," Brother Pasquerel said as he dabbed at Andrew's wounds.

"La Trémoille is no friend to the king," Eve said bitterly.

Andrew nodded. "Simon told me that La Trémoille is on the side of the English. Or the Burgundians. Or maybe himself. He convinces the king to do things that undermine putting France back into his hands."

Eve saw how pale Andrew's face was. His cheekbones stuck out more, probably from lack of food. His eyes had dark circles under them.

"I have to tell you something about Simon's *treasure*," he said, trying to wink at Eve.

"Not now," said Brother Pasquerel. With a grunt, he got to his feet. "You need food and rest."

Eve stood up. "He is right. We can talk about treasure later."

Andrew frowned. "But it is important."

"So is your health," Brother Pasquerel said. He nodded for Eve to leave as he took the bowl and sat it on a bedside table. He gently pushed Andrew to get him to lie down and then tucked him in.

As she closed the door behind her, Eve heard Andrew yawn loudly and say, "But I am not tired."

Eve later found Jeanne in a small chapel in a remote part of the abbey.

Eve entered as quietly as she could. Jeanne was on her knees at the altar. Her hands were clasped in prayer. Eve glanced at the altar, surprised by what she saw there. She knelt next to Jeanne and said a few prayers of her own. Then the two sat on a rough wooden pew together.

In a soft whisper, Eve told Jeanne about Andrew and what she'd heard about La Trémoille.

Jeanne looked at her. With a forced smile she said, "I did not lose Paris because of La Trémoille. I lost it because I did not have both of my angels with me."

"Jeanne, please. You have to be careful with La Trémoille," Eve said.

"I must be careful with everyone," Jeanne said quietly. She was silent for a moment, looking at her calloused hands in her lap. She sighed deeply. "Sweet Evangeline, my Voices have gone silent. I hear only the clamor of the king and his council. What am I to do? I have nothing to offer their world of politics."

Eve's heart ached. "I will not leave you again."

Jeanne nodded to the altar and said bravely, "I have made an offering to Our Lady Mary. I have vowed to follow my king and do as he commands."

Eve suspected that Jeanne was trying to sound positive, but the fire had gone out of her voice. Jeanne stood up slowly, gave a slight bow, and limped out of the chapel.

Eve rose and followed, glancing back at the altar.

Jeanne had placed all of her armor there.

The retreat from Paris had wrecked the morale of everyone who had fought so hard for King Charles. Everyone, that is, except Charles himself and La Trémoille.

Few now doubted that La Trémoille was manipulating the king to his own ends. Many wondered why. There were whispers that La Trémoille had been bribed by either the Duke of Burgundy or the Duke of Bedford—or both.

The king announced that he and his court would be on the move again. He included Jeanne, Eve, and Andrew in his plans. He led his vast court around Paris to the east and then south.

"We are going home to the Loire valley," he said happily.

Eve wondered which home in the valley the king meant. He had a lot of them.

The Duke of Alençon assembled an army of his own to strike into the territories that once belonged to his family. He asked the king to allow Jeanne to go with him. The king and his council refused.

"For you to attack on your own is your right as a duke," said La Trémoille. "For the Maiden to accompany you will be seen as royal approval of your efforts. We must not upset our diplomatic efforts. The king has signed the truce, you know."

Jeanne and the duke offered heartfelt goodbyes to each other. She also bade farewell to the other commanders, who were going their separate ways. Eve suspected Jeanne knew she would never see them again.

Jeanne's brother Pierre, who had been fighting for Jeanne since Orléans, now admitted defeat. "I cannot stay here and watch the king treat you so poorly. I am going back to Domrémy."

Thanking him with a long hug, Jeanne blessed him for his help and sent her love with him to their family.

King Charles commanded Jeanne to rest and fully recover from her various wounds. She unhappily obeyed. Privately she said to Eve that she now feared their drive to reclaim France had been lost.

Over the next several days, the royal court visited the towns of Provins, Courtenay, and Montargis. They even returned to Gien. It was all a blur to Eve.

They finally settled in Bourges, where the king stayed at his residence. Jeanne, Eve, and Andrew lodged at the home of Madame Marguerite La Touroulde, a friend of Queen Marie's. Eve found out that Madame La Touroulde's husband had something to do with managing the king's money.

Madame La Touroulde was an energetic woman in her forties. She was attentive to Jeanne and often riddled her with questions about her life. Jeanne answered politely but vaguely. Eve could tell that she was wary of the woman's motives.

Jeanne was right to feel that way. Eve learned later that Madame La Touroulde would repeat and embellish Jeanne's answers to her socialite friends. She liked to give the impression that she was a *very* close personal friend of Jeanne's.

Eventually Eve realized that Madame La Touroulde was putting Jeanne on display. Guests came to the house to see her, just to say they had done it. A few brought their rosaries for Jeanne to touch and bless. She refused. Their own touches would be as effective as hers, she said.

Madame La Touroulde was also nosy about Eve and Andrew. She quizzed them about where they were from, who their parents were, and how they had become Jeanne's "angels." They tried to answer her questions without really answering at all.

For a while, life was nothing more than a flurry of social encounters and mundane living. After so many adventures, Eve and Andrew both began to feel restless and bored.

Jeanne's wounds, old and new, slowly healed. But Eve noticed that she did not go out into the field to practice with a sword, or even to ride her horse. Instead, she studied Scriptures with Brother Pasquerel and prayed, often for hours.

To Madame La Touroulde's dismay, Jeanne still insisted on wearing a squire's clothes.

After all the battles, Eve thought they had found peace in their lives. She wondered if she would ever return to Hope Springs. The thought made her think of Simon. She remembered her encounter with him on the cathedral steps. She still couldn't believe that he had come from Hope Springs. The odds seemed impossible to her.

She asked Andrew one afternoon what had become of Simon.

"He's disappeared," Andrew replied. "I think he's gone to find Vincent the Ravager."

While Andrew and Eve were in Bourges, a new young man became an ever-present part of their lives. His name was Sir Charles d'Albret. Eve thought he looked familiar, then later realized that he was the one who had held the royal sword at the king's coronation. D'Albret was related to La Trémoille somehow—a half-brother or a nephew or something like that. That made Eve suspicious of him. She wondered if he had been sent to spy on Jeanne or even sabotage her efforts. D'Albret was only in his twenties, but the king put him in charge of the now-shrunken royal army.

"You have work to do," the king told him, then gestured to Jeanne. "You will need her help."

It was October now, and the king wanted d'Albret and Jeanne to reclaim the small town of Saint-Pierre-le-Moûtier. It sounded like busywork to Eve, but Jeanne was excited about the chance to get away from Madame La Touroulde and do something constructive.

Eve had vowed to stay by Jeanne's side. However, Jeanne insisted that she remain behind. Only her squire, Jean d'Aulon, was allowed to accompany her on this new venture.

"You do not need your angels?" Eve asked her.

"This task comes from the king, not my Voices," Jeanne replied.

"You need protection either way," Eve said.

Jeanne laughed. "Jean d'Aulon will give me that."

Off they marched with a modest-sized army. Eve and Andrew waved them on at the town gate. Eve assumed it would be a quick skirmish, and then they'd return. But a week went by, and very little word came back. Then word trickled down to Eve that a messenger had informed the king that the town would not fall easily.

A few days later, a report came that Saint-Pierre-le-Moûtier was taken, thanks to Jeanne's courageous efforts.

Jean d'Aulon returned to Bourges with a wounded foot. He told Eve and Andrew that at one stage of the battle, the army had fully retreated. Jeanne had refused and remained at the moat, trying to build a makeshift bridge to cross it. D'Aulon had raced up to her and asked why she was still there with only a handful of men. She had laughed and said she had *fifty thousand* men at her side. D'Aulon scratched his head. "I counted only five men."

Eve smiled at him. Sometimes the squire didn't understand Jeanne at all.

"What happened then?" Andrew asked.

"She shouted for everyone to 'Lay down wood! Build a bridge! I will not leave this spot until we take the town!' So we did as she said. And we took the town as if we had fifty thousand men with us."

Eve knew it was a repeat of what had happened in Paris. But unlike that campaign, the soldiers obeyed and secured their victory.

When Jeanne eventually returned to Bourges, La Trémoille publicly praised her for adding Saint-Pierre-le-Moûtier to the list of the king's victories. Jeanne replied that she was grateful to have served him.

However, Eve learned that La Trémoille's motives were not pure.

"La Trémoille wanted revenge," Andrew told her as they walked in a field outside of Bourges.

"Revenge for what?" Eve asked. She knew that Andrew was now getting information from servants of the council members he'd befriended.

"The town was run by a mercenary named Perrinet Gressart."

The name meant nothing to Eve.

"Gressart works for whoever pays him the most," Andrew explained. "Right now he's on the side of the English and Burgundians. A couple of years ago, he kidnapped La Trémoille and held him prisoner until a big ransom was paid. La Trémoille has never forgiven him. Now Gressart has his own little kingdom, including Saint-Pierre-le-Moûtier. That's why La Trémoille sent Jeanne there."

"It does not seem like much of a revenge," Eve said.

Andrew frowned. "That's just the beginning. He will send Jeanne off to another town in Gressart's area, where the battle will be bigger and harder."

"Is he trying to get her killed?" Eve asked.

"Killed—or captured," Andrew replied, giving her a worried look.

***

Eve made it a point to stay close to Jeanne in Bourges. If she couldn't protect her in battle, maybe she could protect her there. Eve bristled every time the king or his council summoned Jeanne. The Maiden often returned looking worn out. Eve felt that more and more, the king and his advisers were trying to beat her down. Or worse, she was nothing more than a pet or mascot.

Eve didn't know her history well enough to remember when or how Jeanne was captured.

"I don't remember either," Andrew said. "What difference does it make if we know?"

"We can warn her," Eve told him.

"*Warn* her?" Andrew exclaimed. "We can't mess with history."

Eve stiffened. "I don't care."

Andrew looked stunned. "What? But you're the one who told me that we can't change history, or it will backfire on us—or something like that."

Eve shrugged. "That's what Alfred Virtue said. What if he was wrong?"

"What if he was *right*?" Andrew shook his head. "You once told me that trying to change history is a big mistake. Time fights back. Remember? Alfred Virtue said so!"

"Since when did you become such a rule follower?" she asked, sulking.

Eve knew he was right but couldn't bring herself to admit it. The thought of standing by while Jeanne was captured—and burned at the stake—was too much for her to endure.

That afternoon she saw Brother Pasquerel. He was still teaching Jeanne to read and write. Eve asked if he would hear her confession after their class. He happily agreed.

Sitting down with him in the empty chapel, she began trying to remember her sins since her last confession. After he offered her absolution, she lingered.

"Is there something else?" he asked.

"I was wondering ..." She didn't know how to put it into words. "If a person knows that something bad is going to happen to another person and might be able to stop it, should she?"

Brother Pasquerel looked thoughtful, then said, "We are duty bound to save others from trouble if it is within our power."

Eve smiled.

The priest added, "If I can help you with this person, let me know."

"If I can, I will," she said.

Eve learned quickly that castles were cold in November. The rooms were cold, the chairs were cold, the beds were cold, everything was cold. Fires gave warmth only to those standing next to them.

No matter how many layers of clothes she put on, Eve felt like she was shivering constantly as a damp chill soaked into her bones. At night she slept on her cot under a stack of blankets and furs.

She grumbled that at least Andrew could do things to warm up. He was often racing through the woods, hunting for food, chopping wood, and practicing his skills with swords and staff.

Madame La Touroulde took a dim view of girls doing such things. She insisted that Eve become better at needlework and overseeing a proper household. Otherwise, she was invited to recite Scripture and poetry or play parlor games. Some of the games had boards like tic-tac-toe and nine-men's morris and draughts, which was kind of like checkers and chess. Eve learned various card games, too. But being housebound made everyone a little cabin crazy. Jeanne became the most restless.

Friar Richard had become a mainstay at the house. Jeanne had drawn him close as a spiritual adviser, but lately she began to distance herself from him. Not only did he try to position himself as a spiritual authority to the king, but he had assembled a group of women who claimed to see God in human form, wearing a white gown under a red tunic.

"Like Santa Claus," Eve joked to Andrew.

One of the women, named Catherine, claimed that a woman wearing white with a gold mantle came to her in visions. Catherine had left her husband and children to travel through all the towns in France and raise money for the king's army. She demanded that people give her the money, or the woman in white would expose them to shame. It worked. Donations were up. Even the Archbishop of Reims seemed impressed with her.

Catherine was loud and arrogant and insisted that the king should make peace with the Duke of Burgundy.

Jeanne was furious and said to Catherine, "Our king has done more than enough to make peace. The duke is a traitor and should be met with the point of a lance."

Friar Richard slowly turned his loyalty from Jeanne to Catherine.

One night Jeanne confided to Eve that her Voices had told her that Catherine and her "white woman" were frauds. To prove it, she invited Catherine to stay in her room so she might see the white woman for herself.

The test was a failure. The woman did not appear. Catherine made excuses.

Jeanne lost patience with the fake prophetess. "Go home to your husband and children. I will personally tell the king that you are not what you claim to be."

Catherine turned red with anger. "You will *lose* your next battle," she proclaimed.

Later, Friar Richard railed at Jeanne for her accusation, then stopped speaking to her completely.

Jeanne kept her promise and warned the king about both of them.

It did not matter. The king had lost interest. He announced he would be moving yet again to another palace in the west of France. He did not invite Jeanne to join him.

———————————————————►

Now that she was no longer near the king, Jeanne relaxed. She was still fiercely devoted to him, but his court and council had worn her down. It helped that Friar Richard and his flock of followers left too.

In a side room that served as a kind of library, Andrew admitted to Eve that he'd been thinking about Hope Springs a lot more lately. It was now late November. He assumed everyone would be celebrating Thanksgiving.

"But they're not," Eve reminded him. "It's still the same time there as when we left. Maybe a few minutes later. I don't know what the formula is."

Andrew sighed. "Technically, Thanksgiving hasn't been invented yet. The Pilgrims won't go to America for another two hundred years."

Eve chuckled. "Here's something else to think about ..." She tugged at her hair. "We've been here for months, and my hair has hardly grown. The same with yours. Normally I would need a haircut by now. Why is that?"

"This whole time-travel thing is enough to drive me nuts." He paused, his face alight with a thought. "Hey, what if Simon is nuts because he came from the future but stayed here too long?"

"Why would he stay here on purpose?"

"How should I know? Maybe he lost the stone or ..."

"He fell in love and got married," Eve said.

"Or that." Andrew nodded.

"Or maybe he is just crazy, and the stone is just a jewel that Vincent wants to steal," Eve said. She still thought it was too far-fetched that there was another time traveler nearby.

Andrew looked as if he was on the verge of a pout. "It gives me hope."

"I feel a lot better without hope," Eve said, joking.

But it wasn't really a joke. Eve had been so focused on Jeanne that she had given up on ever going back to Hope Springs. She thought about the message she had left for Alfred Virtue at Chinon but dismissed it as a wild fantasy.

The next day, there was a sudden flurry of activity in the house. Jeanne had been summoned to a battle for the town of La Charité. This time she seemed agitated, even worried, about going.

"We are low on gunpowder, arrows, good crossbows, and supplies. We need to take this town," Jeanne explained as Jean d'Aulon helped put on her new suit of armor. "The king has written from Mehun-sur-Yèvre that he cannot send money to help."

"If the attack turns into a siege?" he asked her.

"Then we must pray for help from the nearby towns that are loyal to the king."

Eve began to pack her own things for the journey.

"No, my angel. You must stay here," Jeanne said.

"Why?"

"I will not have you suffer the bitter cold."

"I want to be wherever you are," Eve replied. "How can I protect you if I do not go?"

"By being my eyes and ears here," Jeanne said.

The king was gone, so Eve did not know what she could see or hear that would help Jeanne. But arguing with Jeanne was not an option. So Jeanne marched off to another battle with the Marshal of Sainte-Sévère and Sir Charles d'Albret.

Eve felt sick while Jeanne was gone. Would the Maiden be captured by the English at this battle?

The days turned into a week. And then another week. Then news came that La Charité was under a miserable siege. The townspeople were comfortable enough, but Jeanne's soldiers were dealing with hunger and the numbing cold.

Eve fumed. "Jeanne took Orléans in only four days. How much time did the king give her to take Paris? *One.* Now she is stuck for weeks at some outpost, all because La Trémoille wants revenge."

Meanwhile, Madame La Touroulde decorated the house for *Noël*, as Christmas was called. Holly and ivy were placed in the windows and around the doors. Rushes and herbs were thrown onto the stone floors. Eve wondered when they would set up the Christmas tree, only to remember that the idea hadn't migrated from Germany yet.

The siege at La Charité dragged on until a few days before Christ's Mass. Word came that Jeanne had launched a decisive attack, though it was decisive only in its failure to capture the town. Sainte-Sévère and d'Albret gave up.

So Catherine was right, Eve thought.

Guests arrived at Bourges. Eve was not introduced properly to many of them. She didn't mind. Together she and Andrew joined them to eat, play games, and watch plays that retold the story of the first Christmas or recounted local myths and legends. On Christmas Eve, a large piece of wood—called the Yule log—was brought in and placed in the largest fireplace. It was set ablaze and left to burn while the household went off to three Masses that night.

On Christmas Day, Andrew and Eve went to Mass again. Afterward, they enjoyed a lavish meal that included goose, duck, partridge, rabbit, pheasant, and fish. Goblets of wine, ale, and punch were served.

Later, Andrew was invited outside to play a game called *soule*, which was like a mixture of soccer, rugby, and hockey. It was a violent game that left Andrew with a swollen lip and a few bruises.

The only Christmas present for Eve was the arrival of Jean d'Aulon. Delighted as Eve was to see him, she was disappointed to learn that Jeanne was first going to

Jargeau and then back to Orléans to attend to some kind of business. He also informed both Andrew and Eve that the king was summoning them to Mehun-sur-Yèvre.

"Us?" Andrew asked.

"Do we have to go?" Eve was not happy. Staying near the king without Jeanne was the last thing she wanted to do. Madame La Touroulde's house had become a comfortable home.

"If you refuse, you will miss the honors," d'Aulon said.

"What honors?" asked Andrew.

"The king is going to present Jeanne with an official act of ennoblement."

───────────◆

The act of ennoblement was the king's way of rewarding Jeanne and her entire family with a special rank in the kingdom, as if they had been born with noble blood. They were given a royal crest to use and were relieved of paying taxes.

Eve was happy for Jeanne and said so often when Jeanne arrived from Orléans. Jeanne admitted that she was pleased for her family but did not care about the honor herself.

"Any honor for me comes from serving God," Jeanne said, then smiled. "Besides, I have my banner."

They stayed a couple of months at the king's residence in Mehun-sur-Yèvre. Spring arrived and lifted their spirits. The truce with the Duke of Burgundy had been extended a couple of times. It was now set to end at Easter. Tensions were still evident, but there was nothing to be done. Jeanne wrote letters to friends and supporters who had asked for her help.

Eve caught herself pacing, distracted by the feeling that Jeanne's capture was coming closer and closer.

Andrew refused to give in to despair. Instead, he tried to fill the time with new games. He actually taught the servants how to play baseball.

"Aren't you afraid of changing history?" Eve teased him.

He smiled. "It won't catch on. It isn't violent enough for them."

Another move approached, and they traveled with the king and his court to La Trémoille's castle in the town of Sully-sur-Loire. The castle had become an important stronghold between central France and the northern areas held by the Duke of Burgundy.

Those around Jeanne were miserable. Living under La Trémoille's watchful eye in his own home was an unpleasant idea. Eve imagined there were secret corridors and spies behind every portrait and door.

"That would be so cool!" Andrew exclaimed. And from then on, he checked every panel and large painting for evidence that Eve was right.

They hadn't settled in very long before letters came to Jeanne from Reims. The people were afraid the English were going to invade. Rumors abounded that the Duke of Bedford, who had crowned the very young Henry in

England last November, wanted to do the same at the cathedral in Reims.

Jeanne wrote back to reassure the people that there was nothing to fear if they shut their gates and refused him entrance. "I will deal with the English before they ever reach Reims.

"Compiègne," d'Aulon said after the letter had been sent.

"What about it?" asked Eve.

"The Duke of Bedford has told the Duke of Burgundy that he may have the entire region around Compiègne if he can conquer it."

"Wouldn't that break the truce?" Andrew asked.

"The truce ends at Easter," d'Aulon said. "They have been gathering their army for the moment it does."

The spring brought more sun and rain. It was also as if France was slowly awakening to the idea of fighting again. Those loyal to King Charles had started an uprising in Paris, but it was squashed. Other towns followed, trying to shake the English stranglehold. Most of the attempts failed.

"This is how it will happen," Eve said to Andrew. "The battles will start again, and Jeanne will be taken."

Jeanne paced around Sully. All of her most trusted military friends were off living or fighting in other regions. How was she to assemble another army?

Her brother Pierre returned from Domrémy.

"I thought you would need me," he said to Jeanne as they embraced.

Eve felt comforted that Pierre had come back. She hoped he would lift Jeanne's spirits. She needed the help.

King Charles was of no help whatsoever. Either he would not meet with Jeanne, or he would not give her any advice or consent when he did. "Do what you must" was all he would say. He alone seemed to believe that there was a peaceful solution with the Duke of Burgundy and the English.

La Trémoille met with Jeanne quietly, encouraging her to take up the cause of France again. But Eve noticed that he always spoke in a way that would allow him to deny it later. She was convinced that La Trémoille didn't want Jeanne to win anything. He wanted her captured or killed.

One day, Eve found Jeanne was in a state of excitement. "My new army is at Lagny, west of Paris," she said. "One hundred horsemen and over fifty archers and bowmen. All commanded by Captain Bartolomeo Baretta of Lombard. He has gathered Italian soldiers ready to take on the fight."

"Why would the Italians fight for the French?" Eve whispered to Andrew.

"I think Lombard was once part of France," Andrew guessed. "Or maybe they just hate the English."

Jeanne commanded Jean d'Aulon to prepare to depart immediately.

Eve pleaded with her again, "Andrew and I must come with you."

Once again Jeanne said no.

"If you will not let us come to the battle, then *please* take us away from here," Eve begged. "I do not trust La Trémoille."

Jeanne thought it over. "If I can find somewhere safe, I will move you," she said.

In the following days, Eve *really* missed having cell phones and the internet. News about Jeanne came to her slowly. One report confirmed that Jeanne had gone to Lagny to meet her new army. Her commanders were Captain Baretta, a Scot named Hugh Kennedy, and Captain Ambrose de Loré, who had fought with Jeanne at Orléans.

The next report stated that there was an intense battle against the Burgundians outside Lagny. Jeanne and the French forces were victorious.

Another report said there was a problem. The story was that Jeanne had captured a Burgundian captain named d'Arras. He had been held for ransom as part of a prisoner exchange. The exchange went wrong, and d'Arras was given to the people to stand trial. He confessed to his various crimes as a captain and, to the shock of the Burgundians, was immediately beheaded.

The Burgundians were enraged that their esteemed captain was dishonorably executed instead of ransomed. They blamed Jeanne and said it was further proof that she was acting not for God but for the devil. Jeanne denied any wrongdoing.

Another story emerged that in a fit of anger, Jeanne had broken the Sword of Saint Catherine. According to one version, Jeanne had broken the sword across her knee after finding unholy women sneaking into her army's camp. Another version stated that Jeanne had broken the sword over an unholy woman's *head*. Either way, Eve had a hard time believing it.

Meanwhile, the king surprised everyone by sending out a royal letter admitting his own failure to find a peaceful resolution with the Dukes of Bedford and Burgundy. He had done all he could, he said, but the dukes had used his good intentions to deceive him. They had taken advantage of the truce to build up their armies for renewed attacks on the king's territories.

Too little too late, Eve thought.

Jeanne and her army continued on through France. They captured a town called Melun, just south of Paris. Then they circled around Paris to the north and took Senlis. Then Jeanne took a break from the fighting and went on a pilgrimage to the Church of Élincourt, paying homage to Saint Margaret, one of her Voices. After this, there were a few other skirmishes at other towns. Eve needed a map to keep track of them all.

Every day she hoped that Jeanne would send for her and Andrew. She didn't.

One morning Eve felt especially exasperated and went off to find Andrew. Various servants pointed her in different directions. She finally found him near the garrison where the soldiers tasked with protecting the area lived. Andrew was walking across a courtyard when she called out to him. He turned, looking as if she had startled him.

"What are you doing?" she asked.

"Nothing," he said. But he looked uneasy, as if he'd been caught doing something wrong. "Why are you down here?"

"I am worried," Eve said. "We have to find Jeanne."

"*What?*"

"I am so tired of sitting around here waiting."

"Do you know where she is?" he asked.

"No. But we can find out."

He gave her an awkward smile. "I have a *better* idea. We should go back to Chinon."

"Chinon!" Eve exclaimed. "Why?"

Andrew took her arm and drew her off to the side, away from the soldiers. He said softly, "That's where Simon has hidden the stone."

Eve pulled her arm away. "You are kidding me."

Andrew caught hold of her arm again and said, "Come on." He gently tugged at her.

She groaned and walked with him over to a large door. They passed through to the garrison's dining area. Only one soldier sat at a table near the back: Simon Le Fantôme.

"No," Eve said and tried to pull back.

"*Please*," Andrew begged, still holding her arm.

Simon looked up at them. He saw Eve, and his face went rigid. Then a wry smile formed on his lips.

"I really don't like him," she said under her breath.

They sat down across from him, and Andrew said, "She will not go to Chinon. She wants to find Jeanne."

"The Maiden is in the thick of battle now. It is pure folly." His eyes went to Andrew. "Vincent will be where there is a battle, looking for me. Perhaps he is looking for you as well. What he wants must be put into safe hands. Do you understand the trust I am placing in you?"

"What does the assassin want?" Eve asked.

"Tell her about your treasure," Andrew urged him.

Simon said, "It will help you."

"Help us *how*?" Eve asked, thinking they might need money in the days to come.

His eyes narrowed and his voice took on a hard edge. "Why do you ask so many questions?" he asked through clenched teeth.

Eve got ready to run out. This was how the old man looked before he acted crazy.

"Is it not enough that I said I have a treasure that will help you?" he demanded.

"Why do you want to help us?" she asked.

"You are ..." He pressed his hands onto the table as if to keep them from turning into fists. "You must repair what I have broken."

"What does that mean?" she asked.

He glared at her. His lips moved as if he did not know how to form the words. Finally, with great effort, he said, "It is impossible to explain until you have done it."

Eve turned to Andrew. "He does not make sense." She stood up and walked out.

Andrew chased after her, catching her in the middle of the courtyard. "Will you stop for a minute?"

"Why do you believe anything he says?" she asked.

"Why do you want to go back to Jeanne when you know what will happen?" Andrew countered.

Eve looked around and gestured for him to lower his voice. She said in a harsh whisper, "How can you ask me such a stupid question? I don't want her to feel abandoned."

Andrew held up his hands. "Okay. I get it."

She frowned at him, ready to walk away.

"Eve," he said gently. "You know you cannot save her. Your name is not in the history books. We are not supposed to be here."

"I have to be there for her," she said, "even if there is nothing I can do."

Andrew eyed her. "But you think there is. You think you can change what happens."

Eve didn't respond.

"Listen to me. We have a chance to go *home*. But we have to go to Chinon. That is where Simon has hidden the stone."

"*A* stone," she said. "What if that is all it is? I mean, if it is like the Radiant Stone, then why doesn't he come out and say so? The words are easy: 'I have a stone that will let you travel in time.'"

"Because he has been here too long," Andrew replied. "He cannot bring together what his memory knows is true but his brain cannot accept. He remembers what the stone does, but his brain cannot make sense of it. It is like his life here has pushed everything he knew out of his mind and locked it away."

"You just made that up," she said.

"This is *all* I have been thinking about!" Andrew cried out. "That is why he is going crazy. He knows there are things he should remember but cannot. What he does remember does not make sense. Our showing up makes it worse. Throw Vincent into the mix, and it is enough to send him over the edge."

"You think Vincent knows what the stone does?" Eve asked.

Andrew shrugged. "I hope not. I hope he wants the stone because he thinks it is valuable. But Simon is right: if someone like Vincent got the stone and traveled through time, he might do some terrible things."

Suddenly Eve felt as if they were being watched. Andrew must have sensed it too. They both slowly turned toward the dining hall.

Simon stood in the doorway. "Let us make a deal," he said. He walked toward them, a look of serenity on his face. "I will take you to Jeanne. If we survive, then we will go to Chinon together."

"*If* we survive?" Eve said.

He sneered at her. "The Maiden is at Compiègne. It is being surrounded by four thousand Burgundians. I am certain Vincent the Ravager will be among them. So we may live, or we may not. If we do, then we will make the journey to Chinon."

"Deal," Eve said.

Everything Eve owned fit into a small satchel. It wasn't much. A few bits of clothes, a makeshift toothbrush, a flask, and a pair of low leather shoes that she started to use as slippers. She slung the bag over her shoulder; then she went to meet Andrew and Simon at the castle gate. Both of them wore the tunics and tights normally worn under armor. Their swords hung at their sides. Andrew suddenly looked very grown up.

"We are walking," Simon told them. "My horse was killed by the Ravager the last time I saw him."

"Can we borrow one?" Eve asked.

"One cannot simply borrow a horse," said Simon. "Nor does one steal a horse. Not without a fear of being executed."

They departed from Sully. Eve had no idea that it would take almost three days to walk to Compiègne. Nor could she know what dangers awaited them there.

36

Along the way, Simon explained that Compiègne was one of the largest and strongest cities in France. It was north of Paris, a vital position for whoever had its loyalty. For now, its loyalty belonged to King Charles, even though the king and his council had given the city up to the Duke of Burgundy as part of the truce.

Guillaume de Flavy, the captain of the city's garrison, refused the king's order to yield the city to the duke. De Flavy replied that the city would remain loyal to the true king of France, truce or no truce. With more than four hundred men in the garrison, no one wanted to force the issue in combat.

La Trémoille, on the other hand, tried other means. He offered a huge bribe to de Flavy. The captain refused it.

Now that the truce was officially broken, Captain de Flavy was considered a hero for holding his ground.

The Duke of Burgundy sent four thousand men to take Compiègne, along with artillery that could fire stone balls larger than any army had used before. He also brought in mortars and a great catapult. His archers and crossbowmen were exceptionally skilled, hitting whatever they aimed at with barbed arrows. In addition, the duke brought in men who specialized in laying powder mines around the town, along with an ancient type of flamethrower to make them explode.

That is what Eve, Andrew, and Simon were about to experience as they approached the city from the southeast. Standing at the edge of a forest, they saw the river. On the north bank, the Burgundian camp spread out on a distant hill and adjoining fields.

"Where will we find Jeanne?" Eve asked. Her heart filled with alarm as she gazed at the city's stone towers that now looked like broken teeth.

Just then, a tradesman and his family came toward them from the city. Eve assumed they were trying to get out of harm's way. Simon hailed them to stop, assuring them that he was not a robber but a soldier seeking information.

As his young children played among the trees, the tradesman explained that the Burgundians now had control over most of the towns surrounding Compiègne. Jeanne, he had heard, was with the Archbishop of Reims and the Count of Vendôme and his army in Soissons to the east. However, the people of Soissons feared any Burgundian reprisals and would not open the gate to the Maiden.

"It has been said that she may be in Crépy-en-Valois to gather more troops," the tradesman offered.

Simon tossed the man a coin by way of thanks. Then he announced to Eve and Andrew that they would stay where they were and wait.

"Wait!" Eve said.

"Crépy-en-Valois is to the south. If she has gone for troops and supplies there, she must pass us here on the way back to Compiègne."

Since the three travelers were not strangers to staying in the woods, they quickly found a comfortable spot near the main road to rest and watch. Andrew caught a rabbit, which Simon prepared and cooked over a modest fire. Night came to them on a cold breeze. A mere sliver of a moon hung overhead. Eve curled up in a ball and fell asleep beneath a tree.

She was awakened by Andrew. "Someone is coming," he whispered to her.

She sat up and listened. The sound of horses' hooves and the marching of many feet was unmistakable. Worried that it might be the Burgundians, they hid behind a grove of trees near the road.

Jeanne, on horseback, came into view. She lifted her hand to bring the column to a halt. Then she dismounted to consult with her officers under torchlight. Jean d'Aulon was there. And a captain with dark hair and eyes whom Eve remembered from earlier battles. The name quickly came to her: Captain Poton de Xaintrailles, a friend of

La Hire's. There were also a few other men Eve had never seen before.

Eve heard Jeanne saying softly that she would enter Compiègne first to apprise Captain de Flavy of their whereabouts. The troops should remain hidden in the forest until dawn.

Eve was about to step out, when Simon moved first and called Jeanne's name. There was a loud rattle as the commanders and nearby soldiers grabbed their weapons. Simon held up his hands and identified himself. He waved for Eve and Andrew to come out.

Jeanne gasped at the sight of Eve, her hands going to her face like a little girl. She embraced Eve, then Andrew, then both of them together. "My angels, my angels! What are you doing here?"

"I was tired of waiting for you," Eve replied.

"Come, then," Jeanne said after thanking Simon for bringing them to her safely.

Jeanne and the three travelers made their way to the city, along with Captain de Xaintrailles and Jean d'Aulon. They entered by a small gateway Jeanne said she had used before. Guards stopped them just inside and then, seeing who it was, welcomed them in. They walked down the darkened streets to a large house. A bewildered servant girl answered the door. Jeanne demanded to see the master of the house, Captain de Flavy.

They were taken to a large study. Jeanne paced while Simon stood with his back to the feeble flames of a hastily made fire. Eve sat down with Andrew on a small sofa. D'Aulon gazed at Jeanne. Captain de Xaintrailles leaned against the wall and watched them all with an expression of disapproval.

Wearing a long robe and looking as if he'd been dragged from his bed, Captain de Flavy entered the room, a sullen look on his face. It was clear that he was not happy about his unwelcome visitors. "You have come back," he said.

"I promised you I would," Jeanne said. "Tomorrow I will fight the English and the traitors of France."

Captain de Flavy groaned. "Not so fast, Maiden. They have tightened their grip around the city. Wait until we can assess their numbers."

Clearly, Captain de Flavy did not know how Jeanne reacted to the word *wait*.

"What will their numbers tell us? We will fight tomorrow," she said again.

He looked at Captain de Xaintrailles for help. "Do you agree?"

"Of course," he said.

De Flavy grunted. "As you wish," he said, snarling, then walked out of the room. The servant girl pulled the door closed.

"Do you trust him?" Simon asked Jeanne. "He is known to be ruthlessly corrupt."

"He has remained strong for our king," said Jeanne.

Captain de Xaintrailles nodded, though Eve wasn't sure what he was nodding to.

"We must rest now for what is to come," he said. "We have only a few hours to sleep."

The captain pulled the door open. The servant girl was standing there, red-faced. She had been listening to their conversation.

"I will show you to your rooms," she stammered.

Captain de Xaintrailles and Simon followed her out.

"Leave us for a moment," Jeanne told d'Aulon. He bowed, then strode out.

Jeanne sat on the couch between Eve and Andrew. "Why are you here?" she asked, her expression serious.

"Like I said—," Eve began to say.

"You should not be here," Jeanne interjected. "It is not safe."

"If it is not safe, then you need your angels nearby," Eve reminded her.

"Perhaps it is best for me not to have my angels at all." Jeanne's eyes glistened in the firelight.

Eve shot a look at Andrew, then took Jeanne's hands. "Jeanne, you are going to be captured. If not tomorrow, then soon."

Andrew screwed up his face and said, "No."

Eve ignored him. "They will capture you and ... and ..." She couldn't bring herself to say any more.

Jeanne smiled at her. "Evangeline, you are saying what I already know."

"What?" from Andrew.

"How do you know?" from Eve.

"My Voices," Jeanne told her. "Saint Catherine and Saint Margaret proclaimed that I would be taken before Saint John's Day."

"When is that?" asked Andrew.

"A month from now," she replied. "So all that I have done, I have done knowing that it might be the last."

With a trembling voice, Eve asked, "Did the Voices tell you anything else?"

"No," she said. "Though I asked to die immediately, without suffering long."

"What did they say about that?" Andrew asked.

"They said only that I must be taken, and so it should be. But I am not to be troubled. I must yield, knowing that God will help me." Jeanne looked at Eve, resolved. "I would rather they had told me something else, but that is what they said. So I accept it, knowing that God is always with me."

Burning tears fell on Eve's cheeks.

"Come what may," Jeanne said, "you have inspired me in all I have done."

"Inspired you? How?" asked Eve.

"By being here."

———————————————————▶

Eve did not sleep that night. She sat across the room, looking at Jeanne on the bed. D'Aulon was sprawled on a cot, snoring softly. Andrew had stretched out on the floor.

Eve prayed, fighting her feeling of helplessness. The words "Thy will be done" kept coming to her. It was what Jesus said. It was what all of the saints eventually said. And without a doubt, Jeanne was a saint.

As the gray dawn filled the room, Jeanne sat up. Stretching, she said to Eve, "I have something for you." She slipped out of bed and went to a bag she normally kept tied to her saddle. It contained the few personal items she carried with her. She took out a leather purse and handed it to Eve. "Take this," she said.

It jingled in Eve's hand.

"If anything happens to me."

Eve tried to hand it back. "No, please."

Jeanne pushed her hand away. "Keep it. You may need it."

Eve looked at the purse, the urge to cry coming upon her again.

Brightly, Jeanne said, "Let us go to Mass."

"Should I wake the others?" Eve asked.

"Let the Holy Spirit awaken them," she said, giggling.

The Church of Saint-Jacques was only a few streets away. Pierre, Jeanne's brother, joined them. He had been staying in the city as a point of contact between Captain de Flavy and Jeanne. After Mass, they returned to Captain de Flavy's house, where Andrew stood, scratching his head.

"You should have gotten me up," he said to Eve.

Captain de Xaintrailles, Jean d'Aulon, and Captain de Flavy were eating breakfast with the newly arrived

Captain Bartolomeo Baretta. Eve thought Baretta had the look of a pirate, with olive skin, a pudgy face, a scraggly beard, and a mop of unkempt hair.

Simon sat off to the side, nibbling on a piece of cheese and watching the officers.

A map had been placed in the middle of the table. Captain de Xaintrailles, who had finished his modest meal, stood and said, "The Burgundians are on the north side of the river Oise. A single bridge from the city, here, crosses to the meadowlands, which go some three-quarters of a mile and rise beyond the slope of Picardy. The meadow is low and often flooded. We remember well what low, wet meadows have done to our armies in the past."

There were grunts of assent. The English frequently won against the French in wet meadows.

"The road to Margny goes off to the west," the captain continued. "It follows the steep slope of the hill. The enemy is there, commanded by Baudot de Noyelles. And north in Clairoix is the commander Jean de Luxembourg and his Picards. In Venette, to the south, we have Lord Montgomery from England. The Duke of Burgundy himself is now only two miles north in Coudun."

Captain de Flavy nodded. "It is good military strategy for them to spread their troops out, forcing their enemies to do the same. It diminishes concentrated strength."

Captain Baretta reached over and stabbed a finger at the mark representing Margny. "Let us attack there. The enemy has had no time to build strongholds. It is small and easily captured. We will make that our outpost."

From his seat, Simon asked, "What if the enemy swings around from the north and cuts you off from the bridge?"

Baretta looked offended. Simon was an uninvited participant and had no right to speak.

"They will not move their forces quickly enough to cut us off," Baretta said.

Captain de Flavy cleared his throat. "I will post archers on my walls to repel any who attempt to block the bridge. There will also be covered boats on the river. Your soldiers may use them to retreat."

Baretta snorted. "We will not retreat."

Simon did not seem impressed.

"You will march out this morning?" Captain de Flavy asked.

"This afternoon," said Captain de Xaintrailles. "They will expect us in the morning. Taking Margny this afternoon will allow us time to fortify it as our outpost before they attempt to take it back in the morning."

Jeanne was silent for the entire meeting. No one asked for her advice or input. Did she trust these men completely, or had she been relegated to the role of a mascot again?

As the day progressed, Jeanne's army made its way from the forest into Compiègne. The troops were told to prepare for an afternoon fight. With the words "Bring me my banner" from Jeanne, they came alive.

Jeanne wore a new set of armor. It was still her traditional white, but was now covered with a vest of rich gold.

"What is that sword?" Eve asked.

Jeanne held it up for her to see. "It is Burgundian. I captured it at Lagny," Jeanne explained. She mounted a gray horse. A young man Eve did not know served as her standard bearer.

Jean d'Aulon climbed onto a brown steed next to her.

"Watch from the city tower," Jeanne said to Eve. "Pray for me as I go—and always, if you do not see me again."

"This reminds me of Orléans," Andrew said as he climbed the stairs of the tower.

Eve couldn't speak. She felt nauseous from her anxiety about Jeanne.

They reached the top, moving to the turrets where Captain de Flavy's archers stood ready. Below, the trumpets sounded, and Jeanne rode out onto the bridge, with Jean d'Aulon, Captain Baretta and Captain de Xaintrailles alongside her. Then came the other horseback riders and four hundred foot soldiers with lances and spears pointed to the heavens. They marched quickly, as if getting a running start for the slope of the hill ahead of them.

Even from the tower, with its view of the meadow and Margny, Eve found it hard to follow the battle as it quickly unfolded. Only when she had time to think later did it become clearer.

The French army crested the hill to Margny and, from all appearances, caught the Burgundians off guard. Victory seemed assured.

Then a strange thing happened. A group of men without armor rode down from the north, accompanied by only a dozen soldiers. It looked as if they were noblemen who had gone off for an evening ride. Eve learned later that they were, in fact, two commanders from Clairoix, including the commander Jean de Luxembourg. It was possible that Luxembourg had come to explore the state of the city. At the sight of the assault on Margny, their horses reared back. Luxembourg shouted, and two of the soldiers galloped away.

"This is really bad," Andrew said. "They are going for help."

A couple of longbowmen released their arrows at the men, but they were too far away.

"They should have taken Margny by now," Andrew said as a column of smoke rose above the town. "Why are they not returning?"

"It is their right to plunder the village," an archer standing nearby said.

Andrew turned to him. "Can you signal them? They have to be warned about the reinforcements."

"I see no reinforcements," the archer said simply.

An agonizing hour went by. The sounds from Margny suggested combat, but nothing like the cacophony of a full battle.

Eve wrung her hands. "Come back. *Please* come back."

Movement to the north caught her eye. Then, with growing fear, she saw the Burgundian army racing for Margny. The Duke of Burgundy was leading them, his banner held high. Suddenly, half of the army split off and rode toward Compiègne.

Only then could Eve see the French soldiers casually emerge from the village. Many carried sacks of plunder. They did not know what was coming at them.

Eve moved back and forth along the turret, searching for Jeanne.

"She will come last," Andrew said. "She would never leave the field while her soldiers are still there."

The Burgundians came within sight of the French soldiers. With frightening shouts, the French dropped their sacks and ran for the bridge into Compiègne. Some angled away, hoping to reach the boats on the river. In their panic, a few stumbled and fell into the water, thrashing before their armor dragged them under.

"Do something!" Andrew shouted at the archers. "Give them cover!"

"We have no orders," one archer said.

"You must help them! Use your arrows! Your cannons!" Eve cried.

"We will strike our own soldiers," the archer snarled at her.

It was true, Eve realized. The Burgundians were now too close to the French soldiers.

A shout came from the wall. "Raise the bridge!" It was Captain de Flavy. He was leaning over the edge and waving.

Eve heard a loud grating sound as the bridge was slowly drawn up. "But our soldiers are still coming!"

"So are the Burgundians," Andrew said, his voice filled with despair. "If they breach that gate, then the city could be taken."

Jeanne now appeared in the meadow and beckoned the French soldiers to turn and attack the Burgundians. They ignored her as the sight of the rising bridge caused greater panic. More soldiers scrambled to catch the lip of the bridge. Failing that, they threw themselves at the boats.

Jeanne spurred her horse toward the enemy. "Go forward! They are ours!" was her rallying cry. But there were fewer soldiers to rally now.

The Burgundians came at her, circled around and behind her like water around a large rock. More Burgundian riders came from the east. It seemed endless. Eve saw that they had completely cut Jeanne off from Compiègne.

"Oh no," Andrew whispered.

Fighting back her tears, Eve asked, "How will she get back?" She grabbed the arm of the nearest archer. "*Do* something!"

Jeanne turned her horse in one direction, then another. Burgundian foot soldiers closed in. One reached up and caught hold of her vest. She pulled away. He grabbed it with both hands and yanked hard. Jeanne came off her horse and disappeared into the mob of men.

"No!" Eve sobbed. She threw herself against Andrew's chest. "It is too hard to watch."

Andrew wrapped his arms around her. "Wait ... Look! Jeanne is on her feet."

Eve spun around. The Burgundian soldiers had spread out. Jeanne now stood in the center, saying something to them.

A single soldier stepped forward and held out his hand. Jeanne turned her sword around and offered it to him, grip first. He took it, then held it up and shouted a single word that eventually echoed throughout all of France.

"Surrender!"

Jeanne was captured.

There were no French soldiers left to fight for her. The Burgundians put her back on her horse and led her away.

Eve swayed. Andrew thought she might faint. He put an arm around her. "It is over," he said and guided her off the tower.

They made their way slowly through the city, looking like they had just come from a funeral. They headed for the house of Captain de Flavy. It was the only place Andrew could think to go.

The servant at the door claimed she did not know them. It was the same girl who had answered the door the night before. She would not let them in without Captain de Flavy's permission.

They went to the Church of Saint-Jacques. Andrew told Eve to go inside. "Pray for Jeanne while I try to figure out what to do."

She looked at him with a dazed expression, as if she didn't know what he was saying. Then she turned and walked to the doors.

Andrew wasn't unprepared. He had thought a lot about what they should do when Jeanne was captured. One way or the other, they would get to Chinon. But for now, they were in a strange town with no money and no friends.

He made his way to the city's garrison, hoping to find Jean d'Aulon, Captain de Xaintrailles, or Simon. Many of Jeanne's soldiers were there, tending to their wounds. The place had a tomb-like silence.

Then Andrew heard one man whisper, "They have taken the Maiden. What will become of France?"

After a bit of searching, Andrew found Simon sitting on a patch of straw with his back against a hitching post. His head was hanging down, and for a moment, Andrew feared he was dead.

"Simon?"

Simon lifted his head, only a little.

"They have taken her prisoner," Andrew told him.

Simon nodded, only a little.

"What about everyone else?"

"Jean d'Aulon was also captured," Simon said. "And Jeanne's brother Pierre. I am not sure of the others."

Andrew crouched in front of him. "Are you wounded?"

Simon's head came up, more than a little this time. Blood trickled down the right side of his face from a gash under his hair.

Andrew winced. "You need a doctor."

"I need to rest," he said.

Andrew hurried into the garrison. A man was attending to the soldiers on stretchers. Andrew recoiled from the gaping wounds and half-severed limbs. The ground was soaked with blood. The screams made him want to put his hands over his ears.

"I need help," Andrew cried out. "There's a man with a gash outside."

"Is he conscious? Able to speak?" the man asked.

"Yes."

The man shook his head. "Look around you. I am too busy to deal with a mere head wound. Take a few rags. Bandage it yourself."

Andrew grabbed a few strips of cloth from a pile on a table. He found Simon where he'd left him. He began to dress the wound, but he bungled the effort. The rag kept falling into Simon's face.

Simon snatched the cloth away from him. "You do not know what you are doing," he snapped, then tied the rag tightly around his head.

Andrew stepped back. "What will happen to Jeanne?" he asked.

The old man snorted. "She will be taken as a trophy to the Duke of Burgundy, probably at his castle. It is in Luxembourg, a dozen miles north of here."

"Will she be ransomed?"

"Not her," he said. "She is not nobility, or even a soldier. They will treat her as something else. A witch perhaps."

"Someone will rescue her," Andrew said hopefully.

"Someone may try, but she is too valuable for the Burgundians—and the English—to lose. They will fight harder to keep her than they have fought for any city."

"But the king—"

"Listen, boy," Simon said. "The only thing the king or La Trémoille or the Archbishop will do is forget that Jeanne ever served them. They will say she brought it on herself somehow. She was too arrogant and willful, they will say. She did not listen to her superiors. And some will say she was never sent from God at all, but from the devil to deceive them. You know as well as I do what the end will be."

"What the end will be?" Andrew asked, waiting to hear a response that would confirm what he suspected.

Simon gazed up at him. "She will be declared a heretic and burned at the stake."

"You *know* that," Andrew said. "You are not guessing."

"I know my history," he said and looked away.

Andrew wanted to drag Simon back to the church. He wanted Simon to repeat to Eve what he had just said. Simon refused to go anywhere. He was tired. He wanted to rest.

"Prepare to leave for Chinon in the morning" were his parting words.

Andrew made his way through the crowded streets, feeling as if he was swimming upstream no matter which way he turned.

The people looked stunned. Women and children cried openly. The Maiden had been captured. How was that possible? France was doomed. So they went into the streets to talk, or to the inns to drink, or to the cathedral to pray—anything to cope with the horrible news.

Eve was still at the church, kneeling in a back pew. Andrew touched her shoulder. She nodded and came outside. Her eyes were red and swollen.

"We have to stay somewhere tonight," Andrew said.

"I saw an inn around the corner."

"We don't have any money," Andrew reminded her.

"Jeanne gave me a purse," Eve said. "I hid it in my room back at Captain de Flavy's house."

"I hope it's still there."

This time they didn't give the servant a chance to close the door on them.

"Our belongings are here," Andrew stated, then pushed past her. She looked startled but didn't try to stop them.

He grabbed a lit lamp from a side table. Then he marched up the stairs to the room where they had stayed the night before. He saw that it had been tidied up. Obviously someone had already gone through the few things Jeanne had left there.

"Please, God," Eve whispered, then went to the canopied bed.

Andrew assumed she had put the purse under the mattress. He braced himself. Whoever had searched the room would have looked there first.

Eve reached up to one of the slats holding the canopy and felt along the ledge. "Ah," she said, smiling. She pulled down a leather purse.

The servant girl watched them from the hallway, a look of disappointment on her face.

"You did not think to search there, did you?" Andrew teased her.

Eve grabbed her satchel. Andrew picked up a shoulder bag in the corner. It was Jean d'Aulon's. He upended it. A few items of clothing fell out.

"The bag may come in handy," Andrew said. "Jean will not need it."

The servant girl followed them to the door. Andrew handed her the lamp on the way out.

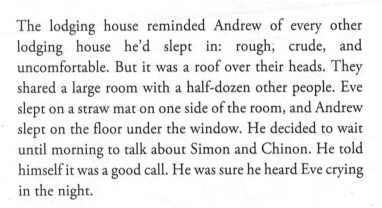

The lodging house reminded Andrew of every other lodging house he'd slept in: rough, crude, and uncomfortable. But it was a roof over their heads. They shared a large room with a half-dozen other people. Eve slept on a straw mat on one side of the room, and Andrew slept on the floor under the window. He decided to wait until morning to talk about Simon and Chinon. He told himself it was a good call. He was sure he heard Eve crying in the night.

In the morning, he was awakened to a clamor of street noise. Compiègne was overrun with soldiers from Jeanne's army and refugees from nearby villages who had come to escape the Burgundians.

"We have to leave," Andrew said to Eve, shaking her gently. She got up without speaking. They gathered their things. He noticed she was wearing the red peasant dress Jeanne had given her.

"Wait," Eve suddenly said.

"What is wrong?"

"What if they rescue Jeanne? We have to be here when she comes back." She pulled a dark cape over her shoulders and tied it at the neck.

Andrew said as kindly as he could, "She is not coming back, Eve. You know that."

"I do *not* know that."

He said firmly, "They will put her on trial as a heretic and burn her at the stake. It will all happen miles away from us. You will not see her. You cannot help her."

"I can try." She gave him a grim look.

"You will die trying," he said. "And what is the point of that?"

------------------------------➤

"We made a deal," Simon reminded Eve outside the garrison. The bandage was gone from his head, but there was a large scrape of dried blood near his hairline.

Eve was still objecting to leaving Jeanne.

Simon was impatient. "Child, *if* you found out where they were keeping her, and *if* you were able to go there, what do you think would happen? They would catch you and burn you at the stake as a witch. It is what *I* wanted to do when I first saw you."

Eve glowered at him.

"It is the color of your eyes," Andrew added, wiggling two fingers at them. "They freak everyone out."

"I will not argue with you," Eve said, sulking.

"As it is, we must go," said Simon. "Captain de Xaintrailles and the other officers are leaving Compiègne. Only Captain Baretta has promised to stay behind with his company. He will assist Captain de Flavy should the Burgundians attack."

Simon stepped back and looked at Andrew and Eve.

"Is something wrong?" Eve asked.

"Weapons?" he asked.

Andrew pushed back his coat to show the sword in the sheath.

"You?"

Eve turned slightly, drawing aside her cape. A knife was tucked into her belt.

They headed for the small gate Jeanne had used a couple of nights before. Emerging into the bright light of day, they stopped to look out at the fields and forest. Andrew wondered how the day could look so beautiful when they felt so bad.

"How long will it take to reach Chinon?" Eve asked.

"If the weather spares us and we walk briskly and avoid trouble, six or seven days," Simon told them.

"I did not think it was so far away," Andrew said.

"It is only as far as it has ever been," said Simon.

Andrew thought about all the moving around they had done since they'd first arrived in France. One day he hoped to sit down with a map to see where all the towns were.

With Compiègne behind them, they entered the forest where they had met Jeanne and her army two nights ago. They walked in silence. Eve sniffled a few times and rubbed her eyes.

Andrew tried to block out the shock of Jeanne's capture—and the cruelty of what would happen to her.

The clip-clop of horses' hooves and the rattle of wooden wheels caused them to turn. It looked like a potter's wagon, with large clay pots in the back and smaller jugs hanging from rope on the side. The potter drove at a leisurely pace, as if he didn't have anywhere special to be.

"Maybe we can get a ride," Andrew said.

Simon's hand went to the hilt of his sword. "Move from the path." He swept them back with his outstretched arm.

"What is wrong?" Eve asked.

The potter's head was lowered, a hood covering his face. He slouched at an odd angle.

The wagon slowed as it came alongside them, the reins pulling back.

Andrew now saw that the reins were not in the driver's hands but around both his sides, stretching to the back of the wagon.

A second later, the potter fell lifeless off the seat. Vincent the Ravager sprang up from the back of the wagon, his sword drawn.

Simon stepped in front of Andrew and Eve, knocking them out of the way. Andrew kept his footing, but Eve tumbled backward.

Simon's sword was in his hand, but he stumbled while trying to avoid the falling dead man. He attempted a first strike at Vincent and missed.

Vincent leapt from the wagon and was now on the path. He thrust at Simon, stabbing the old man in the right shoulder.

Simon swore at the pain but regained his stance.

Andrew glanced at Eve, who was rubbing her head. He reached for his sword, fumbling to get it out of his sheath.

Simon lunged back at Vincent.

Andrew stepped forward with his sword drawn.

"Stay back!" Simon shouted.

Vincent jeered. "Yes, boy, I will deal with you after I have killed him."

The two men exchanged fierce blows, the ring of steel echoing all around. Simon drove Vincent back, and he stumbled into the horse. It snorted at him, moving forward and backward uneasily. The cart moved with it. Vincent sidestepped the animal and blocked Simon's blade with the flat of his sword.

The men fought with equal force. Vincent was younger and more agile. Simon had great strength and years of experience.

Eve came alongside Andrew. She had a long straight branch in her hands. She cut at the twigs with her knife, keeping her eyes on the battle.

Andrew thought, as he often did, that fights in real life were not like they appeared in the movies. All of the smooth routines in action films were replaced by stumbles, grunts, and falling into each other like wrestlers. In no time, both men were on their knees, their hands on each other's wrists as each one tried to get the other to drop his sword.

Eve tucked her knife away. "I have had enough of this," she said, then rushed forward with her newly made staff. Using both hands, she stabbed it at Vincent, hitting him on the side of the head. He shouted and fell sideways.

Simon gave her a grateful nod and got to his feet. He flicked his sword at Vincent's sword arm, catching enough of the wrist to make Vincent drop his weapon.

"Now," he started to say to Vincent, but Vincent wasn't ready to give up. He suddenly rolled toward the horse and spider-crawled under the wagon, kicking up a lot of dust as he went.

"Yield," Simon shouted. He kicked Vincent's sword off the path.

Andrew heard the sound of feet and knees scraping on the dirt path. Simon moved in front of the horse, watching one side of the wagon, then the other.

"What is he doing?" Andrew asked, moving away in case Vincent tried to grab his leg.

"Perhaps the snake has found a hole in the ground," Simon said.

Vincent suddenly popped up at the back of the wagon, a crossbow in his hands. He released a bolt, striking Simon in the chest. Simon staggered back and looked down with an outraged expression. Then he dropped his sword, reeling off balance.

Andrew reached out to catch him. They both crashed onto the dirt road. Andrew rolled to his knees and bent over the old man. The bolt jutted from the left side of Simon's chest.

Panicked, Andrew whispered, "What do I do?"

Simon turned his head. He coughed. A line of blood slid from between his lips. He grabbed Andrew's tunic and pulled him close. "Secret. Pass. Box. Under. Nails." His words were a gurgling whisper. He coughed again. Then more clearly, he said, "A mistake ... Man should stay ... own time."

Those last words were English, spoken with an American accent.

Simon exhaled a long breath, his eyes fixed on something beyond the top of Andrew's head. They stayed there.

Andrew fell back, dazed.

Eve cried out. Andrew spun around.

Vincent had Eve by the hair, a knife pointed at her throat.

"What did he say?" Vincent asked. "He said something to you in English. What was it?"

"I could not understand him," Andrew said.

"Get up!" Vincent shouted, a wild look in his eyes.

Andrew stood. His sword was a few feet in one direction, and Simon's sword was a few feet in the other. Andrew raised his hands.

"Where is the stone?" Vincent said. "Tell me or I will kill her."

"I do not know anything about the stone." Andrew's eyes went to Eve. He wondered if she had a plan to do something to escape.

She merely rolled her eyes.

Vincent jerked her head sharply, as if to get their attention.

"Ouch," she said. "That hurts."

"You know where the stone is hidden! Take me to it!" Vincent shouted.

"It is somewhere in Chinon," Andrew confessed. "Simon was taking us there. That is all we know. You killed him before he could tell me anything else."

"Chinon," Vincent repeated. He yanked at Eve to step back toward the wagon. "You," he snapped at Andrew. "There is rope in the back. Tie her. Then I will tie you. Together we will go to Chinon."

"It is better than walking," Andrew said.

Once Eve and Andrew were securely tied, Vincent lifted them onto the wagon seat. He put another bolt in the crossbow, then set the weapon on the ground. "At least one of you will die if you try to escape," he said. He dragged Simon's body into the woods, then the potter's.

"He has weapons and supplies in the back," Andrew whispered to Eve. "Maybe we'll find a way to escape."

"Escape to where? We have to go to Chinon either way," she whispered back.

Andrew shrugged. "Good point."

Vincent gathered the fallen weapons and tossed them into the back of the wagon, covering them with a tarp. He climbed onto the seat next to Andrew. "Is this not cozy?"

"No, it is not," said Andrew.

Vincent snapped the reins, and the horse lurched forward with a jolt.

Vincent did not allow Andrew and Eve to talk unless he first asked a question. He had a lot of questions. How did they know Simon? Did they know about his past? Did they know why Vincent had been after him?

Andrew answered honestly. He even repeated what he had heard about Vincent killing Simon's wife and Simon stabbing him in the eye.

Vincent sniffed. "Is that how they say it? Simon's *wife*? She was my sister before she was Simon's wife," he told them.

Andrew decided not to quibble. He looked over at Eve. Her eyes were on the road ahead.

"So why did you kill your sister?" he asked.

"It was *his* fault," Vincent said. "Had he given me the stone, we would not have fought. If we had not fought, my sister would not have placed herself between us. She should have known better, but there you are. My knife was aiming for him, and she got in the way."

"Is a stone worth that much?" Andrew asked.

"Do you know that stone? Have you seen it?"

"No."

"When you see it, when you understand its power, then you will not ask such stupid questions," Vincent said.

So he knows the stone isn't a normal jewel, Andrew thought. *But does he know what it really does?*

The forest was hot and muggy, but at least they had shade. The open road now put the summer sun heavily on their backs. Vincent kept the horse moving at a fast pace, stopping only occasionally for water.

He drove around the west side of Paris, since it was country held by the English. Then he continued south. Andrew did not recognize the names of the towns they passed. They trotted along colorful meadows and wild woodlands. They happened upon other travelers on the road, men of trade, beggars, soldiers marching to their assignments. Most saw the one-eyed man and averted their gaze.

Late in the afternoon, they reached an inn, where they watered the horse. A tinkerer nearby questioned Vincent about the two bound children. He gave the man a cold look and said, "They are thieves. I am taking them to justice."

The tinkerer looked doubtful, but Vincent put a hand on the knife in his belt. The tinkerer walked off.

That night, they slept in the middle of a field. To prevent Eve and Andrew from trying to escape, Vincent bound them to the wagon wheel. By morning their hands and feet were so numb, they could hardly use them. It took almost a half hour before they could stand up on their own.

"Stop complaining," Vincent said.

On the second night, Vincent roasted a rabbit he had caught. As he crouched by the fire, there was a loud snap from somewhere in the woods. Andrew and Eve both turned, sure that someone was coming.

Vincent grabbed his sword and shouted, "Come out!"

No one answered or appeared.

Andrew was sure that whoever it was remained nearby. Vincent suddenly spun to the left, his sword pointing in that direction. At the same time, Eve turned to the right.

"What did you see?" she asked Vincent.

"What did *you* see?" Vincent countered. He shouted again, "Whoever you are, *come out!*"

Andrew did not know whether he should be glad or worried that a mysterious stranger was nearby. Maybe it was one of Jeanne's allies. He thought of Louis, or other people they had come to know. Or maybe someone saw what had happened with Simon on the road and was following to help.

Or it might be an outlaw waiting for the chance to rob and murder them.

"Is it Simon? Is it possible he survived?" Eve whispered to Andrew that night.

"No," Andrew said. He would never forget that last look on Simon's face. The life had truly left him.

"Stop whispering!" Vincent said. He was using the wagon as cover. He looked in all directions, his crossbow ready to shoot.

The next day Vincent kept both his sword and his crossbow close at hand, his eyes darting in the direction of every sound.

"Do not be hopeful," he said. "If it is a friend of yours, he will die."

That evening they found another inn to refresh the horse.

Andrew thought he saw the flickering silhouette of a man in a long coat under a torch near the door. The man was watching them.

Vincent followed Andrew's line of sight and spun around. "What were you looking at? What did you see?"

"A man was standing under that torch," Andrew said.

Vincent stared for a moment. "He is not there now." He held the point of a knife close to the kids' faces. "Do not try to scare me. I get reckless when I get scared."

"I did not think a man like you was ever scared," Eve said.

Vincent grunted at her and put the knife away. "This is true."

Andrew noticed that Vincent whipped the horse to a faster pace and looked over his shoulder more often.

The next day, they entered territory held by King Charles. Vincent showed the kids his knife and sword again, just to remind them of what would happen if they tried to get help. His threat was real but lacked confidence. The mystery man was clearly unnerving him.

They were riding to Chinon from a direction Andrew did not know. He searched for anything that might look familiar. The idea of returning to the town was a relief. He realized it was like going home.

"What will happen when we get there?" Eve asked.

"We will find the stone," Vincent said.

"How?" she asked in a bored tone.

"The boy will tell us what Simon told him, and we will search."

"I told you, I did not understand what Simon said to me," Andrew said.

"Speak the words to me now," Vincent demanded.

Andrew groaned. "He muttered something about a pass and a secret and nails and a box. I do not know what it means."

"Why would he speak words to you unless he knew you would understand?"

"He was *dying*. You put a bolt in his chest, remember?" Andrew said. As he spoke, he realized he felt grieved about Simon. Andrew had come to like him in spite of his craziness.

"Think!" Vincent said, pounding his fist against the side of the wagon. "Where would Simon hide the stone?"

"In the castle somewhere," Andrew replied. "He lived in an officer's room. He guarded a box there."

Eve gave him a "Why are you telling him everything?" look.

Andrew tried to give her an "I know what I'm doing" look.

It didn't work. She looked confused.

It wasn't until the afternoon of the next day that the towers of Chinon came into view. Vincent brought the wagon to a halt and took out his knife. Andrew flinched. Vincent cut the ropes that bound their hands.

Andrew and Eve gently rubbed the chafing on their wrists and hands. They compared who had it worse.

"You win," Andrew said to Eve.

Vincent leaned in close. "Say anything I do not like, or do anything to escape, and one of you will die," he warned them. "Both, if I have my way."

Andrew made a face. Vincent's breath smelled of old onions and cabbage.

"How do we know you will not kill us if we find the stone?" Eve asked.

"You do not know," Vincent replied.

He drove the wagon around to the road that wound up to the main gate. Andrew felt comforted by the familiarity of the people and houses and the rushing sound of the river.

Eve sniffled next to him and wiped her nose with her sleeve. "Only a year," she said.

Andrew knew what she meant.

"What is it you are saying?" asked Vincent. "Why are you crying?"

She said, "This is where we met Jeanne. We were with her when she met the Dauphin for the first time."

"Ah," said Vincent. "You are friends of the king."

"Not friends," Andrew corrected him.

"It is enough to serve our purposes," he said. "I had hoped to get into the castle by using the name of Simon Le Fantôme, but the names of the Maiden and the king are better."

"What are you going to do?" Andrew asked.

Vincent stood on the footboard. "Move aside." He dropped down between Andrew and Eve.

They were crossing the bridge to the castle gate when Vincent suddenly swung his fist around, slamming it against the side of Eve's head.

"Hey!" Andrew cried out.

Then Vincent threw his elbow hard into Andrew's stomach. It knocked the wind out of him. Andrew doubled over. Black spots danced in front of his eyes.

Amid the ringing in his ears, Andrew heard Vincent shout out to the guards at the gate. "Help! The king has sent me! I have come from Compiègne with these two children! They were with Jeanne the Maiden! They are hurt! Let us enter!"

The words, the names, and the urgency were enough for the guards to let the wagon pass. Vincent pulled the horse and wagon around to an isolated spot in the courtyard. He put his arms around Eve and Andrew and rubbed their shoulders. In a creepy voice he must have thought was soothing, Vincent said, "There, there. No harm done. Breathe slowly, boy."

To Eve, he said, "Your senses will come back to you. And once you have recovered, we will solve the mystery of Simon's last words."

39

Vincent climbed down from the wagon and walked around to assess the area.

It took a while before the pain in Andrew's stomach had eased enough for him to think clearly.

Eve sat next to him, gently touching the side of her head. "I'm going to have a headache for a week," she said.

Andrew practiced breathing. He slowly drew air in and let it out again.

"I hope you have a plan," she said to him. The side of her face was red from the blow.

"I *had* an idea," Andrew replied. He *had* planned to expose Vincent to the guards at the gate. But now it was undone. They could scream for help, he thought, but Vincent was close enough to make quick work of them with his knife.

Vincent sidled up to the wagon. "If you are well enough to talk, you are well enough to take me to Simon's room."

They walked from the wagon to the courtyard where Simon had taught Andrew to sword-fight. Andrew looked at the many faces around them but did not see any he recognized. He wondered how many soldiers from a year ago had gone away to fight in battles.

"There." Andrew pointed to the door. "Another soldier may be living there now."

Vincent did not seem to care. He pushed the door open, then pulled Andrew and Eve inside. He closed the door behind them.

The room was filled with someone's clothes and belongings, but not Simon's. The new owner was not there.

Vincent grabbed Eve by the arm. In a flash, the knife was at her throat.

"Not again," Eve moaned.

"Find the stone," he said to Andrew.

"But I do not—," Andrew started to protest.

"You know what Simon was telling you," Vincent insisted.

"He does not!" Eve said.

Vincent grunted and edged the knife closer to Eve's skin. "How much pain will you allow before you tell the truth?" he asked.

Andrew gave in. "None," he admitted. "I *think* I know where Simon hid the stone."

"What?" Eve said.

"But do not blame me if I am wrong," he added quickly.

Vincent's mouth twisted into a smile. "Tell me."

"He said 'secret' and 'pass,' which must be the secret passage." Andrew went to the wall, found the hidden latch, and sprung the panel door open to reveal the corridor behind the wall.

"Be careful, boy," Vincent warned. "Disappear and she will suffer for it."

"You have made that clear." Andrew stepped into the secret corridor. It was exactly as he remembered it. The old oil lamp was there, with the flint. The shelves were still covered with dust and cobwebs. He saw the bottles and jugs, the ragged leather pouches, and the boxes with the old tools and ironworks. A knife had been there, but it was gone now. Andrew was disappointed about that. He had hoped to have a weapon. He looked at the rest of the junk, trying to think of a way to escape.

Simon's box was still in its place on a shelf. As he reached for it, his foot touched something on the ground that made a scraping noise. He looked down. The knife was there. He knelt and saw that the latch and lock on a crate had been broken.

"Hurry," came Vincent's voice from the room.

Andrew tucked the knife into his belt, just under his cloak. He grabbed the box.

"This is it," Andrew announced as he entered the room again.

Vincent pushed Eve onto the bed. "Come away from that passage," he said to Andrew.

Andrew did as he was told, taking a few more steps into the room.

"Put it on the bed. Empty it out," Vincent told him.

Eve moved out of the way, dropping her legs on the side of the bed facing the secret passage. Andrew opened the lid and upended the box onto the bed. There was not much to be seen. Some parchments bound with ribbons ... and a small pouch.

Vincent grabbed the pouch.

"Do not touch the stone with your bare hands," Andrew warned him.

Vincent sneered as he lifted the pouch and shook it. Something gold fell onto the bed. It was a wedding ring, embedded with small jewels.

"That is my sister's wedding ring," Vincent told them. He squeezed the empty pouch and threw it down. "Where is the stone?"

"It is supposed to be there!" Andrew said.

Vincent pointed the knife at Andrew. "Where is it?"

Andrew gave him a helpless expression. "I do not know. Maybe it is hidden in the passage." He suddenly had the idea of getting Vincent into the secret corridor and closing the door on him. They could escape while he tried to get out.

Vincent's face turned red. "You are lying!"

Andrew gestured to the passage. "There are shelves in there, with crates," he said.

Vincent looked as if he might fall for it.

Just then, the door opened. A bearded mountain of a soldier walked in. He looked at the three intruders and bellowed, "This is my room! What goes on here?"

Vincent swung his knife around to slash at the soldier.

The soldier was quick and caught hold of Vincent's wrist. "I see. You want violence?" With his free hand, he punched Vincent in the side of the face.

Vincent let out an animal-like noise and threw himself into the soldier.

The two men began to struggle.

Andrew pulled Eve with him into the secret passage.

Vincent saw them and reached out to catch hold of Andrew. But the soldier caught Vincent by the neck and pulled him back into the room.

Andrew grabbed the ring on the inside of the panel and pulled the door closed. He heard the click of the latch. There were bumps and crashes on the other side of the wall as the men fought.

With the light from the room gone, the passage was almost pitch-black.

"Was this your plan?" Eve asked.

Andrew felt around the shelves, bumping the bottles and jars. His fingers came to the oil lamp and the flint. He grabbed the lamp and put it on the ground. Feeling for the wick, he slipped the small ring of the starter around his fingers and struck it against the flint. There was a spark. He tried it again. Another spark. And again.

"What are you doing? We have to run!" Eve said.

"How are we supposed to see where we're going?" he asked. More strikes, more sparks, and then a flame caught onto the wick. They had light.

Andrew stayed on his knees. By the small glow of the lamp, he looked at the crate with the broken latch. "Simon opened this."

"*Let's go!*" Eve begged. The noise in the room had changed. The struggle was coming to an end.

Andrew dragged the crate out and lifted the lid. Inside were old iron spikes.

"Nails," he said. He lifted them out, tossing them aside.

Things were now very quiet on the other side of the door.

"Andrew?" Eve said.

Beneath the first layer of spikes was a small wooden box. Andrew lifted it up. He flipped open the lid. Inside was a large gemstone with facets that seemed to glow, even in the darkness.

Eve gasped. "That looks like the Radiant Stone."

Someone was clawing at the other side of the wall, trying to find the latch to open the door.

"Come on, Andrew!" Eve pleaded.

"Take the lamp," he said. Once she had it, he upended the crate of spikes onto the floor. He hoped they would slow down whoever was about to come through the panel.

He picked up the small wooden box and pointed down the dark corridor. "That way."

They ran.

Following the passageway, they eventually came to the drinking room Andrew had found before. A drunk soldier was leaning against a stack of barrels as they came out. He looked at them with thick-lidded eyes, puzzling over their sudden appearance. As Andrew closed the secret door, he said to the man, "If anyone comes through that door, hit him with a chair."

The man slurred a "Yes, Cap'n."

"To the tower or the gate?" Eve asked as they raced back into the courtyard.

"Not the tower," Andrew replied. "We have to get out of the castle. Vincent could raise an alarm and accuse us of being thieves. Then we'll have a lot of questions to answer."

Eve said, "Down to the bridge. If this stone can get us home, we'll want our clothes."

Andrew nodded. They ran for the gate. There was a terrible crash behind them. They turned to see Vincent stagger out of Simon's old room. His clothes were torn, and his face was swollen, bruised, and scratched. He clutched his side.

Vincent saw them just as they were seeing him. "Stop!" he yelled and limped toward them.

Andrew and Eve ran away as fast as they could. Andrew held tightly to the wooden box.

At the gate leading to the town, he grabbed the guard and pointed back at Vincent. "That is Vincent the Ravager! He just murdered one of your soldiers!"

Startled, the guard turned to look. The two kids raced across the bridge for the road to town. Andrew heard violent shouts back at the castle.

They quickly reached the streets of Chinon itself. Lamps were being lit for the approaching evening. They followed the road that cut through the town to the bridge, passing the familiar shops and buildings.

Rounding a final gentle curve to the bridge, they came to the south gate. Andrew said to the guard there what he had said to the castle guard, just in case Vincent was still following them. They came to the bridge and collapsed against the rail, gasping for breath. The river Vienne gurgled and splashed below.

"We can't stop," Eve said, then launched herself to the right.

They soon reached the path down to the riverbank.

"It's poetic," Eve said, dropping to her knees on the wet bank.

"I remember throwing up on this very spot." Andrew laughed. He looked at the water swirling around the pillars. "The river has risen since we were here last. Getting our clothes could be harder."

"I noticed," Eve said. "It's getting dark, too."

Andrew went to the waterline. He dreaded the thought of getting wet while trying to reach the place where Eve had hidden their bundle of clothes. More importantly, he worried that the current might carry them off.

"Any ideas?" he asked.

Eve didn't answer.

He turned and saw why. Vincent was there. He had grabbed hold of her again, his knife held in the usual place.

"You are more trouble than you are worth," Vincent said. "Give me the stone."

Andrew looked down at the box in his hand. There was no point denying he had it.

"All right." He slowly put the box on the ground. As he did, he stretched the fingers of his right hand to claw a single pebble from the damp earth. He stood up again, the pebble in his palm.

"Move away," Vincent said.

Andrew stepped back.

Vincent shoved Eve toward Andrew. Keeping his eyes on the two of them, he crouched to pick up the box. He opened the lid and saw the gem. "Yes," he hissed.

Eve moved closer to Andrew. Her eyes were filled with despair.

"What will you do with it?" Andrew asked Vincent.

The Ravager lowered his hand to the stone, his fingers poised to grab it.

"Don't touch it!" Andrew shouted.

Vincent jerked his hand back. "Why not?"

"Do you know what will happen if you do?" Andrew asked.

"It will take me to other times and places," Vincent said. "My sister told me."

"Do you know which facets to touch?" Eve asked. "Each one will take you to different times."

"How do you know?" Vincent asked. He grabbed the box, then stood up. He had that wild-eyed look again. "Who are you? Where are you from?"

"The future," Andrew told him.

Vincent looked as if he did not believe Andrew. Then he looked as if he did. "If that is true, you can guide me. You can take me to those places, just as I wanted Simon to."

"We cannot," Eve said.

"You *will*," Vincent threatened.

"We do not know about *that* stone," Andrew explained. "It would be dangerous for us to take you until we know what it does."

Vincent's lips curled. "Then you are of no use to me." He put the box down, then lifted his knife again. He positioned himself to block their escape to the path.

I have a single stone, Andrew thought. *I use that, or I pull Eve with me into the river.*

The stone was his best option. He wasn't going to allow Vincent to leave with that box. But the shadow of the bridge was now merging with the darkness of the night. Vincent was becoming a dim figure to him.

"I know what you are thinking," Vincent said, nudging the box with his foot. "Are you fast enough to grab the box without feeling this blade?"

Eve gasped.

Andrew glanced at her. She was looking past Vincent. He followed her gaze. He saw a shadow move at the entrance of the path.

Vincent must have seen the change in their eyes. He began turning his head to look, then stopped. "You are trying to trick me."

"I wish I had thought of it," Andrew said. He moved his fingers around the stone, getting ready to throw. He had no idea what the shadow was, but the distraction was a good opportunity to act.

The shadow moved forward and took the form of a man in an overcoat and hat. "That would be quite a trick," the man said.

Vincent whirled around with his knife. "This is not your business," he said defiantly as he carefully stepped over the box and reached out for Andrew.

Andrew tried to move, but Vincent caught his tunic and pulled him close.

Andrew wondered if punching Vincent with a stone-filled hand would do any good.

"I will cut his throat," said Vincent.

"Is that your only threat?" the man asked.

"See for yourself, if you dare take another step." Vincent replied.

"I do not need another step," the man said. His hand came up, holding a revolver. He leveled it at Vincent.

Eve whispered, "What?"

Andrew was wide-eyed.

"What is that, pray tell?" Vincent asked. He sounded as if he was not taking it seriously. Why should he?

Andrew did not wait to find out. With a kick, he threw himself away from Vincent, catching Eve in his arms as he flew. They both fell onto the grassy bank.

Vincent's instincts betrayed him. Catlike, he twisted to slash his blade at whatever piece of Andrew he might catch.

A deafening explosion echoed up to the castle walls and under the bridge.

Vincent jerked as if an invisible string had suddenly yanked the left side of his body in the wrong direction. He looked bewildered and furious. His legs buckled, and his free hand clawed at the air. He fell lifeless into the river. The current quickly carried him away.

Still on the wet ground, Andrew scrambled to get between the mysterious stranger and Eve. The man had saved them, but for what purpose?

Only then did Andrew realize that the man was wearing a *modern* overcoat and a *modern* hat to match.

The man pushed the hat back on his head. "Well," he said.

Eve put her hands over her mouth.

"It can't be!" Andrew exclaimed.

They were looking at a face they'd only ever seen in a large portrait at the Old Bank Building and in black-and-white photos in a dusty office.

The man smiled and said, "I am Alfred Virtue."

Alfred Virtue tucked the gun into the pocket of his overcoat. "We have to go. The sound of the gunshot will draw a crowd."

They took the path up to the bridge. They turned away from the town and crossed over to an open field. Walking quickly, they headed for a forest beyond.

The rustling of Alfred's overcoat and even the sound of the soles of his shoes on the ground were different from anything Andrew had heard in a year. He found himself looking at the man from the corner of his eye.

"I'm guessing you are from the future," Alfred Virtue said, "but not my future."

"That's right," answered Andrew.

"Which century?" he asked.

"The twenty-first," Eve replied.

He stopped and looked at them with an expression of pure wonder. "Well, how about that," he said, then started walking again.

They reached the forest and made their way to an isolated spot in a thicket.

"How are you at making a fire?" Alfred Virtue asked.

"Pretty good now," Andrew said. He gathered kindling and wood, then cleared a space. "It might take a few minutes while I get it lit."

Alfred pulled a silver lighter from his pocket. "This will speed things up."

By the light of the fire, they sat on logs in a small circle.

"Now, I would like to know your names." He pointed to Andrew. "You must be a Perry. The resemblance to Ted is uncanny."

"I'm Andrew Perry, his great-great-whatever grandson." He turned to Eve.

"I'm *your* relative," Eve said. "Evangeline. *Eve*. Virtue."

He smiled. "I'll resist asking about your relatives. It's better I don't know. But you have to tell me what you're doing here."

Andrew nodded for Eve to go first. She explained about finding the Radiant Stone in his office and her few time-travel experiences and how Andrew had joined her to meet Robin Hood.

"And here?" he asked.

"This was an accident," she said. "We've been trapped here without the Radiant Stone."

"That's very interesting," Alfred Virtue said. "I've wondered what I would do if that happened."

"We learned that panicking doesn't help," Andrew offered.

Alfred looked down at the wooden box. "Mind if I look?"

"It belongs to you," Andrew said.

He opened the lid. The stone was there, though it had been jostled by all the running around.

"Do you know it?" Eve asked.

"I do indeed." With a gloved hand, Alfred lifted the stone. "This is the Valiant Stone. I acquired it here in France."

He turned the stone slowly so the facets glittered in the firelight. "It was discovered during renovations on the bridge in the late 1800s. A worker unearthed it and took it home. He thought it was cursed because it made him nauseous and gave him terrible dreams. He boxed it up and got rid of it. After changing a few hands and locations, it wound up with an archaeologist I happened to meet during one of my expeditions here. He knew I collected these particular gems, so he sold it to me."

"Did the archaeologist use it to go back in time?" Andrew asked.

"That's the funny thing about the stones. They don't work for everyone," he said. "Not everyone who touches them goes off to other times. Only certain people. I don't know why." He nodded to them. "It works for you two, obviously."

Something caught his eye, and he looked more closely at the box. "What's this?" He reached in and pulled out folded sheets of paper. He handed them around.

Andrew saw that they were handwritten pages of a journal. "Simon's diary?"

"Ah," Eve said and held up a familiar-looking page.

"That came from my notebook," Alfred said.

"You wrote 'Beware' at the top of it. I guess Simon tore it out," said Eve. "If I ever get home, I'll put it back."

"You have my journals?"

"Some of them. I think you hid the rest somewhere before you—"

"No," he said sharply. "Don't say it. I don't want to know."

Andrew fidgeted. "Okay. But there is a lot *we* want to know. Like how are you connected to Simon?"

"And how did you find us?" Eve threw in.

"The first question is easy," Alfred Virtue said. "Simon was a geologist I consulted about the stones."

"The Radiant Stone and the Valiant Stone? Or are there more?" Eve asked.

"A few more," he said. "The more I acquired, the more I realized I needed to consult with an expert. Simon was one of the best in the area. He lived in Denver but often came to Hope Springs to dig around in the caves. I trusted his expertise. But he seemed to change when he found out what the stones could do. He demanded that I take him back to England during the time of Henry the

Fifth. He wanted to witness the Battle of Agincourt, of all things."

"Why there?" asked Eve.

'He loved that period of history. He had to see the event for himself."

"He *demanded* that you take him?" Andrew asked.

Alfred nodded. "He threatened me, actually. He said he would tell everyone about the stones if I didn't do what he wanted. I couldn't have that. I foolishly agreed. I hadn't figured out the Valiant Stone yet, but I knew the Radiant Stone would get us to England during the time he wanted. So we went back to London. Simon actually saw King Henry. But it was *before* the Battle of Agincourt. I kept telling him I couldn't get him to that exact place and time, but he didn't care. He said he wanted to stay long enough to witness the battle. I said no."

"What did he do?" Andrew asked.

"He knew the Valiant Stone had come from France, so he kept asking me to let him test the facets. He believed that one of them was bound to take him to Agincourt. I refused."

"Why?"

"Because he was becoming obsessed. He was irrational and angry. He threatened me again. I called his bluff and told him to go public if he wanted. He marched out of the bank, and I assumed it was over. I wasn't very smart. I'm sure he broke into my office and stole the Valiant Stone. He disappeared from my time without a trace."

"Wasn't his family upset?" asked Andrew.

"He was a widower. But yes, his grown children were worried. I couldn't tell them what I really believed he'd done." Alfred pointed to the pages from the box. "The details of what happened after that may be in his documents. You should read them to see what you'll learn."

"You don't want to read them yourself?" Eve asked.

Alfred shook his head. "Time travel has made me wary of knowing more than I should in the natural course of events. Otherwise, I would go mad trying to alter the future to my advantage. The future is and always shall be God's domain."

"So why did you come back?" Andrew asked.

"Did you find my message?" Eve interjected.

"What message?" he asked.

"I put it with our clothes under the bridge," she explained. "I wrote your name and asked you to come help us."

Alfred laughed. "That was you?"

"You got it?" Andrew asked, amazed.

"I did, but not the way you intended," Alfred said. "The archaeologist who had the Valiant Stone also had what was left of a parchment he discovered. It was over five hundred years old. Most of the message was too faded to read. He contacted me because he saw *my* name written clearly at the top. He wanted to know how that could happen, since the paper was five hundred years old. Obviously I didn't know. Until now." He laughed again.

"What about our clothes?" Andrew asked.

"Sorry. There were no clothes that I know of."

"So you didn't come back to rescue us?" Eve asked.

"Not directly," Alfred said. "I didn't know you were here."

"Then ... why?" asked Eve.

"I have come back from time to time to check on Simon. When he disappeared from my time, I was sure he was here somewhere. I traveled back to England and found enough evidence to tell me that Simon had come to France. He took the name Simon Le Fantôme and gained the reputation of a talented jeweler turned man of war. That made it easier for me to track him. I had found obscure writings about him in this time period. I also knew his life overlapped with Joan of Arc, so I decided to retrace her various battles, suspecting that Simon might fight in one of them."

"More than one," Andrew added.

"Finally I saw him from afar at the Battle of Orléans."

"We were there!" Eve said.

"I may have seen you," he said. "But I couldn't have known it."

"So you went to Compiègne to find him?" asked Eve.

Alfred nodded. "I got there just in time to see him die by the hand of the Ravager. I also saw the two of you. Andrew, you looked so much like Ted Perry that I knew it wasn't a coincidence. I decided to follow you to see what was going on."

"What did you plan to do if you met Simon face-to-face?" Eve asked. "Drag him home?"

Alfred's brow furrowed. "I couldn't force him to go back. And how would I explain the way he had changed after disappearing?"

Andrew asked, "Then why were you searching for him?"

Alfred looked a little embarrassed. "To be honest, I wanted to see the impact time was having on him here."

"He went crazy," Eve said.

"So it would seem," Alfred said sadly.

Andrew gestured toward Alfred's coat pocket. "Do you always carry a gun when you time-travel?"

"Not always. This is the first time I've had to use it."

"I'm glad you did. You saved our lives," Andrew said. "Thank you."

"My pleasure." Alfred shook his head. "I don't think anyone will miss the Ravager."

"Aren't you worried that you've changed history?" Eve asked.

Alfred shrugged. "In my experience with time travel, if the gun was going to change history somehow, it wouldn't have gone off. Time won't let us change some things."

"So I keep hearing," Andrew said, rolling his eyes.

Alfred looked at him with a curious expression.

"*Please* tell us about the Radiant Stone," Eve said. "We know it was from England, but we can't figure out why it brought us here."

Alfred gave it some thought, then said, "Its history goes back to Ireland during the time of Saint Patrick. Then I *think* it traveled to England with Saint Brigid to the Beckery Monastery near Glastonbury. It's possible a monk or nun carried it here to Chinon or one of the many abbeys in France. Or it might have been a thief. I know it wound up in England again later. Some things I don't know for sure."

"Somebody should lock these stones up," Andrew teased. "They're dangerous."

"I'm thinking of building a special vault, for safekeeping," Alfred said.

Andrew and Eve exchanged looks.

Alfred noticed. "Don't tell me."

They laughed.

"It's dangerous for me to be with you," he admitted. "I had better leave."

"You're leaving us? Aren't we going with you?" Eve asked.

"I'm not sure what the Radiant Stone will do with people from two different times. It might take you to my time, not yours. Or worse, it could take us back to *your* time. That could be a problem. I don't belong in the future. It might kill me instantly, or I might die quickly of old age. I would rather not take that chance, if it's all the same to you."

"But won't the Valiant Stone take us back to the moment Simon stole it from you in your time?" asked Andrew.

Eve brightened up. "If it does, then we can use the Radiant Stone to go back to our time," she suggested.

Alfred chuckled. "Like changing trains at a station?"

"Why not?" she asked.

"I'm not sure it works that way. If you take the Radiant Stone from my time to your time, then I won't be able to finish my research."

"Oh," Eve said thoughtfully. "If you don't finish your research, then I won't know how the stone works."

"That could change both our histories in ways we can't anticipate," Alfred said.

"But you said we can't change history," Eve reminded him. "You're very clear about it in your journals."

"Really? Oh." He laughed. "Clearly you know more of what I know than I do at this point."

"What should we do?" Andrew asked.

"Any hope you have of getting back to your time is with the Valiant Stone," he said. "Unlike the Radiant Stone, it hasn't been part of your history. Until now."

Eve looked worried. "Are you sure it will take us home?"

Alfred rubbed his chin. "I'm making an uneducated guess about that. I believe it will take you back to your time because that is where you belong. The stones have an uncanny sense of order and place. The individual facets go backward, but if you clasp the stone with your entire hand, the stone defers to the one clasping it, as if it *must* return you to your true place."

Andrew struggled to understand what Alfred Virtue was saying. "Why?"

"I believe it's because God has so ordered it. The stones are part of the wonder of His creation. He places us in our times and places to serve Him there and then. The stones aren't meant to change that."

"We served Him here," Eve said. "We helped Jeanne."

Alfred nodded. "That may be so, but you were not born to be here. To stay here would eventually drive you insane, like it did Simon. The answer may be in his papers." He stood up.

"What if the Valiant Stone doesn't work?" Eve asked.

"I will come back to check on you." He tipped his hat to them. "With that, I will say goodbye." He gestured to the box and papers. "And I'll say a sad farewell to poor Simon Howard."

"Simon *Howard*?" Eve said.

"Yes. Why?"

"That's the name of a professor my aunt knows."

"A descendant?"

Andrew remembered that Dr. Howard had said his ancestor knew Alfred Virtue and Theodore Perry. "It has to be," said Andrew.

Alfred reached into his pocket and pulled out a small pouch. He carefully removed the Radiant Stone. "It's clumsy trying to carry it without touching it," he said.

"You should design a case for that," Andrew suggested. "Like a pocket watch."

Alfred chuckled. "Theodore Perry said the same thing." He took the glove off his right hand.

"Thank you for saving us," Eve said.

Alfred Virtue smiled at her. "It was a providential accident."

Alfred clasped the Radiant Stone.

"Wait!" Andrew called out. "Theodore Perry *knew* about the time travel?"

It was too late. Alfred Virtue had disappeared.

42

As much as Andrew and Eve wanted to go back to Hope Springs right away, they wanted to return in their modern clothes just as much.

"It's too dark to get them now," Eve said.

They agreed to retrieve their clothes in the morning.

Too excited to sleep, they took out Simon's parchments. Andrew was right: they were his personal journals. Passing them back and forth, they put together his story.

Simon Howard was determined to witness the Battle of Agincourt for himself, and he refused to take Alfred Virtue's *no* as an answer. He stole the Valiant Stone, believing he would go, watch the battle, and then return to his time. The problem was that the Valiant Stone had never been to Agincourt. Instead, the stone took him to Paris the year *before* Agincourt, so he had to bide his time until the battle happened.

He wasn't idle. He used his knowledge of gems, science, warfare, and even his high-school French, to good advantage. He made a decent living in Paris that year and then—*oops*—he met a peasant woman named Catherine and fell in love. Though he knew it was wrong, he married her. To make matters worse, he told her about the Valiant Stone.

At this point in his journal, Simon admitted that he had tried to bring Catherine to the Hope Springs of his time, but the minute she arrived, she began to feel extremely sick. She also began to age very quickly. "She didn't belong there," Simon wrote. So they returned to Paris.

The time for Agincourt grew closer. He was about to journey to that part of the country, when Catherine's brother, Vincent, showed up. According to Simon, the man was "as foul and unworthy a creature as ever allowed by God to exist." Vincent wanted money to buy a commission in the army so he could fight the English invaders. Simon was willing to lend him some, but it wasn't enough.

Unfortunately, Catherine had told Vincent about the Valiant Stone. He believed they could all enjoy a wealthy life if only Simon would use it. Vincent imagined the benefits of investing money in areas they knew would succeed.

Ironically, Simon had refused to help Vincent in much the same way that Alfred Virtue had refused to help Simon. Undaunted, Vincent demanded the stone from Simon. Knives were drawn, and the two men fought. Catherine tried to intercede, and Vincent stabbed her by accident. Simon attacked Vincent, wounding him in the eye. Vincent escaped. But Catherine died a slow and painful death.

Simon wrote, "All of my modern knowledge could not save her."

In his despair and grief, he sought revenge against Vincent. Certain that the fiend would be at Agincourt, Simon went there to kill him. The men came upon each other the night before the battle. They fought again. This time, Vincent cried for help. French soldiers rushed in. Vincent claimed that Simon was an assassin from the English side. The French tried to take Simon prisoner, but he escaped.

Knowing that Agincourt would end in a decisive victory for the English, Simon joined their forces. After the slaughter, he departed from France, knowing the poverty the long war would bring. He returned to England with Henry's troops and was welcomed as a hero. Again Simon used his modern knowledge to good advantage and became a royal jeweler, armorer, and soldier. He fought in battle like a man who didn't care whether he lived or died. He knew he would encounter Vincent again and eventually fulfill his obsession for revenge.

Simon also began to realize that being a man out of time had affected something else. He was aging more slowly than everyone else. He speculated he could live for another hundred years. But would he want to?

After this, the journal entries became more random. Andrew and Eve concluded that Simon was losing his mind. He wrote again and again about forgetting things he should remember, and the nagging sense that he belonged somewhere else. In his growing madness, his knowledge of history became little more than instinct. He could sense what was going to happen without remembering that he once *knew* what would happen. He chronicled how he reread the earlier parts of his journal and decided he was insane for believing what he wrote.

Meanwhile, he fought for the English against the French, until he saw firsthand what English rule was doing to the French people. He could not justify England's claim to the throne or the country. He placed his allegiance with the Dauphin and journeyed to Chinon. He'd heard about *la Pucelle*, and the memories began to torment him. He *knew* about Joan of Arc but couldn't explain why. Then in his last scribbled note, he admitted that he saw two children arrive. He was sure they were of the devil. It filled him with an unexplainable rage.

"He forgot to mention how he attacked our sneakers," Eve said.

At first light, Andrew and Eve went back to get their clothes. They made their way down to the riverbank. The water had receded enough for Andrew to climb the pillars and supports and pull the sack from the space where Eve had stashed it.

Hidden by the bridge, they changed into their modern clothes. Then Eve decided to put the sack and her note back in their hiding place.

"That archaeologist will find my note years from now and contact Alfred Virtue," Eve said. "He won't know what it means, but it'll be a fun mystery."

"This stuff gives me a headache," Andrew complained.

They looked at each other's clothes and the way Simon had mangled the stitching.

"Are you ready?" Eve asked.

Andrew held open the wooden box. *Please let this work,* he prayed.

Eve took Andrew's hand, then wrapped her fingers around the Valiant Stone.

"I hope—"

But Eve didn't get to finish her sentence in fifteenth-century France.

"—it takes us back to our own time," Eve was saying when they arrived.

Andrew was looking down at Simon's box. It was still in his hands. Then he looked around.

"Oh no," Eve said.

They weren't in Alfred Virtue's office in the Old Bank Building. They were standing in what looked like the living room of someone's apartment. The style of the furniture and decorations were old-fashioned, maybe from the early twentieth century.

"Did it take us back to Simon's time?" Eve asked.

The sound of a horn outside sent them both rushing to the window. They were on the second floor of an apartment building across the street from the Old Bank Building. The sign declared that it was the home of the Virtue Curiosity Shoppe.

"And the cars are modern," Andrew said.

Eve gave a sigh of relief. "Thank God."

"But whose apartment is this?" Andrew asked.

Looking around, they spied a picture on the wall. It was Dr. Vince Howard at a ceremony. Next to the picture was his framed master's degree from a university in Denver.

"This is Dr. Howard's place?" Andrew was beginning to feel nauseous.

"His name is Vincent," Eve noted. "I knew there was a good reason not to like him," she added.

"But why did the stone bring us here?" Andrew asked.

Eve pointed to another framed photo of a young-looking Simon Howard sitting on a side table.

"Maybe it was Simon's apartment then, and Vincent stays here now when he visits Hope Springs," Andrew suggested. "So the Valiant Stone brought us here because ... Are you feeling sick? I'm feeling sick." Andrew felt as if he was turning green.

"I am too. But we can't throw up in here. It isn't ours."

They suddenly looked at each other and realized that, at the moment, they were guilty of breaking and entering.

"We have to get out of here," Andrew said.

They tiptoed as fast as they could out the door and down the stairs to the front door of the complex.

Eve carefully put the Valiant Stone in her pocket. "Remind me not to touch that," she said.

Not wanting to be seen from across the street, they found a rear door leading to a parking lot. They navigated around the apartment building and across the street to the Old Bank Building, then slipped through a side door by the stairwell.

Eve's Aunt Catherine and Dr. Howard were still talking in the main area of the shop. Eve and Andrew crept down the stairwell that led to the vaults and Alfred Virtue's private office.

Once inside again, Andrew dropped the box on the desk and collapsed into Alfred Virtue's old chair. He felt better now. The radonite was doing its job.

"Home again," Eve said happily.

Andrew looked at the Radiant Stone. It was sitting where it had been a few seconds ago. Then he remembered that more than a year had gone by almost six hundred years ago. He groaned.

"This stuff gives me a headache," he said again.

Eve looked up at the wall. A framed photo of Alfred Virtue looked back at her. "We met him," she said proudly.

"And Joan of Arc," Andrew added.

Eve held up her hand. "I don't want to think about that right now. It breaks my heart."

"All right," Andrew agreed. "But you have to admit, these stones are making our lives really weird."

Eve found a cleaning cloth and used it to take the Valiant Stone out of her pocket. She looked around. "Where should I put it?"

"In Simon's box," Andrew suggested. "Then hide it in one of those file drawers."

Eve put the Valiant Stone into the box and set the box on the desk.

Andrew could hear Mrs. Drake and Dr. Howard coming down the hall, talking. Mrs. Drake peeked into the office. "I was just showing Dr. Howard the vaults." She stepped aside so Dr. Howard could look in.

"This was Alfred Virtue's office," she told him.

Now that he knew Dr. Howard was related to Simon, Andrew could see a resemblance in the eyes and mouth.

"Fascinating," Dr. Howard said. He looked down at the desk. "What is this box? May I see it?"

Eve put her hand on the top. "No."

"Don't be rude." Aunt Catherine spoke politely but with a "Let him look if he wants" edge.

"I have some personal things in it," Eve said quickly. "It's embarrassing."

Dr. Howard was undaunted. "The wood, the hinges. It looks medieval. That's quite a thing to put personal items in. Where did you get it?"

Eve shuffled nervously. "It was mixed in with Alfred Virtue's stuff."

"He collected all sorts of things," Aunt Catherine said. She touched Eve's shoulder, her fingers tugging at the crude stitching on Eve's pullover. She looked at Eve with an unspoken question.

Dr. Howard scanned the desk. His eyes landed on the Radiant Stone. It was still sitting in its open case. "What is that?" he asked as he reached for it.

"Don't touch it!" Andrew and Eve cried out together.

His head jerked toward them even as the tip of his finger touched the stone.

He disappeared.

Aunt Catherine shrieked.

"Oh no." Andrew stood up. The stone was still on the desk. He looked at Eve.

"He went without the stone." Eve's face went pale.

"What have you done with him?" Aunt Catherine cried.

"I haven't done anything with him," Eve said. "He touched the stone. He went somewhere in time."

"Well, *do something!*" Aunt Catherine sputtered.

Andrew looked at the stone. In a worried tone, he said, "He didn't take it with him."

"What does that mean?" asked Aunt Catherine.

Andrew swallowed hard. "He can't get back."

Aunt Catherine put a hand on her hip and wagged a finger at Eve. "Then you will have to go get him!"

"Which facet did he touch?" Eve asked Andrew.

Andrew took a closer look. "I think it was *that* one. Or maybe it was that other one. I don't know. We'd have to dust for fingerprints to find out."

"Magnifying glass," Eve muttered and searched through the desk drawers and shelves. She found one, wiped the dust off on her pant leg, and checked the stone.

"Well?" Aunt Catherine stood with her arms folded, her foot tapping.

"Was he eating any candy?" Eve asked.

"He had one of my homemade strawberry pastries."

"Powdered sugar?"

"Yes!" she said, obviously annoyed. "Please stop playing Sherlock Holmes and go find the poor man!"

Eve looked at Andrew. "It's this one. But I don't know where it goes."

"Touch it and we'll find out," Andrew said.

Eve picked up the case holding the Radiant Stone. She draped the chain over her head and around her neck. "Here we go again."

"Where were you before?" Aunt Catherine asked.

"I'll explain when we get back." She held out her hand for Andrew.

He grabbed it.

She carefully touched the facet with Dr. Howard's sugary fingerprint on it.

The office—and the world as they knew it—disappeared.